Praise for the novels of Meg Elison

"*Number One Fan* is a tense ride from the start as we're introduced to one of the most deeply unsettling villains I've encountered in a long time. It's about fighting for who and what you are when it would be easier to simply give up and be someone else's idea of you. It's about pain and resilience and redemption. In short, it's terrific."
—Richard Kadrey, *New York Times* bestselling author of *Sandman Slim*

"A tense, creepy, and deeply spooky thriller that locks you down and wrings you out in the best way possible. I had other things to do today, but I couldn't put this down— so those things didn't get done. All Meg's fault. I hope she's happy, drat her."   —Cherie Priest, author of *The Toll*

MEG ELISON

NUMBER ONE FAN

mira

ISBN-13: 978-0-7783-8615-5

Number One Fan

For questions and comments about the quality of this book, please contact us at CustomerService@Harlequin.com.

Mira
22 Adelaide St. West, 41st Floor
Toronto, Ontario M5H 4E3, Canada
BookClubbish.com

Printed in U.S.A.

Recycling programs for this product may not exist in your area.

Dedicated to TNC: as we are, as we were, as we will be.

We were the best thing I ever had, and you all got the best out of me.

1

The car rolled into view, the lit decals on the dashboard letting Eli know that her driver was typical: working for all the rideshare services at once.

Gotta hustle, she thought as she quickened her pace away from the airfield. She hoped he hadn't been waiting long.

"Elizabeth?" He seemed bored, not even bothering to turn around.

"That's right. I go by Eli, though."

"Sure," he said, tapping his phone.

She settled in, her satchel beside her. "Thank you."

The car was air-conditioned against the cushion of heat that pressed against its tinted windows, and as they headed toward the freeway, she finally began to relax. She was grateful the driver didn't seem to want to talk. She was tired of talking from the event, and her throat was dry and sore.

"There is a cold drink there in the cup holder. Down in the door." His voice was low, a raspy baritone.

"Oh, cool, thanks." Eli reached down and felt the blessed condensation on a plastic bottle. She pulled up a blue Gatorade and wrenched it open, suddenly very thirsty. She drank half of it in huge gulps, disliking the weird, salty taste of the electrolyte mixture, but unable to stop herself. It felt good, after hours of talking and the dry air of the flight. She breathed deep and drank again, coming close to finishing it off.

Must be the heat, she thought. That and the two miniature bottles of Jack Daniel's she'd had to calm her nerves on the plane.

Her phone vibrated in her pocket in an unfamiliar cadence and she slid it out to check.

Her notification from the rideshare app blared.

Brenda has canceled the ride for reason: no-show. You have been charged a cancellation fee of $5.

Eli frowned at her phone. Had she summoned two cars by accident?

She unlocked it with her facial scan and checked. The app showed only one ride: a black Prius driven by Brenda, which had arrived five minutes ago and canceled four minutes after that.

It wasn't a busy day at the airfield. It certainly wasn't curbside pickup like at SFO, but it was still possible that she had gotten in the wrong car.

But he had known her name.

She leaned forward to get the driver's attention. "Hey, just clarifying—you've got my info, right? I just got a cancellation from another driver, and I'm worried that I got someone else's ride."

The driver tapped his phone and his eyes darted between it, the rearview mirror and the road. "Elizabeth Grey. Headed to the Sailing Stones, right?"

The phone displayed a highlighted blue route along the freeway. It was a map program, rather than the rideshare's software, but Eli had seen drivers toggle between those before. She glanced up at the rearview mirror, but his eyes were on the road and he had put on a pair of dark glasses.

"Right," she said. "Huh. Wonder what happened."

Eli settled back into her seat. She stared out the window and thought of home, of the deep gray fog rolling down over the hillsides and the wind coming in, salty from the Bay. She was homesick. Even in the same state, the air felt wrong on her skin. Los Angeles had been an endless parade of palm trees against a blameless sky, and the tacos were so good she could barely stop shoveling them in, but the traffic had left her feeling exhausted upon every arrival.

And then there was the way that people looked you over in Los Angeles, deciding whether you were famous or fuckable or useful in some other way before sliding on to the next thing. Her audiences had been lively and engaging but draining, and after each of her events, she'd wanted nothing but some dinner, a hot bath and sleep. Maybe a couple fingers of bourbon over ice.

Traveling always left her wrung out and unmoored. It didn't help that the sun was so all-encompassing outside the car it could have been anywhere, anytime of day, the hot, white light blinding. She couldn't look at a surface other than the black asphalt without squinting. Living in San Francisco gave her what she had thought was a passing acquaintance with the sun, but the glare as the 10 freeway led out into Kern County and the high desert landscape was just too much.

How are people here not dog-tired all the time? Doesn't the heat suck all the life out of them? How do they ever leave the house? Christ, it's March. Imagine later in the year. I gotta get some sunglasses.

She set the phone beside her on the seat to avoid pawing it in and out of her jeans. She belatedly buckled her seat belt as

they picked up speed. Out the window, the freeway was sliding past, one unfamiliar mile blending into the next.

The driver turned his radio on. It annoyed her at first that
he had not asked, but then she reminded herself that he probably spent the whole day in his car. She wasn't talking; he
was probably both lonely and bored. Let him have his Oingo
Boingo.

He changed lanes to get into the faster flow of traffic and
the motion of it made her feel a trifle ill. This heat had produced all kinds of new feelings. She ignored it, drinking the
last swallow of the Gatorade.

She looked around for a polite place to deposit the bottle.
The motion of her head made her dizziness worse and she tried
to blink it away. "Do you have a spot for trash?" she asked
him. As the words slid out of her mouth, she realized she was
slurring like she was very, very drunk. She was horrified to
realize she was drooling, too.

Eli tried to get ahold of herself. She pushed with her palms
and worked to sit up straight, but found that she could not.
Her head felt far too heavy for the wet noodle of her neck to
have ever supported. Her abs were slack and her spine was a
worm. She sagged against the seat; the seat belt the only thing
keeping her from sliding to the floor.

"Whass going on?" The words seemed to take a long time
to reach her ears.

Oh shit, I'm having a stroke. An old classmate of Eli's had
had a freak stroke event a week shy of her thirtieth birthday.
Frantically, she tried to recall the diagnostic that the woman
had posted on Facebook right after. She couldn't speak clearly.
She couldn't lift her arms at all. Her hand flopped uselessly in
the direction of her phone.

"Ooogoada tachme to ahspital," she slurred at him in molasses-
thick nightmare slowness. "Shumding wruuuuunnnnng."

"Relax," he said clearly, his voice less deep than before. "You are fine."

With her last spasm of strength, Eli pulled at the door handle, intending to tumble out of the car. The child safety lock held her in place.

I'm not fine, she thought with her last clear and lucid moment. As her eyes fell closed like heavy curtains, she finally registered that they were going the wrong way. The steely spike of panic that stabbed at her heart was almost enough to counteract the soporific effect of whatever was wrong with her, but not quite. Fighting, terrified, she slipped out of consciousness.

2

A rumbling sound. Flashes of bright light. A thin jet of icy air. A roll of nausea, then another.

Eli Grey had brief moments of something approaching being awake, but she couldn't make sense of what was happening. She was on a plane—or was it just the memory of a plane? No, she was in a car. She was very hot, and when she could force her eyes open, dust motes swirled past her face into a blurry field of vision. She groaned and went back out.

When she came to again, she was in a bed and under covers. It was not her bed, and the covers did not feel like that industrial foam-plastic stuff she knew from hotels. Deep breaths brought more strange smells: cleaning fluid, ant bait, an unfamiliar soap. She thought hard.

Did I hook up with someone after a reading? Did I get hammered last night? What's the last thing I can remember?

But all she remembered was the tiny plane that had flown her across the Southern California desert, and the creases in her hands when she had let go of her death grip on the Naugahyde seats.

Deep breath. Figure it out. You're okay. You're alone, for now.
Deep breath.

Eli remembered fidgeting in the cramped airplane seat. She had badly wanted another drink. When she thought about the series being almost done, about the eighth book coming out, there was a small panic somewhere inside her. The success of her book series had brought her financial security: a little house and a little money, her debts paid off. When this series ended one day, she knew what she wanted to write next. There was a little thrill in her belly when she wondered whether people would like it as well as the Millicent Michaelson books or not. Her other books out of the series had done well, but not blockbusters.

The craft had bumped and bounced to a stop, and she breathed a long, shaky sigh of relief. They began to taxi around the small airport and she knew her drinking window had closed.

Airport personnel scurried out to roll one of those old-fashioned staircases to the tiny plane's door, and Eli emerged, blinded by the sun and taking the heat of the Mojave to the face like the first volley of a pillow fight in hell. Blinking and pulling her sunglasses down, she turned her phone back on.

She tweeted:

Back on solid ground and it feels so good! Thank you, Los Angeles!

She attached a selfie in the big gray headphones, with the tiny plane evident in the background. Eli wrote in the caption about her private plane experience; not glamorous like a G6, no flight attendants to bring drinks and no luxurious seating. But it had been only her and the pilot, unable to speak over the roar of the engines. She had also gotten a shot of the city she had taken in the air, added it to the gallery post. Immediately, likes and retweets began to roll in. She muted the notifications and pocketed her phone. She thought about texting her assistant, Joe, who was going to check in with her at SeaTac tomorrow, but decided it could wait. The kid deserved a day off.

On the ground, the pilot had found her and wanted to shake her hand. Eli adjusted her satchel to hang between her shoulders and shook back.

"Thank you for the safe flight. I was pretty nervous about such a small plane."

"No trouble. I make that run all the time," the man said through his gingery beard. "I was wondering, though, if you'd sign my wife's book for her. She's just crazy about that Millicent."

Eli grinned broadly. "Sure, I will, of course. Do you have it handy? I've got a copy in my satchel—"

"No, no, it's here in my car. If you'll just wait a second." He jogged off, holding up both hands. "Back in one minute."

"No problem," she called to him. She pulled her phone back out and began to look at her odds of getting a car back to her hotel. Small towns in California had fewer options than San Francisco, which seemed to dream up a new, disruptive transportation solution every two weeks. She checked her favorite rideshare app and was surprised to see a handful of drivers active and nearby. She put in her location and the address of her hotel, and saw that she had correctly guessed it was going to be a while before her ride showed up. She stowed her phone again and spied the pilot jogging back to her.

"Here we go!" He was holding a first-edition paperback copy of *The City under the City*, her debut novel. She knew it was the first edition on sight, because she had been published the first time by a tiny press with no design budget, and the cover was homely and humble. It gave her a funny twinge in her heart to see it.

"I haven't seen one of these at a signing in about five years," she said, smiling and taking the book from him.

"My wife has been a fan of yours since back then," he said, grinning back. "She used to tell all her friends, her book club ladies, you know, that you were gonna be the next big thing. She says she saw it right away. She wanted me to make sure you knew that she was loyal from the very beginning."

Eli opened the front cover, noticing how worn this copy of *City* was. "I can see this one has been well-loved. Are you sure I can't get her a new copy? I could have it sent to you."

"No, no. This one is her treasure. She says it's her proof that she's your biggest fan. She'd be here herself, but we just had a baby and she's still lying in. Stitches, you know."

Eli nodded, bracing the book gently against her belly and uncapping her good fountain pen, a Montblanc she had picked out to celebrate hitting the bestseller list. "Should I just autograph this, or make it out to her personally?"

"Oh, she'd just die. Please make it out to Adeline, and say something nice. Or clever. Or both, I guess." He was grinning and Eli could not help but grin back.

"That's *A-d-e-l-i-n-e*?"

He nodded.

Eli wrote carefully, mindful that years of typing were eroding her script into a barely legible scrawl.

To Adeline, my number-one fan, with my thanks and friendship.

Below that, she laid out her practiced author's signature, tall and wide and cocksure. She had modeled it on all of her heroes' autographs and hoped it looked like it belonged: *Eli Grey.*

The pilot smiled again, taking the book back. "She's gonna be so happy. She didn't believe me when I said I was gonna be flying you."

Eli smiled back, but she saw an attendant flagging her down

from the edge of the parking lot nearby. "I think my ride is here."

"Oh! Okay, great! Have a good one!"

She raised a hand to him and began to walk briskly away.

And then I was in the car, she thought, her heart pounding at the memory of that ride. Her stomach dropped the way it had when the small plane had banked a turn.

And then I was here. So where is here?

Upon her first deep breath, Eli immediately began to cough like she'd just smoked her first cigarette. She whooped in big breaths, her head pounding with the effort. She found that she could not sit up, or even hold herself up on one arm.

Once she could breathe, she peeled her dry eyes open and looked around. It was a bedroom, but the extreme gloom and lack of windows told her it had to be a basement. The bed was low, but soft. There was a dresser and a small closet without a door on it. Looking around, she saw that the room had two doors. One she guessed was the bathroom, on the right. On the left, a flight of concrete stairs without a banister led up to a door at the top.

That must be the way out.

With her notice of a bathroom came a sudden and pressing need to pee. She pulled the blankets off herself and realized two things:

The first was that she was wearing someone else's nightgown. It was a long, pink silky thing, hyperfeminine like something the dame in a detective novel might be wearing when the cops came to tell her that her husband was dead under mysterious circumstances and she had better answer their questions. Eli tried hard to remember what she had been wearing before. It came back slowly as she blinked to clear her head.

Black jeans, cuffed at the ankles. My custom oxfords. Sports bra.

A white undershirt and a white dress shirt over it. My good black blazer. Remember, I was too hot. Wanted to take the blazer off, but didn't. Why didn't I?

The second thing she realized was that her right ankle was shackled to the bed with an old-fashioned leg iron, like a handcuff.

Her sense of unreality deepened. Had she woken up in someone else's life? No, that couldn't really happen. Was this a dream? No. Surreal, but too real. Where was she? How had she ended up here?

There was a terrible significance to these two alien objects when her mind combined them in just the right way, but she wouldn't let that thought in. Not yet.

The door she had correctly guessed was the way out opened. She stared up at it, riveted. There, standing in semidarkness, was her driver from the airport.

I know you. The thought drifted across her mind and out to sea. She knew him from somewhere; was it just the airport? Was her short-term memory affected by whatever drug she had been given? He was familiar, but why?

He drove you. That's why. That's all it is.

She was piecing it together. She knew how she had gotten here.

"I saw you were awake, and I wanted to come greet you properly this time."

She peered up at him as he began to descend the staircase, all legs, like a stilt walker. "What the hell is this? Unlock my ankle right now."

He looked pained as he reached the floor, drawing his long arms up as if threatened. He came toward her with that same hurt expression on his long, horsey features. She took in his face carefully now, studying it just as she had ignored it in the car. He was young, maybe all of thirty-five. Only a few years younger than her, she thought. His face was unremarkable, with dark hair cut short and a deep shadow under his carefully shaved cheeks. His beard around that, dark and wild but closely clipped. Dry skin, like he exfoliated but never moisturized. Oval glasses in black wire somehow made his face seem more civilized.

He was incredibly tall. Eli blinked hard, trying to get her sense of proportion to settle right. She was low to the ground; the metal frame was only about six inches off the floor. Even allowing for the extreme angle, she had seen the way he stooped coming through the doorway. She remembered how he had sat in his car, hunched over the wheel like there wasn't room for him behind it.

His hair, dull, wavy and wild as well, brushed against the acoustic popcorn on the ceiling in the room. Was the room small? His arms and legs seemed terribly long, like a spider's. He wore dark jeans and indoor shoes, and she saw the bony knobs of his wrists poking out of the sleeves of his flannel shirt, and inches of sock showed between his pants and his shoes. The effect was startling: Abraham Lincoln in lifts, a daddy longlegs in eyeglasses.

He stepped toward the bed, wiry muscle looming over her with elbows cocked, and Eli flinched away involuntarily. His glasses shone in the overhead light, and for just a second she felt like a clam watching a crab scuttle over, ready to rip her apart.

"You are not really in a position to tell me what to do, are you?" His smile was small, almost gentle. A kindergarten teacher reminding you to say *please* and *thank-you*.

"What do you want? Do you want money? Let me call my assistant and he can wire you money. I'm not loaded, but—"

He looked offended. "I do not want your money," he scoffed.

Eli struggled against the ankle chain a bit, testing it. The bed frame was made out of joined steel pipes, she could see now. Getting out of this would not be easy.

"We can release you from the lock, if you will just agree to abide by the rules."

"We?" She fought rising panic. She was still forcibly holding her mind back from doing the math on what this man almost surely wanted from her. Eli steeled herself.

"I'm not going to play any games with you. I'm not interested in your rules. Just tell me what you want."

He looked her over. "I can see that you are not in the mood to talk about this now. That is alright. I will come back later."

He turned, climbed the steps and closed the door decorously behind him. She sat staring at the door for several minutes, numbly trying to figure out what had just happened.

He doesn't want money.

You know what he wants.

Think, godsdamn it.

He had said that he *saw* she was awake. Looking around the upper corners of the room, she spotted a round black camera above her, pointed down toward the bed.

Okay, so he can see me. Probably watching right now.

He was the driver.

Her real driver must have been the one who sent her that cancellation notice. Brenda. She felt like the stupidest person in the world, the girl in the horror movie who suggests they all split up and walks right into the basement.

Didn't I notice the driver was a woman? That never happens. But I just got in the car that showed up. Didn't check the make or the plate.

That hardly mattered now. She had gotten into his car. She had assumed, and trusted herself to a stranger. She did it all the time—everyone did. Why not?

Okay. He wasn't really a driver. He was just a guy who…who what? Who knew where I'd be, and then just showed up and got me? How could he know where I was?

She was hyperventilating.

Am I stuck in some guy's basement because he knows who I am and tracked me down? Or because this guy just likes to stalk women? Maybe kill women. How many other women have worn this nightgown?

She was shuddering, unable to slow her breathing. Her eyes swept around wildly. She needed something to ground her or she was going to scream.

Her breath caught in her throat like a door had slammed.

Opposite the bed, a large sheet of paper was taped to the wall. On it was a list printed in large bold letters that she could read from where she lay.

THE RULES:

YOU ARE NOT REAL; YOU ARE THE PRODUCT OF MY WORK.

YOUR LIFE IS MEANINGLESS IF YOU DO NOT SERVE OTHERS.

YOU WILL BEHAVE WELL AND BE TIDY OR THERE WILL BE CONSEQUENCES.

WE WILL BE VERY HAPPY TOGETHER.

YOU WILL LEAVE THIS ROOM WHEN YOU HAVE A PERFECT UNDERSTANDING OF YOUR PURPOSE.

She stared at it, uncomprehending. She read it again. And again. The words stacked up like a pyramid, immovable proof of the trouble she was in.

Oh fuck. I am so fucked.

The rules were familiar to her for a reason. They were a parody of the rules she had written for the Maginaria, the magical school Millicent Michaelson attended in her book series. The originals ran a little differently:

MAGINARIA RULES:

MAGIC IS NOT BORN; IT IS THE PRODUCT OF WORK.

YOUR GIFTS ARE MEANINGLESS IF THEY DO NOT SERVE OTHERS.

YOU WILL PERFORM TO THE BEST OF YOUR ABILITY OR YOU WILL LEAVE.

WE, THE MAGICAL FOLK, ARE STRONGER TO-GETHER.

YOU WILL LEAVE THIS SCHOOL ONLY WHEN YOU HAVE PERFECT CONTROL OF YOUR GIFT. THIS PROCESS TAKES AS LONG AS IT TAKES.

That's intentional, right? It's got to be. Has he read my books, or does he just have a sick sense of humor?

Either way, he definitely knew who she was. Rational thought retreated behind a wall of screaming, illogical, fight-or-flight reaction. She pulled hard against her ankle cuff, straining and yanking, trying to spring it or break the eight or so inches of chain that connected it to the post. She reached down and pulled at the footboard of the bed, thrashing and trying to shake it apart. She breathed between her teeth, struggling. Her head swam again.

Okay. Okay. Okay. A crazy person has me. That's what I know now. I don't know anything else, even if I suspect it. I got myself into this. I'm going to have to get myself out. I have to think. Must think. Can't give in to panic. Fear is the mind killer, right? Fuck off. Fuck OFF. Think, godsdamn it.

She fought for a long moment to get ahold of herself. She shook all over, adrenaline washing through her, making her tremble like a spooked Maltese. She forced herself to take long, deep breaths.

I can do this. I have to do this. I'm all I've got.

Eli took a quick and despairing inventory of her life. No partner. No family. No friends she spoke to every day, or even every week. Nobody was house-sitting. Nobody was waiting to hear from her.

Fuck. How am I going to—JOE.

He sprang into her mind like the hope of heaven. Joe, her assistant. He would notice she was gone. He would tell someone.

But Joe wouldn't realize something had gone wrong until tomorrow afternoon. She was supposed to arrive in Seattle for her next event. When she didn't show, the event coordinator at the bookstore would call her, then him. That was what the email chain directed them to do, anyway. Joe might notice that Eli had failed to check in before then, but maybe not. Eli was not great about touching base. That was not a particularly useful thought at the moment.

I can live through this for a couple of days. He wants something. If this guy didn't want something, I'd already be dead. If he isn't planning to kill me right away, then there's got to be a way out.

She shivered again and thought again about how bad she needed to pee. She didn't want to wet the bed, since she was stuck in it. She looked around the room and saw no receptacle, no good option. She couldn't hold it much longer. There was an almost insurmountable mental block here: she couldn't hold it and she couldn't imagine doing it anywhere but a toilet.

Maybe in the woods, she thought, recalling one miserable camping trip with a girl who had insisted it made for a romantic third date. *Some romance. Poison ivy on my ass. But where am I supposed to piss? There isn't even a potted plant.*

She shifted from side to side, trying to fool her bladder. She flexed her pelvic floor, trying to gauge how long this stalemate could continue. *Really, knocked out like I was I'm surprised I didn't wet the bed. That would almost be a relief.*

She called out tentatively, pitching her voice toward the ceiling. "Hey? Hello? I have a small problem here."

No answer. She hated the feeling that she was asking him for anything, especially this. Shame welled up in her like a flash flood too quick for the warning. How long had it been since she had to ask someone before she could go to the bathroom?

The defiance of that idea was enough to move her past it. *Fuck him*, she thought. *Fuck him for making me ask, for leaving me with nothing.* Mindful of the camera above, she hiked up the long nightgown and balanced her hips out over the edge of the low bed. The floor was stone and quite cold. She pissed a long time, feeling relief steal through her. She had nothing to wipe with. After a few seconds of air-drying, she gave up and scooted back into the bed.

She examined the cuff around her ankle. A bruise was fading in where she'd tried to bust out of it. The irons were the kind used by corrections, but they seemed old. Maybe from a surplus store, or inherited from someone. His father? Had this guy once been a cop? A prison guard?

This line of thought seemed more productive, and she seized on it. What could she know about him? What could she learn? What could she do to help herself here? She consulted that inner diagnosis center again, as she had when she had thought she was having a stroke. None of her Facebook friends had posted a helpful "How to recognize your kidnapper" flow-chart. She thought back to the research she had done to write *City*. She had learned a lot about police procedure and had read some profiling and victim psychology papers. She thought for a long time about the dehumanization techniques she had learned from her research into human trafficking. It wasn't where she was, but it was something.

And if he did snatch me because of who I am, if his rules are based on mine, then we have a connection. I can talk to him knowing that he's familiar with my value in the world. I don't have to end up being some bullshit true-crime podcast after I'm dead. Or worse, a book someone else gets to write. The Girl in the Basement. The Pervy Spider Guy's Wife. The Untold Story of Me, Pissing on the Floor. *Fuck that. Fuck that entirely.*

Remind him that I'm a person. Use my name. Tell him I have family and feelings.

That sounded like bullshit to her now, caught as she was in waves of panic threatening to drown her. Anything that wasn't an all-out fight seemed worthless. She held on tight to thoughts that made sense, that helped her feel like she was doing something.

The door flew open and the driver came back in, angrily carrying a handful of rags and a steaming pot of water.

"I never in a million years thought you would do some-thing so disgusting and disrespectful!" He was yelling at her, but staring at the puddle.

She tried to stop herself from shrinking back into the bed in terror. Her heart was pounding again, and her mouth went so dry that her tongue stuck to her teeth.

Speak up! Don't let him cow you so fast, so easily!

"I had to pee!" She didn't know what else to say. The shame returned, immediate and all-consuming, some radioactive relic from childhood. She hated that; she wanted to feel defiant again and found she could not. She had, after all, just pissed on the floor.

Come on! He has the same biological needs as you! Make him sympathize!

She tried again. "I'm locked to the bed, with nowhere to go. You put me here with no other options. I called for you. What was I supposed to do? What would you have done?"

He poured out a stream of hot water and knelt down to clean up the mess. "Certainly not that. Just disgusting."

He was not looking at her. The tone of his voice was like someone training a puppy.

"What's your name?"

He did not look up.

"My name is Eli, and I have lots of friends who call me that. Even my family calls me that, now."

Nothing. He scrubbed, scowling, wringing out the rags in the hot water.

"I know you know who I am. I'm an author. You know my books, don't you? That's how you picked me up, right?"

Nothing.

He was sweating just a bit, and she could smell him. They were very close to one another. He smelled clean, but goatish. Musky. Unpleasant. Heavier by far than the smell of her own urine.

Hunched down, he was still so long and tall. She could see the bumps of individual vertebrae between the twin sheets of muscle down his back, even under his flannel and an undershirt. She tried again to get a sense of his height, in a room where she had never stood. Was he six-five? Six-*six*?

She straightened up and tried to get ahold of her breathing. She pried her tongue off her teeth and tried to scare up a lick of moisture in her mouth. She blew the smell of him out of her nostrils and stopped trying to describe him to a police officer who wasn't there.

"This is probably just a misunderstanding. Maybe you don't have any idea who I am. You didn't mean to bring me here. You could give me my clothes and my bag and phone, and I could go get a cab and just be on my way. Nobody would have to know."

He stood up with the pot, slopping the wet rags into the water. He walked back to the bathroom door and turned to face her.

"I know exactly who you are. This was not a mistake or a misunderstanding. You were always meant to be here, with me. And the next time you need to use the ladies' room, you will ask me, using exactly those words. Is that clear?"

She looked up at him, dumbstruck. Her eyes strayed to the Rules poster on the wall. *He set this all up for me. He's telling the truth there.* "Why am I here?"

"Is that clear?" he repeated.

"Why did you bring me here? How long have you been stalking me?"

"Is. That. Clear?"

"Look, dude. This isn't going to work. You're not going to get what you want out of me, so you might as well quit while you're ahead." Her eyes were wild and her head was hammering. His biceps bunched up and his elbows bent fast. He shot the pot out in both hands and hot water and piss flew through the air. Most of it caught her in the chest. The wet rags slapped down on the bedclothes. Eli gasped as it hit her, pulling water into her mouth and sputtering it back out. Her shock was total.

He righted the pot, his expression unchanged. She sat there, soaking wet, knowing the hot water would soon go cold. She smelled her own piss, diluted in the water, all over her.

"Are you ready to talk about the rules? If you understood the rules, you might not be so surprised by your punishments." His face was strangely calm through all of this, almost boyish. She half expected him to shrug and smile, as if none of this was a big deal.

"What the fuck?" She held out her dripping arms and stared up at him, her mouth open. "What the fuck is wrong with you?"

He did shrug then, but only with one sharp, pointed shoulder. His mouth slid to one side, as if disappointed with her. "Your choice."

He turned around, the pot dangling from one arm as his shadow loped up the stairs. Dirty water dripped from the end of Eli's nose.

She did not see him again for eight hours.

August 2

TO: *elizabethgrey@gmail.com*
FROM: *leonardlobovich@aol.com*

Dear Ms. Grey,
I just wanted to tell you that I absolutely loved The City under
the City. *The world-building reminds me of the classics of the*
genre, and you have created such an unforgettable character in
Millicent Michaelson.

Rarely has a book touched me so deeply. I cannot wait to
read more of this wonderful series.
Sincerely,
Leonard Lobovich

3

The water turned cold sooner than she expected, but she was already busy by then. Eli pulled and kicked the blankets and sheets down, peeling the layers off the bed and pushing them down by her feet. The mattress itself was also wet, but it hadn't soaked all the way through yet.

She found a dryish spot and sat for a minute, trying to get ahold of herself.

What the actual fuck just happened? How is this real?

She breathed shakily, the only sound in the room.

That's not useful. Denial is going to get you killed. It doesn't matter, and you don't have to make sense of it. You need to move on to the next step. And what is the next step?

Unbidden, lines of dialogue from *The City under the City* came to her mind. *"Rage is the forge that turns you into an instrument for justice."*

Jesus fucking Christ, that was corny. People send me pictures of that line. They get it as a tattoo, for fuck's sake. I wrote that when I was just a kid—I can barely stand it now.

But it was working on her just the same.

Alright. Alright. What can rage do that denial can't? What can I do?

Eli looked around the room again.

The floor is a weapon. The walls are a weapon. But only if I had the leverage to use one of them.

Shifting her weight from one hip to the other, she tried to peel the wet nightgown off her skin. The springs made a grinding, metallic noise beneath her. She looked down at the loops of stitching across the mattress's wet white surface.

There's an idea.

She crawled all over the mattress awkwardly, with her one ankle stuck in place. She was looking for a frayed seam and finally found one, her thoughts racing as she worked first one finger and then two into the small hole to enlarge it.

She curved her body around her work, giving her back to the camera. Her entire being was focused on this one task: getting into the mattress. Her knuckles reddened as she fought the synthetic machine-stitched thread. The hole was tiny, and she had no tools but her own body. She bent down and bit savagely at it.

Springs are sharp as fuck. Get poked and never forget they have those razor-sharp edges. Get ahold of one and bend it until it breaks. Get a sharp piece, just enough to hold in my hand. He comes close to me and I'll poke his fucking eyes out.

Her teeth helped more than she dared hope. She spit out a piece of fluff and stuck her fingers back into the enlarged hole. She ripped back viciously and the stout stitches parted with a rough purr. She shoved aside the multicolored lint-like filling and groped at the springs beneath.

Eli's head still ached, and she was exhausted and weak all over. Her hands began to hurt immediately from ripping the fabric, and the endless work of pressing and pulling on the slim bits of metal was making it worse. She was grunting and moaning and barely heard herself.

How many times did we make that joke? You get told your whole life not to get into cars with strangers, not to take candy. And what do we do? Summon strangers from the internet, get in their cars, take anything they give us. You're so fucking stupid. Was that Gatorade even sealed?

She thought it had been. She thought of the bottle's top and collar popping free of one another as she opened it eagerly.

Not impossible to get something into it, even so. You just don't think. You just slid right in, drank what you were given. And this is what you get. You get to fight with a mattress in Buffalo Bill's fucking basement.

She collapsed forward for a moment, panting, on the edge of tears. Her arms felt overworked, though they had done almost nothing. One spring was just beginning to show signs of abuse. She breathed deeply, slowly.

Two days before I miss my flight to SFO. Joe won't hear from me—what then? What will happen? Who will notice?

If she didn't tweet for a day solid, her friends said they assumed she was dead. The irony was less enjoyable from here.

Nella. She might notice.

But just thinking about Nella made her heart hurt. Nella Atwiler, her only real friend. Nella, the best writer she knew, who had just hit her big break and was on her way to literary stardom. Nella, who was completely sick of her shit.

Eli flashed back on the shining mass of water flying out of the pot, hanging in space for just a moment, headed for her. What had made him do it? Why dress her up like this just to spoil it by throwing toilet water at her?

You know why. It's not about sex—it's about power. He wants to humiliate you. To take something from you.

Eli blinked her eyes and realized something was missing.

Her contact lenses. She could see close-up without them, but she was leaning too far forward to see the work. Anything far away was going to be a challenge, unless it was printed in large letters. *Does he know I'm nearsighted? Is that why the rules are printed that way?* She was squinting. She put her fingers to her eyelids and felt nothing there—no telltale bluish edge at the rim of her iris.

He took my fucking contacts out. He put his fingers into my eyes.

The thought was too disturbing to entertain. She went back to work, pulling harder on the spring. But panic was making its way through her body. She was whimpering low, under her breath like a scared animal. The metal was looking very abused now. She thought she could get a piece the size of her pocketknife.

That broke open another thought.

What does he have? My phone, but he can't get into it. Plus if he used it, they could find me here. My satchel. My wallet and ID, my pocketknife that was in my bra. My good fountain pen.

The thought of him unhooking her bra with his long, spidery fingers while she was unconscious made her feel cold and rubbery all over, like something poured out in a factory and molded into something fuckable. Her sense of herself was eroding.

From his command center somewhere above her, Leonard Lobovich sat in his plastic-wrapped desk chair, peering at Eli's laptop. It was password protected, but he was confident that he knew her well enough to break into it. He had a list of things to try, and another list of the most common passwords he had found on the internet. She was anything but common, but it was still possible. He went down his list first, confident he'd figure it out. He barely glanced at the monitor streaming footage from the camera in the basement as he worked.

Some problems were easy to solve. Her password, surely—and her clothes. He had gotten rid of her strangely masculine clothing and was glad she had fit the dress despite her weight gain. Worse was that business of making a mess down in the basement like an untrained puppy.

When he had planned all this out, he hadn't thought about her needing the restroom.

He exhausted his list of passwords, and then the list of the most common passwords, as well. The computer remained frustratingly locked. He would just have to make her tell him.

He had been researching long and hard on how to do this correctly. There were others just like him out there, and he had found them online: men pushed to the edge of their endurance, pushed to desperate measures by an unfair world that wanted to make them weak and small. They, too, had shared their plans as "thought experiments," shared their careful steps to do the things that most would never dare to do. He couldn't have gotten as far as this without them.

He opened the file of links he had compiled on enhanced interrogation. His favorites were at the top, the subtler things he believed would bring her into line and help her understand her destiny without too much pain or ugliness. Toward the bottom of the list were his less favored methods: the things that would harm her, or cause permanent damage.

"Hurting is not harming," he whispered to himself. "Hurt is for your own good. Harm is the sacrifice you make for safety."

It was a line from *Captive Prince*, the sequel to *The City under the City*. Millicent—always Millicent, never Millie—lived through her first heartbreak in that wonderful story, leaving behind her first love, Marcel, to attend police academy training.

Leonard was not an orphan like his favorite character, but he was alone, and on a quest to find his true self, just as Millicent was. They were on an intercept pattern that would bring them together. He hoped she would come to understand that in the same way that there was a bigger destiny in place for them both.

He imagined sitting calmly on the bed beside her. She wasn't leaning away from him, and her face was calm.

"I am doing this for us. Can you understand that?"

She said yes and she dimpled. Emboldened, he came a little closer. "Good. Soon, there will be no reason to keep you restrained."

He imagined her voice, girlish but strong, like in the movies, telling him she was ready. She was ready for everything. Her eyes shone and he leaned forward, coming close to her, inhaling an imagined scent.

Unwatched on the monitor over his shoulder, Eli kept pulling apart the metal inside the mattress.

Cold, exhausted and wrung out, Eli finally wrested a four-inch section of spring from the bed. She badly scratched her forearm in the process and could hardly feel any triumph at having done it. The nightgown was sheer and thin and still wet, and she felt naked. She shivered in the direct blast of dry air from the air conditioner vent and the motion of her body made her headache worse.

What did he give me? Like, a roofie? Or something worse? How did he get it? Does he have more?

She examined the possibility that she might not be able to eat or drink anything he offered her. Maybe she could get him to drink first and prove it was safe. She was already so thirsty.

Like he'll do that. So fucked. So boned. So fucking screwed. And that's if he intends to keep me alive for more than a day. For more fun. For whatever he's got in mind.

She chased the useless thought down and made it be still.

Not helping. Need to concentrate on useful thoughts. Useful thoughts only.

Eli curled her knees up toward her chest, holding her jagged metal prize between her palms. She felt the beginning of a UTI, just the lowest setting on a stove burner, beginning in her. She shifted away from it, knowing it would only get worse with her trapped the way she was. In her mind, she went to her secret stronghold. Fitfully, thinly, she began to sleep.

Eli woke, having kicked off her covers. He was standing there, head cocked to one side, staring. *How long has he been standing there, watching me sleep?* Cold crept into her, bypassing her taut muscles and her clamped courage.

She sat up, holding the piece of metal on the far side of her body, putting her hand down on top of it.

"You're back," she said in a croaky voice.

"I am back. We have to talk about something."

"Come over here and talk to me, then."

He walked across to her.

"Why don't you sit down with me and tell me your name."

He sat down on the edge of the bed, where it looked dry. She scooted closer to where her leg was trapped, bent awkwardly on the bed. She was stiff with fear at being this close to him.

You can do this. You must do this. Smile and get him in close. Very close.

"I think we got off on the wrong foot," she started, trying to smile. "My name is Eli, like I told you—"

"I know who you are. What is your password to your laptop?"

"What?" She blinked at him in the dim light.

He was looking at her, unblinking. He wasn't kidding. He was waiting. "The password to get into your laptop. I want it."

"Why? I don't even have my laptop with me. Just my satchel and my phone." She shook her head, not following.

Eli had left most of her things at the hotel in LA, since her flight to Seattle was out of LAX. She was supposed to spend half a day at Sailing Stones Books, then pick up a rental car and drive herself back. The short flight had been a courtesy, and a real indulgence to make her schedule work better. When her publisher had offered her the same conveyance back, Eli had balked. If it only meant losing two or three hours of sleep, she would rather drive.

That half smile crossed his face again. "I took the liberty of gathering your things from your hotel room. And I answered the texts from the bookstore you were scheduled to visit that your flight had made you ill and you could not attend. It is all taken care of, do not worry. The password?"

She sat in shock for a moment, trying to put that together.

My key was in my bag. Was the name of the hotel on it? How did he know the room number?

Her thoughts swam.

Stay on target.

"If you have my clothes, then why am I wearing this? Why did you change me at all?" She steeled herself, her hand closing around the broken spring.

He sighed. "Because your attire was not appropriate."

Is this the fight we're going to have? You should try to relax him. Get him talking.

But fear and indignation won out.

"What's appropriate attire for me, then? Why is that up to you?" She squeezed the metal across her palm so that the last few inches pushed upward from her fist, like a second thumb.

He was watching her face.

He's not looking. He doesn't know you have it. Get him closer. Closer.

"Those clothes were hiding who you really are. You may not see it yet, but I do. You are the perfect woman. I used to think that Lady Jessica was the perfect woman, but now I know it is you."

This guy is deeply crazy, and I am going to die here. The thought dropped like a stone into the water of her consciousness, whole and heavy. Everything rippled out from that, and the ripples made the clear reflections of the future she saw for herself distort, dissolve, disappear. What was left was a flat certainty: *I am going to die here.*

She decided immediately to fight. Fight now, before things could get any worse or weirder. The nearness of gruesome, violent death filled her with killing rage that was a form of relief unto itself. She was so glad to be filled with something that was not terror that she seized it. She wanted to use it. This might be her only shot.

I decided to fight when I stuck my hand into this mattress. I was always going to fight. Alright, motherfucker. Let's fight. Let's do this. Let's do this right now.

She had to bear down to continue having the conversation. *Make it sound good. Get him relaxed, just a few notches more.*

"Lady Jessica? You mean from *Dune*?" She said it like she was genuinely interested. She just wanted him distracted. She had been trained for this her whole life: to feign interest in a man's opinion.

He bit.

"Yes. Lady Jessica chooses her love over—"

Now.

She brought her arm up in a savage arc and stabbed him in the cheek with the broken end of the steel spring. She felt the edge grind against bone before he could pull away. She had wanted the eye, but this was good. Very, very good.

He screamed long and high, rising like a teakettle. He twisted toward her, long-fingered hands grappling with her arms, slipping on the blood that had leaked steadily from the wound on her right hand and wrist. She yanked the spring out and tried desperately to stick him again. She succeeded in scratching him deeply across the chest before he rolled his weight on top of her and she lost her grip.

He took the piece of metal in his closed fist and brought up one solid, bony knee to kneel on her chest. The pain was excruciating.

They stayed that way a minute, locked together. He was panting, dripping blood down on her face. She writhed, turned her face away. She could not move.

"You continue to disappoint me," he panted, wiping blood off his face with the back of his hand. It ran in shocking red strokes across his pale skin toward his mouth, making his face even longer. His glasses were askew. His eyes rolled and his thin lips puffed out as he struggled to regain control of his breathing.

"Fuck you," she wheezed, trying to buck him off, to turn to the side and get away. His skeletal knee ground against her breastbone in a bright graveyard agony.

He reached back with one mile-long arm and slapped her hard with his bloody left hand, knocking her head to the side, slipping in his own blood on her face. His glasses jumped again and he crammed them back down on the blade of his nose.

"Tell me the password."

"Fuck...you..." She had to pull two shallow breaths to say those short words, but she didn't care if they were her last. Her vision swam. Her head pounded. She wanted those words bad enough to fight for them. Her ribs ached with the pressure of his body on hers. Her heart was like a live pinned butterfly in her chest.

He leaned over, shifting more of his weight on to that one knee. She thought for sure one of her ribs would break. She saw stars.

She was pushing at him, clawing at his chest, trying to fight him. Her arms grew weaker and weaker as everything but the need to breathe deserted her. They fell at the sides of her head, useless. She was graying out.

He delicately picked up her right hand and held it. She barely registered this strangely gentle contact. Then, his grip tightened and he brought his other hand over and slowly, thoughtfully stabbed the metal shard into the tip of her pinkie finger, mingling his blood and hers.

She opened her mouth to scream but only a high, breathy sound came out. The pain was intolerable. She couldn't breathe, couldn't think. Her legs kicked weakly, involuntarily, like a dead frog stimulated by electricity. The world was only her burning lungs, and the distant point of white-out pain in her finger.

He saw the slackness in her face and let up off her chest long enough for reflex to draw a deep breath. Then he came back down, heavy as the earth. She tried to pull her hand away from him, but his grip was iron. She sobbed dryly, losing hope.

"Password."

"Fuckyou123," she said. "All one word." She wheezed and spoke again. "Capital *F*."

He moved the shard to her ring finger and stabbed again. She felt blood running down both digits into her open palm. Her hands shook. Her lower lip quivered. She sobbed and tried feebly to roll away, to get away, to reclaim her hand.

"I do not want to hurt you, but it is important that you learn the rules. When I ask you a question, you answer. It is the only way I can help you. In the end we are going to be so happy."

He was smiling, almost beatifically. The effect of it stretched the wound in his face and made it bleed more freely around a feeble clot. His glasses slid down his nose, slick with blood.

She stared up at him. She tried to close her hand. "Get the fuck off me, you crazy piece of shit."

He stabbed her middle finger next, and a lightning bolt ripped down her arm. The metal had jabbed into the soft, membranous bed under the nail. The nail lifted up and pulled away from her dry skin there. It was pain beyond anything she had ever felt, even as she knew it was more panic than damage. She could survive this, but she could not live with it.

She saw red. She screeched from the thin, cramped space in her rib cage. She was something brainless, spineless, without higher cognitive function. She was a worm cut in half by a curious child with a piece of broken glass.

"Password," he said, smiling again. He wiggled the piece of metal savagely against the nerves there. She gibbered inarticulately, yanking her arm back with diminishing force.

"Aida!" It was out of her mouth before she could think to stop it. Her voice was too high. "Aida1992."

He withdrew the metal. He came off her chest with one final, sickening downward push. She lay stunned, bleeding. She curled up instinctively, pulling her hand against her belly and cradling it, hiding it.

"Now you have spoiled everything," he said. His tone was aggrieved, as if she had ruined a surprise party. "Look at this! Blood all over. Your nightgown is disgusting. My face is a wreck. I am going to have to wash everything and start all over. You are a mess. Did you know that? Were you trying to make a mess?" He gestured tiredly to the rules posted on the wall, and despite herself, Eli's eyes landed on number three:

YOU WILL BEHAVE WELL AND BE TIDY OR THERE WILL BE CONSEQUENCES.

Eli watched as he pulled his crabby hand back to wipe blood off his own face, fascinated and trembling with exhaustion. She had cut him up pretty bad, but his focus had returned.

He seemed not to notice how badly he must be hurt, or her wounds, either.

He cares about order before anything else. The dirty nightgown. Not the fact that we're both bleeding. The mess.

He walked around the bed to where the linens had been kicked to the floor. He gathered them up, blotting his bleeding face on them as he rose.

"Give me your nightgown."

"No," she said at once.

"I have to wash it. Take it off and give it to me or I will come take it off you," he said. His smile was gone now.

Her hand hurt almost as bad as it had when he had jammed the spring in. Her head throbbed. The UTI was worse now, an ache on top of the constant heat. She could feel it like a deep itch in her pelvis, a localized fever. She knew that the next time she urinated, the liquid leaving her body would feel like fire. There was nothing she could do for it; she couldn't wash or even piss when she needed to. She was pulsing with pain all over, like the rippling of a caterpillar. She couldn't think of another course of action that wouldn't lead to more pain, so she slowly hiked the gown up while staying curled in on herself, and threw it over to him. The shame she had felt before intensified, coupled itself with the vulnerability of being naked in front of a stranger. She expected him to leer. She expected him to put his hands on her. Everything inside her shrank away from what would follow.

I will simply leave my body, she thought, the process already beginning. *I will not be here when it happens.*

He added it to the pile, looking her over. She noticed he did not leer. He was almost prim in averting his eyes. "There, now. That is more like it. Now you think about what you have done here, and how you can do better in the future. I know you can."

He left. She was keenly aware of the sound of him above her. She heard a washer start to fill and then agitate. She heard him in his bathroom, running the water for a long time as he tended to his face. She did what she could to shield herself from the camera, turning her back to it and keeping her thighs pressed together tightly.

I can do better than that in the future, you fucker. I know I can.

Shock was settling in, as welcome as the sunrise. She was not quite in herself. Looking at her bleeding hand dreamily, she thought about her bracelet. She had been wearing it when he snatched her; he must have taken it off her at some point.

She had never mentioned the bracelet in an interview. She didn't want anyone trying to steal it from her at a convention or in an airport security line. She had chosen the design for its blandness: a black leather band with a plain, wide metal clasp. At a glance, it looked like something that might count steps or vibrate when you got a text message. Unremarkable.

Even when he unsnapped it, he couldn't have seen the USB connector. There's no way he sprang the hidden catch.

Eli believed in that precious piece of hardware the same way she believed in the cash she hid around her house, or the two forms of ID she always carried with her. It held all her books, including the unpublished one. All her notes for the rest of the series. Everything.

The bracelet was as much a fetish as a rabbit's foot or a rosary, and it carried the same weight. She would never be caught unawares. She would never lose her work to a dead laptop or a thief. No cloud was secure enough to suit her. She was safe as long as she had that formidable, unassuming piece of armor on her wrist.

She pulled her wounded hand against her chest, thinking about safety. About armor. About that fucking monster walking around over her head. About what she had that he couldn't predict. The springy, meaty feeling of the metal going through his cheek.

He doesn't know he's got it. Whatever he is looking for on my laptop, he's got in a bracelet that he may have tossed in the garbage for all I know. And I'll never fucking tell him. Because he'll never ask, so he can't get it out of me.

He can't break me. Not all the way. I am going to get out of this alive. He has no idea what kind of trouble he got when he picked me.

She jammed her wounded fingers into her mouth, with her back against the wall. She didn't have to stay in this basement, and she knew it. She had a secret basement of her own. She called up its memory, its scent and its dimensions and left herself as completely as she knew how. She went to her secret fortress in her mind. The comfort of that mixed with her shock and she began to drift. After a time, she slept.

4

Standing over the bathtub, he poured peroxide into the deep, narrow wound. He thought he could get along without stitches, but applied three careful droplets of cyanoacrylate to close the skin over the wound. Next time, he would have a better plan.

He imagined her standing in the doorway of the bathroom behind him, looking anxiously over his shoulder.

When she understood his plan, she would beg his forgiveness. There were forces inside her that she could not control, like an infection. Like possession. He had to free her from them. He had to help her see what they could be together.

He washed again, the long and pristine white basin of the tub splashed with bloody water.

He imagined her closing the distance between them, laying a cool hand against his back. He felt the clinging of the wet spots on his shirt and told himself, *Her hand her hand her hand.*

She whispered near his ear. She said again the words he longed to hear. She would give herself to him, more completely and more permanently than any woman had ever done to any man. This was part of her magic, and something that only she could do. This was the gift of her blood. She asked him to remember her testing, her blood dripped into the vial of milk.

"I remember," he said to the echo of the tub.

She patiently explained that the work had already begun. This was the magic that would free them and unite them. Blood magic. Hers spilled and his spilled and mixed together.

He looked down at the pink as it swirled toward the drain. "Blood magic."

She nodded behind his back. *It is the way we become one,* she said. *Just as when a man fathers a child and mixes a bloodline. So, too, have we mixed. Like John Donne's flea. Bloodtalking. The change is at hand.*

Leonard Lobovich smiled with just his lips. "I can use that in the book," he mused.

You certainly can, said his muse.

In her thin dream in her basement bed, Eli was at a convention. She couldn't tell which one; all those windowless hotel ballrooms and convention center conference rooms looked exactly alike. She was on a panel, and someone had asked her a question, but she had no answer.

She looked from her left to her right and saw the faces of authors she knew, but she couldn't come up with their names. They looked at her off-center, zeroing in on specific parts of her face like she had a massive zit or a snot bat in the cave of her nose. One seemed to angle his head to look into her mouth, at her teeth.

"Well?" the questioner was prompting her. "Are you going to answer me?"

She looked out into the yellow-lit room and saw that the man with the microphone was her captor. She could tell it was him immediately, despite the fact that the lower half of his face was covered by a bandanna, like a robber in an old Western film. She saw his eyes.

"What do you want from me?" The words were nearly impossible to wrench out of her mouth. Everything was slowing down. He was closer to her with every heartbeat. The second row. The first. She couldn't breathe. She could smell him.

He was standing just on the other side of the conference table with its heavy pleated skirt. He was pressing the microphone against his mask and moaning into it, making a sound like a low, deep vibration.

Eli awoke.

She was very cold and disoriented. She had forgotten where she was again. The room's sole overhead light fixture was controlled by a switch somewhere above. The basement was fully dark, except for the glowing red eye of the camera above the bed.

As soon as she moved, she realized how much pain she was in. Her hand ached horribly from where he had stabbed her fingers. Her chest felt like it had been run over by a car. Her head ached worse than ever now, and she figured she must also be dehydrated.

The vibrating noise continued, seeming to come from above her and travel down all the walls at once.

"What the hell is that?" she croaked, her throat and chest barely cooperating. The sound kept up for a few minutes, then quit.

Vacuum cleaner, maybe? A drill?

There was nothing to look at in the darkness. There was nothing to focus on but the dry, cold air and the pain. Even the noise had gone. The room was so silent that her ears rang. She tried to make herself work on the problem.

He didn't want to kill her. If that was what he wanted, even distantly, it would have already happened. He must want something from her that he could only get with her alive.

He didn't even look when I was naked. Barely glanced. So what is it, if it's not that?

He had wanted the password to her laptop, but had acted uninterested in money. The money was what she had always worried about if her laptop were stolen. If someone could get past her initial password, she had saved her log-ins to her bank account and her investment accounts. Someone could access her quarterly statements from her publisher and rob her broke on the right day.

If this guy had wanted to do that, mugging her would have been easier. That was not the aim here.

He had gone to the hotel and gotten her clothes. Why?

Doing it this way makes it look like I checked out on my own. If I had disappeared without my clothes and my work, then it's foul play. This way it's...

It's what? A sudden urge to roam?

Unbidden, an interview she had just done for a women's magazine replayed itself to her.

"I don't like feeling like I've got a leash on. Sometimes I like to just disappear for a day or two," she had said dreamily to the interviewer. "Just go to some town where no one knows mc and walk their waterfront. Eat something I've never eaten before. Live something new and shake the dust off."

The answer had been in response to a tiresome question about writer's block.

It's just that. Just disappearing.

Eli really could disappear without anyone noticing for a while. *How long?*

She thought of Joe again, trying to renew that sense of relief in the idea that her assistant would blow the whistle and get help. Right now, that feeling would not come. Eli dug deep.

Joe was the best damned assistant money would buy, and she was lucky to have him. The kid had come up through internships at publishing houses and had learned all the author liaison stuff. But the business was rough, and he hadn't been able to get a full-time gig.

He had reached out to her through her agent. She had answered back directly, intrigued. He had been brassy and smart and asked for a meeting in person. His emails were professional and polished, but still audacious. She had said yes.

He had set them up at one of her favorite bars in San Francisco. When she arrived, there was a beaded glass on the table containing her favorite cocktail, and a hot plate of charred duck hearts laid over fans of pickled pineapple had just landed. He gestured to the booth bench and she sat with him.

"This is impressive," she had said, taking a duck heart while it steamed and popping it in her mouth.

"What I'm going to say may sound crazy," Joe said, pushing his long black glossy bangs off his face and smiling at her. "But you need an executive assistant."

Eli ate another heart. "That's not crazy. What's crazy is thinking that any author, even a very good one and a luckily successful one like me, can afford it."

Joe tittered nervously and adjusted his bow tie. He was a stocky fellow, with the look of a big, friendly dog. He classed up his natural goofiness with a natty aesthetic: suspenders, tweedy bow tie, expensive haircut. He was unfashionably soft for San Francisco, but still fit right in. Beneath the edges of his cuffs, Eli could see the outer lines of tattoos.

She had liked him at once. She sipped her cocktail and found it excellent. "This is all very coordinated," she began.

He raised a finger to speak, but interjected smoothly in a way that did not feel like an interruption. "I've read every single one of your books. I've also read every single one of your essays, your short stories, your Instagram posts and tweets. I came here an hour early and had a conversation with your bartender. She had no idea that you were famous, just that you were a regular and a good tipper. I know what your schedule is like. I know that you'd need me most in months leading up to and following a book release, and that your volume of mail goes up significantly after you publish a short story or say something controversial. I can chart your weekly productivity, if you want. I can disappear when you don't need me as much."

She drank again, giving him a skeptical look. "Alright. You've got my attention. Plus I'm pleasantly creeped out. Please go on."

"I also know that you can't afford a full-time assistant. Neither can G. A. Hangerton, or Jeff Busch. They're… Well, I don't have to tell you. They're the giants of your field. I don't represent just anyone. I represent people whose work I love. Whose work has changed me. I don't want to just do the drudgery for someone. I want to righteously obsess over the details so you can make art. There have been people throughout history whose job it has been to be close to the seat of power, of genius, but to serve it. The power behind the throne. All the greats had one—Nabokov had Vera, Wordsworth had Dorothy. You could have me."

His face had taken on the glow of fanaticism, and Eli could see it. She drew back, just a little. She set her drink down. He saw it and fixed his face. He cleared his throat and took a drink of water before going on, slower and in a more even voice.

"That's why I work for them, too. Look, an assistant is a coordinator. A scheduler. A handler. A gofer. And none of you need any of those things all the time. You all have agents and publishers and PR, plus your own friends and fam and independent workflow. I can handle the extraneous stuff, with polish and attention to detail. I know the business, the publishing houses, the events and the nitty-gritty stuff. And since I work part-time for several authors, I'm surprisingly affordable. I'm adding another client and I only work for writers whose work I love. I want to work for you."

Eli had met Hangerton. The woman was a star on the convention circuit: bright red hair and eccentric fashions to go with her enormously popular series on Romani vampires. Eli thought of the older woman as one of those people who wasn't constantly impersonating a grown-up. Hangerton actually seemed to have her shit together. Naturally, that meant she was hiring out the small stuff.

Eli set down her empty glass. "I'm supposed to be at a convention in two weeks," she said.

"In Boulder," he supplied, his eyes bright again.

Eli thought idly that he looked like the kind of young man who usually showed up at the door with tracts or works of scripture.

He went on, "You're speaking on four panels and giving a talk about movie adaptations of novels for aspiring writers."

Eli was impressed, but kept pushing. "Anna Narendra is going to be there. I have always wanted to meet her, and I know she's looking for someone to headline her anthology of mother-and-daughter stories."

"She is," Joe agreed, taking a sip of water. "But I think she may go to Gia Wong. They've worked together before."

Eli nodded. "So what I was hoping to do was get coffee with her at this convention and feel her out about it."

Joe signaled their waiter and hot, house-made potato chips arrived with dipping sauce. "One moment, please," he said. He brought a small tablet onto his side of the table. He typed as Eli munched with satisfaction, tapping the glass for another drink when the bartender spared her a glance.

Joe pulled out his phone and dialed. "Hello, Mr. Bacon," he said warmly. "It's Joe Papasian. I don't know if you remember me, but we met at—" Joe gave a fetching giggle, interrupted, "Yeah, that was me. You were so lit I didn't think you'd know your own name the next day... Well, thank you! Anyhow, I'm calling to talk a little business, if you don't mind. How's Anna's schedule at Boulderon?"

Joe briskly tapped out a few notes while the person on the other side of the line spoke. "That's not too bad. One of my clients is a guest of the con and was hoping they could do coffee." His voice was warm like caramel cream as he slid glibly between turns of phrase.

Joe paused. A small smile tipped up the corners of his lips. "Eli Grey."

Another pause. "I'm so glad to hear that. So, I know Anna's got a ridiculous sweet tooth, and there's a patisserie not far from the hotel. Can I set them up there?...Sunday? Great. I'll send you the invite. Thank you so much...Oh yes, we must!... Alright, thank you. Bye!"

He smiled and set his phone down. "She's yours."

Joe slipped his tablet back into his slim bag.

"The point of that wasn't access. It's your name that opens the door, and you know that. The point is that you shouldn't have to handle that kind of thing yourself. The point is that even though your name is good enough, it sounds even better coming from a crisp professional who works for you." He folded his hands on the table, showing a neat and recent manicure.

Eli looked at her own nails, considering. He was efficient, but obsessive. At least he was obsessive about her.

"More importantly, everybody should know that they don't talk to you without getting through your people. That's the level that you're at now. I know you have your agent and your publisher, but I would love to be your littlest gatekeeper."

The kid smiled. He was good. Eli sipped her second drink as soon as it arrived.

"Let's talk about rates," she said. Joe pulled his tablet back out, smiling still.

He had worked for her ever since.

It had been four years since that good first day. She had been able to give him a raise every year and a gift every holiday and birthday. She had grown to like him very much and trust his instincts. When she didn't show up, Joe would have all the proof in the world: her itinerary, her many confirmations, her habit of checking in with him not constantly, but with fair regularity from the road. How long would he wait before going to the police? How long before they believed him?

He's not family. My friends know I'm on the road for almost another month, and they're not exactly close to me.

Her stomach dropped and her throat tightened as she had to admit to herself that nobody really was close to her. The idea that the only person who would really miss her was her assistant was depressing.

I don't even have a cat that somebody has to feed. No plants to water. I don't ask anybody to sit for my house. My mail piles up in my PO box and I don't sweat the rest. Not going to cry. This is not a thing I'm going to cry about. I have bigger problems.

Isn't that the life I wanted, though? Nobody to answer to, nobody's bullshit to schedule myself around?

The answer was yes, but it was more complicated than that. She had been lonely, but not lonely enough to settle into a relationship that didn't suit her completely. She spent most of her time alone.

And why? Because Nella points out when you drink too much?

Because she asks you when you're going to see a counselor? No crying. Because you have no old friends and you can't trust new friends?

With success had come a thousand hangers-on, people from high school who suddenly felt nostalgic and wanted to catch up. People from college whom she had hated all of a sudden saw four years of heinous classism as water under the bridge and wanted to invite her to their kids' birthday parties. It had all seemed so phony, so contingent on money and fame.

A few writer friends understood her. Nella was one of them. Nella had been unpublished back then, but talented and very disciplined about submissions. Eli had never stopped believing she would make it and she was right. Eli had offered to blurb Nella's first book, but in the end Nella's editor had gotten her someone even better.

Eli remembered the first time Nella had come to her place just to hang out. It had felt surprisingly awkward to have someone in her space who was not a lover or a prospective lover.

"This place is dark," Nella had said.

"Sorry, I'm a vampire," Eli had joked, hastily whipping open a few of the heavy drapes, watching the dust lift off them and swirl in the sudden shafts of light.

"How long have you been here?" Nella was still standing, turning, taking inventory of the room. She held on to her purple skirt as if concerned that she might come away coated in dust.

"About four years," Eli said, sitting down. "Why?" She offered Nella a cup of tea.

Nella sat finally and took it, one eyebrow up. "Nothing on the walls. Generic furniture. It looks like nobody lives here."

Eli had tried to laugh it off. "Well, I keep my Supernovas in the office. I suppose I could bring them out here."

Nella had shrugged, as if to say that wasn't going to be enough. "It feels empty. Like nobody lives here. Or a serial killer. You know?" Nella had a husband who adored her to go home to, someone who appreciated her warmth and her sense of humor. Of course she found Eli's place empty. Compared to her own, it was.

Eli knew what Nella was feeling, but she couldn't explain herself to so new a friend. She had made some lazy joke in the moment, and Nella had dropped it. They had talked about writing, which was easier than talking about life. Which was why Eli wrote fiction in the first place.

This is a hell of a time to psychoanalyze myself. My lifestyle is not the issue. The problem here is that nobody is going to call the cops.

But it was all the same thing, and Eli knew it. She had made her bed, and she was typically relieved if not happy to lie in it. She had never considered who would report her missing if circumstances required it.

I take care of myself. I don't need anybody complicating my life. But right now...

She looked around the room desperately, wishing she had been better at becoming real friends with Joe. He had certainly kept the door open, but she had never gone through it.

He has a boyfriend. What's his name? Pete? Pat? Fuck. Am I gonna die here because I don't have roommates anymore?

Come on, Joe, you know me. You know I wouldn't just blow you off. Go get help.

But Joe did not expect her for eighteen more hours. She would have to wait this out until then. And maybe much longer than that.

5

Joe Papasian knew something was wrong long before he let himself admit it.

He was miffed when Eli missed her check-in, so he texted her. No answer came. He logged in as her and saw that she had not checked in for her flight. His heart beat faster when he discovered that she had canceled her event at Sailing Stones. When he found that she had not answered an email or tweeted or signed in to her Facebook in over a day, he raised an eyebrow and said aloud, "Sober up, doll. We have work to do." Inwardly, he knew that this show of bravado was for his own benefit. He was scared.

He signed into the app she had allowed him to install on both their phones that made them a family group and let him to track her location, and she his.

"I'm never gonna use this," she had said. "And if I start seeing someone new, I'm probably gonna turn it off."

Joe typed in her nickname: Queen of Tales. He had set up their avatar photos, using her book jacket portrait and one of himself in Hawaii in his senior year in college where he thought he looked young.

"It's really just in case you're lost or in trouble, so I can find you," he said. "Also, when you're driving and I want to know how long you're gonna be and instead of you yelling at me that you can't text behind the wheel, I can just check you out myself."

"Fine," she sighed. "I'm sure this is some big privacy thing that I should fight you about, but I actually don't care. You run my life anyway—it's not like you don't already know where I am. I could probably die and you could keep up the illusion that I was alive for years before anyone knew."

"And cash your royalty checks," he said sweetly, handing back her phone.

That had been almost a year ago, but the app was still doing its job. He pulled up the map and zoomed in over LA. He saw the pink line showing that she had made the flight to Mojave. She was supposed to go back to her hotel from there, but she hadn't. She had driven north on some freeway for an hour or more, and then switched off her phone.

Joe frowned at his screen.

He checked her email and saw the form letter from the hotel thanking her for staying there and knew she must have checked out.

He looked over her recent activity. The last sign-in to her account had only been about an hour ago, on her own laptop. In fact, she had been signing in and out of that account all day, as if she were checking for something important to come through.

But her phone hadn't signed in for over a day.

Joe was very sure at this point that something was wrong. His hands unsteady, he activated the app's find function, which would turn it on even if it were powered down and set off a shrieking alarm that could not be silenced without a code.

He hoped that it would turn on, wherever it was, and he would see her pop up on the locator app in that same moment.

The app displayed a thumbs-up, indicating that somewhere, it was screaming to be found. But nothing appeared on the map, even as Joe refreshed it over and over again.

She had turned her GPS off. Or someone else had.

That was when he was sure. Joe kicked the other apps off his screen and thought hard. He pushed back in his chair and called Paul into the room.

"Yeah?" Paul was drying his hands on a dish towel, clearly busy with something else.

"Listen, you know my client Eli?" Joe looked up at his boyfriend.

"Yeah, the one you fucking, like, worship? Yes, I know Eli."

Joe sighed. "Okay, fair. So I think something bad may have happened to her. But she doesn't really have anybody. Should I call the cops?"

Paul's Spock eyebrow went up. "You think it's that serious?"

"I don't know. I have a feeling. It's not like her to miss a flight. She's supernervous about it and obsesses over the procedure for days before."

Paul set the towel down on the desk and put his hands on Joe's shoulders. "Trust your gut. The worst thing that happens is you look silly. You'd regret not saying something when you were worried if it turns out to be legit."

"You're right," Joe said. But he still felt like things were more dire than he could say out loud. If Eli died, he didn't know what he would do. She wasn't just his boss—she was his favorite writer of all time, and someone whom he genuinely liked. "I'll call in the morning, if I haven't heard from her."

Joe stopped talking, but he didn't stop thinking about it. He was looking up the rules of how long he had to wait to report a missing person. Eli was an adult, and he wasn't her family. The answer was not entirely clear. But Paul was right: better safe than sorry. And Joe was feeling sorry already.

6

Leonard Lobovich was relieved to finally get access to the computer, but he hated that the process had been so ugly.

He had never expected her to become violent. She wasn't violent in the books, not at all. She never had fistfights; she carried no gun. She solved her problems with her brains and her magic and her quick, witty words. He had thought she would try to talk her way into his good graces. Instead, she had acted like a wild animal caught in a trap.

The laptop, at least, was orderly. Her files were perfectly labeled. Her in-box was sorted according to sensible categories. He signed in to her social media accounts, to which the passwords were helpfully stored, and was startled at the number of notifications he found waiting for him there. Hundreds of people in her timeline took the care to tell her how much they loved her and her work. They told jokes and asked questions. They took pictures of themselves with the book and at the movies, and took the time to tag her in them. Some of them were nonsense or even occasionally hostile, but the love was like a wave that washed over him.

His own laptop sat beside hers. He pivoted to it and ran back the video interview he had seen with her just two weeks ago, when he had made his decision.

She was wearing another black blazer, sitting on a tall stool talking to the host of a morning show. The lights were bright and she was smiling, running her fingers through her terribly short hair. She was slouching, and her lack of discipline showed in both her posture and the pooch of her belly as she struggled to look comfortable on her perch.

But when she smiled, he could see right into her. Who she was…what she could be.

The host leaned over in his stool, speaking to her as if there were a secret between them despite the cameras. His perfect white teeth shone.

"So, when can we expect that next Millicent Michaelson book? When are we going to hear about what happens after the big wedding?"

She smiled, looking down for a moment. "It's written," she said, grinning. "It's ready. I'm sending it to my publisher on April 1. It's a tradition of mine. That's the day I sent in my first novel. I figured if they hated it, I could always pretend I was just joking."

The host smiled and wagged his finger at her self-deprecating joke. The woman to his right laughed like a parrot that had heard actual humans laugh once or twice in its life. "We'll be right back," she said. The clip on the website ended.

It was here. He could barely contain his excitement. Everything he wanted was right here in this house. The book was written. It was still his, because it was only March, so she hadn't sent it in yet. But he searched and searched through all the documents, looking for the file. He found nothing.

He was so close to what he wanted. He walked to the monitors to look in on her and soothe himself. She was right there. She was where she belonged. He had everything under control.

Leonard began to pace. Getting the first password from her had been awful, just awful. She might be smart enough to figure out why he had wanted it.

She hadn't recognized him. He was sure of that. He had made substantial changes to his look, not just for her, but to preclude the possibility of ever being recognized by anyone. Nothing in her face had suggested she knew they had met before. But he would have to proceed very carefully.

Leonard Lobovich had read the first Millicent Michaelson book when he was a junior in college, and it had reshaped how he saw the world. Before that, his favorite book had been *Dune*. Since first reading it in seventh grade, he'd spent hundreds of hours thinking about Lady Jessica. What would his life have been like if she had been his mother, or if she were his wife? She had sacrificed tradition and loyalty and all she had to devote herself to her great love, Duke Leto, and bear his child, Paul Atreides. She had given Leonard the thing he treasured most as a child: the Bene Gesserit litany against fear. Jessica had helped him learn to shed his vulnerability and shame and become something more.

But when he got old enough to fantasize about women in *that* way, he couldn't picture Jessica. She was maternal, remote, her vitality and power taken up by the husband and son she loved so desperately.

Millicent Michaelson, on the other hand, crackled with energy. She was a thinker, and she worked hard in both the cowan world and the magical world as a helpmeet, making life better and easier for so many. She rebuffed coarse advances, readily and often, from would-be suitors who were impolite or vulgar. His beautiful Millicent had rejected even Master Ignus, the greatest sorcerer in the inverted city. He was so obvious: handsome, strong, talented and arrogant. Leonard had blushed when Millicent had felt his sizeable erection against her when they danced. She had told him he was disgusting and walked away.

Her life had captivated him from the first. In her first adventure, Millicent uncovered a vast network of magical criminals called the Sceleris, who preyed mostly on cowans—the word she used for nonmagical folks—procuring children for human trafficking and protected by rites of sacrifice. She used detective work to locate their magical fortress: an inverted church in the caves beneath the city's oldest cathedral. In it, she rescued a young girl who had been chained to the great stone altar, her blood consecrated to the dark god who protected the Sceleris and their work. It was dark stuff, drawn from her own history and embellished with a magic and a kind of hope she had always wished for when she was a child, but had never found.

The big reveal, the thing that really burned Millicent's story into his mind, was of course that she was also a sorceress. Her unknown parents must have been quite powerful, because when Millicent's abilities manifested they were notable even among the magical elites. She believed that her defeat of the Sceleris had been just police work done diligently and good luck. Magical authorities, however, sought her out after she had destroyed Sceleris' labyrinthine locus of dark magic and freed their slaves to ask her how she had done it.

In a tense midnight meeting, Madame Olitti had pricked Millicent's finger and whispered to the ruby drop of her blood that it must reveal its secrets. The drop of blood was dripped into a long, thin flute full of milk given at the new moon. An ancient house's magical sigil had displayed itself there, red in white, announcing that Millicent was the last known scion of a long-lost ruling house of powerful sorceresses. Millicent had no desire to rule, but wanted to put her unique powers to use helping those who could not help themselves. She applied and was accepted into the Maginaria, the magical law-enforcement academy, and mentored by their greatest and oldest teacher. The journey of Millicent Michaelson began as one of adventures in the magical and mundane worlds paired with parallel ones of self-discovery.

Best of all, she developed a secret love for her cowan partner, Charlie Schrader. He was like her first love, Marcel, but he was a better man: a quiet, decent policeman. Could he ever be taught what it meant to her to walk in both worlds? Could she give him the gift of sight? In the most recent book, she had said yes to his devastatingly romantic proposal, and their wedding was set to take place. Leonard couldn't wait to hear about the consummation of their love.

Millicent went right to the heart of him, reading his roommate's book there in their dorm. As an MFA student, he had noticed the work that went into the book. He didn't like to think of the author, but of the effort as a whole, perfect world that came together as naturally as water turns to ice. It was a perfect book. The mind behind it had to be perfect, as well. What would it be like to have access to that mind? The adventures, the art, the *understanding* that might be found there?

The campus bookstore had had the first two volumes, and he had bought his own copy of both that same night. The author eventually came to his campus for a signing event at their bookstore, but he hadn't wanted to go. He assumed she would be like most celebrities: mean, conceited or dull.

He stood at the back of the line, watching her smile and sign books and listen patiently while people told her how much they loved her work and why. She looked genuinely happy to see each person in line. She thanked everyone for reading and buying the book; she kept saying that she was living her dream life.

All at once, her smile became winsome as she looked down the line. She was rapt in a moment of absolutely breathless delight. She fully felt how lucky she was to live the dream. She was walking in a whole new world. He looked back at her, nakedly longing to take part in that feeling. And that was when it had all come together.

She didn't look right; she dressed wrong and wore her hair wrong and even her eyes were the wrong color. She was thinner back then, but not the sexy slip of a girl who could wriggle through a tight secret passage in the Maginaria. But she was Millicent. She had to be. He saw to the core of her, and he loved her.

When it came to his turn, he smiled and asked her to just sign his books rather than making them out to him. He said he wanted to preserve their resale value.

Her smile had faltered a little at this and his soaring heart had throbbed all the harder. She wasn't in it for the money. She wasn't thinking of what her signature was worth. She was really in it for the love of art, like him.

He hurried away with his treasured books and never opened them again. They were only paperbacks and he knew they wouldn't last. Instead, he bought two more copies and read them exhaustively, waiting for the next to come out.

After her third book, *Well of Onyx*, he had seen her at a convention for writers in Los Angeles. She was talking on a panel about what it was like to work on a series, but she was the least well-known author on the dais. She was nervous and spoke only when someone asked a question directly addressed to her. She seemed flustered and jumpy. It was strangely exciting to him to see her troubled this way. As if she might need his help.

The convention took place over a weekend and there were parties each night after panels broke up. He checked her Twitter all evening to find out where she would be, but she didn't tweet anything until nearly midnight.

Her tweets were error filled, clearly drunk efforts to apologize for her disappointing appearance earlier that day. They gave the name of the bar where she was hanging out, and invited anyone who wanted to chat with her to meet her there.

Leonard had already been in bed in his hotel room, but he got dressed and immediately headed out.

It was never really night in Los Angeles. The lights were always on and the smog-filled sky reflected the orangey glow of the city and its bright, brittle denizens.

The bar was old and draped with long fabric banners to disguise earthquake damage. It was both too loud and too crowded to be a good place to talk. He spotted her right away, sitting alone at the bar with her head in both hands. A whiskey with one giant ice cube sat before her.

He wedged his way toward a gap near her and ordered club soda with lime. He didn't drink, but knew from experience that this combination would make it look as though he did. She was close. If he had reached out his right hand, he could have touched her. The space between them vibrated with potential, a hot cushion of air.

He had finished college by then and had begun his own career. He knew now that she was only two years older than him, but he tried not to compare his accomplishments to hers. What she was doing wasn't even really fiction, when you got down to it. She was just writing about herself.

Someone sat on the other side of her and Leonard busied himself with his phone. But he listened intently.

"Hey," said the woman on the other side of Eli.

"Hey, Nella," Eli said, obviously miserable.

Leonard had gathered through internet gossip and the tone of their conversation that Nella was at the convention promoting her new book; a runaway hit about a Brooklyn mage who had discovered a book of magic that had the power to create new worlds. Eli had hyped it endlessly, telling readers of the *Maginaria* that they would love it, but Nella hadn't needed her help. The book had scored incredible reviews and been a breakthrough in her career, selling her backlist and bringing TV and movie people sniffing around. Nella was riding high on the wave, and he could see Eli's distaste at dragging her down.

"I heard what happened."

Eli took a drink. "I know I shouldn't let it get to me or ruin this conference for you. I just wasn't ready to deal with it."

"I can't believe you're here at all," Nella said, scooting her stool in closer. Sidelong, Leonard could see that this woman was older, with a huge puff of kinky black hair that spread out all around her head. He knew her work, and his mouth opened when he realized who she was. She caught him looking and he quickly looked away.

"How was the marginalized-voices panel?" Eli asked.

Nella sighed. "You know, if white writers came and sat in the audience for that, it would be a really good thing. But you folks never do."

Eli grimaced. "I'm not in good shape."

"Sure, at this con. What about all the others? All I ever get asked to talk about is diversity. Marginalization. Never my work. And you get to talk about your work. And you don't even show up to my shit."

"You're right. You're right. I'm sorry. I'll be there next time. I'll bring someone with me."

They sat in silence a moment.

She leaned slightly toward Eli. Her face softened. "Eli, your mother died. That's real, but you need to get your shit together. You're an adult. You shouldn't be here drinking alone.

You want to come back to my suite? Angela and Candace are up there, too. You should have somebody to talk to."

"I don't want to bring you all down," she said, her voice hitching. "I think I'm just going to finish this one and then go cry it off. I just didn't expect to feel like this."

"You're allowed to feel how you feel," Nella said, but she was making a face. "Are you upset that you didn't contact her before she was gone?"

Eli sniffed again. "No. I'm upset that she didn't want me to."

Nella had hugged Eli awkwardly, from the side. Eli didn't move.

"Alright, then. There's no fixing that. But when you want to move on and come back to living, you know where to find me."

"I do. Thank you."

Leonard felt rather than saw the other woman go. He saw the crowd part to let her through.

He sipped his club soda. He didn't want the author to leave. He could smell her from here. Whiskey, yes, but also some clean, citrusy cologne. Her clean skin. Herself.

She set her glass down and slid it toward the inside of the bar. The bartender noticed and refilled it at once.

When she had done this a half dozen more times, he told her gently he couldn't serve her anymore. She smiled sadly and closed her tab.

When she got up to leave, Leonard gave her a head start. He threw down six dollars and went after her once she had entered the dancing throng that separated her from the door. People bumped and shouldered against one another, and he knew that if he reached out and touched her now, she'd never know it. She would think it was the movement of that many-limbed collective body on the dance floor. For that matter, she was so anesthetized she might not notice at all. He might be able to get a handle on her.

But that wasn't what he really wanted. It would be empty. A meaningless moment without true connection.

Drunk as she was, she had hailed a car on her phone and slid into it, slumping in the back seat as neatly as a rabbit going back into a hat.

He stood there a moment, transfixed, as she unquestioningly entered that tiny, closed world. How she trusted the shadowed man in the front seat to take her to her hotel, rather than parking somewhere secluded and having his way with her in her insensible state. How childlike. How simple.

He walked back to his hotel. She canceled her appearance on the following day, but he wasn't that disappointed. He already felt as though he knew her much better. Leonard disliked hearing Millicent talk about herself in the third person, anyway.

I don't remember those moments, she told him calmly, sitting across the table from him.

"I know you don't," he assured her.

You could make me remember them, if you wanted to, she said, putting her head in her hand and smiling at him.

"I don't think I want to do that," he murmured.

She assured him that he really did look different. But not quite different enough yet. The change was not yet obvious.

"I know that. I know. It needs to happen slowly."

She reminded him that the shoes she had been wearing would never fit him.

"I know that, too, my love."

But you can read the tag in them and order another pair just like them, in your own size. It will help. Magic tools to achieve magical results, remember?

He did remember. He tapped out the name of a website where he thought he could buy them.

That's my love, she told him, circling around to put her arms about his neck.

"Say my name," he told her in a low voice.

Eli Grey. Eli Grey. Eli Grey.

He was still saying it when the author's phone began to ring. Full of a rush of confidence, he answered.

7

Joe Papasian had spoken to four different people on the phone at the FBI before he reached someone who seemed to understand what he was saying.

"So she hasn't tweeted in a couple of days. That's not the same as proof of foul play. Maybe she ran off to an ashram or something. She's a writer. Who the hell knows?"

"With all due respect, ma'am, I am only laying that on the top of the rest of my proof. She hasn't touched money. Hasn't checked her email or answered her phone. Hasn't caught the flight she was booked on. Something is wrong, I'm telling you."

Joe's nerves had him biting his nails, despite the fact that he had gotten a manicure two days ago.

The agent went once more through the basic vital statistics of the individual he wanted to report missing.

"Name?" Her voice was bored, but gaining in focus.

"Elizabeth Grey. Goes by Eli."

"Occupation?"

"Bestselling and award-winning author."

"Okay, writer. Got it. Date of birth?"

Once she had enough to go on, Joe asked for her direct contact information.

"Look, I don't want to impugn the honor of the FBI or anything, but I need to know who I can call if I get any more info. Not just your office. You."

There was an audible sigh on the line.

"Agent Silvestri, Mr. Papasian. What did you say her Twitter handle was?"

"@eligrey," Joe spelled out slowly to her. He had read that FBI agents were notoriously ignorant about the internet. He anticipated having to explain all this at its most basic level to the officer.

"Yeah, I've got her account up right now. She just tweeted something, like, five minutes ago."

Joe had not looked at his phone since the call began. Now, he tore it away from his face to check the notifications, forgetting entirely that someone was expecting him to respond.

There it was. Eli had tweeted an eerily filtered picture of the sunrise, with the caption: "Daybreak."

That was it. No location was attached. The horizon in the photo was featureless desert, unrecognizable. Dirt, rock, sky.

"She didn't take that picture," he said, still staring at it.

Small and tinny from his phone: "Say again?"

He pulled it back to his face. "Sorry, I said Eli didn't take that picture."

"How do you know that?"

He couldn't answer. He knew it instinctively and with certainty, but he could not say why. Maybe it was the perspective from which the shot was taken. Maybe it was the tone of the caption: not at all like Eli's usual snarky, sharp Twitter voice. Maybe it was merely the mounting paranoia the last few hours had instilled in him, screaming inside his head that he had already waited too long, that she was already gone. But Joe knew that even if he was being paranoid, Eli had not taken this picture. She had not.

"I don't know. It's a feeling. I know this woman. I shop for her clothes. I read most of her emails before she does. It's a gut thing, but I swear there's something wrong here. I think someone else has her phone."

Agent Silvestri knew a hunch when she heard one. She respected it. Still, this wasn't much to go on.

"I'm going to do some checking on this," she told him, gentler than before.

"Thank you, ma'am." Joe hung up, feeling only slightly better.

Silvestri, seeing that the author had just tweeted and thought that perhaps Mr. Papasian was a codependent drama queen who had just been terminated by a boss who couldn't face the actual firing process, decided that she could spend a little time getting him an answer to put his mind at ease.

She looked at the time stamp on the Instagram photo and the author's last tweet. She sighed and dialed the writer's cell phone number.

There was an answer after the first ring. "Eli Grey."

The voice was low and musical. "Ms. Grey? This is Agent Silvestri with the FBI, in the San Francisco office. How are you doing today?"

There was a beat of silence. Silvestri was accustomed to surprise on the other end of the line when she had identified herself and the Bureau. She waited it out.

"Uh, hello there, Agent... Silvestri, was it? What can I do for you?"

Silvestri sighed. "I'm calling because I've received a call from someone close to you who worried that you might be in danger."

A small laugh on the other line, something between a rueful chuckle and a scoff. "Would that be Nella Atwiler?"

Silvestri looked down at the info she had taken from Papasian. That was the name of the writer's closest friend.

That checks out, Silvestri thought. Out loud she said, "No, it was your personal assistant."

"Ah. She always worries, poor thing."

Silvestri's eyebrows went up. She hadn't misheard; she was sure.

"He was concerned that you'd missed an appointment in Seattle and thought perhaps something had prevented you from coming." She listened carefully.

"Oh, my *assistant*," the voice on the other end of the line said quickly. "I thought you said my *agent*, thought you meant Michaela. I apologize. No, I just decided to take some time off with someone who means a great deal to me. I do not want to publicize it, but I am going through some stuff. It is quite personal, you understand."

Silvestri's notes from Papasian's assiduous information stated that Grey's agent was indeed named Michaela Griffin, but that she went by Mickey with everyone who knew her. These mistakes plucked at Silvestri, making her begin to think the assistant was not overreacting after all.

"I wonder if you could get in touch with your assistant. Mr....uh..." Silvestri trailed off and shuffled papers as if she could not recall his name and were searching for it even now.

"I am not interested in making contact right now," the person on the other end said smoothly. "Frankly, it is none of his business. He works for me, not I for him. I will get ahold of my assistant when I am ready. Is there anything else, Agent?"

Silvestri took a gamble. "Did you turn off the GPS capability in your cell phone, Ms. Grey?"

"That is not a crime. It is my business whether I share my location or not."

"Of course it is," Silvestri said at once. "But if I wanted to have an agent from the local field office drop in and verify that you're not in any danger, it would be helpful to know where you are. It could dispel any confusion, make sure that there's no reason to follow up on your assistant's report."

"I am not interested in supplying that information at this time. And this conversation has reached a natural endpoint. I am done here. Good afternoon, Agent."

The line went dead.

Silvestri tapped the phone a few times to call up the recording of their conversation. She listened to Grey's responses again—if indeed that had been Grey on the line.

She pulled up an interview with the author on YouTube. The woman's voice was quite low, somewhere between sultry and obviously gay. She played the recording on her phone again. She alternated between the two voices, listening carefully. The lab would be able to tell her for sure, but to her ear the two voices were not the same. The person on the phone had sounded stilted, a little formal. The woman in the video was easier, much more natural. The person she had spoken to by phone was a passable imitator, but they were not Eli Grey.

Sighing, Silvestri got up out of her chair and began to set the wheels of this investigation in motion.

September 3

TO: eligrey@maginaria.com
FROM: leonardlobovich@gmail.com

Dear Ms. Grey,
We have not met yet, but my name is Leonard and I am an aspiring writer. I have sold a few short stories and I have been working on my first novel. I am a great admirer of your work and I wanted to reach out and ask you if you have any advice for someone who is just starting out. I know you must get asked this all time, but it would mean the world to me if you would lend me a little of your view.
Sincerely,
Leonard Lobovich

★ ★ ★

TO: leonardlobovich@gmail.com
FROM: eligrey@maginaria.com

Dear Leonard,
I know how tough and impenetrable the business can seem when you're just starting out. Somebody helped me get started, so I always try to pass that kindness on. I went and looked up a couple of your stories. It looks like you've published mostly fanfic? There's nothing wrong with that, but it's highly unlikely to lead to anything saleable.

However, if you've got a novel to pitch, my advice is to start looking for a good agent. The right agent will make all the difference in the world to the kind of attention you can get for your work. I suggest making a Twitter account—if you don't have *one already—and following authors you respect, whose work is like yours. Find out who represents them and set your queries up based on how they prefer to be contacted. This process is long, but it yields the best results.*

Thank you for writing, and for reading my work. I really appreciate it.

Best,

Eli Grey

Eli's response was copied and pasted from a template she kept in her online documents folder, because she got this exact email about twice per month. She had made a cursory search for this man's work, then hastily added the lines about his fan fiction to show that she had checked him out. Occasionally, this kind of contact turned her on to a real up-and-comer, but this hadn't struck her as one of those times.

After she sent the response, Eli filed it to a part of her memory that she didn't anticipate having to access ever again. It wasn't the same as forgetting, but it made remembering much harder, if the story became important later.

8

When he came down the stairs, Eli was ready. She had been breathing deep and even for long minutes, working on getting control of herself. She had taken classes in meditation a few years ago. What they had told her to do had never worked; the visualizations of a great blue pearl or a set of rainbow stairs had never materialized in her mind. Just once, someone had instructed her to remember a place where she had felt at peace.

What she did now when she needed to get calm was to go there. The place was complete and rich in sensual detail, and she could call it to mind whenever she needed. This was hard work in the moment. Eli's hand hurt desperately and she could barely slow down her breathing. But she knew it would work now, because it had helped her a great deal in moments of rage.

She had rage now, oh yes. But she needed to be even and calm with him. She needed to be in charge of herself. She needed to establish herself as someone he would have to talk to in a reasonable manner.

He appeared with the same nightgown as before, fresh from the dryer, laid over a small box.

"Would you like to get dressed again?"

"Yes," she said. "I'd also like some socks and shoes, and maybe a jacket. It's too cold down here to go without those things. Are you running the air at, like, 45 degrees?"

"We shall see about that," he said, laying the silky nightgown down.

She pulled it over her head quickly, wanting the shortest possible time when she couldn't see him. "I also need medical care. You hurt my fingers quite badly, and it would be easy for them to get infected. I've got a urinary tract infection, as well. I need to go to an urgent care."

"I will take care of you," he said, almost tenderly.

She looked up at his brown eyes. How harmless he looked. How normal. She could hear his neighbors now, as the cops bagged what was left of her body. *He was always quiet, neat. Kept to himself.*

"I'm not comfortable with that. I need to see a professional."

"Your voice sounds terrible. You must be thirsty." He pulled a bottle of water out of the box and held it out to her.

She stared at it.

He set it down on the floor where she could reach it. He also pulled out a bowl of canned peaches and cottage cheese, a single thin slice of unbuttered wheat toast and three little round white pills that she thought might be aspirin.

"I do not have one of those breakfast-in-bed trays. But you get the idea."

She looked it over. She was very hungry. She was terribly, dangerously thirsty. So much so that this one bottle would not be enough. Her throat felt like a twisted-up piece of notebook paper when she swallowed. Her head still ached, and she could feel every pulse in her scabbed fingers. She wanted the aspirin badly enough to think she would take it before the food, her stomach lining be damned.

"I'm not going to touch any of that until you taste it first," she said.

"That is your decision," he said. He took the empty box with him and left the room.

She sat looking at what he had left her. The bowl and the bottle were both plastic. Breaking one and making it into a weapon was going to be hard, much harder than with glass or ceramics. She picked up the aspirins and examined them. They were small, round, white caplets, marked like generic Tylenol. But she couldn't be sure that was what they were.

She needed the water. She thought she might just take one big gulp and then wait to see how she felt. She put it off as long as she could, then drank. She set the bottle back down and took a few breaths. She couldn't make herself wait any longer. She had been without water for the better part of two days, had bled and fought for her life in that time. Her body overruled her logical thought and snatched the bottle back up again to drain it. She swallowed the three pills and then found she could wait. The effect of the painkillers came on quickly and she nearly cried with relief when the awful tension began to drain out of her.

The peaches had been rinsed of either the syrup or the juice they had been preserved in. They were sweet enough on their own, but for a moment she wondered why he'd gone to the trouble. It was so much easier just to plop them out of the can. The cottage cheese was clearly the low-fat variety, tasting like nothing remotely creamy or cheesy. The toast was some whole-grain garbage, barely registering as bread and badly in need of butter or jam or both. She was too hungry to care too much about any of this, but she couldn't help noticing. Every piece of information here was valuable.

Is he trying to demoralize me with shitty food?

She was almost finished eating when the rest of it hit her. It was worse than it had been in the car, possibly because of her weakened state. She was nauseated immediately and fought to keep down the food and water. She rolled around in bed, trying to shake it off. She finally did vomit, realizing that it might slow down or stop the absorption of whatever it was into her bloodstream.

Above her, Leonard watched closely to be sure that she did not choke. He fingered a thin Cross fountain pen, taking comfort in its cold steel body. When she was motionless but still visibly breathing, he put the pen down and grabbed his large plastic tote and headed back down.

Stepping so lightly—how he loved her grace and poise!—Millicent followed down behind him on the stairs.

This isn't going to be like the other times, she told him soothingly.

"It will not be," he agreed, setting the tote down on the floor and looking over the slack body on the bed.

Because this time you understand the secret, she said. She was behind him. He could not see them both at once.

"I will not do the ungentlemanly thing," he told her. "Because it disrupts the magic."

Yes, she told him. *It always has. The magic is in becoming. I showed you how. It was in the books. You studied so carefully, and now you see the pattern.*

"The pattern is becoming. Millicent must become herself."

Correct, she said. *And Eli must become himself.*

He nodded, setting out his tools.

"I know that," he said. "And it is time to begin."

September 12

TO: *eligrey@maginaria.com*
FROM: *leonardlobovich@gmail.com*

Dear Ms. Grey,
Thank you so much for taking the time to answer my letter! I know how busy you must be and I perceive it as no small honor that you would bother with one such as me.

I have done as you suggested regarding Twitter and beginning my agent search. Of course, my top pick is your own agent, Ms. Michaela Griffin. However, as she is not accepting new clients at this time, I shall have to focus my efforts elsewhere.

Incidentally, I assume that you have heard that Ent Books is seeking a replacement for the great Bernard Armour so that a new writer can finish the Hand of Fate series. I must confess I am a rampant, deathless fan of those books. I can think of no author more qualified than yourself to take up the task. Have you thrown your hat into the ring, as it were?

Thank you again for your guidance. I hope to meet you one day as your colleague.
Sincerely,
Leonard Lobovich

★ ★ ★

FROM: *eligrey@maginaria.com*
TO: *leonardlobovich@gmail.com*

Dear Leonard,
Thank you so much for your interest in my work. Letters like

*this make the whole job worthwhile, and I appreciate that you
took the time to send it.*
Best,
Eli Grey

PS I have not expressed interest in the Hand of Fate *series.
Too much pressure to be like Armour, in my opinion.*

9

The third time Leonard had met Eli was when everything had gone wrong.

Millicent Michaelson was a bona fide hit. The fourth book, *Name of the Faceless*, had hit a chord at just the right time: Millicent was up against a corrupt police chief and a semifascist regime in the inverted city at the same time that an election had been won by a nativist conservative president. Book bloggers and reviewers noticed the similarities and credited Eli with prescience and political forethought, a rare credit in genre writing.

As always, readers loved her plucky heroine, and Eli started getting some real airplay in national media. People bought so many copies of the first books that they went back into print, under a new deal with a new publisher. The press called it Harry Potter for grown-ups. She hated that comparison, but it was flattering all the same. Eli was suddenly everywhere: a profile in the *New York Times* and interviews on National Public Radio.

Thousands poured onto the forums and subreddits for Millicent fans, finding out there had been a community all this time. Leonard was a founding member of several such message boards. These new bandwagon fans would have driven him crazy, but his energy was directed elsewhere.

Leonard had found his own small fame by writing purple prose and very decorous romance and erotica fanfic in another fandom, creating an alternate universe where the beloved starship commander Captain Ampari had become the shameless concubine of an alien king. The pieces were lush with a focus on prosody and fussy euphemisms for the acts in which the players engaged. Ampari was starry-eyed in love with King Gorlan; so much so that she forsook her oaths to her people and her commission in the Royal Stellar Navy.

Ampari wanted one thing: to be loved and owned by this captivating man. Gorlan's species was powerfully telepathic. He had picked up immediately on the captain's need for release through servitude. He used his powers to hone her desire until she was the ultimate vessel for his will, living only to serve him. Their relationship was perfect, seamless, a fetishization of true love and the perfect monogamy it brings. The digital cover for the story was just a close-up of Ampari's blue-white neck featuring the jeweled collar she wore as a symbol of her total submission, her gift.

The *Ampari Unveiled* series was polarizing: people either loved or hated it. Commenters either told him it was starkly erotic or baldly regressive. He told his online friends that he never read bad reviews, but the truth was he read them all. Sometimes more than once. He thought they would cease or at least slow down when he was nominated for the Supernova award for best fan work, but that only seemed to enlarge his audience on both sides. He was both more loved and hated as a writer than he had been prepared for.

He had gone to the awards ceremony at the Nova convention in Wisconsin. It was the third convention he had attended where he knew the author of Millicent Michaelson would also be present. She was projected to win the prize for best novel, and his own nomination paled beside his desire to see her receive hers.

He was booked for one panel on fan writing, but the crowd was dismally small. Four people sat dotted around the room, despite the moderator's invitation to come closer to the front and make this feel less formal. They got through introductions and the moderator's rote and uninspired questions—"Where do you get your ideas?"—before opening it up to the room.

One woman shot immediately to her feet and began speaking without being acknowledged. "I just want to say that your depiction of Ampari Trowbridge completely robs her of her agency as a character. I think choosing to submit sexually is a valid choice for any woman, if that's what she wants. But the truth of it is that she's only with that guy because of his mind control."

"W-well," Leonard stammered. "It is really that he just unlocks something in her that allows her to—"

"Yeah, I know, we all wanna be dominated deep down or whatever. I just want you to know that we see you. There's a whole community of women who see you for what you really are. We finally get one woman captain in the RSN, and you just can't handle it. You take her out of command and put her into a whorehouse the very first chance you get. Because that's what men want."

Leonard opened his mouth to say something, but he didn't have a chance.

The moderator, an older man who had worked in the fan creation community for long years and had a nine-foot train of fading con badges to prove it, had tipped his microphone closer to his face.

"It's incredibly offensive and damaging to generalize to all men. You coming here to attack this creator just proves the liberal thought police will show up to complain anytime a woman happens to be beautiful, or particularly well-endowed." He punctuated this with a grand gesture of both hands, sculpting breasts like basketballs in the air in front of his chest.

He laughed a dry, hateful chuckle before continuing. "You know fan writers make no money, right?"

The woman began to speak again, but he cut her off.

"Leonard has the right to express himself, the same as anyone. If you don't like it, you don't have to read it. You have no right to come here and malign him, damage his reputation or accuse him of destroying anything. Fan work often places familiar things in unfamiliar circumstances. If you don't get that, then this really isn't the place for you."

Leonard relaxed. There was some small laughter. The woman stalked out of the room, leaving the pitiful crowd even smaller. Conversation turned to mirror universes. Leonard did not speak again.

That night, Leonard got a message from the other woman who had been in the room for that conversation.

TO: *leonardlobovich@gmail.com*
FROM: *m.torrez@gmail.com*

Dear Leonard,
I thought that was really unfair today. I like your work and I wanted to reach out and tell you that. Don't let the haters get you down.
Best,
Manuela

The note had included the girl's phone number. They had breakfast at the con hotel the next day. Manuela was a nice, shy girl. She had smiled at everything he said. They had spent most of the day together, and then agreed to stay in touch after the event ended.

On the final night of the conference, Leonard sat at the special reserved tables for awards nominees. He was starstruck in the extreme, surrounded by the great writers and artists who had created his favorite characters and universes out of nothing but impulses and energy. At the far end sat Millicent's creator, flushed with drink in a dark green suit cut like a riding habit. She held her date's hand, a willowy redhead in a white gown. Leonard turned his head so he could see the author, but not her companion.

When his name was called for best fan writer, his vision went gray for a moment. He couldn't believe this was really happening. He staggered to his feet and made his way to the stage, where he was handed the statuette and the judges shook his hand.

He had no acceptance speech. He hadn't expected to win, knowing how many people disliked his work. He had heard rumors that people had gamed the nominations and pushed a slate, trying to force certain undesirables out of the running. He had thought that might work in his favor, but not to this degree.

He stepped to the microphone, his mind racing, trying to come up with something on the fly.

"Thank you so much," he began. But he stopped.

Hissing was issuing from around the room. Long, sharp, sibilant hisses began in one corner and were taken up in another. The hissers were too subtle to be spotted, and the sound seemed to come from everywhere at once. As the volume of hissing increased, a general clamor of applause rose to drown it out.

It was only then that Leonard realized that most of the people in the audience were ready to tear each other apart. The story about the weighted slate of nominations for the Supernova awards was just the tip of the iceberg. What he was seeing was a legitimate culture war.

He looked desperately to his favorite writer's face, hoping to see some support there. She and her companion had their heads down in private conversation. The author seemed desperate not to signal agreement or disagreement, just to pass through the moment unscathed.

Leonard returned to his seat on the dais with shaky legs and found he had to wipe his sweating palms on the edges of the tablecloth that lay in his lap. The event emcee tried their best to move the ceremony along, but the tension in the room did not break.

When the third Millicent Michaelson book was announced as the best novel of the year, the room erupted. People sprang from their seats and clapped riotously, crowing and whooping as the author made her way to the podium.

She accepted the statuette and the room was breathless, beaming and glowering, to await the political import of the words she would say next.

"I want to thank my agent and my editor for helping me get my books out into the world," she said, slurring her words slightly. "And to all of you for voting for me, a newbie. I know there's a lot going on here tonight and that we don't all agree with each other. So, I hope we can put this behind us and focus on bringing more good stories into the world. Thank you."

Half-hearted applause carried her back to her seat and the closing remarks commenced hastily. No one seemed satisfied with that as a cap to the evening. The after-party crowd seethed and rumbled as they cleared the room, already separating into factions at the door.

Leonard watched the winners go, many stumbling drunk and arm in arm. There was a special party to which he was now entitled to go as an award winner, but the convention had made him defensive and unsure. He felt exposed and out of control, and he loathed it. He did not follow the crowd.

Instead, he walked casually over to the chair where the author had been sitting and draped his hand across it, feeling the warm spot where her back had pressed against the upholstery. After a moment he sat, inhaling deeply. He dreamed.

After his win, the people who had nominated Leonard for his fanfic writing found ways to let him know that he was one of them, that they had chosen him. They found him through email and on forums, striking up casual conversations about sexual domination with hardly any preamble. He was polite, he was appreciative, but he was ultimately uninterested in joining them. The animosity of the awards ceremony had unnerved him. He had imagined the literati as a well-behaved and generous society of brilliant people, not a sniping nest of bullies who did nothing but tear each other down. His first introduction to the life that the professionals in this industry lived left him reeling. He did not know how to adjust his expectations to reality.

He sought out the groups that had helped push the slate that made him a winner. When he found them online, he was disappointed. Their message boards were coarse, full of base pornography and rough language. He couldn't possibly belong among them. What he created was art and beauty, not some kind of statement on how all human relationships should be. It had nothing to do with their animalistic desires. He couldn't see himself the way that they did.

He could, however, see himself with Manuela. Manuela emailed him every week at first. He assiduously read through all of her social posts from the beginning of their existence. He clicked Like on her prom photos from ten years before, her Christmas cards and old Facebook rants. He dug her abandoned journal project from college and quoted it back to her in his emails. He learned details about her friends and family and asked astute questions about them when it seemed appropriate.

When she stopped answering, he reached out to those friends. He wrote them his concerns that something might have happened to her. This was the girl who had broken her leg at Girl Scout camp and tried to play it off, after all. Maybe she wasn't answering him because she was in trouble. She disappeared off Facebook. She deleted her old blogs.

He sent flowers to her home address—after discovering it through a fairly simple means, which anybody could have done—and verified that they had been delivered, but heard nothing. He called her work and they hung up on him. He called her parents' house and received a very direct and unhappy dressing-down from her father, who instructed him to never contact Manuela again.

People began sending him screenshots from posts Manuela had made on various forums, claiming she wasn't safe and that she was afraid he would show up at any moment. He tried to get ahead of the damage, explaining on his blog and his Twitter that all of this was a misunderstanding. He posted screenshots from their conversations, showing that she had contacted him first and continuously, so how could he have been victimizing her? He tried pointing out that if Manuela really thought she was in danger, then why didn't she go to the police?

When he did contact her again, it was under another name, and another set of accounts. He could keep an eye on her that way, make sure she was safe. She need never find out.

He learned from that interaction to diversify his identity. He wrote his fan work under his own name and had to keep that intact, but he used false names at conventions he attended in a participant capacity and created a few dozen sock-puppet accounts on various sites. He had only used a few of them on the author of Millicent Michaelson. He had never threatened her. He would never be that foolish, or that vulgar. He had, on occasion, dropped by to admire or compliment her.

It wasn't until he had really gone pro that she had paid attention to him at all. But there were a few years between Captain Ampari and his big break.

The between time was not easy for Leonard. The next convention he attended was the disaster. He hadn't realized how far the story of Manuela had spread. When it combined with the enmity some people held against him for the Ampari stories and his win, it came to define him to the community. This convention taught him his new place in the universe. He attended this one with a few readings and panels booked, so he traveled under his real name. Upon registration, he was instructed to report to one of the convention facilitators in a second-floor room.

He assumed he was being referred to special instructions or services for panelists. He was incorrect.

The person with the clipboard who greeted him was very tall, wearing a Utilikilt and a jawbone headset, and immediately intimidated him.

"I'm leading the dragon corps of this con. My name is Eldritch."

Eldritch was wearing a *No Touch* badge ribbon in red, just below a white badge that read *They/Them*. Leonard understood the red, but not the white. He looked up and smiled, not offering to shake as a gesture of comprehending the no-touch signal.

"Pleased to meet you, Eldritch. I am—"

"I know who you are," Eldritch said, beginning to mantle around Leonard like a vulture. "I flagged your registration because I want to let you know that you're on my watch list."

"Watch list?"

Eldritch considered their clipboard. "You've been reported to the community as a harasser and/or abuser from previous events. I'm not on the registration team, but if I were, you'd have been refused admittance, let alone space on a panel. However, I am in charge of security. I want you to know that if there's even a shred of possibility that you violated the code of conduct for this con, I will not only permaban you. I have many friends in local law enforcement, and I will find a way to make sure you're in a jail cell when you should be boarding your flight home. Do I make myself clear?"

"This is all a misunderstanding," Leonard began. "I—"

Eldritch cut him off again. "Believe me when I tell you that I am not interested in your version of events, now or ever. If I hear something about you, I am not going to come to you and hear your side of it. You don't deserve the benefit of the doubt. Are we clear?"

"Yes," Leonard said stonily, his face aflame.

Eldritch wordlessly pointed him to the door, and Leonard went.

He performed and appeared when he was scheduled, but otherwise Leonard stayed in his room. He ordered pizza and Chinese takeout, keeping out of the hotel restaurant and even avoiding the Denny's across the street. He did not want to be out among people. He felt threatened. He didn't emerge from his room until the final party of the con, and that was where he saw her.

The author was dancing with a group of colleagues, smiling and probably fairly drunk. Leonard worked his way through the crowd toward her, trying to get close enough to hear their conversation, to smell her again.

He half danced his way across the floor, staying casual, keeping her at his side instead of openly approaching her. Her friends were shrieking with laughter, some of them singing along to the music. He smiled to match them, but kept his distance.

He felt slightly better, being out of his room. They had no right to treat him this way, based purely on rumors and conjecture about who they thought he really was. They had caged him with shame, but he had broken out. That was good. That was just.

He had just reread the entire *Maginaria* series before this con. He had so many questions that he wanted to ask her. He looked sidelong at her, dreamily, imagining having her to himself somewhere quiet and really getting to talk. He had some theories about where the series was going. He ached to tell her.

At that exact moment, someone knocked into him on his unguarded side. The person was inches away from falling and grabbed Leonard on their way down, pushing him violently so that his cocked elbow landed on the side of the author's face.

She looked over, shocked at the tumult beside her. Leonard helped the man who had fallen up from the floor. His friends appeared to carry him out.

She looked up at him, recognizing him hazily. "Oh, sorry, Leonard." She apologized in that way that women often do, when they have done nothing wrong.

She had said his name. He could scarcely believe it. Turning back to her, through the din he said, "No, that is entirely my fault. Forgive me, Millicent."

She heard him. He could see the confusion in her face when she heard him. But the music was loud and she was pretty wasted, and she could be made to doubt it later if it came up.

All the same, he knew he was caught. Leonard went out after the man who had fallen, pretending to try and catch up.

It was the only time they had seen each other when he thought he might remain in her memory. In the morning, he was gone before he could find out whether she had made a complaint to Eldritch or any of their team. When he landed back at home, he saw that she remembered the incident only hazily and had tweeted about it in a way that indicated that she thought it was funny.

Leonard was relieved. Later, reliving their rare moment of connection, he realized that she had remembered his name. He was elated, and cherished that knowledge for years afterward.

At the same time, Eli became embroiled in a minor scandal on Twitter as people reacted to her nonstatement about the award or the controversy. Leonard supported and defended her from sock-puppet accounts, but she did not seem to notice. Indeed, she seemed to withdraw from the platform altogether, to seek peace while the issue blew over. He realized that she was wise to do so. Those people were not open to discussing things reasonably or with any logic. He couldn't imagine having to stand up to the kind of criticism authors of her caliber were made to answer to. He hoped she would come back to Twitter soon, and resume sharing pictures and details of where she would be, and when.

December 10

TO: *eligrey@maginaria.com*
FROM: *leonardlobovich@gmail.com*

Dear Ms. Grey,
We did not really get a chance to talk, but we saw each other at the Nova Awards. I wanted to congratulate you on your win for novel of the year, but it was such a chaotic night. I won for best fan writer, which is a small thing compared with your triumph. I really admired the way you avoided the political nonsense that so colored the event. I had hoped I would get to shake your hand, but alas. Perhaps another time.

I saw that you had some trouble on Twitter from people who felt that you should have made your acceptance speech more political. I have always admired how you kept the art pure and separate from life, letting the story speak for itself. Pay no attention to those fools who try and argue that you should be other than you are. You are an artist. They are nothing.

I wanted to write and let you know that I sold my first novel after my Nova win. I still don't have an agent, but I am very excited to show the world *The Moon's Harsh Mistress*. My publisher instructs me that I should inquire as to whether any of my professional friends would be willing to read the manuscript and provide a cover blurb, and I can think of no one who would lend the work more prestige than you. I have attached it here, for your convenience.

Thank you again for your early encouragement in my career. I would not be where I am today without you.
Sincerely,
Leonard Lobovich

Post scriptum: I spoke with an editor at Ent about the search for a replacement for Armour. They still have found no one suitable. What a shame.

★ ★ ★

FROM: *eligrey@maginaria.com*
TO: *leonardlobovich@gmail.com*

Dear Leonard,
I'm sorry, I'm not able to offer cover blurbs at this time. My schedule simply doesn't allow for this kind of work.
Best,
Eli Grey

When Leonard's debut novel hit the market, he could not help but notice that another book by Nella Atwiler that was released on the same day featured an effusive bit of praise from Eli Grey on its front cover. What had begun to smolder in him was now burning outright.

When Eli finally made her statement about what had happened at the Nova awards, it was in a massive joint blog post shared by all the luminaries in science fiction, fantasy and horror, and published at the same time. They roundly condemned the slate voting and co-opting of the Nova awards by political factions. They announced changes to the way voting was distributed and calculated, and outlined a better future without naming names.

None of the posts mentioned Leonard Lobovich, winner for best fan writer that year. In the scheme of this struggle and these changes, he was insignificant.

The post was the same, verbatim, across the internet. Leonard read each one carefully nonetheless, convinced that one of them would mention him. When they did not, he sought out various forums on the internet and attempted to find his name in the arguments and screeds of either side of this literary firestorm. No one mentioned him.

Lobovich's debut, *The Moon's Harsh Mistress*, did fine. It sold a few thousand copies and got mostly good reviews in minor outlets. The Supernova scandal overshadowed it, he was sure. He had been unlucky. He would be better next time.

Leonard aimed himself straight at the heart of this world. He saw the tight-knit knot of celebrity writers at its center. He saw the way they tweeted at one another, the photos of them drinking together at convention hotels. Their blurbs on one another's books, their chummy sharing of links and boosting of good news. He felt like he was pressing his nose against a warm window and he was desperate to come in out of the cold. He would be one of them one day. He had to be.

He began to focus on finding a way in.

10

Leonard felt for the pulse in her neck, concerned that he hadn't been careful enough with the dosage this time. He wanted to have enough time to do everything he needed to do. The pulse was slow but strong. He didn't have any medical training, but he had read a significant amount of literature on the internet about the effects of Rohypnol. He was fairly certain it wouldn't kill her after the first time didn't trigger an allergic reaction.

He was able to move her to the bathtub fairly easily, with minimal bumping. He ran the water and got to work quickly, not knowing how much time he might have. He shackled one ankle to the pipe below the faucet and spread out the shaving cream. Slowly, humming to himself, Leonard Lobovich began to shave Eli's legs, deep in thought.

Manuela hadn't been the first girl who had gone crazy on him. Leonard was just the sort of fellow who had bad luck with women. He had kept himself from giving in and doing the ungentlemanly thing until he was almost twenty-five. He kept files on his favorites, operating dozens of accounts to keep an eye on them, give them advice, listen to their troubles and help them to fall in love with him.

Most of the time, he never met them in person. But each time he seemed to want a little more. These minor interactions were never enough.

Manuela was the outlier in that she had seen him in the flesh before their relationship began. That made Leonard uncomfortable; he preferred to remain unknown as a suitor until the right moment. That was what he had done with Jessica. He had started to follow her on Instagram. Cosplayers were common, but Jessica chose uncommon subjects for her art. Her favorite was her namesake, Lady Jessica Atreides. It was the first time Leonard had realized how easy it was for a creator to eclipse a character, to become her. He watched Jessica's short videos over and over again.

He had worked carefully for months, sending her poetry and obscure lines from the *Dune* saga, praising her gentle beauty and feminine crafts. At the same time, he had posed as a fellow cosplay artist just starting out, too shy to show anything yet. One hand beckoned while the other hand sighed about the rarity of true love. It all worked like a machine, like an orderly, perfect process.

When he had finally met Jessica, she was exactly as he had envisioned her. On the very first night of the convention, he had caught her alone in a corridor. He had offered her a bottle of water, seeing how much she was sweating. The water bottle he had made helped her to fall asleep so that they could be together, peacefully and perfectly.

The night he had spent in her hotel room with her warm and yielding body had been paradise on earth. He wrote about it immediately in exquisite detail, using pieces later for his *Ampari Unveiled* series.

But it wasn't quite right.

Afterward, he had felt a certain emptiness when he thought about her. He relived that night over and over and grew disgusted with himself over his conduct. He was a dashing, romantic lover. Why, then, could he only recall rutting and panting like a dog in the throes of his passion?

The second time he did the ungentlemanly thing, he had already been in love with Millicent Michaelson. He had met a Millicent cosplayer online and employed the same strategy to woo her: talk about the books and romance her with the beautiful prose, while posing as a good friend who listened to her gush and encouraged her to give herself over to a whirlwind romance. Life is too short! If you love him, go to him.

She had come. He had picked her up at the airport in Palm Springs and driven her back across the stretch of miles to his home, passing the tall, weird wind turbines and pointing out the sights to her. She wasn't dressed properly when he saw her. Her hair was the wrong color; her eyes were the wrong color. She wore jeans and a holey old T-shirt. There was something hollow about her, and it upset him to see her so untidy.

When he asked her about it, she seemed blank.

"I wear a wig when I cosplay. Contacts, too. Did you think that was my everyday look? You saw my Facebook photos."

He had seen them. But he had told her to come and be his Millicent. Didn't she understand what that meant?

In the end, it was clear to him that she did not understand. She was only eighteen, and had basically used him as a way to run away from home. His online friends' warnings had been right. She was only interested in his money, his home. Still, he had tried to fix her. She would not obey the rules. The basement had been built for her, his first Millicent. She was inexcusably filthy toward him, calling him Daddy in a way that turned his stomach, and offering him acts Millicent had surely never even heard of.

She reacted poorly to training or any kind of correction.

He had punished her by putting her out naked in the middle of the night. He had expected crying and begging and pounding at the door. Instead, she had wandered off in search of neighbors. There was no one for miles around him. He had waited too long to try to follow her, and he lost the tracks of her bare feet somewhere out among the Joshua trees. He had come home around dawn, worried but still convinced she would find her way back. After three days, her things went into his fireplace, stinking of plastic and creating a mess in the grate.

The rest of her was out there, somewhere. He had seen the bleached skulls of donkeys and birds out under the sun. He didn't like to think about it.

The last time he had done the ungentlemanly thing, he had been markedly better at it. Practice had helped, and he had begun to devote more time to planning and research. He had attended a convention to meet one of the best Millicent cosplayers in the world. She looked right: like a dead ringer for the actress they cast in the films. He had wooed her online, but without much success. He had posed as a friend on a sewing forum, and again in a Millicent fan group, but she had never taken the bait. He had watched, frustrated, trying to find out why.

When he managed to find the right sock puppet that she would friend on Facebook, he figured it out. She had too many friends. She was too independent. When he was honest with himself, he could admit that she was distastefully conceited. She needed to learn some humility. She had to learn that she needed someone like him.

He had worked for months to go through the steps he had been carefully crafting online. He complimented her skillfully, remembering to playfully point out flaws or suggest improvements. He was dashing, then unavailable. He made allusions to his popularity, casually posted about going on dates and rock climbing. She still didn't take the bait. Her life went on exactly as it had, making his efforts seem insignificant.

That hurt terribly, but he met her at the bar in the hotel anyway. She laughed in a huge circle of friends and made great jokes.

He got his club soda and lime and hung around the edges of their group, looking for his moment.

"So then he admits he never read the seventh book," she said, laughing the whole time. "And I just slaughtered him. I went point by point on the reasons why he was wrong and he's just like, 'Uh, I haven't gotten that far yet.' So I said, 'Why are you trying to argue this with me?' It was glorious, just glorious." Millicent stirred her drink with her fingers, something brown with cherries afloat.

He laughed along with the crowd.

A short bald man leaned in closer to her and said, "Well, actually…" in a mocking tone of voice. Those around him laughed harder.

"Oh my, book seven totally explains why Dumbledore is gay!" Leonard was in his nicest shirt, grinning his best grin. "What a fool."

A few heads turned toward him. Millicent looked up. The laughter died down.

"Sorry, I just could not help but overhear. And I love a good takedown." He gestured with his glass in a half-toasting way toward Millicent, who wore a short peach dress and sparkling peridot earrings.

"Ha ha, okay," Millicent said, not looking at him. "Anyway, are you guys going to see Ava in *King Lear*? I already have tickets."

Another woman in the circle blushed prettily and pushed a lock of dark hair behind her ear.

"No pressure," Ava said. "I'm just excited about it, because the director has this really fresh take on the whole thing."

Leonard jockeyed around the big table, trying to interject or appear in Millicent's eyeline. She deliberately avoided him. Everyone took their lead from her.

He did not give up after that night. He had bought tickets to every night of that production of *King Lear*. He bought a bunch of fresh flowers and waited every time to see Millicent show up. She came in with the short bald man and a handful of others, dressed in a pink sheath dress and an impeccable vintage fur shrug.

Leonard lit up when he saw her. He stayed after to congratulate Ava and give her the flowers. She accepted them warily, looking around as if to ask who he was with.

"I am just a fan," he said, smiling at his Millicent. "I wanted to tell you how great you were."

"Thank you," Ava said doubtfully. The group of friends formed around her protectively and started to push outward, talking about going somewhere for a drink.

"How about Kinsey's?" Leonard called after them. "On me!"

"No thanks, dude," the bald man called over his shoulder. And then she was gone.

It was months before he was able to see Millicent again, outside of a few covert glances in her grocery store or at her gym. He bought tickets to SeamstressCon and eagerly marked up his schedule to attend every event she was part of. He clapped appreciatively for her magnificent rendering of the ballgown she had worn to her first Witches Ball in *Captive Prince*. He attended her panel on reversible pieces and pretended to take notes intermittently to disguise the fact that he looked only at her, no matter who was speaking. He was dying inside.

He just needed a moment alone with her.

He found her in the hotel bar, late into the second night of the con. She was still in uniform, and he appreciated the way the stiff fabric hugged her slim hips and perfect breasts. He worked his way down the bar slowly, taking over one stool and then another as more and more people knocked off to go upstairs and sleep.

Millicent was very drunk, but most of her friends were gone. She was tapping on her phone, uploading and captioning photos. He got close enough to read them, close enough to smell her.

She was very tired, and the endless stream of old-fashioned cocktails wasn't helping her at all. She mistyped over and over again, working hard to fix her captions before hitting Done. She left her drink unattended for just a minute, sliding off her stool to the tune of "ladies' room" and staggering down the short hallway.

Leonard closed his own check and waited. She closed her own tab, then slipped off her stool.

"Help you to your room?" he asked shyly. "You don't seem to be in the best shape."

She smiled sloppily at him and mangled the line about the kindness of strangers.

He offered her his elbow and she took it, leaning heavily. It was no trick at all to help her open the door and follow her in, to hang up the Do Not Disturb sign and lock the door. She was helpless by that point, barely able to make it to the bed without support. He watched her slip off her shoes and crawl into the bed. Tenderly, he lay down beside her, telling her all the romantic things he had been waiting to say. He had been practicing for months, imagining for when the moment would be right.

That, too, had been a disappointment. She couldn't make any of the responses from the book, even when he gave her the easy ones. She had flinched when he touched her, asking him who he was, never really fully compliant, only slack and resigned. He had been the same disgusting animal again, unsatisfied even when he had enjoyed himself with her body several times. When he slipped out of her room, he had known this memory would be good for nothing. It wasn't enough.

Something was missing.

This time would be different. This time, he had the real Millicent at last. Not a girl in a costume, but the real deal. He had seen her in the flesh. He knew her life intimately. He had been gathering information for years. He would find a way to make her love him. He would take his time, spare her his base instincts until she was ready. He had something so very special in store for this one; something that would make all the others pale beside this one true love.

She wasn't really Millicent, his mind Millicent said from somewhere over his shoulder.

"Of course she was not. The real Millicent is here, in my bathtub."

And you are on your way to becoming real, as well, she reminded him.

"Returning to real."

She did not answer.

As he finished shaving and trimming the body lovingly, he congratulated himself. Here she was, laid out helpless and welcoming before him, yet he did not use her the way she was made to be used.

Leonard was a gentleman. A romantic. He had left behind

his boyish ways and was ready to be worthy of real love. He was purifying her to be ready for him, too.

Soon, they would be one. Artist and muse. Creator and creation. Pygmalion and Galatea.

He ran his hands down her smooth legs, bringing them primly together.

"I shall wait for you, my darling."

Like the hero on the cover of a romance novel, he lifted her out of the tub and held her tenderly to his chest. Overcome with emotion, he kissed her on her forehead.

April 21

TO: *eligrey@maginaria.com*
FROM: *leonardlobovich@gmail.com*

Dear Ms. Grey,
I am so excited that I just have to tell someone, but I am not permitted to make a public announcement yet! I have been chosen to take over the Hand of Fate series for the late Bernard Armour. The honor is so great that I can scarcely muster up the words to describe it.

I applied after The Moon's Harsh Mistress *received some favorable reviews. The editors at Ent had me write up some sample chapters and an outline of where I wanted the story to go. I had some stiff competition—I heard Nola K. Henderson and Shannon MacConkey were both on the short list. However, in the end I won it. I am thrilled beyond measure and cannot wait to begin.*

I would love to get some other writers together and discuss what we loved most about Hand of Fate. *Some professional banter about the future of the series could be very beneficial to me. I am happy to work around your schedule, if we can make this happen.*
Sincerely,
Leonard Lobovich

★ ★ ★

TO: *leonardlobovich@gmail.com*
FROM: *eligrey@maginaria.com*

Dear Leonard,
Congratulations on landing the whale! I'm afraid I must decline your kind offer, but thank you for thinking of me.

I wish you all the best with your future endeavors.
Eli Grey

11

Eli did not dream, exactly. She swam in memory, trying to tie what was to what would be.

Never would have gotten into this fucking mess if it weren't for the movies. I had readers, sure, but in the tens of thousands. The movies put it over the edge. Probably this asshole came on board then.

There it was again, that feeling that she knew him. It hit her heart like a certainty, like a word trapped on the tip of her tongue.

You just think that because you know the statistics. Most women who experience this kind of violence know their attacker. So you think you must know him.

But was that it? She tried to return to the first moment she got a look at his face. Familiarity coiled deep into her, insisting that she knew him.

I know too many fucking people. Conventions and signings and every time someone acts like I should know them, I freeze. Maybe he's just a crazed fan and you've seen him in the signing line a hundred times. That would be enough to make his face familiar, but not enough to actually remember, right? Maybe you saw him at one of the movie events.

Eli's days on the set of the film adaptations of her books had been bizarre and made her feel very far from herself. The premieres had been like movies themselves; her memory was all flashing lights and clothes that felt like costumes. She could have met god herself during that process and wouldn't likely remember it.

The first day on the set of the Millicent Michaelson film, Eli had been trying to work past her initial disappointments.

The version of the script they had sent her was all bad. The dialogue was toned way down. Pivotal scenes had evaporated and new, lengthy ones had been introduced in their place, positioned to solidify a romantic subplot that wasn't supposed to exist until book three. The essence of the story was slowly leaking out of this thing. She had insisted to her agent that she get to consult on the script, at least. She knew that since she had never written one before, they wouldn't let her have a crack at writing the screenplay. The sale was too big and the studio was too powerful. But she wanted to be sure that they didn't destroy it.

Despite all this aggravation, it was fun to be on the set. She felt like some kind of pseudocelebrity, not famous like the actors or even the director was famous. Famous like someone from a smaller country, some hometown girl who made good and got to take a tour of the big city.

As she sat, thumbing through the offending, blue-bound script in her folding chair, Eli had looked up into the wide green eyes of one of the world's biggest movie stars.

Alice Stample beamed down at her, her veneers and perfect skin, everything about her just begging for a rewrite with heavier romantic overtones. "Are you the author?"

Eli stood up and offered her hand. "Guilty."

The energetic waif slammed her into a frantic embrace. "I love this book so so so much. I begged my agent to get me this. You don't even know."

Eli laughed with relief, hugging back gently. The girl felt tiny and insubstantial, like a couple of coat hangers wrapped in a warm silk dress. "I'm very flattered. Also, you have to know that your interest in this project made it happen at this studio. You're the reason for all of this. Including Mr. Oscar over there," she said, gesturing to the dour director.

Alice held her at arm's length, smiling beatifically. "I was *born* to play Millicent. I literally dreamed about it years ago, when I read the book. Thank you so, so much for writing such a bad-ass character."

"I'm glad you feel that way," Eli began diplomatically, "because I'd really like your help as an advocate for the integrity of the script."

Alice had applied herself to the task immediately, and Eli firmly believed that the film was far better because of their coordinated efforts. In the end, the director had settled for an introduction of a slow-burn romance and a renewed focus on the mystery of Millicent's true nature mirrored by the city above and below the ground. Eli was terribly proud of the film, and Alice had signed on immediately for the rest of the series when the deal for the remaining rights was cemented.

It had certainly done well. Eli had made more money, far and away, from the option and bonuses on the films than all her books' sales and royalties combined. It had catapulted the series into the stratosphere, sales wise, and brought a whole new generation of readers to the books. Eli noticed that interview questions had begun to shift, to ask her what her book meant to girls and young women who were looking for role models. How she felt about her legacy.

Shit, legacy. She was thirty-two years old.

Eli and Alice had not really become friends. They were too different. But they loved working together on the films. Alice would invite her for long talks on set, in the actress's palatial trailer, to discuss the finer points of who Millicent really was. Eli got to talk deep plotting, the stuff that never made it into the books but that she as the author still had to know to write the story.

When the second film earned Alice a nomination for a Golden Globe, the occasion had found her between boyfriends and she invited Eli to be her date.

Eli, who had hated dresses her entire life, got a tuxedo tailored to wear to the event. She got a sharp haircut and tried to transcend the shabby, schlubby aesthetic of the novelists who were only occasionally invited to these things.

Alice was simply ethereal in a seafoam-green gown that made her small form take on gravity like a star being born. For the first time, Eli looked at her not as a pretty girl who did alright in films, but saw her as a leading actress with a powerful magnetism and presence of her own.

Eli emerged first from the limo and offered her hand to Alice, to usher her on to the red carpet. The gesture felt perfectly natural, even practical. Alice wore high, tottering heels to increase the sweep of the gown. Eli was trying to be helpful. Flashes washed over them both as Eli paused and turned as they walked, trying to be gracious while still heading toward their destination. Alice's small hand was warm against her chest as they posed like a couple of teenagers at their senior prom. It was a golden, perfect night. Eli was flash-blind for nearly a minute inside the dark theater, sliding her feet along the carpet and trying to act cool until her eyes adjusted. Alice sat beside her and squeezed her hand when she was overwhelmed by what her work had become.

There had been a party afterward that Eli could scarcely recall. It was as if cymbals had crashed behind her every step all night. She went to bed around dawn, every cell in her body humming with success, glory, fame, glamor. This was not the same universe where she had been born, Eli knew. The tornado had come. She was over the rainbow now.

In the morning, the gossip sites were all running something in the vein of "Alice in Ladyland" or "Muff Divers from the Maginaria" with the pictures of them arriving at the event, clinging to one another, Alice's hand on Eli's tuxedo shirt.

Eli had to admit that she looked rather dashing in the photos, mostly because Alice had perfected the twin arts of becoming an object and making everyone around her look good. But it wasn't great for a starlet's image to show up with a butch novelist who nobody could name on sight. If she were to date a woman, better that it was an artist-DJ from Europe, or even—stop the gossip rag presses—another actress of similar magnitude.

Eli had called up Alice as soon as she saw it. They had never spoken on the phone before, but she thought this was more sensitive than texting. Alice picked up on the first ring.

"Eli, look, I know what you're going to say."

"Yeah, I just wanted to talk about it before—"

"I had no idea they would think that. I am so sorry if you're embarrassed at all. I know you're not used to being looked at or dissected like this and it can be kind of a lot. Sometimes they're really mean. At least you looked great."

Eli went blank for a moment, not sure what had just happened.

"Eli?" Alice sounded worried. "Are you there?"

She snapped back in. "Actually, I was calling to apologize to you. I didn't mean to make you look gay, I guess."

"Oh, that." Alice's voice broadened, becoming dismissive and mocking all at once. "I don't give a fuck about that. It gives people something new to talk about. Some dried-up old biddy at the *Times* compared us to Marilyn Monroe and Arthur Miller."

"That's...kind of a compliment?" Eli laughed and put a hand on the back of her neck.

"I'm so glad you're not freaking out." Alice laughed back. "I was so ready for you to be mad at me."

Eli rolled her eyes. "Yeah, I'm superpissed now that the world thinks I'm dating a gorgeous, talented movie star. How will I ever show my face in public again?"

"You tease," Alice said. "Showing up dressed like Prince Charming and you didn't even try to touch my slippers."

They had both laughed it off. About a week later, Eli received an email from her brother. They hadn't talked in a long time. They could not, in fact, talk most of the time.

Eli was absolutely cloistered about her personal life, always sliding away from questions about her upbringing and declining to tell stories about herself that began anytime before college. She didn't need people to know that she really had no family. Once those questions started, it was all sob stories and rags-to-riches bullshit. She had gotten enough of that in college when she had been honest with people as a method of making friends.

She remembered their horror: "You lived without power in your house for over a month? How did you do it? What was wrong with your parents?"

Their pity: "I can't imagine what that must have been like. You poor thing."

And their sudden need for inspiration porn when considering the trajectory of her life: "I mean, you made it. You made it against all odds. You're such an example to people like you who started out with nothing. You're the American dream."

Eli had seen enough people break down and cry for Oprah,

cry for Barbara. She had no interest in being one of them. She didn't tell anyone her story. She told Millicent's instead.

Eli wanted, more than anything, to write a book that exploded the relationship between fantasy destiny and parentage. She wanted Millicent to defy convention, to do something only a mother could do without having a child, to have a child on her own terms and in her own time. It was an impossible problem in real life. In the work, Eli could fix it. She could subvert prophecy. She could break the chain between mothers and children and tell a truly new story. She made that the focus of the end of the series, and poured her heart into it.

Millicent was a magical orphan, which was more blessing than curse in fiction. It freed Millicent from controls as a teenager, and allowed her to discover her own identity as a young adult. It added weight and drama to the question of whether she'd become a mother. It created mystery.

Eli's parental estrangement, on the other hand, had caused mostly misery. Her father had left their family penniless and without a clue when Eli was old enough to feel the sting, while her brother could only cry. Her mother was constantly drunk from that time on, and the kids were on their own. Eli remembered coming home one day to find Benny wailing on the front porch that the house was burning down and he couldn't wake up Mom. Eli had run straight to the sound of the beeping alarm. She had taken a forgotten teakettle off the stove, engulfed in flames, with a branch she had to search for outside while Benny continued screaming and running in small circles. She had thrown the kettle into the sink, put it out, then poured salt on the stove, killed the gas and turned off the smoke detector. Eli had soothed Benny with a Popsicle and set him down in front of a movie. Their mother had not stirred from her facedown sprawl during any part of this operation.

Another day, she had come home to find her mother too drunk to walk straight, staggering around the front lawn. When Benny had asked her if she was okay, she had tossed her cup of cold coffee at his face. He had cried more out of humiliation than pain, but Eli hated her mother as if she'd slapped the boy.

The household had decayed along the customary lines of abuse and neglect. Eli had tried hard to hold it together, but she was only a child and couldn't change how poor they were or whether their mother stayed sober enough to pay the electric bill.

Eli had called child protective services herself when she realized that no one at her school was going to do it, no matter how dirty and hungry she and her brother appeared to be. She hadn't known it would tear her away from her brother, permanently, until the deed was done. She had found him again when she was of age and on her way to college, but it was too late by then. He knew she had been the instrument of their undoing and he couldn't forgive her.

Immediately following their removal from their mother's home, Eli had been able to arrange to see him for an hour in a public park, with his social worker present. She could picture the table: iron with blue rubbery plastic covering the metal, the whole thing made of eyelets that stared up at them. She could feel it carving the backs of her thighs into bites of flesh, putting its pattern into her skin.

"How are you doing, Benny?"

He wouldn't look at her. He fiddled with his sleeves, looked at the sky.

"I hear you're with a family that has two other boys now." The social worker nodded at her, trying to encourage her. Eli ignored the woman.

Benny said nothing.

"Benny, come on. I worked really hard to make this happen. I miss you. Please say something."

It wasn't until Benny looked right at her that she realized that his eyes were exactly like their father's. They had the exact same pitiless gleam in them. He had never looked so adult.

"This is your fault," he said, his voice quavering with venom. "If you hadn't told, we'd still live with Mom. Mom was better than this."

"Benny," she had begun, trying to explain. But he had cut her off.

"Now I have nobody. I don't even have you, and you suck. I'm all alone."

Eli had teared up, devastated already but trying to save something. "I've been all alone, too, Benny. I was trying to save us."

"You ruined everything," Benny said stonily. He rose up off the blue table. "I'm ready to go," he said to his caseworker.

The woman had shot Eli a look of apology. Eli had walked back to her last foster home, crying her heart out the whole way. Benny never let her in again.

As adults, they had tried to maintain the typical points of familial connection. He invited her to his two weddings at sleazy chapels in Las Vegas. She had missed the first and shown up to the second just in time to see the police break up a fist-fight between bride and groom. The cops had suggested they postpone their nuptials. The couple had indeed postponed. Six hours later they were married.

Eli had tried going to Benny's house for Christmas, replete with a Santa Claus sack full of presents for the kids. Benny's wife, Maureen, had been roundly pregnant and clearly resentful of the class differences between herself and her sister-in-law. Benny tried to make jokes about it to ease the tension, but became more and more artless as the day wore on and his tower of empty beer cans grew higher. Eli had begun to immediately dream up ways to escape. She had even stayed sober so she could avoid having to call a cab on Christmas Day.

Dinner was a long, messy show of day-old KFC served to children who seemed to evaluate their choices as ammunition rather than as food. Maureen desperately tried to get the kids to put on their "company manners," but to Eli it was clear that these children were nearly as feral as she and Benny had been at their age. She made the best of it until she could not.

After she had said her hasty goodbyes, Benny had walked her out to her car.

"Thanks for the presents for the kids."

"Yeah, don't mention it." Eli opened her car door and stood behind it like a shield.

"I know they're wild, but they're good kids."

"They're a lot like we were." The accusation that he was no better as a parent than their own parents had been hung there in the air. She wasn't sure if he heard it or not.

"You gonna see Dad today?" He heard it.

"No."

Benny looked at the ground, his hand on the back of his neck. "You gotta forgive him sometime. He's gonna die, you know."

"Then why does it matter if I forgive him or not?" Eli's nose was ice-cold, though her breath was hot and fast.

"Well, he's your dad." Benny seemed very far away, as though he had something important to say, but did not know how to say it.

"Yeah, thanks for having me, Benny."

His face turned mean all at once, pulling in on itself exactly as their father's had done when his happy drunk was over and the reign of the angry drunk was about to begin. "Maureen's right. You do think you're better than us. You won't even stay… You won't even say hi to Dad…"

Eli felt herself go cold all over, exhausted from trying and pushed over the edge. *I don't owe them anything.* "I don't need this. I'm done with this."

"Yeah, of course you are," Benny said, stumbling forward a few steps. "Just run away from your problems, like you always do. You wanna call CPS on us, for old time's sake?"

Eli slammed her car door and hurriedly backed out, hands shaking as she put the car into Reverse and then into Drive again.

Fuck that, she thought the whole way home. *Fuck that entirely. Nobody needs that.*

They had tried phone calls and Facebook chats since then. The results were about the same. Benny occasionally wrote to browbeat her about making peace with their parents. More than once he asked for money. Eli would say nothing in response, but anytime he asked she mailed him a check for a thousand dollars.

There were a lot of ways to say *Fuck you.*

After the pictures of Eli and Alice had hit the press, an email arrived without salutation or signature. She knew it was Benny by the email address, but easier than that to identify was his tone: belligerent and drunk even in brief text form. She'd have known it was him if it had been written in the sky above her apartment.

So, what, you're a dyke now?

Eli thought about saying yes. She would enjoy the shock, the moral superiority of getting to call him a bigot when he couldn't handle it. She thought about saying no, but that might make him think he had gotten to her, which she would not allow. She thought about telling him it was none of his business, and a pretty ballsy question from somebody she was supporting financially whenever things got tough, no questions asked.

She thought about asking him how it felt knowing that her life was orders of magnitude better than his; that she had gotten out and went to Hollywood parties and lived exactly as she pleased and he was stuck repeating not only his own mistakes, but his parents' whole wretched lives for the next forty years. She thought about ignoring his question and asking him whether he didn't want better for his own kids. Maybe the best way to say *Fuck you* would be to open college accounts for each of his brats and let him know she had done it for their sake, since she was a rich dyke now and could do for them what their daddy would never be able to.

She stared at the screen a long time. She thought about teaching him to tie his shoes when they were small. She remembered watching Saturday-morning cartoons, just the two of them and a box of dry, sugary cereal. Remembered his voice in the night, asking for a story. She deleted the email unanswered. She mailed a check the next day.

12

Eli was vaguely aware of being wet. More than that was the sensation of warmth, and of gravity being not quite what it should have been. Normally, these pieces would have snapped together in her mind as conditions of a bath, but the drugs in her system had made the normally contiguous continent of her thoughts into islands that only dimly glimpsed one another through the fog.

Panic shot through her, punctuating a languid sense of well-being with that frantic feeling that she ought to be doing something, that doing something was important. It produced only a fluttering of her eyelids and a squeaking noise in her throat.

Once, she saw through the netting of her eyelashes that she was bleeding from one ankle. She tried to lean forward, but her abdominal muscles fired spasmodically, pulling on one side and not the other, succeeding only in sliding her downward from her half-sitting position against the back wall of the tub.

She slid down far enough to inhale a few milliliters of water before being shoved roughly back upward. Drips of it came out of her nose, but more went deep into her lungs.

Minutes later, she felt the solid, meaty weight of her own biceps pressing against her ear, followed by a tickling pressure in her armpit. The other side repeated the same way, a few moments afterward.

The panic pulsed again, like someone hammering on the pipes of a dead furnace. Adrenaline would not rise. Conscious thoughts floated through like flotsam.

Trouble...

Naked...

Drowning...

Naked...

She knew these things were true but couldn't even raise her wounded hands to cover her breasts. Wholly undefended, she slipped back into the underwater part of her mind, beneath those islands and down nearer to the volcano that had made them.

The space between dreaming and seeing the real world was so thin, and she made the switch without knowing it. She was at a book signing and he was there. Filing forward, behind grinning fans. The leg irons were in his hands. "I wanted you to sign these. For the resale value."

When she awoke, she couldn't really remember the bath, just the change of scene and sensation. She saw that the bed was made, her hands were bandaged and she was dressed in a new nightgown, this one green satin with lace at the V-neck. She had been dried carefully, but she could smell herself and knew that something had changed. She smelled something flowery, like some old-lady perfume she couldn't place or escape.

She looked around the room, trying to figure out how much time had passed, or how he had gotten the bed made without her noticing.

Her fingers were tightly bandaged, each a fat fluff of gauze bounded in with athletic tape. They didn't hurt at all. Nothing hurt, in fact.

She turned her head too quickly and everything swam in her skull, like a melting Jell-O mold sliding inside its Tupperware.

Oh, I am hella stoned.

It was close to the feeling of the drunkest she had ever been. As a freshman in college, someone had let her pull endlessly on a gallon jug of coconut rum that tasted like candy lit on fire. She had felt the customary shame that the child of drunks feels when she begins to drink, but also their customary curiosity. How good could it be? How bad? She had no previous experience with drinking, and didn't know that beyond that pleasant, buzzing numbness lay an untold hell of sickness and spins.

This was worse than that. She felt like the room wasn't spinning, but agitating like a washing machine. Swapping top for bottom and back again, then whirling along no particular axis. Every movement of her head was sickening. Moving her hand in front of her face produced a trail of color and light that smeared across her field of vision.

That's how. That's how you're dressed and the bed is made. Just like how he got you here.

She kicked at the covers, fighting for control of her body. That movement produced a sensation so singular she knew at once without looking that her legs were freshly shaved.

There was nothing so silky, so all-encompassing as the feeling of shaved skin against clean sheets. Even in the depths of the involuntary bender she supposed she was on, she knew it in a microsecond.

She struggled to throw back the blankets and have a look, but the exertion was nauseating. When she finally got a leg free, she saw that she had been shaved and moisturized. The skin glistened and glowed. There was a small Band-Aid near her heel.

Blood remember blood like strawberry syrup in vanilla ice cream I was bleeding?

Abruptly, she yanked up her green nightgown and saw with horror that her pubic hair had been neatly trimmed, as well, with the far edges shaved smooth. There, too, her skin had been lotioned or oiled.

With her uninjured hand, Eli cupped her vulva, testing for the ghost of friction there. She clenched the muscles of her pelvic floor. That sensation, too, was perfectly singular. She had no sense that she had been raped. Violated, oh yes. But nothing substantial had been inside her recently.

Shaking, she began to tug viciously at her chained ankle. She was crying before she knew it, the sensation of heat in her face unbearable on top of this swimming, sickening high.

The cuff dug mercilessly into her skin, sliding against the oil to catch at the bone of her ankle and bite there.

Eli began to moan at the horror of it all. It was overwhelming, and she knew she was coming to the edge of her own endurance.

She forced herself to stop. To slow down. To breathe. With breathing came thinking.

A single, still image came slowly to the forefront of her mind. It was her safe place, and she thought of it only when she was truly panicked. Her meditation destination. It was an old linen closet with small, controlled points of light. It had been another basement, in another time. A therapist had helped her pinpoint it in memory: a place where she felt safe and protected. She went there now.

Breathe deep. Smell mildew and brick dust and old plaster. You're safe. Nothing can get you in here.

She came back to herself slowly, her heart rate still not right but manageable, given the circumstances. She cleared her throat and tried to clear her head.

Work on the problem. Think about getting out.

The leg iron was made exactly like a handcuff, with a swinging jaw that ratcheted into itself. It was bright steel and looked new. The links were chunky and seamless. She followed the chain to the other cuff, which was fastened tighter around the steel pipe frame that held up the bed.

The pipes were threaded and the joints were screwed together. Eli had made simple plumbing repairs before, and knew that they might be sealed with plumber's tape, or they might have been heated or even welded together. She wrapped her hands around the pipe to test for give when she thought about the camera.

Above her, its red eye glowed malevolently.

Does it record when he's not watching? Or just a live feed? When he's gone for a while, does he review it? No way to know. When is he gone? Does he have a job? Does he ever leave the house?

She sat back on the bed, her mind racing, working.

I've been here at least a day. The last place I was officially was the airfield. They think I checked out of my hotel, but I didn't. Can anybody prove that?

Without windows or a clock, she could not even be sure whether it was night or day. She might be underground or underwater. Her breath was speeding up again and she forced it to slow down. To deepen. As she tried to change the pattern, she triggered a hacking cough that nearly made her vomit.

I'm probably still in California. It's a big state, and I don't think I was out that long. Arizona is a possibility, or Nevada, I guess. The AC is always running, so maybe I'm still in the desert.

I never hear anything outside. Not cars passing, not coyotes howling. Nothing. Is that because of really good insulation, or are we in the middle of nowhere? If we were in a suburb, I'd hear neighbors. Where the hell are we?

The windows up near the top of the basement were the type that opened up just above the dirt, but they were covered completely on the outside.

Siding? Just boarded up? Does that look suspicious from the outside?

He lives alone. I've heard no one else upstairs. It's been two days, I think. How long was I out?

Her lungs burned. Her body felt greasy, like something she had picked up secondhand. She rubbed her skin against the sheets, trying to cleanse herself in some small way. The coughing fit returned, and her mouth was slimed with throat mucus.

"Shit," she said, blotting her mouth on the blanket nearest her.

What if I'm dry drowning? Secondary drowning. Like those horror stories lifeguards tell mothers at the beach.

She remembered through a haze that she had inhaled water in the tub, but hadn't been able to rouse herself enough to really kick it back out. She wondered how much would be enough to kill her.

Footsteps came pounding down the stairs. Eli began to cough again.

He appeared in the doorway, alarm clear on his face.

"I inhaled water when you dragged me into the bathtub, asshole." Eli wheezed for breath as the coughing fit subsided. "I think I'm dry drowning. You know, like kids do in the summertime."

"I am sure that is not what is happening here," he said, clearly terrified that that was it.

"I don't want to die here," she said. "Take me to a hospital so they can fix this. You can just drop me off at the emergency room and drive away. I'll say I don't know how I got there."

"No," he said quickly.

Eli coughed again because she saw the effect it was having on him. The irritation was near constant at this point, so it wasn't hard to get a good one going. His eyes were huge and he crossed his arms across his chest.

Good. Let's keep this scare going.

"Do you have a plan for my body?" Her voice sounded strange to her. She used it against the fear and pressed on, talking to him as if it were not her own life she was arguing for. "It looks to me like you have a plan for captivity, but maybe not anything else. You've got my DNA all over you, your house, your car—"

He blanched and took a few steps toward her.

"You'll clean up but you'll never get it all. They'll find you, and then they'll find me. And I don't think you have that all worked out yet."

"You will not die."

She coughed again, really dragging it up. She considered bashing her fingers against the wall to get them bleeding again, but thought that she might feel the pain of that even through the numbing effect of the drugs.

"I can take care of you." He was smiling now, and the sight of it stopped her completely. It was a warm smile, utterly guileless, like a child looking into a hamster cage.

"I know you have always taken care of yourself. But now, I am going to take care of you. Is that hard to imagine? Well, get used to it. I am going to take care of you better than you ever dreamed."

She stared up at him. Unreality yawned wide around her and that dizzy feeling of the room as a washing machine agitator returned.

Still smiling, he poured out a spoonful of cough syrup.

What he had just told her was a line of dialogue, word for word, from the second Millicent Michaelson movie. It was a line that she had hated. Had, in fact, told the screenwriter that it dripped with cheese like a plate of truck stop nachos, but he hadn't cared. He said it would have them weeping in the aisles, these independent women who saw themselves in Millicent.

He had been right.

Eli sat there, utterly stunned. She watched the bowl of the spoon fill up with the blue-green, viscous liquid.

Not smart to take anything he gives me. But fuck it.

She let him put the bowl of the spoon in her mouth, hating how childish it made her feel. He tried to hold her eye as he did it and she looked away pointedly, looking at the spoon in his crabbed, spindly hand. She gulped the stuff and thought longingly of real alcohol as its faint warmth lit up her throat.

She did look up at him then, mouth set in a line. "So I gather you're a fan."

"Oh, I am more than a fan," he said, his voice filling out with a wistful romanticism. "You are very important to me."

"Um, good? That's good. I like to be important. So, you were quoting from one of the Millicent movies just then."

"Your story," he said, capping the cough syrup and sitting on the bed beside her.

She worked hard not to lean away. "You know I didn't write that, right?"

"You did not have to. You lived it." He was wiping the bowl of the spoon and balancing it on top of the bottle just so, making sure of it before letting go.

"Ha ha. Yeah. I kind of did. I was on set for some of the filming. I met Alice and everything."

"I am not interested in that," he said, moving his hand through the air as if dismissing a notification for a spam email. "I want to know more about the Maginaria and where the series is headed."

Eli cleared her throat and thought about her USB bracelet

again. "I can tell you about that. I know how hard it is, waiting on a series to be finished, wanting to know what happens next."

He smiled at her like she was a gamboling lizard in a terrarium.

Eli bore down on her friendliness, her desire to be liked. She pressed it into this macabre service.

He's a fan. Treat him like a fan. Let him in on some secrets. Use it to get him to see you.

"I dreamed up the Maginaria when I was in college," she began. "Because all I wanted was a well-run bureaucracy with endless money and power that would never make anybody beg for financial aid. It was literally my dream school."

He nodded, his eyes bright and eager. "Wish fulfillment. Sure. That drives so many fantasy writers. It certainly drove me, when I started."

Eli flinched and shook her head, confused. "Oh, you're a writer, too?"

Her captor ducked his head suddenly, as if feeling modest. "Oh, not like you. Not at all like you."

She watched his face close up all of a sudden.

What is he hiding, besides the obvious? Why does he look familiar to me? Do I know this motherfucker? How could I forget someone who looks like Slenderman?

The oft-repeated statistics surged again into Eli's mind: you're more likely to be raped by a friend, you're more likely to be killed by an intimate partner and most of the violence you will know in your lifetime will come from the other side of the bed if you are a woman.

You have to know all that and do it anyway. You can't treat all men like the enemy, even though the enemy is always a man. Open up and let them in and don't be a bitch, but also if you get hurt it's your fault. If he hurts anybody else, it's your fault because you didn't report it, because you didn't keep him satisfied, because you didn't know better. You are supposed to know better. Why didn't you leave and why didn't you warn somebody before he let his violence spread beyond the acceptable sphere of your body and into the world?

Do I know him? He acts like he knows me. Is that the fan's belief that they know the writer because they read the work? Or is there something else? How did I bring this guy to me? How do I bring him closer?

"What do you write?"

He looked away from her. "Oh, fan fiction mostly. Fantasy. I dabble in science fiction."

Eli tried hard to smile, but if she could have seen herself she would have been horrified at the effect. "I got my start writing fanfic. You have a good memory, pulling up lines like that. It must help."

"Oh, that is nothing," he said, warming visibly. He turned a few degrees in his seat, coming to face her more fully. "I can recite whole long sections of *Dune*. I will never forget Herbert's prose."

"Is that the universe you got started writing in?"

He nodded, his long face slicing through the air. "It was the best book I had ever read. I wanted to be part of it. Mostly to write about Lady Jessica."

"Fear is the mind killer," she told him, looking into his eyes, her mind killed over and over and still ticking away.

"Exactly," he said, his mouth softening. "I always knew you would understand it. I have dreamed of talking with you about this so many times."

Eli forced herself to lean forward like she couldn't wait to hear more. Her muscles were sludgy, unresponsive. Her head was still fogged with drug. She licked her lips and tried to sound fascinated. "Well, today's your lucky day. Here we are. So, *Dune* fanfic. What else?"

He looked back at the balanced spoon, as if he were planning to stand up and leave.

Eli took a risk. "I used to write Harry Potter slash," she said, trying to muster up a blush. "Did you ever read any of that, back in the day?"

He looked back at her, his mouth drooping to one side. "There was an awful lot of perversion on the slash fiction boards. Harry/Draco. Sirius/Lupin. Unnatural pairings. I could never stomach it."

Of course, Eli thought bitterly. *Of course he's one of those.*

"I wrote a lot of Hermione/Snape," she said quietly. It was true; she had. She wasn't proud of those taboo tales of teacher-student romance. She was even less proud of her own history with the same.

Is this how the universe works that out? Does fantasizing about a fucked-up power dynamic call it into being?

He was nodding. "That makes sense. They would have so much to teach each other."

Eli nodded back. "Right. He was so lonely, growing up. He was in love with Lily, but never got to be with her. Hermione was like a second chance."

"Second chances," her captor sighed. "What a wonderful idea."

"Is that something you're hoping for in life?" Eli looked at him steadily, trying to make her eyes sympathetic.

"I do not have to hope," he said. "I have you."

And that's a line from Well of Onyx, Eli thought wonderingly. *What kind of fantasy is he living in?*

Eli considered the plot of *Captive Prince*. Millicent Michaelson had to give up her newly discovered magic powers in order to learn more about her own origins, and to prove herself to the Maginaria. She had to rescue the prince with nothing but her human cunning.

The Mage Prince was imprisoned in an enchanted palace, she thought, looking around. *A gilded cage where he wanted for nothing.*

As if on cue, her stomach growled. *That is not what's going on here. Fuck it—why not try?*

Eli found herself very resistant to the idea of diving into his fantasy of her books, but she had to use the advantage. "The Mage Prince's captors took good care of him," she said. "He was never harmed. Or hungry."

He was standing, gathering the bottle and spoon. "Of course. One cannot mistreat royalty."

Her sick smile came again. "Well, I know I'm not royalty. But I would really appreciate something to eat, to settle my stomach after taking that medicine."

He held up the bottle, considering it. "There are almost a hundred calories in a single dose of this medicine." He turned his gaze to her. "Did you know that?"

Eli grimaced, trying not to yell back at him. "How about some soup? That's the thing for sickness, isn't it?"

He looked her up and down, slowly. Her skin crawled.

"I am afraid I must decline," he said, a weird half smile quirking up the side of his face.

He turned and climbed the stairs, leaving Eli to wonder what in the hell he had meant by that oddly formal turn of phrase.

Upstairs, Leonard Lobovich watched the clip of the movie again and again, trying to see if he had gotten the inflection right, the timing. He preferred the book to the film, of course. But the movie had brought the story to life in such an incredible way.

He reread all their correspondence. He mined it for phrases that had cut him, that had wounded him to the quick. He tried to think of ways he could turn them and use them against her. He held in his hand his best, most expensive pen. His grail pen. The black sheen of its body like the feathers of a corvid; the mellow gold of its nib exquisitely impregnated with deep violet ink. The pen hovered above an immaculate, cream-colored sheet of Tomoe River. He did not touch pen to paper. He could not make a mark without being certain.

She was opening up to him. He could see her slowly giving up and making room for him in her heart, in her work, in her life. He was close to getting what he wanted. So very close.

You can make the books better, you know.

Not a thing had changed, but there his muse was, sitting beside him.

"Of course I will make them better. Without me, they will not even go on."

She shook her head. He watched her long blond hair move hypnotically. He took the time to really see her, her perfect uniform in houndstooth, her flawless skin.

Leonard worked his short brass Kaweco fountain pen between his long fingers, twirling it with the ease of long habit. He dropped the weight of it into his palm, feeling the heft of words yet to be written. So much potential. His destiny ahead.

The mistake you made last time was imitation. Imitation is always a mistake.

He nodded. Armour's voice had been so unlike his own. He had itched to tune it up, to make it more precise. He went back and reread his own debut, *The Moon's Harsh Mistress*. He had longed to return to his own convoluted prose style.

But the Armour estate—and the contract he had signed— was wholly unforgiving. He had to stay within the parameters and accepted word lists that came with the job. The books were outlined and the style was prescribed. It would make his career, but his voice would hardly be in it at all.

You can bring your voice to Millicent. There is no reason to imitate the voice of the author. That is part of becoming.

He loved how calm she always was. How she always knew what to do.

"My muse, you are so right."

I can't wait to be with you, she whispered, leaning across the table as if she wanted more than anything to reach out and touch him.

"Your body is coming along," he told her.

You simply have to break its will. The spirit within is much more pliable once the body is disciplined. She looked at him, her eyes so large, so real.

"You think I should move to the next stage."

She nodded. *The body is strong,* she told him. *You must do more. You must do it faster. We have deadlines, my love.*

"The work," he mused. "The work is of the utmost importance. The work must come along." He put the Kaweco back in its home and ran his fingertips down his rack of pens. Their burnished gleam comforted him. The work awaited, and he was ready. His instruments were sharp. He could shape the world to suit him. It was his destiny to write his desire into existence.

You are coming along, too, she reassured him. *Eli, Eli, Eli.*

He smiled. The name felt as if it had always been his.

13

There was nothing to do but wait until he returned. Eli was maddened with boredom, counting blemishes in the concrete floor, or thinking over old sitcom jokes in her mind. She tried not to think about her body, but all its needs were present and pestering. The cough came and went, and her head began to ache again.

Can't drink any water. Can't trust him not to drug me again. But if I don't drink, I'll die. Shit, if I don't eat, I'll die. That last spread he brought me was maybe three hundred calories, and I threw most of it up. A hundred calories in a dose of NyQuil. Balls. I'll get too weak to fight.

Maybe that's what he's after.

She stared up at the camera, trying to spot a logo or a brand name.

I want to remember what brand of water bottles he buys. What label of cottage cheese. Who made that camera? I never want to see any of this shit again, once I'm free.

She turned her mind back to the problem of his identity. It had the maddening quality of the thing that was almost grasped before it swam away, slippery as a fish. It was a word on the tip of her tongue, a song stuck in her head without words to anchor it to memory.

The doorknob at the top of the stairs rattled and her eyes snapped to it. A second later, her captor slipped through the doorway.

"Did you bring me anything to eat? Or drink?" Her voice was rough and pained.

He had brought her a plastic bucket where she could relieve herself.

"This is so that we don't have another mess on the floor," he said primly, setting it beside her bed.

"I have to drink," she said. "I'm sick and I'm going to get sicker without some fluids."

He left and returned with two small bottles of water. He left them at the foot of her bed, where she could reach.

"Hey, why don't you tell me your name? What should I call you?"

She was speaking to his back. He was already on his way out.

"When it is time. Names have power."

"Where are you going? Come back here!"

He was gone again.

Eli drank a few swallows of water, but hunger gnawed at her. Boredom returned at once, after he had left the room. Her mind brought her commercial jingles and scraps of dialogue from old TV shows. She recalled vacations and trips she had been on like someone reviewing home movies. Click: her week in Spain. Click: the month she had stayed in Tahiti when she realized the money wasn't going to dry up anytime soon. Click: the time she had driven to the Grand Canyon by herself, on a whim. Freedom of movement. Stimulating views. Her own time.

Even the smallest self-determined entertainments felt like keen losses. Like almost any adult, she had been addicted to her phone. She badly missed reading the *New Yorker*, her Twitter feed. Even the endless cringe that was her Facebook timeline would feel like a miracle right now. Boredom was the killing thing. It kept her sleepy, gave her nothing to think about but the problem.

She slept only thinly, however. She was constantly alert for the sound of him leaving the house. She hadn't heard it once yet, not for sure. She was hoping she might hear a car pulling away from the house or something definitive. Then she would try the pipes.

He walked, sometimes. She was fairly certain she heard the creak and roll of a desk chair above the opposite side of her room, near the bathroom. Once, she heard the chiming alarm of an expensive refrigerator door that had been left open.

He's got money. That fridge was two grand, at least. He writes on the side of a real job, maybe. What else can I tell? What can I hear?

Once she noticed that, she was able to pick up on the cloyingly peppy high-pitched tune that his dryer played when its cycle ended. She looked closely at the sheets on her bed and the sexy, slippery nightgown she wore.

All were good quality. All breathed softly of money, and plenty of it.

Money buys isolation. Money buys a big house with a secure basement. A camera system. Money buys leg irons and drugs.

She had been thinking about the drugs for hours, worried about the water she had drunk. So far, nothing.

What the hell has he been giving me?

She had limited exposure to anything beyond the socially acceptable inebriation lent by alcohol and marijuana. She knew that it was some kind of downer, since it knocked her out and made short-term memory nearly impossible. But it also made her heart race and her stomach flip, and she didn't associate those things with downers at all.

Some kind of date-rape drug.

Thinking the word *rape* made her close up like a clam. He had stripped her, bathed her, shaved her and carried her around without her knowledge. He had certainly manhandled her, hoisted her up like so many pounds of potatoes to kidnap her and move her around. He had been too familiar with her, far too close and acted like he owned her.

But he hadn't raped her.

Like the question of murder, she had to wonder: *If he hasn't done it yet, why not? Is it because he can't get up his nerve yet? Or because he wants something that he can't get from me afterward?*

If I knew who he was, I'd know what he wanted.

She thought about the way his face had looked when he asked for her laptop password. *Why in hell did he want that so badly, if not for money? If he's just a crazed fan, does he want the book? To what end? Just to read it? Why bother? What in the mad-hattering fuck does he want?*

Chasing her tail, she fell asleep.

The first alarm scared her so badly that she sat up screaming. A bright green-blue light flashed from everywhere at once. It was under the bed, it was above and below her and it snapped on and off in a blinking strobe that she could see even with her eyes closed.

The strobe light started seconds before the Klaxon. It was a tooth-shattering sound. Eli could feel it vibrating the pipes of her bed frame. She clapped her hands over her ears and clenched her teeth. It went off at a regular interval, arrhythmic and heedless of the flashing light. Her ears rang between blasts so that it never really seemed to cease. She wanted to cram a pillow or blanket against her head to muffle the noise, but she couldn't bear to let go long enough to snatch it.

The light stopped first. Then the Klaxon.

Eli removed her hands from her head slowly, carefully. She looked up at the camera.

"What the fuck?" She could barely hear her own voice, though she knew she had screamed it.

There was no answer.

She lay, twitching and impotently enraged, for a long time. She drank some water and drifted off to sleep again a long while later.

She had just fully dropped into a deeper state of sleep when it started again. Lights first. Then the Klaxon, just as loud as the first time. Total sensory overload chased away thought. When it ended, she felt right on the edge of tears. She sat up in bed, pulling the top sheet out and using it to wind her pillow crudely around the back of her head. She wrapped the sheet over and over until it covered her face and muffled her ears, which still rang.

She had to think. She yanked up the part of the sheet that covered her mouth to get deep breaths.

Sleep deprivation. This is going to keep happening. He is trying to weaken me. Break me. For what?

When she was in grad school, Eli had had a partner who was obsessed with game shows. Lee paid for the big cable package specifically for the Game Show Network, which Eli despised immediately and grew to eventually loathe. Lee loved it all: competing for cash, for celebrity dating arrangement or for fabulous merchandise.

"It's just human society on a soundstage," Lee would say, eyes shining and smile wide. "Everything we wish we were, everything we're afraid we'll never be, is right there. On the wheel. On the board."

Eli had rolled her eyes, and for the most part not watched. She was always working anyway, either reading and writing for school, or reading and writing for her first disastrous novel. TV was a time suck, so she let it be background noise.

Except for one show that she could not ignore: *Solitude*.

The first time Eli had realized what was going on, she thought that there was no way the show was real. It must have been scripted and staged somehow, because nobody would have allowed that to air. Many game shows traded in humiliation and even physical pain, but this one seemed to be selling literal torture as entertainment.

The participants were sealed in their own isolation pods, without any interaction with other people. They spoke only to a malevolent, indifferent robot voice named Mal. Mal suggested insidiously that they were weak, doomed or unequal to the task of being the last man standing—which was how the game was won.

Of course, that wasn't enough for a game show. A reality show, maybe. But the game was that anyone could opt out at any time by striking a big surrender button. Mal taunted them about that, too, goading them to quit. She insinuated that others had quit already, and each player might be prolonging their agony for no reason at all.

What agony? Why, all kinds! The players were served strange food, underfed and overfed. They were made to watch horror movies while taking notes or counting certain elements. They had to sit in tubs of ice water. The game stole their few personal possessions from them and sometimes allowed players to taunt each other via Mal, their heartless companion.

The episode Eli remembered the most clearly was one that introduced sleep deprivation. Each pod was dark and contained one fitfully sleeping person who had not had any human contact for weeks. An alarm would sound and a floodlight would fill the room. The person had to enter a long numerical code into the computer in order to deactivate the alarm.

They could make no mistake. The code got longer each time the trap sprang. If they made a mistake, the light and sound continued indefinitely.

Most of them got it right at least once, but by the end of the night they were broken, stumbling like overtired toddlers, incapable of playing the game anymore. Eventually, they all curled up in the maddening light while the alarm sounded loudly enough to distort in the overhead microphone.

Some cried and some feigned stoicism.

"That's some prisoner-of-war shit," Lee had said gravely. "That's what you do when you're trying to break a person."

Eli's prediction that this would happen throughout the night was correct. She thought that the interval was around fifteen or twenty minutes, but it also seemed to coincide with her actual lapse into deep sleep.

He might be watching me and setting it off. But then, he'd be just as fucked up by the end of the night.

But it didn't end with the night. In the dayless, thoughtless basement, there was no night. No day. No ebb and flow. And the alarm and light did not stop.

Eli tried counting each occurrence on her fingers, but her mind lost hold of the number at once. She had nothing to make tick marks with. The walls were concrete block and she couldn't scratch them. She thought of scratching lines into her skin, but recoiled, recalling the pain in her fingertips.

She became badly disoriented, unable to tell up from down in her first waking moments. She hallucinated, finding herself asleep at the wheel and waking to the sound of an oncoming truck. She held the pillow against her head and screamed helplessly for a time. When she could think of anything at all, she thought of the keypad that the people on the game show had used. It had given them some tiny piece of order, something they could control. That was what had kept it from being torture, really. That and the fact that they could free themselves at any moment, losing only money that had never really been theirs in the first place.

Eli had no buttons to push. No Mal to taunt her. No lists to make. No way to surrender, even if she wanted to. In a lull, she shrieked up at the camera that he had to come down there and talk to her like a person, that he could not do this.

Leonard was not at home to hear any of this.

He knew that the sleep program would be upsetting to watch, so he had taken his car and gone to town. He'd arranged for a hotel room and drew out his errands for two and a half days.

By the third day, Eli was sure she would die. Her water was long gone and her eyelids scraped over her eyeballs like sandpaper. She could not think straight about anything. When the alarm sounded, she had begun reciting anything she could think of.

"'I pledge allegiance to the flag of the United States of America...'"

Fifteen minutes.

"'By the shores of Gitchee Gumee. By the shining Big-Sea-Water...'"

"'Down, down, baby. Down by the roller coaster.'"

Her voice was a creak and a croak without much else. She pinched at the skin on her hands and watched the pinch roll slowly out.

"Dehydration," she whispered. "I know you."

Leonard unlocked the door to the basement and came down. Eli didn't hear him at all.

She lay on her side, dryly crooning, "I know you."

"What?"

She felt the vibration of his speech in the room more than heard him. She sat up slowly, laboriously. She pulled the sheet and pillow cocoon off her head. She blinked up at him, not sure at first if he was really there.

"I know you."

He stepped forward with a bottle of water and her hands shot out as though she were falling.

She looked awful. Her cheeks and temples had sunken, and her eyes looked sick. Had it really been this bad in just a couple of days?

He handed her the water bottle and watched her claw the lid off, gulping it down.

She threw up water a second later; her head whipped to the side to vomit mostly off the side of the bed.

She drank again anyway, trying to make herself drink slowly.

He waited. He was worried that she really did know him. He tried to keep from thinking his own name, as if she could pick it up out of his brain waves.

"Let me go," she croaked.

Leonard shook his head.

"Then kill me," she said simply. "I can't do this anymore. I'll die. Just get it over with."

"You can't die," he said. "Someone like you can never die."

"I don't know where you got that idea," she rasped at him. "I am literally dying of thirst right now."

"You're not real," he said, his smile spreading across his face like relief. He pointed helpfully to the rules on the wall. She did not look where he pointed.

She gulped water as if to defy that pronouncement.

"You had my blood all over you just a few days ago. Was that real?"

He looked away from her. She saw his beard in profile, looked over his face. He looked so normal.

"I stabbed you in your fucking face. Was that real, you fucking lunatic?"

He said nothing, pointedly moving his face to show that he was ignoring her.

"If I wasn't real, how did you kidnap me? I have a whole life outside of this basement, and you know that. You must, because it's how you found me. I have friends and lovers and dentist appointments. I'm real, chickenshit."

She began to cough again, as though the sickness that had been lying low in her chest had been reconstituted—just add water!

She sputtered water droplets across the pink pattern on the bedspread. Despite the return of her cough, she was amazed at how much better she felt just getting something to drink.

"I also need to eat," she spit at him. "Once again, because I am real. I have all kinds of needs you don't know anything about."

His smile was faltering. "I know everything about you." He fixed his gaze down on her.

"I'm going to bleed out of my vagina in about two weeks. Did you know that? Do you have a plan for that, or is this going to be like when you realized I would piss all over your floor? Do you have a box of tampons, or just a vat of roofies upstairs?"

He recoiled, his lip curled back.

"I'm not fucking around with you." Her eyes were wild. "I know what you're trying to do. I won't let you."

He backed away from her, toward the stairs. He held his hands up in front of him as though she could offer him any threat.

"Get back here, asshole!" she yelled after him. Her ears rang. She sat blowing air hard out of both nostrils.

I'm glad to find I'm still spoiling for a fight. Why won't he fight me? He fought me before. What the fuck does he want?

But that last time you fought him, you put a hole in his face. He won't forget that. That's why he's trying to get at you indirectly now.

Fuck that.

The alarm.

If the schedule was still the same, the alarm would go off any minute. She was still loopy and exhausted, not seeing clearly. Adrenaline would desert her and she would fall asleep again. The alarm would roll again.

I will go crazy, she thought simply. *It's long overdue. I will check the fuck out.*

But the alarm didn't sound. She did not fall asleep quickly, as she expected. She began tearing the sheets off the bed again. She pulled the comforter through her hands at the edge seams, examining every inch of it. Her senses felt heightened. She could see the tight weave of the cloth, the serged seams. She came to the manufacturer's tag and read every word, flipped it over and read them again in French. It felt so good to read something that she almost smiled.

She began to bite at the seam at the corner, where she could see the end of the serging ran out. If she pulled enough of it free, she could maybe garrote him when he came close.

With her hands full of freed string, she fell asleep.

Leonard knew she was running a fever. He saw the strange brightness in her eyes, even in the dimness of the basement, the spots of color on her cheeks like blush.

He wasn't sure whether this was good or bad. It would probably further weaken her so that his program would work better, which was good. It might make her less receptive, which was bad. He stared up at the monitor, trying to guess whether she was asleep. It seemed that she was. She had been busy like a caged rodent for a few long minutes, but the resolution wasn't good enough for him to tell what she had been doing. When she had been still for five minutes, he got his water pistol out of the freezer and headed back down.

String. There was string all over her hands; she had torn open the edge of her comforter. He pursed his lips. He would have to fix that. But he decided he would do it later, when she was compliant.

He shot her in the face with the icy water in four rapid trigger pulls. She came awake, sputtering and gasping.

"What? What?" She was shrill and confused, but he heard no threatening tears in her voice.

"You're not real," he told her calmly. "Say it."

"Fuck you," she said, wiping her face with the back of her hand.

"You're not real. Say 'I'm not real,' and I'll go up those stairs and leave you alone for eight whole hours."

"No," she said. "Go fuck yourself."

He shot her in the face again. "You're only making this harder on yourself. I can go back to my nice warm bed and turn the alarm program back on. I can leave it on for days."

"I'm going to kill myself," she told him calmly. "I'm not going to let you torture me indefinitely. When it gets too bad, I'm just gonna opt out. I have everything I need to do it right here."

"You would never do that," he said, looking uncertain. His eyes darted to the pipes of her headboard.

She almost smiled.

"I absolutely will." She was staring straight up at him. "You obviously need me alive, and I don't want you to have anything you want. So try me. Keep fucking with me and see what happens."

He shot her in the face again, staring down dispassionately. She put up her hands. When he stopped, she looked up at him.

"Well?"

He said nothing, turned and walked upstairs.

He did turn the alarm system back on. It ran for the next forty-eight hours. At one point, he opened the door at the top of the stairs and rolled a succession of water bottles down to her. She was able to capture several of them and drank thirstily.

Her fever worsened. Her cough deepened. She slept in snatches between alarms. She used the bucket when she had to empty her bladder and gritted her teeth against the cresting, white-hot pain of her UTI asserting itself. She breathed through her teeth.

Can't get clean. Don't want him washing me again. Cranberry juice, for fuck's sake. Anything. It burns.

On the second day, she ripped the comforter open enough that she could crawl inside it.

She had meant it when she threatened to kill herself, but she didn't actually have a plan.

I could just bash my head into the floor or the headboard, but I might pass out before I was really done. Just hurt myself for no reason.

From her position inside the bag of cotton fluff that had once been her comforter, she hunched up over the edge of the bed.

Her right hand was still bandaged and the fingers hurt quite badly when bumped or when she curled them past halfway. She held her right palm open against the frame for leverage. With her left, she bore down to see whether she could loosen a two-foot length of pipe.

She strained and grunted, trying to grip tight and keep her hand from sliding. Nothing budged.

The alarm went off and she started to laugh. The laugh was jagged and hooting, nothing like her normal laughter. She couldn't hear herself over the wearing din.

She drank another bottle of water all at a go, thinking about a baked-egg sandwich at the ferry building in San Francisco. About the good cheese shop. About blackberries in season and a carnitas taco dripping with lime juice.

Dying of sleep deprivation is slow.

Dying of hunger is slow.

This motherfucker.

Leonard watched the camera off and on, waiting for her to reach one of the spiked bottles. He knew she was under when the alarms didn't wake her. He deactivated the system and headed down.

September 4

@the_spice_flows: Greetings, @eligrey! Wondering if you would lend us your view on the new "Hand of Fate" novel. Did you get an ARC?

@eligrey: I think I did, but I've been too busy to write reviews, tbh. I've always been a fan, and I hope the series does well under the new author.

@the_spice_flows: Oh, I had so hoped to hear your opinion on it. I am a great admirer of your work. "City Under the City" is a work of genius.

@eligrey: Thank you so much, that's very kind

@the_spice_flows: [photo of a signed first edition of The City under the City, autographed by the author] My most prized possession!

@the_spice_flows: Cannot wait to read the new Hand of Fate!

@the_spice_flows: Wow, the leading lady in Hand of Fate reminds me so much of Millicent Michaelson. Anyone see the similarity? @eligrey?

14

Eli was dimly aware that she was coughing, but not awake quite yet. Her lungs felt wet and cold and sore, but breathing in big gulps of hot air was a slight comfort.

Really hot air. Like a mouthful of steaming coffee. The same heat was digging into her hip and her elbow.

The heat was so all-encompassing that she didn't register it as temperature at first, only as sharpness and pressure. She thought maybe she had torn up more of the bed and was lying on the bare, sharp springs.

She couldn't open her eyes.

She stirred weakly, not really able to move. The sick, swimmy feeling was back in her head and she knew she had been drugged again.

From far away, she could hear a voice.

"You said you wanted to kill yourself."

The voice was slow and low, with long pauses between words. The words floated down to her like they were being shouted through the mouth of a cave and she was miles below.

"Here's your chance."

With great effort, Eli forced her eyes open.

She assumed she had been blindfolded, since she could see only baffled white light. She felt her face and put her hands directly on naked skin.

Naked. She was completely naked, not a stitch on her. Even her ankle cuff was gone.

She wasn't blindfolded. Her eyes adjusted and she saw that she was lying on a bare gray driveway. Flecks of quartz winked up at her, picking up the sunlight like diamond dust.

Outside. I'm outside.

She pushed herself up and looked over her shoulder. She saw she was beside a house. There was siding from end to end, and no windows on this side.

She fought her way to her feet and cried out at the way they burned, pressing against the scalding pavement.

With laborious effort, she circled around to the other side of the house. There were windows here, and a front door. No numbers or signs on it gave any clue to where she was. Speakers mounted up under the eaves spoke to her.

"Go on. Run out into the desert and kill yourself. You're free. Go."

Eli spotted a red Jeep Cherokee, a few years old, sitting on oversize all-terrain tires a few yards away from the house. She ran toward it on feet that were already burning their way toward numbness.

It was, of course, locked up. She pounded on the windows with her curled fists, sure she was hurting her fingers but not caring. With the bandages gone, her fingers looked like bruised fruit. They were fat and purple and swelled around her nailbeds where blood crusted between skin and keratin.

She put her bad hand over her good and tried to smash the driver's side window with her elbow.

Her arm bounced painfully off the hot glass.

She was sobbing, but didn't know she was until the hot tears shocked her dry face.

She ran again, away from the house. There was another car parked in front, a small sedan. She fumbled with every possible point of entry, trying to break into it.

Can't drive it. Can't even start it. Don't care. Get in there and stay in there. Make him come after and fight him.

The speakers on the house were saying something again, but she couldn't make it out from here. That was good. Good.

How far from a road? How long before someone else comes along? Where are we?

She ran away from the house, trying to get her bearings. The sun was low in the sky, but she couldn't tell whether it was early or late. She looked in every direction, trying to make sense of what she was seeing.

There were no other houses in sight. The horizon was empty, dotted with cacti and Joshua trees, but featureless otherwise. In one direction, there was a suggestion of hills.

The house behind her sat at an intersection of two streets. The roads were packed, but not paved. Green street signs sat at the crossing, naming these roads after women: Johanna, Miranda, Christina. She stared at the signs, confirming over and over that they were real.

Why the fuck are these roads marked, but there's nothing here?

Eli began to get a sense that this was a planned subdivision, but that the work had not yet begun. *Clearly there's going to be a neighborhood here. Just not yet.*

She looked again at the green street signs. They were not new; they showed wear around the edges and the color had faded in the sun.

Eli gave up on figuring it out. She picked a direction and ran. Her feet picked up goat's heads and hit sharp bits of rock. She passed a desert tortoise with barely a look.

If that thing is alive, then there's water out here somewhere. Has to be.

Birds wheeled overhead as if to support her hypothesis. She tried not to look up and see them too clearly. If they were buzzards, she didn't want to know.

She found that she couldn't run well. She was exhausted and her lungs were burning. She coughed as she struggled to breathe deeper, but she did not slow down.

There has to be something. Some place to hide. Some weather station I can fuck with and the forestry service will show up. Something.

She ran with the sun to her back. Her shadow stretched out before her, long and juddering, naked and bouncing and bizarre. She could already feel her pale shoulders and scalp beginning to burn. She reached the edge of the unpaved streets and looked back. The house was still there, malevolent and gray in the distance. She saw no movement.

Eli turned and ran again. The Joshua trees looked like nothing she had ever seen before, and nothing that belonged on earth. Their round, stumpy, undulating branches reminded Eli of some sinister Dr. Seuss drawings, or a *Star Trek* set from the original series. Scrubby bushes and cacti dotted the ground right at the edge of the road, and Eli had to look where she was going to avoid them. She tried not to think about how far she might be from a main road.

He drove me here on the freeway. There is a freeway somewhere nearby.

She stopped a moment and tried to calm her panting, to listen for the sound of cars. The wind stirred. She heard nothing.

Doesn't matter.

She jogged on, losing speed. She was flagging and gasping for air, coughing badly. She had slowed to a normal walking pace when she heard the sound of a motor.

She looked around wildly, trying to place it. It was definitely coming from behind her.

The Jeep! He got in the fucking Jeep and he's coming after me!

Eli began to run again, desperately looking for someplace
to hide.

Dig a hole! The ground is powdery and you can cover yourself.

It was a stupid idea, but she wanted to give it a chance anyway. She dug her toes experimentally into the dry, hot dirt. It
was hard as rock less than an inch below the silt.

Eli swore under her breath. She jogged on, looking for
anything that could hide her. There was nothing. She was a
naked woman alone in a desert. Exposure made her turn her
toes in and wrap her arms around her body.

The sound of the car drew closer. She could see the dust
trail the vehicle was raising behind it.

You fucker.

She looked around now, searching for a rock she could
throw at him when he arrived. Maybe she could knock him
out and take control of the vehicle.

*Get behind the wheel and run him the fuck over. Don't stop until
I find help.*

It wasn't a bad idea, but she couldn't spot a rock anywhere.
She jogged again, zigzagging, looking for any sign of difference on the ground or in the distance. Heat shimmer made
it impossible to tell what lay ahead before the brown moun-
tains ate up the horizon.

The Jeep was almost upon her when she saw them: three
round stones lying against each other, each of them small
enough to hold in one hand and throw. She stood looking at
them, then looked back at the car.

It was the Jeep. The dust trail had kicked up considerably,
and the wind was stirring the dirt in its wake. It looked like
the car was dragging a storm.

Don't pick it up. Not yet. Don't let him see that you're ready.

The car stopped fifteen feet away from her. She waited.

Eli's captor came out slowly, holding a bottle of water like a peace offering. "Are you ready to come home and be a good girl?" His glasses reflected the sun, becoming white ovals in his face.

She squinted at him. "Bring me that water and we can talk about it."

He walked toward her.

When he was close enough, she steeled herself. She knelt quickly, clumsily, and groped for the stones with her right hand. He saw what she was doing and ran to close the distance.

Her fingers wrapped around the hot smoothness of the rock for one perfect, blessed moment.

I am going to smash your fucking brains out.

It was the last thing she thought before the scorpion struck at the outside corner of her wrist, stinging three times in rapid succession. She lost consciousness almost immediately.

Leonard watched her go down, not having seen the sting and not understanding why this was happening. Her whole body jerked and she cried out as if she'd hit an electrical wire in the dirt. She reached for the ground even as she collapsed to it, crumpling and writhing there for a minute before going slack. He stood a moment, making sure she wasn't just playing possum. He lifted her and carried her to his car, counting himself lucky that he hadn't lost track of the author completely.

He checked her all over for injuries, noting the redness of the soles of her feet. He found the sting site on her right hand and wrist and put together what must have happened.

Back at his house, on his Wi-Fi, he looked up how to care for a sting, guessing it could have been one of the many species of desert spiders. He gave her liquid baby Tylenol and applied ice to the reddest area on her arm.

He hadn't counted on this going so well. He had known the desert would defeat her, and that she would gain a more accurate sense of the position she was in. But this had worked far better than he had planned, costing him no more than half a day.

He looked the author over. The exercise had likely done her some good. She was already losing weight.

His lady was going to need another bath.

When Millicent came to him again, she was in a shimmering white gown. It was so out of place in the bathroom that he left the arm he was holding slip through his fingers and dunk back beneath the water.

It is time to tell her, she said in her beautiful voice that did not echo off the tiles.

"To tell her who I am?"

No, not that. Not yet. Tell her first who she is. Who I am. Who we are. Help her assume her correct role. Help her see what we will have when this magic is done.

"But the change."

The change is still coming, she told him. *Maybe you should take a step in the right direction. Shave. Practice talking about your work. Get her talking about the work and listen to how she says it.*

"If she talks about the work, she will feel as though the work is hers."

The white gown made no sound as Millicent walked. *She will feel powerless,* she said. *She will give herself to you. Her power is draining away, already flowing into you. Can't you feel it? Even now, she is helpless before you and you remain a perfect gentleman. That is true power. The power of self-control.*

He nodded. He could feel the power of transfer between

them. Soon, he would have everything that was once hers. He had done everything right. She did not even know his name.

Tell her what her name is. Only then can you begin to take your own.

Leonard let his head fall back, exposing his throat. He closed his eyes. "Say it again."

Eli Grey. Bestselling author, Eli Grey. Herbert award winner. Respected author. Creator of Millicent Michaelson. Now, take your pen in hand and show me how you made me. Show me, Eli.

He did.

October 30

@LeonardLobovich: *Prince Vantan rides again! Today, we return to the glorious saga of the "Hand of Fate." Thank you, readers and Ent Books for trusting me with this world and this story. Debuted on the* New York Times *and* Amazon *bestseller lists! [a photo of author Leonard Lobovich holding the seventh book in the series:* Vantan's Burden*]*

@gassygoat34: *Thank the lords of story! I can't wait to return to the Vale of Varia! [RT]*

@kimsimkins: *At last… I have been dying for the show to go on… [RT]*

@frsrcrnsrzr: *HELLO 911 MY PREORDER HASN'T ARRIVED YET [RT]*

@3littlemades: *After book six, anything is going to seem great. What a joke.*

@alexbundy: *2/5 stars to Vantan's Burden on Goodreads [link] Armour is dead and nobody can take his place.*

@LeonardLobovich: *I want to take a moment and thank the authors I admire for helping me to achieve my dreams. Thank you, @peterrothfisk, @jeffbusch, @eligrey, @niallhimself, J. R. R. Tolkien, Piers Anthony and Frank Herbert. Of course, I cannot forget the late, great @bernardarmour. It is an honor to be in your company.*

@jeffbusch: *Congratulations, man. That's one hell of a debut!*

@peterrothfisk: *You lucky bastard! No, seriously, you've earned it. Enjoy this.*

@FrankHerbertfans: *He'd be so proud of you! You are the muad'dib! [gif of sandworm]*

@niallhimself: *Happy book day!*

@bernardarmour: *What is remembered lives. [gif of a hand adding a stone to a cairn]*

15

Eli dreamed, so she knew she was not dead.

In the dream, Eli was a child again. She and her brother were hungry. They had not seen each other for years and could not get along, but the thought of those days still made her heart move up into her throat and swell and swell.

Benny was four years younger than her, born at the perfect time to be constantly in her charge, but not enough for her to be good at it.

Like most poor children, they both faced a perfect hell in school. Benny's clothes were loose and baggy, while Eli's frayed and stretched as she grew. Their shoes fell apart and they tried to patch them with glue or tape, but wet days left them both cold and humiliated. Kids pointed and laughed. They made up mean songs about the free-lunch kids, the latchkey kids. They made a terrible thing worse.

"Why can't you fix them so that they won't leak?" Benny was furious with Eli, since he couldn't be furious with the root cause of his embarrassment.

Eli couldn't answer that. She also couldn't stand letting him go hungry. She could make him dinner out of instant oatmeal, or ramen noodles, or the last eye-sprung potato in the house.

But Eli dreamed of a period when they had nothing, not even the kind of canned vegetables that no kid would eat.

They had been evicted from their home. Their mother had disappeared for a couple of days. Their father was long gone. They had no money and there was nothing at all in the house. During the week, they got free breakfast and lunch at school. Eli had pocketed a roll and an apple at lunch on Friday and had split them both with Benny on Saturday morning.

And then there was nothing to do but wait for Monday.

Hunger in the dream was hunger in real life. Eli hadn't eaten in days, and her suspicion of what little water she got was costing her. She stirred weakly in her sleep, felt herself tightly wrapped in blankets and fell deeply back into her own mind.

In the dream, Benny followed her around the house, yelling that he was hungry.

"I'm sorry," she said over and over. "I'm sorry. There's nothing I can do. I'm sorry."

Her mind gnawed at the problem as her stomach growled. She could shoplift. She could beg something from the neighbors. Terror kept her from acting. They circled the apartment in a never-ending hallway. There was nowhere to go.

"I'm hungry," Benny said behind her. "I'm hungry and you won't do anything."

She looked over her shoulder. The person behind her was wearing Benny's thrift-store clothes, and speaking in his voice. But his face was the face of her captor.

"I'm hungry," he cried plaintively. "I'm so hungry."

She began to run, but running in dreams was rarely an efficient expression of the urge to escape. She ran slowly, groggily, pushing along the wall to keep upright.

"I could just eat you," her captor spoke thoughtfully from just behind her. "I could eat you, and then I'd be fine."

Eli opened her mouth to scream and found that only a low groaning was coming from her lips.

She was awake but not awake. Her body was weak and confined. She fought stark terror for a long moment, remembering previous encounters with sleep paralysis. This was like that dreadful state, but much worse. When she had suffered in the past, she had merely soothed herself back to sleep to awaken in a better condition.

She whooped in a deep breath and began to cough weakly. She couldn't raise her arms or move her legs. She could feel the foreign yet familiar pressure of the cuff around her right ankle.

Fighting to open her eyes rewarded her with an awful stabbing sensation when the light hit them. But it also confirmed what she knew somehow, through some other sense: he was there with her. The basement was the same. Same stairs. Same bed. Same door. Same hateful rules on the wall. She wanted to cry with frustration that she had not woken up somewhere else. Anywhere at all would do.

"Who the hell are you? Why didn't you leave me out there to die? Why did you let me run in the first place? What was the point of that?" Her voice was a dry croak.

"I do not want anything to happen to you. I just needed you to understand what it is I am trying to do here."

"And what is that?"

"I am trying to help you understand what you are." His voice was gentle and awful, cozening.

"Here," he said. "I brought you some soup. It will warm you up."

She struggled to look at him, but she couldn't tilt her head and the angle was awkward for her eyes. She saw that he had shaved his fastidiously kept beard off. It made his face look even longer, but more familiar. She brushed that aside. She had to focus.

It smells so good. So what if I'm under again? At least I ate. What's the point?

She fought anyway.

"Even if I wanted to take anything you brought me, which I don't, I can't even lift my hands to eat that."

She pulled back deeper under the blankets and tried to will herself back to sleep. Sleep seemed so near, between the lasting effect of the drugs and incipient heat stroke. But his proximity kept her alert, kept her on the edge of fight or flight, though neither was really possible.

"Look," he said.

She pried her eyes open and saw him take a bite from the steaming bowl. It looked like pea soup. Despite the brittle weakness in her limbs, her body cried out for it. The hunger of the dream resurfaced as a sharp sensation of emptiness.

Eat it. For Christ's sake, eat it before he takes it away.

But her hands would not obey the command to get it to her mouth.

Eli worked hard to pull one arm out of the wrappings and then let it fall, panting. Her wrist and fingers were bandaged again. Vaguely, she recalled the sensation of getting stung. That whole arm ached. She fought again to free her left hand instead.

He watched her do it.

It was an odd sensation to want help, to need it badly and to be absolutely opposed to asking for it from the nearest human. If he touched her, she would scream and never stop.

She kept her eyes on him. Aside from the shave, it was the same face as ever. Familiar, but so terribly keen that she felt she must look away. The hole in his cheek, revealed now with his bare skin, was healing and looked much better than the

wounds in her hand did. She left it lying where it was and focused her clumsier—but uninjured—left hand. It crawled toward the bowl like a wounded bird. Plucking the spoon from
it wasn't too hard, but she couldn't go through the range of
motion to fill its small stainless steel bowl.

Instead, she brought it to her mouth with only a thin coat-
ing of pale green substance. It was loathsome to think that this
same spoon had just been in his mouth, but this entire mode
of living was loathsome. She licked the spoon morosely, but
was unable to deny the rush of need that rose in her.

She dipped the spoon again and again, getting only the tiniest dribs and drabs of food. Still, it helped sharpen her wits.
She felt warmed. Enlivened.

He sat beside her bed the whole time. Watching. Frigid air
drifted over them, falling from the vents.

The most natural thing to do would have been to help her.
She felt it all along, that discomfort of watching another person struggle. In any other instance it would have prompted an
automatic gesture: opening the door for someone with their
hands full, or picking something up when it had been dropped.

Their proximity was growing its own mutated form of intimacy, Eli realized. She was able to steal glances at his face
when he was in the room with her, but he was always staring
at her. Some men have a way of eating you with their eyes,
and she had been gobbled up before. She knew that look. He
wouldn't look anywhere but her face. He blinked slowly, like
a creature of the depths of the sea that rarely saw the sun.

She kept raking over his frame and his body, trying to find
the anomaly or the oddness that had made him into what he
was. Trying to nail down what it was about him that seemed
familiar.

Even the most dangerous serial killers just look like normal people.

Think of John Wayne Gacy or Ted Bundy. Those normal subur-
ban dudes look like tellers at the bank, or junior high school teachers.

Eli wondered if this guy had a job. He showed up in the
basement at all hours, but she had been out of it so deeply and
so often it was possible that he was gone eight hours a day and
she wouldn't know it. Not yet.

In a flash, she realized she had no idea what day it was. She
tried to place how many days he had had her and couldn't.
She had been on her book tour yesterday. She had been in this
basement since the beginning of time.

Joe, tell somebody I'm missing. Do your good-ass job, like you
always do.

All at once, Eli began to cry. There was no way to stop
it. She had no inner resources left. She cried like an uncom-
forted child.

I have to hope that my assistant—someone I pay to look after my
bullshit—will report me missing, because nobody else will. There's
no one in my life who knows me better than Joe, or might notice I'm
gone. He's not even mine full-time. Shit, if Hangerton or Busch has
a book release this week, I'm going to die here. He'll be too busy with
other stuff to notice.

Please, Joe. Please.

The need to beg him was so real she almost said the words
out loud. She tasted her own tears when she licked another
half swallow of soup.

This is pathetic. I'm bawling in front of this crazy bastard. I have
no control whatsoever. I'm so, so fucked here.

She couldn't eat any more soup without being sick. She
dropped the spoon in the bowl with a clatter and tried to wipe
her face. She felt an absurd urge to thank him for the food,
a reflex from another incarnation. She clamped down hard
on the idea of that. The knowledge that she could normalize
his behavior for him came glowing at the center of her con-

sciousness, radioactive. She could get used to this. She could get used to anything.

She sniffled raggedly and tried to focus. *What is productive to say right now?* "I must be in pretty bad shape."

"Yes," he said softly.

"That's why you've got me all wrapped up." She tried to struggle to emphasize this point, but found that she was too weak, every muscle either feebly flexing or refusing her demands outright. Her terror deepened.

"Yes," he said again, looking over the cocoon of her body.

"Are you going to kill me?"

"I could never kill you, Millicent."

Eli blinked. There were two of him in her vision, sliding apart and back together again. "What did you call me?"

"Millicent Michaelson. That is rule number one." His face broke into a smile and he pushed his glasses up his long, thin nose. "You are not a real person. You are a fictional character. You will tell me your name is Millicent Michaelson."

Her blood did not turn to ice water. Rather, it was more like the vast, branching network of blood vessels and capillaries throughout her body froze instantly into a crystalline structure. She was rigid and cold. Her face was hot. Her back cramped feebly, trying to stiffen her, to sit her up, to prepare to fight.

"I'm not Millicent. Millicent's not real."

His smile widened. "To me, you are. You are more real than anyone else. The realest girl in the world. Come on, Millicent. Say your name."

Her weakness felt awful. The swaddling confinement wrapped around her was unbearable. She was beginning to cry with frustration and fear. She realized too late that she could not even brush the tears away from her hot, welling eyes.

"I'm not Millicent. You said my name. You said it when you picked me up. You said Elizabeth Grey. I heard you say it."

I heard you say it. The thought echoed back from some disjointed time. She thought it was the scrambling action of terror on the brain and waved it away.

"I had to say that," he said quietly, his smile fading. "That is who you think you are. That person does not exist. That is all made-up. What is real, what we make together, is Millicent."

He came closer to her and reached out a hand like a fry cook's spatula, tucking one of her shoulders back into the bandage-wrapped bedding. The gesture was tender, and he held his hand against the back of her shoulder just a beat too long.

"Get the fuck off me! Don't touch me. Don't." She tried to glare up at him, but she could hardly see. Her teeth were bared, neck corded.

"Hush now," he said as though talking to a baby. "You need to rest and get better."

"I'm not going to rest," she said, already sliding into sleep.

Medication took its hold and she drifted away like an unmoored boat.

Leonard sat and watched her sleep.

Millicent lay her hands on his shoulders as he sat. *This is good*, she told him. *We are getting closer. The body is going to break so that the spirit can prevail.*

He waited, watching the body sink deeper and deeper.

"What do I do now, my Millicent?"

She leaned down to whisper in his ear. *Now you must become. Now is the time to prove who you are. This is the new moon, the hour of bloodtalking.*

Leonard went up the stairs alone.

16

Dosing an unconscious person with antibiotics was a gamble no matter what choices you made. Allergies were common and often deadly. Even smart, trained people making an educated guess were capable of making serious mistakes. Millicent did not appear and help him. He was on his own.

Still, despite the dangers the internet warned him about, Leonard was sure this was the right course of action. With Millicent pliant and asleep, he was able to examine her carefully.

Her breathing sounded ragged, and there was a slight whistling tone to it. He laid his ear against her bare skin and listened to her heart for a few minutes.

He examined her injured fingers again, feeling the swelling heat in their tips. He felt the nodes in her neck and found them swollen, as well. There was nothing else for it; he was just going to have to dose her with the one he thought was safest. He needed to give her fluids, anyway.

The YouTube tutorials had helped him prepare, but the reality turned out to be terribly messy. He blew out two veins in Millicent's elbow before he was able to establish an IV line. He whistled to himself as he worked, stopping periodically to listen to her breathing.

Millicent stood above her own prone body, looking at him with a direct and frank desire. *You are so safe now*, she told him soothingly. *You have been so careful. You handled that FBI agent just right. She will never be able to prove she didn't talk to her*, she said, gesturing to the body. *She said she was here of her own free will. No matter what happens now, you will always have the benefit of the doubt.*

Leonard nodded. He just needed a little more time. A few more days, or a week. Millicent was stubborn; he knew that from the stories. But she was also adaptable. In time, she would see. She would understand, and they would be able to work together. He would not need the benefit of the doubt.

"She will come to me willingly. She will give herself to the change."

Millicent crossed her heart and leaned down to kiss herself on the brow. Leonard watched the tenderness of the gesture, his heart swelling for the beauty he had created.

Later, he knew he would write that touching moment into one of his stories. But now he had to focus on the task at hand. Leonard had done the dosage math several times, using the calculator in her phone as he consulted the bottle of erythromycin. He set that up in the drip, then added another of sedative to keep her under while she got better.

The catheter was another matter entirely. He detested the feeling of the Vaseline, of struggling to get it placed and inserted correctly. It slipped and slid; her body seemed to resist it though she was as limp as a noodle. He noticed he had caused some indecorous bleeding, and he found that very distasteful. He watched the YouTube video over and over again, but it was shown on a rubber model. Very orderly. Not like this. His failure to insert it disgusted him even more than the mess.

His second choice was the adult diapers. Those were distasteful, as well, but he had at least done that before. His baby sister's diapers had been a responsibility of his when he was a teen. He remembered the careful, detailed work of cleaning feces out of her tiny folds and crevices. Surely, he could be that loving and painstaking to Millicent, when the time came.

Eli mostly did not dream. She swam somewhere black and viscous, separated from conscious and unconscious thought by a long delay. It took time for anything to reach her, no matter how urgent the signal seemed. It dissipated in the molasses pool she corkscrewed through.

When dreams did come, they were isolated, puny things. As lost and pitiful as a single ant, images marched toward her uncertainly, disconnected. A candle flame pulsed and flagged as though in a strong wind. A car sat on flat tires. Her feet burned like she was crossing hot blacktop in the summer without shoes.

That sensation brought her brother. She couldn't see him, but his voice was there.

"So you're a dyke now?"

"Benny, tell somebody. Tell them I'm here."

Benny's laugh was mirthless, derisive. "Remember that time Mom put out a cigarette on my arm?"

Shame covered Eli. She wanted to hide somewhere darker; she dived into the molasses and struggled to exhale the bubbles that would keep her from sinking.

"Do you remember that?"

Speaking up toward him now. "Yeah, I do. I should have done something."

"Yeah, you should have. Still, that's the way out of this. You've got to do it like you always did with Mom."

"What, by not saying anything?"

Benny was somewhere near her, swimming in his ten-year-old body, the burn on his arm hissing as it touched the hot, sticky darkness.

"Yeah. By making it normal. By acting like it's normal. That's how you do the everyday. Not the underneath."

Underneath. Eli sank. The candle flame guttered and she knew it was important, but she couldn't care.

Time had no meaning. Pain had no teeth. She had no needs, and even the terror couldn't touch her. When thoughts recurred and she knew for sure that she was still in the basement, she swam gratefully away back out into the black. There was nothing she wanted there.

Once, she dreamed a hospital in cruel clarity. Her mind pulled out every stop: the antiseptic smell, the constant beeping noise. The murmur of voices nearby and the intercom system overhead.

The intercom called for Elizabeth Grey, but she didn't have to answer it. She turned away from it sleepily, relief welling up in her like an intensity like she'd never known. It was like every safe plane landing she'd ever had, the feeling when her credit card went through, the fall into a comfortable chair with her bra off at the end of a hard day all rolled together and sharpened into a needle.

The chart at her feet was clipped to the old-fashioned metal bed frame. It identified her as Millicent Michaelson.

Eli sank back into the black, letting the hospital pop like a balloon. There was no relief. There was the basement, and the tar pit of unconsciousness was the only escape.

It might have been hours and it might have been years when Eli came to. She had no way of knowing. She was not swaddled anymore, but stunned to find herself in a camisole and a diaper. She had to touch it with both hands, patting its puffy plastic surface to confirm that to herself.

"A fucking diaper?" Her throat was so dry and her voice so unused that she hardly recognized it. That scared her badly, but not as much as the sudden certainty that he had been changing her while she was out.

Moving stirred the IV lines in her arm and they ached fiercely. Nauseated, beginning to yell already, she reached over and pulled the needles out of her arm. She saw black-and-blue proof there that one vein had been blown out, maybe two. But that had not been there when she had gone down; she had been sure.

How long have I been out? The thought was frantic, insane. She hadn't even made scratches in the wall when she was conscious. She looked around wildly to see if anything in the room with her had changed and something else caught her eye.

Her hair. It had previously been very short, shaved on the sides and long on the top, but never long enough to hang into her eyes, even if she combed it straight forward.

Eli could see her hair. Some of it hung low over her eyebrows and she snatched at it with both hands.

Not only was it long, but it was *blond*. Eli had been black haired from birth; it was as black as her eyes and shone as only thick and well-oiled hair can do.

He had bleached her hair. It felt alien, dry and porous. Her hands shook as she grabbed it over and over again, trying to slide it off her head and reveal her true self still beneath. She pulled it finally, frustrated and feeling deeply displaced from herself.

It was her hair. There was no question about it.

How much growth? How long has it been?

At home, she had a standing appointment for a trim every four weeks exactly. In the fourth week, she was always convinced she was as shaggy as a sheepdog. Eli knew that her hair grew quickly; she was both proud and wary of it. Back when she had worn it long, it had been healthy, shiny and thick, falling down her back like a long, heavy bundle of silk cables. She had cut it during her third year in college.

Boredom was her constant companion in the basement; more constant than terror and far more reliable than her captor. She found herself drawn back into the past quite often, imagining what had been rather than her usual pastime of imagining what could be. Boredom took her further into the details of who she had been than any yearbook ever could. Holding her bleach-ruined hair, she could remember every detail.

It was the same year that she had started writing for the university newspaper, publishing a series of firebrand opinion articles against the rampant and acknowledged gender bias in the school's graduate programs. She had finally found a way to stand out among these rich kids who could not be her friend. She went after the administration with ambition sharpened by alienation. She was reckless and crass, but she could write.

She had coaxed some of the women she knew who had hit the glass ceiling hard after refusing to sleep with one particularly powerful professor into talking to her and a few other reporters, then lambasted the administration for having tried to bury the problem.

Her columns had caught on, partly because the news was hot and happening to big-name colleges all over the country, but also because of her cogent arguments and tight prose. She had been syndicated by local and then national newspapers, bringing just as much attention to Eli as to the problem itself.

Her classes had suffered somewhat, and Eli remembered being taken to task by her creative writing instructor.

He was much older, more emeritus than professor. Retired in his late fifties but still a jewel in the university's crown.

He had been a literary prizewinner in years that had left him with pictures of himself in wider lapels, shaking hands with his own dead heroes. When he called Eli into his office—she had still been Elizabeth then—she was pretty sure she knew what to expect.

"Your work is slipping," he told her. He drank openly in his office with the frank privilege of his position. "That last story was a first draft. Don't try to bullshit me, kid. I know a first draft when I see one. I'm seeing one right now."

She shot him as blazing a look as she possessed at that tender age. Her heavy hair was in a long braid that lay over her shoulder. She fiddled with the loose end.

"I don't know if you've noticed, Professor, but I've been busy producing work for a national audience. Besides, aren't you here to provide feedback? Should I submit a fully finished draft and then let you tear it apart?"

He leaned forward, elbows on the desk. "You should let me tear apart these so-called columns of yours. Sensationalist nonsense. You're no better than Thompson with this junk."

She glowed with pride that he had compared her to Hunter S. Thompson, no matter how he meant it.

That was, in fact, how he had meant it.

"You have real talent, kid. I teach small groups of privileged whiners every year. I see maybe one in a decade who has a real shot at producing anything of worth. You will. I know you will. You're like Raymond Chandler and William Faulkner had a disobedient daughter."

She tilted her head to the side and smiled at him. "Wouldn't at least one woman writer be more apt for that metaphor?"

He tilted his back, looking at the angle her neck made with her shoulder as a vampire would, and smiled to show his fangs. "There are many different kinds of fucking."

Professor Emeritus was correct in that assertion, but they

started fucking in the usual way that same week. He was re-markably virile for his age, though as unconcerned with her orgasm as any man of his generation would be. She didn't ask about his wife and he didn't belabor the rather obvious paral-lel between what they were doing and what she was writing about for the newspaper.

The day she caught him fucking a different undergrad, she did the labor for herself. She dropped his class and cut her hair with her roommate's pair of art scissors. She changed her byline from Elizabeth to Eli. Her column the next day was a viral smash.

He sent her a brief note the day her first book was pub-lished, congratulating her in a way that made it very clear that he was claiming partial credit. She had wished she had kept the braid so she could answer his note with a parcel of her own dead hair.

Eli's brow creased deeply as she looked up at the ends of her hair. She pulled them far out, wondering if he had any idea what he was doing. Running her hands over it, it felt heavily processed all over, dry like a broomstick.

Did he get my roots? Did he use a box job, or pick a shade and a developer? How fucking bad does this look?

She knew she wasn't asking the right questions. She needed to focus on *How fucking dare he?* and *Where is he going with this?* But she didn't. It scared her to the point of physical pain to ex-amine that edge of her predicament too closely, so she pushed it away. She thought about author photos and TV appearances. She thought about her image. She remembered her manicure routine to keep her nails brutally short and perfectly smooth, just to clearly signal to the men she met that she wasn't in-tended for their use.

That brought her out of her reverie. She dropped her hair and looked at her hand.

Her fingers had healed almost completely. The middle finger still had dark marks beneath the nail, and a few had a deep red to purple spot where the tiny stab wounds had been, but they were closed. She drummed her fingers against the other forearm and felt only the ghost of pain. The bite or sting or whatever it had been was gone.

She drew a deep breath and found that her lungs did not ache; the urge to cough was nowhere in her.

He must have given me something while I was out. Maybe a couple of somethings.

With that realization came a vague but suddenly noticeable burning sensation stretching from her vagina to her anus.

Antibiotics. I've got a rager of a yeast infection, I can feel it. And probably diarrhea. That's why I'm in a diaper. Oh fuck, this is gross.

That brought back the deeply uncomfortable image of him wiping her, cleaning her. One knee up on his shoulder, his face close enough to inspect her sex and tend to it. She shifted uncomfortably, trying to pull away from the heavy, soggy thing that was wrapped around her.

One hand thrust down into the damp diaper confirmed what she suspected.

He waxed me bare. Or shaved me. Oh shit. Last time it was just a trim. This son of a bitch.

The red light of the camera shone on and on. She knew he must be watching, and that he must have noticed that she was awake.

As if the thought called him forth, he opened the door at the top of the stairs.

He carried water bottles and a box of baby wipes, plus a long cardboard carton.

"I see you're awake. Say your name and I'll give you a bottle of water."

Her mouth was dry, but she knew her body was hydrated

by the IV line she had yanked out. Blood crusted in the needle holes, new on top of old.

"Elizabeth Katherine Grey."

"Millicent Margaret Michaelson," he answered evenly.

She looked him over, hoping to see some of the strain of keeping her captive for this long. He seemed utterly relaxed. His long frame sagged slightly forward at the hips. His narrow, knifelike shoulders were relaxed, despite their burden. He was, once again, freshly shaved.

"That's not my name."

"It is, honey. You'll see that soon."

"Don't fucking call me honey."

He set the water bottles down against the opposite wall, then turned around to face her at a distance.

"I have been thinking about this," he said meticulously. "If I decide to just leave because you have made me unhappy, you would have a horrible death. With no one to care for you. All alone. You would die of thirst, right there. Can you image what that must feel like?"

She stared up at him with her mouth open for a moment. Then she considered. "You might not even have to leave. What if you fell down some stairs, or died of food poisoning? I'd die either way. And if you keep me in this fucking basement much longer, I have to assume you're going to kill me. So why should I give a fuck how it happens?"

He sighed, looking at his feet and pushing his glasses up his thin nose. "I would never choose to harm you, Millicent. I do not want to leave you, either. Nothing is going to happen to me."

"I'm not Millicent," she said as calmly as she could, though she was nearly rent by a lightning bolt of horror branching through her body. "An author is not the same person as her main character. Surely you know that. I wrote another book, one about a young boy named Alfred. Did you read that one? Do you think I'm Alfie, too?"

He smiled his oddly boyish smile. "Of course. *The River Is My Backyard*. Not as good as my Millicent books, but still excellent."

"So, you understand that my books are works of fiction." She tried to sound rational, still very calm.

"Of course not," he said at once, prim as a schoolteacher. "They are not your works, and they are not fiction. Not really. You did not write Alfred. I did. He is based on me as a small child."

She gaped at him. The world threatened to swim away again and she seized it in a tough mental grip. She bore down. "You abso-fucking-lutely did not write Alfred," she said. "I wrote that. Just like I wrote Millicent."

"In time," he said again, turning away from her, "you will see that that is just not true. I wrote Alfred, and I created you. I created Millicent. You exist because I built my own perfect magical world and wanted you in it. You are getting closer now. Soon, when you look like yourself and live according to the rules, you will see. You are my Millicent. And it is time for me to write your next chapter."

She stared at him a few moments longer. "Give me the water."

"Say your name." He looked perfectly cool and at peace with himself. Unthirsty. His dull blue eyes never wavered.

"Alfred was based on my brother, Benny." Terror was beginning to have its way with her now; there was no way around it. Her voice shook. "That's Benny's stutter and Benny's story about how he broke both of his arms and lied about how he did it. Benjamin Ashford Grey. He's a few years younger than me—"

"Millicent does not have a brother," he cut her off. "She

has a long-lost half sister, but no other family. She's an orphan, like heroes always are. You're an orphan."

Eli felt herself beginning to cry. "I know I say that in interviews," she began. "It's because I was on my own at a really young age and—"

"And you began your magical course of study at the Maginaria, under the tutelage of Madame Olitti, after you graduated from the cowan police academy." Leonard's voice was dreamy, faraway. He began to hum the theme of the film, the one that had been up for the Oscar but had lost.

Eli cleared her throat. *Try to get ahold of yourself. Be calm and rational. Bust up his fantasy.*

"The Maginaria's not real, dude. Millicent had magic powers. She solved crimes using omens and bloodtalking. She had a shapeshifter for a partner. It's fiction. You know none of that's real, right?"

He looked blankly at her. "Just because it is not real does not mean it is impossible. Everything that happens in our heads is really happening. Like Dumbledore said."

Eli's voice sounded like a rusty hinge. She sat up tall and tried to make her face behave, to shed the quiver and softness of her vulnerability. "Dumbledore isn't real, either! He was created by another author, a woman author like me. Joanne Rowling. You understand that, don't you? The difference between real and make-believe? I'm real. Millicent is make-believe."

He smiled his boyish smile. "This is why I have to write your stories from now on, Millicent. They are all based on you, but you just cannot believe the way you used to. You need me. You need to feel the power of surrender. I can tell. The last book was so much duller, so much sadder. So much of the wonder had gone out of it."

She tried to gather herself. "That's because I'm building

up momentum toward the eighth book," she said as calmly as she could. "The origin of magic has been discovered and is controlled—"

"By the Sceleris," he finished. "That's where book eight begins. The search for the Tear of Ymir."

"Like hell it is," Eli said, relieved to be feeling furious again instead of just scared. "I wrote that book, and that is not where it starts."

"Where is book eight?" Leonard was moving fast to close the distance between them.

"Somewhere safe," Eli said, staring up at the predatory intensity of his eyes.

"Is it on your laptop?"

"You've got my laptop. You tortured me to get my password. You tell me."

"No," he said, looming over her, bending his strange, long body like a cane. "You are going to tell me, or I am going to hurt you." His face was very near hers now. She could smell his breath, minty and impeccable. Perfectly hygienic as if he had brushed and flossed just before coming down the stairs.

"That terrible scene we had before when I had to hurt your fingers… I will not ever lose my temper like that again."

"You said you wouldn't hurt me," she said, hating the babyish tremble in her pointless assertion.

"I said I wouldn't choose to *harm* you. We writers are terribly precise with the words we choose. Some words have very specific meanings, Millicent."

Fury returned. "I know the difference between hurt and harm, you cunt. I can't believe you went to all the trouble to kidnap me here just to mansplain my job to me in an environment where I can't escape your bullshit."

He stayed close to her face for a moment, his features impassive but his skin flushing.

She didn't back away.

He turned his back to her, pivoting neatly. "I can see that you mean to be difficult. I want to start small. All you have to do is say your name."

"Elizabeth Grey," she said again, relishing this rebellion that was not a rebellion at all. "Eli to my friends, but you are not one of those. Ms. Grey if you're an asshole who has bleached my hair and drugged me in a fucking basement."

Leonard reached his long arm into the cardboard carton and withdrew a spindly device, about a foot long. Eli had never seen one before and couldn't identify it. It looked like a fireplace lighter with a forked end. Or a really strange bar-beque tool.

"Say your name." He moved back to stand beside the bed.

She sat up all the way and thought about the length of her reach. "What is that thing? Don't come near me with it, you fucker."

"Say your name."

"The Second Earl of Go Fuck Yourself, Esq." Eli gritted her teeth, baring them to him.

Can't change this. Can't stop this. Can't fight. Can't talk him out of it. Might as well give him hell with the last weapon I've got.

So Eli sharpened her mouth.

Leonard casually reached over with the device and pressed its double end into Eli's left shoulder.

She moved to knock it aside before receiving an immobiliz-ing electric shock. She screamed involuntarily, short and high.

"Say your name."

"Is that a fucking cattle prod?" She was gasping from the sudden shock and the pain that rushed like water into the vac-uum the jolt created inside of her.

He shocked her again. Her body went rigid all over and she bit her tongue. She tasted blood and ozone. She steeled herself and found she was not steel at all, only meat. Eli cursed her body for a traitor as the meat began to writhe.

She told herself she would not cry, would not beg him to stop. All that turned to dust around the twentieth time he jammed the end of the prod against her skin. She groaned and keened higher and higher, shrieking through her teeth before losing control and screaming full-out. Her arms fell weakly and she could not defend herself. He pushed the forked tool savagely against her inner thigh, her wrist, her nipple as he worked to break her will. She tried to shrink against the bed, to scoot away, to curl up like a shrimp. There was nothing she could do.

"Say your name."

I will not. I will not fucking tell this man—

Thought short-circuited. Pain was the ruler of the universe. Pain was impossible to anticipate or absorb. She tensed herself to be shocked and he would wait. She anticipated a break and he would shock her again without any refractory period. She tried to block the prod or grab at it and he shocked her hands until they would barely obey her.

Throughout, she tried to pry her eyelids open and look up at her captor. His expression was mild, almost one of boredom.

None of this is affecting him, she wondered from somewhere in the depths of near delirium. *He's not fazed in the slightest by what he's doing here.*

"Miss Mary Mack," she shouted through her sobs. He shocked her with the prod.

"James Tiberius Kirk." He prodded her on the side of her neck.

"Spartacus!" The prod sought her hip bone, protruding now through her thinning frame.

"David Bowie." He jammed the prod between her toes and let her have it. Her whole leg cramped in response and she could not unlock it. She lay gasping as he loped toward her on his stilt-long legs, walking up close to her face again.

"I am going to put it in your eye," he said calmly.

She didn't answer. This was not defiance, merely inability.

The pain hit her face as a combination of bright, burning blue-white light and an agony of the same quality. He hadn't shocked the eyeball itself, but he had come perilously close and Eli felt as though the vitreous fluid in it was boiling, ready to pop. He moved to do the same to her other eye when she began to scream.

"Millicent Michaelson! Millicent Michaelson!"

It had taken less than a quarter of an hour.

He prodded her in the soft hollow of her cheek and gave her a quick jolt.

"What is your middle name?"

She wheezed like a detuned squeezebox. "Margaret. Millicent Margaret Michaelson."

"And has Millicent ever written a book?" His voice was low and comforting.

"Never," she whispered.

"Who is my good girl?" he cooed in that low voice.

She did not answer.

He retrieved the water bottles from the other side of the room and came to set them gently at her bedside.

"I hope we never have to have this conversation again." He turned to walk up the stairs.

Eli couldn't regulate her breathing. Phantom voltage ran unpredictably through her body, replicating the sensation of being shocked again and again. She twitched and writhed, she tried to straighten her still-cramping leg. Her right eye was a ball of fire and she could not open it. Her diaper was wet and she loathed the feeling of the sodden mess rubbing against her as she struggled.

I am going to fucking kill you. She thought it as loudly as she dared. Following that, she thought *Elizabeth Katherine Grey* over and over again. She pushed her foot against the pipe footboard and wrench-flexed it against the cramp. It unlocked, finally.

Look, it doesn't matter what you say to him. Say anything you need to say. Stay alive. In here, you'll still be Eli. You're Eli.

She held desperately to that voice inside her as she wrapped her arms around herself and tried to calm down. She didn't touch the water. Somewhere above her, he pulled the switch to plunge her into darkness. She stared up at the only light in the room, the red malevolent eye of the camera.

I am going to kill you. I am going to find a way.

She lay awake for a long time.

Joe Papasian worked quickly, efficiently, with calm running out of him like sand through a sieve. He poked around in a few hacker forums to find out whether it was possible to pull location data off an Instagram photo.

It was not.

He was pretty sure it wouldn't be, or celebrities would have dumped the app a long time ago, but it was worth a shot.

He went through her emails, her bank account, her texts sent through Google that would be logged in her account, and everything else he could get his hands on. It gave him the willies at first, but he was able to set it aside when he considered the kind of trouble he was sure she was in.

Famous authors do not get kidnapped. Few were even credibly threatened. If someone had held Eli for ransom, the asking amount would have to be pretty modest for her people to pay it.

Eli was the kind of author that did get threats, however. She got fairly regular Twitter threats of the vague and infantile variety: *die U cunt* directed at her from a minutes-old account with an egg for a face. She had gotten a handful of more credible threats over the years, most of them relating directly to her more overtly feminist works or her comments on the same. With the film, her profile had gotten higher and the quality of threats against her had improved somewhat.

Digging through her cloud storage, Joe found her file marked FBI. It contained copies and screencaps of threats dating back to the beginning of her career. She had told him that she kept it because a more famous friend of hers had said she should. Just in case there was a clear pattern or a stalker should arise.

Once he found the file, he was staggered by the size of it. There were hundreds of pieces of mail, over a thousand screenshots of tweets, Facebook and Tumblr messages, as well as a lot of photographs. Some were of Eli herself, photoshopped into pornography. Others were pornography involving her characters, typically Millicent bound and gagged and being hurt or humiliated in some way. Joe's face twisted as he clicked through these and on to the gallery of unsolicited dick pics.

He remembered the day she had told him about this archive. She had described it as small and not that shocking.

What in the hell would count as shocking? He found a photograph of someone ejaculating on Eli's signature on a first edition of the second Millicent book.

"I'll go back and read some emails later," he mumbled to himself with disgust.

According to her bank, Eli hadn't touched a penny in her accounts in over a week. She'd had two royalty checks drop in since Joe had heard from her. Eli had savings, but she spent like the money wouldn't last and had to be shoveled out the door as quickly as it came in. What's more, she usually tweeted some veiled reference to payday. A gif of Scrooge McDuck, a rapper making it rain. Something.

But Eli hadn't tweeted anything since that one sunrise photo that gave Joe the chills just to look at.

If she was dead, what was the purpose of trying to pretend to be her online? If she was alive, what was happening to her right now?

"Fuck," Joe muttered, and dialed Agent Silvestri again.

"Silvestri." The phone had only rung once.

"Hi, Agent Silvestri. My name is Joe Papasian, we spoke a few days ago about a missing person?"

"Grey, right? The writer?"

"Ms. Grey. Ms. Elizabeth Grey. Eli. That's her name."

Silvestri sat back in her chair and ran a hand over her hair. She stretched her back and buckled down, knowing this was not going to go well. She had her suspicions about who she had spoken to, but she wasn't sure what the assistant could or should know.

"Right. Mr. Papasian, I called your boss. She picked up right away and spoke with me for a few minutes. I got the impression that she was fine, but just wanted to be left alone for right now."

Joe was silent for a moment. "She picked up?"

"She did. I'm sorry if this is hard for you to hear, but I have no reason to believe there's anything else at work here."

Silvestri sighed. She was doing her best to sound sympathetic but bored. The truth was that the lab hadn't gotten back to her about the voice match yet. She had a feeling that they would tell her it was no match. She didn't want to let Papasian go, but she also couldn't tell him her suspicion. She thought he might know more than he was saying. Most of the time, a woman in trouble like this knew the man who had put her there.

"Did you have any additional information to offer?"

Joe jumped back in without hesitation. "I do have additional information. I have a major Barnes & Noble event that she has missed. She's never missed or canceled a live reading. Ever. I have five additional days in which she has contacted no one. Not me, not her agent, not her friends. I've been blowing up her phone and I doubt I'm the only one. I have five additional days when she hasn't touched any of her money. I have five additional days in which she has not hired a car, ordered a pizza or existed on the grid in any perceivable way. I know this woman, I'm telling you. I can tell you that she does not carry cash or peel her own carrots. I don't know who answered her phone, but I don't think it was Eli. I swear to you something is wrong."

Silvestri began to type. Joe could hear the faint click-clack through the line and knew she was using a mechanical keyboard, like Eli preferred at home. "Tell me again where she was the last time you could locate her."

Joe led her through all the details. Silvestri knew all this and had the timeline down. She was working to see if Joe's story would waver, or if he'd produce something he had previously left out. Nothing had changed.

"Is there any person you know who would want to hurt Ms. Grey? Has she ever been threatened? Is she maybe in a relationship with someone you don't know about?"

A little hesitation on the line. "You talked to her on the phone, but you're asking me about enemies?"

Silvestri sighed again. He was smart. He wouldn't be easily gotten around. But his intent felt pure. His concern sounded real. "Just to be thorough. I don't disbelieve you, Mr. Papasian. But I need something to go on here. This is all incredibly vague, and I got an answer when I called her phone. You see the position I'm in?"

Joe thought of the file full of vile pictures and threats and his voice broke as he spoke. "She keeps a file of all the awful things people have sent her, just in case there's a stalker or something. I never saw it until today. Until today, I would have told you that everyone loves her."

Silvestri heard the emotion in his voice. She believed he knew his boss as well as he said he did. If this man was faking his distress, he was very good. Still, he should have mentioned this sooner.

"Can you forward that to me?"

"Of course," Joe said, and took down the email address she provided.

"Have you involved any of Ms. Grey's family in this?"

"Ms. Grey is not on good terms with any of her family," Joe said delicately. "If she went missing, they'd be the last to know."

"Can you get me any of their contact information?" Silvestri had this already, but wanted Joe to feel as though she trusted him, that she would follow up on his suspicions.

"Certainly," Joe said, relieved that he was getting some traction at last.

"Does Ms. Grey have a boyfriend?" Silvestri listened hard. Not just to what Joe said, but how quickly and how forcefully he said it. Was he jealous?

Joe scoffed. "No. Not for a long time."

"A girlfriend?"

"Not for over a year," Joe said. "I can give you her last partner's information, as well."

Silvestri didn't already have that, and she asked for it. Joe read it out of his address book. "Veronica Chandler. She lives in Palo Alto." He read out her address and phone number.

"I'll be in touch," Silvestri said, and hung up without saying goodbye.

The Kern County Sheriff's Office was responsive and quite helpful. By the end of the day, Silvestri had spoken to the pilot who had flown Grey back to Mojave. He was the last person who had been able to confirm they had seen her; the people at the hotel said she had checked out electronically. Silvestri asked the deputy on the line to get ahold of the security footage from the day Grey had checked out and try to pinpoint the last keyed entry to the room. That would take time. Silvestri felt like every phone call was a timer she cranked and left running. All around her, pieces of this case ticked and ticked while she waited for one to go off.

Getting the pilot on the phone right away was a huge relief, and she dug into that feeling, relishing the traction of it, smashing the timer unset in her mind.

The pilot—Andy Warbach, white male, fifty-four, heavy on his feet—was a jolly, dopey sort of man. The noise in the background of the call was terrible. She pictured him standing in a hangar, finger of his free hand jammed in his other ear.

"How did Ms. Grey seem when you last saw her?"

"Good," the pilot said at once. "She said she was a nervous flier, but she never freaked out or anything. She even signed a copy of her book for my wife."

Silvestri could hear enough of his voice over the roar to pick up on the notes that mattered: sincerity, guilelessness, genuine liking. He did not give her the feeling he was involved, or even that he'd ever used his little plane to run drugs. His voice was squeaky-clean. "That was sweet of her. Did she take drugs to make the flight easier?"

"I saw little bottles she had with her. She took a nip or two was all. She seemed fine when the car came and got her."

"A taxi?" Silvestri began to type again, moving her dark hair off her forehead. She kept it just long enough to cut down on the dyke jokes at work. Her hair was a habit from her days as a marine. Her personal life was not something she wore on her head.

"Nah, one of them Lyfts or Ubers or what have you. I don't recall what kind of car."

"Did you get a look at the driver?"

Andy hesitated. Silvestri thought he was working out a lie, then realized it was just sheepishness. This guy really just wanted to be helpful. She pictured his car with one of those shield stickers they give you for buying tickets to the sheriff's ball.

"Not really. A guy. He was wearing a ball cap. And kinda hunched in the seat, the way a really tall fella has to."

"That's pretty good for not much of a look," Silvestri said, encouraging and rewarding at once. If she made him feel helpful, he would be even more so, she knew.

"Well, I thought for a second someone else famous might have been there to pick her up. So I looked. But it wasn't a nice car or anything, so probably not."

"I see. And did she have anything with her?"

"Yeah, a leather satchel. Black, looked kinda old. Had her initials on it."

Silvestri took this down. "Thank you, Mr. Warbach. If you remember anything else, can you please give me a call?"

"Is that writer in trouble?" More concern than suspicion in his voice. Silvestri found herself liking Warbach.

"Some folks are trying to find her," Silvestri said carefully. "She didn't show up at her next gig like she was supposed to."

"Better tell my wife to take good care of that book, then," Andy said amiably.

Silvestri thanked him for his help and gave him her number before hanging up, in case he thought of something else.

She spent the next twenty minutes in the cursory searches necessary to make sure Grey wasn't dead somewhere. Her DNA wasn't on file, but she didn't match the description of any Jane Does found in the states where she might have gone missing.

Silvestri had filed the missing persons case already. She knew that the author's name would catch some attention on the wire; someone who was even just mildly famous could do that. She asked one of the office techs to watch for any stories that showed up in the media and text her if it looked like it was going to be big news. It was impossible to guess.

Carla Silvestri had worked high-profile cases before. In the FBI, everyone did sooner or later. In her first couple of years after becoming an agent, she had handled a murder case involving a senator's son—stabbed and dumped in the river by his rival in a love triangle—and the kidnapping of a pair of twins whose parents ran a big tech company. The former had been covered with salacious glee, while the latter had elicited sympathy, comparisons to the Lindbergh baby and professional acclaim for her and her partner. The tech twins had been found alive. That had been good for her, and for her career.

Getting into her car, she thought about the way these cases had taken on bizarre dimensions as public opinion was brought to bear. So much about an investigation had to be kept quiet, and having reporters lurking everywhere made that very difficult to maintain. Silvestri's nerves were steely, tempered over three tours overseas. But she knew that even with all this in her background, a big-name case going bad at this point could sink her. She was hoping to make deputy director someday, and a memorable kidnapping—if that was what this was—could make that happen for her. If it went well.

But it wasn't enough for her that she could catch the person who was holding Eli Grey, even pretending to be her. She had to get the writer back, alive. Imagine the gratitude, the statements to the press, from someone who wrote for a living.

Silvestri was not vain, but she was mercenary. She wanted Eli alive for a lot of reasons.

Silvestri got on the freeway and drove herself the two hours down to Palo Alto. Traffic was bad and the wind off the bay was cold. She had been turning the case over in her mind for a few miles when she realized she hadn't read the book, but she knew the name from the movie. She could picture the dark, lush visuals of the magical world beneath the city above. Silvestri didn't generally like movies or TV shows about cops. Like most law enforcement, she had seen the flaws in the way the work was presented. But she had liked this movie, since the inclusion of magic seemed to take it out of the realm of the familiar and excuse some of the inconsistencies. She had liked the tough, resourceful heroine, of course. Even in a magical world, a good cop who was a woman and didn't take any nonsense from anybody was still rare.

Silvestri's phone pinged with an email from her digital lab tech. The two voices were no match at all. The person she had spoken to had not been Eli Grey.

"Shit," Silvestri said as traffic came to a stop again. "Oh, shit."

Her phone lit up in its cradle on her dashboard again. It was Joe Papasian. She let it ring through to voice mail.

Joe had started fielding calls from media and friends of Eli's as soon as the story went out over the wire. His professionalism wore thin as the day dragged by. He was calling Silvestri with every piece of information he came across.

When she reached the address Papasian had given her, Silvestri wasn't sure where to park. The house had a private drive, but no gate. It looped in front of the house, and she could see two Teslas and a Bentley staggered across the space. The house itself was like a cliff made of glass. These people had money beyond money. My-daddy-built-Google kind of money.

She stepped on to the porch and the bell rang itself. A young Hispanic woman came to the door.

"Can I help you, Agent Silvestri?"

Silvestri drew back, alarmed. "Do I know you?"

"I'm Rita. I work for the Chandlers. They use a facial-recognition camera," she said, pointing upward. "It identified you as you walked up. It's usually accurate."

Silvestri squinted up, seeing an array of small cameras covering the wide entry to the house. She wondered briefly at the legality of it, but figured that on private property, money like this could get away with anything. And all her information was available through the Bureau.

She shook it off and cleared her throat. "I'm looking for Veronica Chandler. Is she here?"

Rita nodded. "You've caught her at a good time. Wait here, please."

Silvestri nodded back and looked around the porch. The house was all glass, but it had a snowy, frosted effect. It shone flawlessly, but she couldn't see in at all. Instead, she checked her reflection. She was always convinced that people knew she was armed before they saw anything else, but it wasn't as obvious in this jacket as it would be in some others.

It had been like this, in the kidnapping of the tech twins. Fortresses and secrets, followed by the haughtiness of people who lived in the shelter of both. Carla stood up straight and reminded herself not to be an asshole, no matter what. Eyes open. Ears open. Nothing gets past.

The door opened again and a dishy older woman walked out, closing it behind her. "Agent Sylvester?"

"Silvestri," she said, stepping forward and showing her badge. "Veronica Chandler, right?"

"Right," Veronica said, moving a silky section of brown

wavy hair away from her gray eyes with an elegantly lacquered finger. "May I ask what this is about?"

"I'm investigating a missing person, Ms. Chandler. Do you know Elizabeth Grey?"

Something tightened around the older woman's mouth. Silvestri wasn't sure if the woman was feeling defensive or just vulnerable. "Eli. Did she drop off the face of the earth?"

"Kinda, yeah. Does that not surprise you?" Silvestri watched the woman's body language closely.

Veronica crossed her arms, her very expensive watch catching the setting sunlight. "Not really. She ghosted me when we broke up. It was pretty efficient. If I didn't know better, I'd have thought she was dead."

"And when was that?"

Chandler did not look away. She did not turn her body. She did not touch her face, did not waver. She was not working through a lie; Silvestri was fairly sure. Just being guarded. "Over a year ago."

Silvestri tapped out notes quickly in her phone, trying to spare the woman the intensity of her scrutiny for a moment. Peripherally, she watched to see whether Veronica Chandler relaxed visibly when eyes weren't on her. She did not. "Are you married, Ms. Chandler?"

Veronica turned over her left hand, her trinity of diamonds winking again in the sun. "Yes, for eighteen years."

"And your partner—"

"Husband," Veronica corrected her.

Interesting. "Your husband. Was he aware that you were seeing someone outside your marriage?"

Veronica looked over her shoulder, showing taut neck skin that would be the pride of any plastic surgeon.

"My husband and I practice a rather evolved form of non-monogamy, Agent Silvestri. He knows everything."

"I see. Was he jealous?" Silvestri knew this type. Maybe it wasn't cheating, but people still had feelings about it. Particularly husbands.

"Not at all," Veronica said, her mouth flattening into a line. "Just as I am never jealous of his dalliances." She said the final word with a broad *A* sound, much more like a British accent than her own American one.

"When was the last time you heard from Ms. Grey?" Silvestri looked away again, carefully. She looked up casually from her phone, when it seemed natural.

Veronica gave a dry, humorless laugh. "We saw one another for about six weeks. I was really into artists at the time. We had this wonderful Bohemian thing going on. I was staying in the city and she didn't really know who I was. The first time I brought her here—" she gestured around to her home "—she froze up and wouldn't talk to me. Two days later she had blocked me and disappeared."

"Do you know if she dated anyone after you?" Silvestri smiled. The conversation was shifting to pleasant things; why not? She wanted to see if Chandler would match her.

"No idea," Veronica said, smiling back. "But I'm sure she must have. That girl is a black hole. She'll always need somebody."

Silvestri thanked Mrs. Chandler and walked off the porch, feeling satisfied about their whole exchange. Chandler wasn't lying. She certainly had feelings about Grey, but she didn't hate her. She didn't seethe, and she wasn't scorned. She was simply an ex who had felt too much to let go.

Silvestri switched gears in the car, moving on to the next lead. She looked up the address Papasian had given her for the author's brother. It was in Suisun. She checked the GPS and decided she could make it there before it was too late.

As she drove, Silvestri reviewed their history. She knew the siblings didn't speak, saw the difference in their financial status. She knew that when the FBI showed up at his house to ask about his sister, Benny was likely to be less than eager to help.

Silvestri parked her car at the curb and took stock of the place. The house was dingy, looking in desperate need of a paint job and a general cleanup. Kids' toys lay all over the dirt and brown grass yard, some of them broken or rusting into the earth as though they had lain untouched for a season or more. The big picture window that faced the street had a comforter tacked up as a curtain. Upstairs windows were accessorized with stickers and decals that children would choose, backed with foil and cardboard.

The door juddered open and a man stepped out shoeless in a faded pair of jeans and a black T-shirt featuring the logo for a popular energy drink. He blinked a few times as Silvestri approached. She guessed he had just woken up, despite her showing up around dinnertime.

Benjamin Grey ran a hand over his hair and tried to stretch out his rumpled shirt. It sprang back into the exact same rumples as before.

"Mr. Grey?"

"If you're a process server, just hand it over. I don't have to tell you who I am."

Silvestri pulled out her badge and let gravity flop the leather fold open. She knew at once he was going to be a different kind of trouble than the Chandler woman. He had been inside; that was as clear to her as his height. "Mr. Grey, I'm Agent Silvestri from the—"

"You got a warrant?" Grey's tone was nasty and preemptive.

"I'm not here for you, Mr. Grey. I want to ask you some questions about your sister, Elizabeth Grey." Silvestri let the classic cop sound creep into her voice, knowing he would respond to it. Maybe back down a little, submit.

"You can't come in my house, though," Benny said, looking back over his shoulder warily. He shrank a little, slouching so that he was shorter than her.

"That's fine, Mr. Grey. We can talk out here, if you'd like." Silvestri did not smile. She hooked her thumbs through her belt loops in a stance she had picked up from other men at the Bureau. It squared the shoulders and put her hands close to her weapons.

He looked back at her, his brow settling down into a scowl. He crossed his skinny arms and slouched a little more. Message received. "Fine."

"When was the last time you saw your sister?" She held eye contact. He did not look away, but he didn't challenge her, either.

"I don't know, like, five, six years ago. At Christmas. She didn't even come to her mother's funeral."

"Your mother, too, right?" Silvestri watched his mouth, looking for twitches of indecision.

"Yeah, but I was there." Grey's face showed the telltale signs of alcoholism when the light hit it. Silvestri could see the broken blood vessels in the man's cheeks. He was angry at his sister. Was he angry enough?

"So you were teenagers when you last had contact?"

Grey shrugged. "We've had contact. Couple emails. I talked to her after she got famous and all. She wasn't interested in seeing me, knowing my kids. She was too good for all of us. Never came around for holidays or anything."

"I thought you said you last saw her at Christmas." Caught in a lie, maybe?

"Yeah, well, I mean since then. And that was Christmas, like, years ago. Like I said."

Not quite a lie. "Did she have a boyfriend that you know of?"

"Nah, she was dykin' with that actress. The one that was in her movie. I saw it in the papers and tried to ask her about it."

"Your sister is a lesbian?" He was mad about that, too.

"I don't know. She used to date boys. I figure it's those Hollywood types got her messing around with god knows what."

"Would anyone want to hurt her? Did she have any relationships that went bad, or anything like that?"

"Hell, I have no idea. I wouldn't be surprised if someone beat the shit out of her for her man-hatin' nonsense on the internet. All of her books were the same, too. This man's bad and that man's bad. All that crap that's forced into fantasy and comic books and stuff nowadays. Yeah, she's one of them social justice warriors. I always figured there was a baseball bat out there with her name on it." Grey's face had a strange lack of animation, even as his voice grew more impassioned. Silvestri found herself associating him with key identifiers from criminal case studies she had read in the academy.

"Do you have a bat, Mr. Grey?"

He smirked at her. "If I was gonna beat my sister, it wouldn't be over politics. It'd be her attitude. Shit, we were kids together. She went and wrote a book about me. Proved she didn't know a thing about who I am. Just who she thinks I am. Still. She's family. I'd still beat the shit out of anybody who touched her."

"You said your mother had passed away, but your father is still alive, correct?" Silvestri checked the notes on her phone. She kept him in the edge of her vision, tilting her head just so that he knew he was still being watched. He didn't move.

"Living in Texas?"

"I think so. It's been a while since I saw him."

"How long?"

Grey looked back at his house for a long minute and said nothing. His feet did not stir.

"Mr. Grey?"

He looked back. "Two, maybe three years. My dad... He... he has a drinking problem. He's not in such good shape."

"I see. Would your sister maybe be trying to track him down? Maybe have a last conversation with him before he passes, as well?"

Benny grimaced. "Lizzie hasn't once spoken to Dad since she called CPS and broke up our family. 'Cause he didn't come get us when they called him. She was sixteen then, I was thirteen. I know she tried to talk to Mom, but she never looked back once with Dad."

"Why is that?"

"You know how teenage girls are. Are we done here?"

"No, not quite. Does your sister help you out sometimes? Financially?"

That did it. His feet broke their solid contact with the earth and he took a half step forward before thinking better of it.

"I never asked her for anything," he said, rage clear in his voice.

Silvestri gave him a full step forward in response to his half. She came into his space just a little, to remind him that she could. She was maybe an inch taller, but she pulled her chin up and took a wide stance. She filled out the limits of her frame effortlessly, expanding into her immediate power. "That's not what I asked you, Benny."

He shrank again, but did not step back. He looked down. "Yes'm. Sometimes. Sends me a check, is all."

"You ever ask for more? Ask about her will?"

He looked up at her then, still angry but also wounded. She looked back, flat and pitiless.

"I never asked anybody for anything that wasn't mine. I work for a living. Never went on welfare, never stole in my life. I'd never ask if I was in my sister's will. Her money ain't my money."

Silvestri noted this, but did not soften. She did pull up her phone again.

"Mr. Grey, your sister is missing. Possibly in trouble. You said you would help her if someone were to threaten her. Do you know anything that might help me find her?"

Benny made a face like he saw that someone had been pulling his leg. "Yeah, but she's not threatened. She's just a runner. Always been that way. Used to run away when we were kids, come home after a day or two when she was hungry or tired. That's all it is. She's not really missing at all. She's doing it for attention."

Silvestri didn't want to admit that she'd had similar suspicions, but she noted that she didn't like the sound of it coming out of this man's mouth.

"Thank you for your time, Mr. Grey. If you hear from your sister, would you give me a call?"

Benny took her card. "You can't fix up a ticket for me, can you?"

The Dallas field office sent someone out to Edward Grey's house to ask him the same questions. The agent there found the man blackout drunk and unresponsive on his couch. The responding EMTs knew the old man by his address and ungently brought him around. He could not answer the agent's questions. The Dallas field office reported that the missing writer was definitely not at her father's home.

Silvestri looked over all of her research and work on this case. Elizabeth Grey had no current partner, no close friends, no real family and no employer in the traditional sense. Only her assistant was sure she was missing. The last person to see her alive remembered almost nothing about where she went. And someone was answering her phone and pretending to be her.

"It looks like no case at all," Silvestri muttered. But the assistant had been insistent, truthful and worried. The agent was sure he was right as she sat and sipped a little coffee.

The person who had answered the phone and identified themselves as Eli Grey had made mistakes; it was true. But did that mean impersonation, or was the author having some kind of breakdown? Silvestri thought again of the ex-girlfriend living in the glass palace. She had not made Eli sound stable.

Silvestri, deep in thought, started when her phone rang. She picked up right away. Kern County sheriffs had gotten back to her with the footage of the person who had packed up Grey's hotel room and dropped off her key card. They sent it over while she was still on the line.

The footage wasn't great quality, and Silvestri couldn't see the man's face at all. But he was very tall, with a slightly hunched look to his shoulders. He wore a ball cap that partially hid his face.

Silvestri followed up with requests for footage from the hotel's parking lot. Fingerprinting the room would have been a lost cause even a week ago; hotel rooms were a nightmare of unwashed surfaces and hundreds of layers of prints. For the first time since Papasian had called her, Silvestri believed that the writer's assistant had acted too slowly. They were probably already too late.

Just like the pilot described. Match. Match. He's got her.

When the plates on the tall man's car came back, the computer told Silvestri they belonged to a large red truck rather than the white sedan they were on. They were both rental cars, however, registered to the same company.

"Switched plates in the lot," Silvestri muttered. Kern County, still on the phone, asked her to repeat. She thanked them for their help and hit the button to hang up.

Switched plates with another car. Why? It was a weird move. A rookie move. Like a bad liar trying to make their story more believable.

Like impersonating someone by phone and making mistakes about names and nicknames. Silvestri chewed the stylus from her tablet.

She watched the footage again, trying to match the case and bag the man was carrying to the description the assistant had given her. It wasn't Grey; she was sure. It was someone much taller. There was something unsettling about the way the man moved. Silvestri trusted her gut, and this guy sent sensations crawling around in her abdomen like cemetery bugs.

Would she have sent him to clean up after her, to get her things? Is he a boyfriend? Maybe, but why the stagecraft with the license plates? He's got something to hide. Someone.

Silvestri stopped the recording and examined the frame.

He has her. I talked to him on the phone. He's got that author, somewhere.

She forgot Palo Alto. She forgot the brother. She forgot the assistant. She focused like a bird of prey on her quarry: the man in the video.

March 14

TO: *eligrey@maginaria.com*
FROM: *paulleto@protonmail.com*

Dear Ms. Grey,
I have been a fan of yours for many years, and I have reached out to you a dozen times to tell you how much I love your work. I am distressed to find that you do not answer fan mail. How sad. Your fans love you so deeply, and they directly contribute to your fame and fortune in material ways.

Why is it that you will not respond to messages via email or Twitter? Do you think you are too good to have to? How very disappointing. I once thought so much of you.
Regretfully,
Paul Leto

★ ★ ★

TO: *eligrey@maginaria.com*
FROM: *harkotheclown@anonmail.com*

I cannot wait to be with you, my Millicent.

★ ★ ★

TO: *eligrey@maginaria.com*
FROM: *arrakis@protonmail.com*

You really need to lose some weight.

★ ★ ★

@handmaidsfail: Hey @leonardlobovich, what's the holdup with the next Hand of Fate book? We're dying out here!

@leonardlobovich: I am sorry, publishing is a really complex business. As soon as I know, you will know.

November 20

@leonardlobovich: It can be soundly argued that fans own the story. Once a writer writes, it is no longer entirely under their control. We feel as though these stories belong to us because they do.

@nostaljajaja: Do you read Hand of Fate fanfic, now that you've gone legit @leonardlobovich?

@leonardlobovich: @nostaljajaja That is how I got my start! I learned to perfect my writing by claiming ownership of the worlds and characters that I loved.

@nostaljajaja: @leonardlobovich do you still write fanfic in other universes?

@leonardlobovich: @nostaljajaja Why not? It has brought me everything I ever wanted in life. I cannot say which, however. Now that I am a professional, it is too much a risk.

@debauch17: Quit writing girlie shit and get back to Hand of Fate, Lobobitch.

17

Eli was awake. She was deeply sore and swollen all over from the prod. She could not sit with her back against the headboard of the bed, she found. Her ankle cuff was too short. But she could sit up in the middle of the mattress with her legs nearly beneath her. That felt revolutionary after so much time on her back.

She stretched her arms and rotated her wrists. She said her full name out loud to herself a handful of times. She gave the red eye the finger. Her right eye ached and would not open unless she forced it. When she did, the vision she got was blurry and nearly useless. She didn't want to think about whether that damage was permanent. Neither the UTI nor the yeast infection were clearing up; she thought the former had snaked up and become a bladder infection, possibly run to her kidneys. If the drugs he gave her didn't touch it, it had to be out of control. Eli had never had a problem like this before, but she had always had the ability to care for herself.

Is this common for women who are bedbound? Do they just put up with this all the time?

Her whole vulva ached and burned. She itched and knew that scratching would only make it worse. It was humiliating; it made being born with a vagina seem like an ongoing work order. Something always needed to be done to it. Her period hadn't come. Small favors.

I can't ask for a tampon. I sure as hell am not going to ask for a Monistat. I can't even keep him off my name.

Eli took a deep breath. She pissed through the pain, trying as best she could to wipe herself clean. She stuttered the bucket away. She tried to think.

He got me to say words. That's all. He didn't break me. He cannot break me.

She tried to put together everything she knew about the man who held her. He still had no name. He was tall, strong, white, and wore glasses. He knew her work and her habits intimately. He was willing to hurt her, but clearly wanted—needed to keep her alive.

For what?

He had wanted the password to her laptop, but there was only so much damage he could do with that. All of her site-specific passwords were saved; he could clean out her bank accounts. He could impersonate her, she supposed. But to what end?

He could get to my next book, she thought. He couldn't steal it. Her agent had read it already, and they could prove he was a plagiarist.

He could leak it on the internet. That one hurt. It would just about kill the book, and possibly fuck up the movie franchise, as well.

But if that's what he's after, he could hack it. He could hire hackers better than him. He wants me, in the flesh, for something he couldn't get any other way. Kidnapping isn't easy, and it's a huge risk.

Wasn't it easy, though? Eli's face and chest grew hot at how trustingly she had gotten into his car, accepted what she was told, drank what she had been given, all in a contained environment controlled by some stranger. Some strange man.

But he's not a stranger, is he? Have I met this guy before? Has he maybe been stalking me? Her unconscious mind was trying to tell her something, but it would not surface. She had that maddening sense of affiliation; there were feelings associated with this sense of almost knowing, but not a name. The feelings were...complicated. Cringing awkwardness was one of them. Secondhand embarrassment was another. Pity lurked in there somewhere. *Am I just developing Stockholm syndrome? Fuck.*

She pushed that aside. *Focus.*

If he was going to rape me, he would have done it already. There it was. She was pretty certain that she was correct, both about this guess and about the fact that it hadn't happened while she was unconscious. The evidence just wasn't there.

Why, then? If he was planning to eat me, he'd feed me more. She was always hungry, and she could see the knobby bones of her wrists and knees and ankles announcing themselves against her skin, more prominent than ever. She hadn't had a drink or a cheeseburger in...

How long has it been? This was the question that bothered her most. The divisions of her time did not fit the known mold of a day. The sun did not rise or set here. She had been about two weeks away from her next period when she was abducted, but it hadn't come on. Then again, under these circumstances, it might not.

A bubble broke open inside her and delivered rage. Rage was good; rage was useful. It came as unsorted goods. She wanted eggs Benedict and a mimosa. She wanted a shower. How fucking dare he? How many stories had she read of women held in basements for months or years at a time? How had any of them gotten out?

She had read a lot of police procedurals as research for the Millicent books. She had started off with what she thought was a good draft of the first book, but she had done almost no reading about cops. Her writing group at the time had been made up of women she had hoped would become her friends.

Only one of them had. Nella had turned out to be one of her good friends, tolerant of her silences and good enough to always feel like her equal in talent, drive and dedication.

Nella had showed up to the meeting after the entire group had read the first book. The feedback was generally good. People liked Millicent; they cared about what she wanted and whether she got it. Eli knew she had something that would sell, but it still felt good to hear it. Only Nella had been silent through critique.

"So, what did you think, Nella?"

Nella had sighed, rolling her tongue around inside her cheek. She adjusted her head wrap and would not meet Eli's eyes.

"What is it?"

Nella finally looked at her. "Do you know anything at all about cops?"

Eli had been taken aback for a moment. "I mean, I've watched them on TV."

Nella had laughed, throwing her head back and showing the tiny diamond she had had put into her right canine tooth.

"You know that's not the same thing, right?"

Eli had rolled her eyes and started to disregard the statement. Who the hell was Nella, anyway?

"Listen," Nella said, and her voice was clear and true and Eli could not look away from her full lips. "This is good. Really good. But the parts that you don't know anything about drag it down. You can fix this and an agent is gonna snap it right up. But you need to swallow your pride first and real-

ize there are things that you don't know. Like what a year at
the academy is really like. How two rookie cops talk to each
other when there's nobody around. Think about it."

Eli had stewed about it for days, unable to get past the criticism. Who did Nella think she was? Eli had reread all the
manuscript sections that Nella had shared, picking them apart
for the tiniest flaws and looking for a way to get back at her.

It took two weeks for her to realize that she was being ridiculous. Nella's book was great, and she had given good advice. Eli's book was full of holes, and most of them were in
the shape of a badge. She had swallowed her pride and taken
the advice. She had read case files. She had bought lunch for
the kind of detectives she wanted Millicent to be. Slowly, she
came to understand how wrong she had been. She apologized
to Nella. Nella had rightfully laughed at her, and they had
been better friends because of it.

She began to rewrite all of the sections where Millicent
was supposed to be a good cop, not just a gifted witch. She
read first-person accounts of high-profile criminal cases. She
studied the parts and procedures of a murder investigation and
she found herself making hundreds of small changes, enrich-
ing the work with real-world details.

Some of the cases she had read most carefully had been
kidnappings, in preparation to write *Captive Prince*. Eli had
shied away from the worst details in most of those cases. Kidnapping and holding a person was a terribly intimate and lin-
gering crime. She quit reading case files and delved into the
first-person accounts from people—mostly women—who had
been kidnapped and held for months or years at a time. They
were locked in dog kennels and sheds, outbuildings and basements. They had, one and all, not written directly about the
worst outrages committed against them, body and soul, and
focused on how they kept sane and how they got out.

Every single one of those narratives gave a detailed and climactic account of her last day in captivity. They were written as carefully and unstintingly as how-to instructions. Each one was clearly written with the idea in mind that someone reading the story might need to know this information one day, and not because she was writing a book.

Eli thought of them now, those last-day stories. She was one of them now, those basement girls. She thought about their desperation, their insistence that they weren't good or bad, that this was just a thing that happened. Their focus on any opportunity to make it out alive. They had all escaped in the end because someone slipped up, or guilt convinced their captor that they needed to see a doctor.

What about the ones who never wrote a book? What about the ones who carved marks on the wall until they stopped?

But that was not a thought she could entertain. She would not die here. Would not. Would not.

All she needed was an opportunity. One lucky moment. One knock at the door.

They got lucky, or the guy got sloppy. He left something unlocked, or she managed to slip a message to someone on the outside. That's almost always it. I have to get lucky. He has to slip up. One of these days.

But she had had that moment, hadn't she? She had run out into the desert. She had had her freedom. She just hadn't been able to keep it.

Shit.

Eli thought about Nella. She had always been the kind of friend who would sit you on your ass and tell you the truth. Eli didn't have many friends, but she treasured her connection to the few who stuck by her.

What would Nella tell me to do now?

She pictured Nella's serene brown eyes, her bitten-down fingernails. But Nella would not speak.

Nella would never have gotten into this mess. She's careful. She's always on her guard. Remember that time she told you she wouldn't go into a restaurant where there were only white people? Remember how she always sits where she can see the door? The knife in her bra? She would have been ready. She'd never be in this basement in the first place.

But guilt was no good. She made that up all on her own. She needed help. Help, damn it. Who could help her?

Eli thought of Millicent. The name was like bile in her throat, but she swallowed that down. *Not his Millicent. Mine. My Millicent would focus. She would be about her business. She would set her feelings aside and fall apart later. Magic is focusing your intent toward making change, right? Millicent didn't always know how to use her magic, so she thought like a policewoman. All those reports. All those painstaking re-creations of how people did what they did.*

Eli had an idea.

She got up on her knees and flopped awkwardly on her belly, straining against her bonds. She put her hands against the pipes of the footboard again. Her bleached, too-long hair hung in her face. She puffed it away with her breath.

She bore down with all her strength on each vertical foot-long piece of metal.

He didn't weld them. Son of a bitch didn't weld them. He didn't think of it. They're not water pipes, so he didn't—

One of them rotated ever so slightly. Less than a quarter of a turn.

She pushed again and it gave a quarter turn more, slowly and reluctantly. But it turned.

It wasn't the vertical she was cuffed to, but if she could get it started, she knew she could take the whole fucking thing apart.

She just needed an opportunity. Another one.

Eli sat back up, slowly. Leisurely. Just in case he was watching. She stretched her neck.

I can take a section of pipe with me and brain him with it. If the door at the top of the stairs is locked, I'll just wait there until he opens it. Maybe start howling, see if he comes down. Then, I let him have it.

She remembered the burning sun outside the house.

Steal some shoes. Find his keys. Drive to the freeway. We can't be that far from something. Find your phone. Steal his. Use GPS. Call the cops. Get the fuck out of here.

Millicent would find a way. Don't think like yourself, asshole. Think like her.

Eli sighed heavily and made a face at the hair that still hung over her eyes. She pushed it back with her hands, then pressed her palms against her eyes. Her hands were warm in the cold room and it felt like a form of privacy. A place her captor could not invade. She breathed slower and deeper.

One thing at a time. If I can get out, get upstairs, get to a phone or a computer or that radio, I will find a way to get help here.

But I'll have to kill him. I can't just hurt him and sit on him until they get here.

Despite everything, she shrank from the idea of having to do more than knock him out. In the books, Millicent couldn't kill anyone because Eli couldn't face the finality of it. All life, all possibility seemed to rest in the individual spark. Life was something good that was hard to make and easy to destroy. Even with the most evil villain, she shrank from it.

Maybe I could cuff him to something. Assuming there are more cuffs. Assuming he's knocked out.

Can't think of that, either. I'll figure it out when I get there. I don't know what kind of resources I'll have.

I have to think like Millicent. Not become Millicent. Not fucking look like her. Not perform whatever weirdness he's trying to push

me into. I have to get out of here. I have to think like a protagonist.
Have to. Have to.

But rage was ebbing. She was settling back into that hateful state of frightened complacency. She tried again to count the days to keep terror at bay.

Upstairs, Leonard Lobovich was hard at work on a gift for Millicent.

He was particularly pleased with himself for having talked with the agent by phone. The call had put him at ease; no one was going to look for his Millicent after that. Eli had answered for her whereabouts. He had grown bolder, composing more tweets in Eli's style. Millicent had stood at his shoulder, encouraging him. He used quotes from the books, shared a short story written by a colleague and some safely inane videos of an iguana wearing a top hat. He scheduled them to go out later, easy peasy. Everything looked perfectly fine. Which, of course, it was.

So it was time to celebrate with a little gift. Something that showed her how he felt. He had her leather satchel, and it was a handsome thing. He suspected it had been a gift from her mentor at the Maginaria, where costly gifts were common. However, Madame Olitti must have picked the item up used, because it bore some other person's initials.

Her Montblanc was a thing of beauty, and he stroked the enamel of it. It had a tiny ruby embedded in the clip and he turned it this way and that, watching the facets catch the light. He unscrewed the cap and made a few cautious strokes on a piece of paper. The action was smooth and lovely. He capped it, setting it precisely beside the paper, and turned his attention back to the satchel.

Leonard loved YouTube. He loved the tutorials, the long, ranting fan theories about his Millicent, and the access that it gave him to the world. There were videos he couldn't stand to watch, certain titles that made him look away from the screen and fumble to click away, scroll away. But he had mostly learned to avoid those.

He hated to leave the house. His house was a perfect, clean and climate-controlled island in a sea of chaos. He stepped out of it as seldom as possible. But the world came to him in all these streams. When he wanted to know what Millicent was up to, he could watch her Snapchat story over and over again. When he wanted to hear more of her voice, he could watch different videos of her speaking to bookstores, to classes in schools, or even on a few news shows. He liked to hear her talk about the book, to repeat what she said. To revise it. To practice sounding like her. Her voice was quite low; it wasn't that hard. To become.

It wouldn't be long now until it was his job to talk about Millicent's magical world. Her topsy-turvy movements between magical folk and cowans. Her dark jewel of a world. He wanted to be ready.

He also watched videos about how to bind someone so they couldn't escape. How to dose someone with sedatives. How to perform small medical procedures. He could learn to do anything. The whole world was at his fingertips; the great and small parts of it were all open to him.

YouTube also unobtrusively linked to a person's email account, so that you could see what they had liked and listened to over time. Leonard could use Millicent's profile and review her choices. It looked as though she used YouTube as a jukebox; he could find her favorite songs.

Some of them were too rough for his taste, using coarse language and talking about ungentlemanly things. But some she had listened to again and again were beautiful, melancholy songs that reminded him of her stories. They were perfect. He could listen to them and imagine her there beside him, head on his shoulder, sighing along to the music.

Leonard picked up the emptied satchel. He watched the tutorial on debossing the leather again, but with the sound off. Sound he reserved for the lovely sad songs.

As he worked, his brow furrowed as he contemplated how slowly Millicent was coming around. She was starting to look like herself again; he had helped her and cured her, tried to train her behavior so that she could return to her real life. But she was so stubborn. The life she had been living when she forgot herself had really taken its toll. He hated to be discourteous to her, but it seemed that she had to learn everything the hard way.

She will love this, mind Millicent said. Her voice was dim, as if it came from another room. *This will help to facilitate the change.*

"I know it will," he said somewhat testily. The work he was doing was precise, and he wanted to focus on it.

This is a talisman, she said.

"Keep quiet," he told her. And she did exactly what he asked, as always.

The old silver ink on the initials washed away easily. The heating and pressing of the scuffed leather went just fine. The old lettering was almost erased. Leonard tilted it against the light and saw only the ghost of EKG. He watched the video again on how to emboss the new letters, the MMM he had ready at hand.

He was getting so close now, so close to what he wanted. He ran his hands over the leather satchel, thinking of her hands on it, the way it would hang close to her body.

She knew who she was now. It was only a matter of time.

18

Eli had been alone long enough that she had worked to systematically disassemble the footboard. She didn't remove any pieces; she just worked the individual sections of pipe loose so that when the opportunity presented itself, she could seize it and do the rest quickly. She was working on one of the last sections when she heard the basement door open.

She scooted back against the headboard, trying to look unconcerned with her ankle cuff.

Leonard appeared too focused on what he was carrying to notice her hurry to rearrange herself.

"I have a surprise for you, Millicent."

She worked to keep her face impassive. "A large pizza? My fully charged cell phone? A fucking magazine to read instead of slowly losing my mind?"

Leonard frowned at her. "You must try to be nice to me, Millicent. You will see it is for the best."

She said nothing.

He stepped forward, turning her leather satchel in his praying mantis arms so that she could see the embossing job.

The lettering wasn't as skillful as it had been before, but she could see what he had done. Her monogram was gone. The print now read MMM, like a Roman numeral.

Fuck.

"See, now it has the right initials instead of those old ones that belonged to someone else. I taught myself how to do it." He smiled with his head cocked to the side like a cat delivering a dead bird.

She stared up at him one-eyed, hot with anger and a piercing sense of loss.

"Well," he said in such a joking tone that she could have killed him with her bare hands. "Not even a smile?"

"That satchel," she began through clenched teeth, "was the first thing I bought myself when I got my first advance. For my books. I've been carrying it since then. It was the first thing I owned that felt like it belonged to a writer—"

His mouth settled into a straight line. "You are not a writer. I am a writer, not you. You can use this bag to assist me when we—"

"Listen to me, you dumb motherfucker. You tortured me into lying to you. I'm still me. We've sat right here, in this bed, and talked about writing. You know this is the truth."

He let the satchel drop to the floor. "You do not appreciate a single thing that I do. I have taken care of you. Given you medicine. Cleaned you. And now I make you a gift and you do not show an ounce of gratitude. Not a shred."

"You *kidnapped* me. You *tortured* me. I don't need to be grateful for any fucking part of that."

"Millicent," he said, stepping over the downed satchel. "You need to get these crazy ideas out of your head. You have been very sick and your memories are incorrect. Try to remember with me. You have always lived here, with me. I wrote my stories about you, because you are my inspiration.

You are the ink in my pen. I could not possibly do it without your help."

"Don't come any closer," she said in what she hoped would be a menacing tone. "I'm not the ink in your fucking pen, you loony piece of shit."

Change your approach, Millicent said in his ear, where only he could hear her. *Try appealing to her feminine weaknesses. Remind her that she needs you.*

"You must be hungry," he said, coming closer still. "I should bring you something to eat."

"Yes, you should, you shit-sack. I've been hungry for a long time."

"If only you would obey the rules," he said regretfully. "Then I could be so much sweeter to you. If you were a good girl who deserved it." His cheek twitched as he watched her.

"What do you want from me?" Her voice shook. The mention of food had made her antsy. She didn't want to give an inch, but she badly needed something to eat.

"Smile for me."

It's a small thing. Just pull the corners of your mouth up and hope for a sandwich.

She attempted to comply, but she could tell by his face he wasn't buying it.

"The day that you learned about your parentage, when you realized that you had magical powers. Remember that? Smile like that. Smile for me."

Nope, not for you.

Instead, she thought about Nella. Nella, who would never have gotten into this situation in the first place. Nella, who saw her clearly and who she was taking out to brunch immediately when she was free.

Eli managed something like a real smile. Leonard smiled back.

"Now, it is time we talked about your weight," he said gently.

"What?"

"You have been losing some since you arrived here, and I am so proud. But you are still far above your target range. Thirty-four pounds overweight for your height, to be exact."

Eli stared up at him, dumbfounded.

"I know we lack a running track, like you had at the academy. And we lack the more imaginative facilities of the Maginaria. So we shall have to control it with diet. We can do that."

Leonard drew closer to her, bending like a stick insect to examine her more closely.

Don't look at the footboard, don't look at the footboard, don't look don't look don't look.

She forced her eyes back to his and hated his avid appraisal of her form with an intensity she hadn't known she could muster in her current state.

"I can really see the difference in your face, Millicent darling."

Eli's rage was so complete that she felt capable of leaping out of her body as a murderous specter and killing him with the power of her thoughts. She had been focused on the pipes, ignoring his prattling insanity, until this last. It snapped in her as cleanly as a stick of uncooked spaghetti.

"You can see. The difference. In my face."

Leonard nodded, his face beatific with sympathy. "I know it must be hard for you to pass up all those carbs and alcohol at gatherings with your fellow officers. Cops and doughnuts, after all? Right? But your willpower is strong! You can undo this damage you have done and reach that perfect body. Think of your medal ceremony, when you freed the captive prince! You wore that green silk gown—"

"That was Alice Stample. She is a film actress. She is professionally thin. That is her job. Millicent isn't real, and I'm not her. I am an author, and my body is my fucking business."

His mouth pulled down at the corners. "Well, since I am the one feeding you, that really is not true, is it? I can help you. You can be healthy and beautiful, just as you were meant to be. Just as I dreamed you."

If he starves me until I'm as thin as Alice, I'll never be able to fight him.

Rage would not fade. Eli was white-hot. She had endured the garden-variety fat jokes and tactless comments that are casually lobbed at women who are only slightly overweight, but she had never felt anything like this. She looked up at him with murder clear in her eyes.

He turned and loped up the stairs.

The second the door shut behind him, she began to twist apart the pipes that kept her ankle locked to the bed.

Not much time. He's probably microwaving a bowl of cabbage or some shitty diet food. Lean Cuisine. Focus. Don't have much time.

She struggled with the uprights. The ones she had loosened seemed to have settled somehow. They leaned at odd angles, putting the pressure of her weight on the bed against the threads and making them almost impossible to budge. His brief interaction with her had made her palms slick with sweat, made the muscles in her arms and legs shake with adrenaline and disuse. She had planned for this to go quickly, but the minutes were spinning away as she struggled against the bed and her own body.

Eli freed one upright, groaning with frustration, and concentrated on the joint pieces. Each was as stubborn as the first had been. She began to cry, but she did not give up. One by one, she grapevined closer to the one with the ankle cuff.

Upstairs, Leonard was making haste. He wanted to rejoin her, not to lose what ground he had gained with her this morning. He worked quickly to make her a bowl of soup. But haste makes waste, as any tidy person knows. Leonard splashed soup over the rim of the bowl and stopped a moment to wipe up the mess on his countertop and the inside of the microwave. Once neat, he set the timer for two minutes.

Downstairs, Eli frantically pulled the closed loop of her ankle cuff off the final upright, wrenching it around the joint and putting both feet on the floor for the first time in what seemed like ages.

She stood for a moment, wobbly and disoriented at the new perspective on the strange room. Her head swam dizzily and she had to clench her teeth to keep from fainting.

She looked down for a second at the satchel. It gave her a small pang to leave it, but only for a second.

Not really mine now.

She walked past it, a foot-long piece of steel pipe in her hands. She made for the stairs on feet that felt very unsure. When she stepped forward, her dragging leg iron caught up with her and hit the other ankle. Her bad eye made her paranoid, twisting always to her right, thinking she might be vulnerable on that side. She tried not to yell. Her pulse pounded in her gums.

Leonard thought a moment, checked his calorie calculator, then popped one slice of wheat bread into the toaster.

At the top of the stairs, Eli faced a terrible moment when she was sure the door would be locked.

Has to be. Has to be. Got to stand here and wait for him to open it. Hit him with the pipe. No, push him down the stairs! But he could catch me and pull me down, too. Hit him, then push him when he's shocked.

But her experimental turn of the knob opened the door.

She was in a short hallway. Ahead, she could hear the sounds of him bustling around in the kitchen. To the left, a dark doorway.

She shot left, landing on the padded front of her foot, trying to be as silent as possible. The ankle cuff clattered after her, and she bit her lip.

She reached back to see if she could hold it in her hand as she went, but it was too short. She had to settle for dragging it behind her. When she crossed over into the carpeted part of the house, the noise was less. She moved fast toward it, looking behind her as she went.

The living room was wide and dark, with an old-fashioned sunken look. Two carpeted stairs led down into the pit of it. Her depth perception was way off, down an eye and in an unfamiliar place. She stumbled. The muscles in her thighs trembled.

Can I make it out of here? Christ, can I drive with my vision like this?

The door was within sight. She could make it. She could get out the door.

And then what? No shoes, no plan. I'll die. Where's my phone? Where's his phone?

She looked around desperately, hoping he had carelessly laid her phone down somewhere and she could just dial 911.

Even if I don't get a chance to talk, the line stays open and they have to investigate the call. They have to. Have to.

His phone is in his pocket, you idiot. Look. Look for something useful.

Her one good eye swept the room.

On the wall beside the doorway, she saw something that stopped her. She had seen her own books displayed in bookstores in a dozen countries. She had seen her own portrait on the back cover a million times. She saw it now: her face framed by short dark hair. Her smirk that was not quite a smile. Eli wanted to see herself there on her books and feel grounded and could not. Nothing could ground her. Nothing here made sense.

Between a shelf of *Royal Stellar Navy* novels and framed signed headshots of a dozen big-name actors on one side, and a matching *Lord of the Rings* setup of similar magnitude on the other, Eli was drawn to a centrally positioned bookshelf like a magnet. Everything else about this declaration of nerdiness she had seen a dozen times before; how many friends had crossed lightsabers on their walls? What she had never seen before was a shrine erected to her own universe: *The City under the City.*

The books were on a short shelf that had been mounted to the wall, with several pictures of Eli tacked above it. Some were pencil drawings, some were photos, but others were more elaborate works. There were four or five of her, and almost a dozen of Millicent. It wasn't Alice the actress as Millicent, however. It was Eli's face with Millicent's character imposed on it.

Eli's sense of unreality deepened as she took in this strange gallery. It was all arranged as a peculiar altar, culminating in a triptych of seminude paintings of Eli/Millicent, awash in that pre-Raphaelite glow that suggested a dream or a fantasy. Eli had known there was something like this awaiting her in this house. What was this all about but obsession, after all? He hadn't snatched a random woman off the street. He had chosen her. Here was the inescapable reason why.

Eli walked closer, not wanting to know more but absolutely needing to know everything. She bumped against the shrine, hitting it sooner than she perceived she would. The shelf below the Millicent books was different. There was a collection of framed fan art pieces, but these were clearly from disparate sources. Marker drawings executed by teens appeared beside more professional, digitally created offerings. A few were renderings of specific artifacts that Eli recognized right away: these were all faces and locales and swords from *The Hand of Fate.*

He's a big sci-fi and fantasy nerd. He's into all the usual stuff. I'm sure Glamdring is around here somewhere. Or Sting. Or Ice.

She walked closer, frowning. Something was tickling at her memory, begging to be let in. It wasn't normal nerd-altar stuff. There was something different here. Something like an insider would construct. A professional nerd.

And then she knew. It blew open like a bloated corpse, baked in the sunlight, exploding on the beach inside her mind.

The Hand of Fate. *Oh fuck,* The Hand of Fate. *It's him.*

In the late '90s, Eli and everyone else who read science fiction or fantasy had all been deeply engrossed in a long series called *The Hand of Fate.* The *Fate* books had everything. The world was gorgeously built; an intricate high-fantasy story of a lost prince on a lifelong quest. The characters were true to life; a ride-or-die band of friends following the prince through his journey to his first tragic mentor, his first love, and then slowly fighting and propelling him toward reclaiming his usurped throne.

It was the kind of series that everyone loved and continuously wondered why the story hadn't been made into a blockbuster film or an absolutely killer television series. It was the next big thing, always rumored to be in development hell or contract negotiations to hit the big screen. Kids dressed up as hero Prince Vantan at conventions; a young prince might pass by his older self ten times in a day at one of the big ones. Cosplayers worked to re-create the series's armor, its incredible bestiary and the untamed manes of Vantan's riders. Filkers sang his songs and fan sites re-created the hearty stews and courtly pastries described in the books.

Eli remembered dream-casting this imaginary film with friends, their choices changing over the years as actors got too old or died. How often had someone said that *Fate* was why they wanted to become a writer? It was cited nearly as often as *The Hobbit*, and people got into screaming matches over whether the author of the *Fate* books, a recluse named Bernard Armour, was as good as Tolkien. Armour, they said, was the real lost prince. Tolkien's throne rightfully belonged to him.

Armour's writing was lush, original, lifelike and enchanting. His settings were the stuff of info-dump dreams, and fans couldn't get enough of the in-world family trees, maps and lore. Despite the excruciating level of detail in each book, Armour's plots were also page-turners. Once a reader started, they couldn't quit until they knew what happened, how it all came out. He had the kind of gift that suffused escapist fantasy with a cool, logical realism that made adults fall in love with a suspension of disbelief they hadn't enjoyed since they were children.

Magazines and newspapers celebrated the work as a cultural moment, a great unification of the reading public, and eagerly awaited the conclusion of the long and beloved adventure. Academics warmed to the books despite their recency, debating their eventual importance to the canon of American popular fiction. No book series for adults had been so universally beloved in a century. Armour had the world on a silver hook that sank through the eyeballs and caught in the heart.

Eli was unable to stop herself. She put her hand up to touch the framed photo of Armour. His face was fatherly and kind, round in the cheeks like Santa Claus. She looked at her own portrait and saw a flash of her reflection in the glass of the frame. Her cheeks were gaunt. Her right eye was a red, swollen egg.

Who the hell is that? Who's pretending to be Eli Grey?

The discomfort with her own image made her turn back to Armour's instead.

She remembered that the celebrated author had died tragically young, his work left unfinished.

An aggressive form of testicular cancer had taken the man out in his writing prime, his late forties. There were five books in the *Fate* series, but all his outlines and interviews had promised that there would one day be ten. His agent and editor had been able to cobble together book six and publish it posthumously, but they knew they couldn't pull that same feat off again.

But a writer like Bernard Armour could not die, just as Frank Herbert, V. C. Andrews or Robert Jordan could not be allowed to rest unmolested whilst the fan base still had spendable cash. The publisher had held something like auditions to see who could do the best Armour impression on paper. They had made a public spectacle of this star search: Who was America's next great fantasy bard?

The worst mistake in literary history had been selecting Leonard Lobovich, a small-time sci-fi, fantasy and erotica author, fanfic enthusiast and *Hand of Fate* megafan to take over for Armour.

The seventh and eighth books had come out on schedule. With great fanfare, Lobovich was heralded as a faithful inheritor to Armour. Reviewers took photos of Lobovich among Armour's books, but the heir to the intellectual property had granted few interviews. Lobovich, too, turned out to be a recluse who shunned all launch events and interviews, saying that the work could do the speaking for him. It did exactly that. Lobovich stopped going to conventions once he hit the big time.

Dimly, Eli recalled hearing from Lobovich. Maybe on Twitter? He was somewhere in her orbit, always. Had he been at conventions or had she seen him at some big party or another? Not for years, certainly. He was thinner now, with a beard and glasses and...

How could I be so stupid? This is literally Superman to Clark Kent level subterfuge and I fell for it. I've known this guy since the minute I laid eyes on him, but he looks just different enough... After all that he told me?

Eli gave herself no allowance for her circumstances: she had been drugged, beaten, starved and terrified in every moment in his presence. All she knew was that she should have known and she did not. It was every moment when she had ever forgotten a name or lost track of her keys magnified with the scorching shame of not having known enough to protect herself.

Still, the revelation was unfolding. There would be time to blame herself later. She hoped. Flashes of light went off in her head like bombs exploding.

The fanfic. The bullshit about Dune. *The quotes. Fuck me sideways. Lobovich.*

She thought back to the years after he had taken over the series. No, they had never really known each other. She had known *of* him. Clearly, he had known her better.

Longtime *Hand of Fate* fans weren't elated, but the masses were satisfied by Lobovich's effort. The books were caricatures, and the prose was a flowery parody of Armour's lyric voice. No one could have truly taken over for Armour; the man was a talent whose time comes seldom on this earth. But the new books did what they could to scratch the itch that irritated every reader who just wanted to know what happened next. The books sold, the series went on and the publisher promised book nine would be out any day now.

Long silences grew longer, and cosplayers moved on from Prince Vantan. Furor to see a movie of the *Fate* series died down as people turned their attention elsewhere. The core fandom had always been suspicious and began to whisper rumors. Maybe Lobovich wasn't real and the books were written by an algorithm. Maybe the series was cursed because the author hadn't wanted anyone to write in his place. Maybe Lobovich was real after all, but had died of the same virulent cancer that had taken Armour.

None of these things were true, but the publishing world moved so glacially that no one knew it until the book was more than a year late.

Then, the bombshell: Lobovich was a plagiarist.

The story hit all the papers and blogs on the same day, told by a fan-turned-investigative-journalist when the rumors pushed her to analyze and search the prose of books seven and eight. She found that Lobovich had stolen multiple whole-cloth sections of narration and dialogue from well-known fan fiction writers on Fic & Fan and other communities to which he had belonged before landing the replacement gig. The aggrieved authors had tried to make the case as soon as the books had come out, but each had fallen silent in turn. The newspapers were careful to use the words *alleged* and *accused*, but the evidence was as clear as day. The work had been stolen from high-profile online works, and inexpertly knit together into the lackluster additions to the beloved series.

Eli remembered the unrelenting shitstorm that had ignited on Twitter. It went from the single reporter who figured out the story, to the rumormongers, to the clearinghouses for genre gossip. Then it made the jump to the press, ultimately winding up in a place of prominence in the *New York Times* that a fantasy author could never have dreamed of landing under good circumstances. The fallout was incredible.

I didn't hear from anyone who knew him, though. Nobody tried to defend him. Nobody even seemed worried that he'd kill himself, even though it was what we all said we would do in his place.

The publisher paid out settlements and tried to extract promises and enforce gags. Rumor had it that each of the plagiarized fic writers had received credible death threats just before the story broke. Nobody knew whether Leonard had been behind them, but he was fired and blackballed, banned from the writer's guild and summarily disowned by both the literary and fantasy communities.

He broke the one real law we have, Eli realized, looking around at the room. *He'd have an easier time explaining that he kept me in a basement for a year than he did rationalizing plagiarism. Nobody in this business will believe one word you say after that.*

Writers will tolerate drug problems. They will cheerfully promote alcoholism. They'll overlook years of blatant sexual harassment, make excuses and carve their statuettes in the likenesses of great men who just happened to be raging misogynists or racists in their free time—or on the page. They'll squabble over politics and they'll pretend they never heard of pedophilia when they see that one guy at a party, because no one likes a scene.

But the one thing they will not do is suffer a plagiarist to live among them. And Lobovich had stacked two mortal sins on top of one another: he had plagiarized, and he had ruined a beloved and profitable thing.

Eli knew who had her as soon as she saw that pitiful shelf of eight books where ten ought to be. She knew everything at once, and the knowledge was sickening. She knew why he had snatched her. Why he wanted her passwords. Why he wanted her unpublished book. No pain or indignity that had come her way before now compared to this crashing, sickening agony. He had probably been planning this for years. It nauseated her very soul.

This wasn't even about her. She was not a player here but an object, and maybe even less than that. She was a means to an end; Lobovich was desperate for a way to redeem himself, a chance to make people see him the way he wanted to be seen. But he couldn't do it alone. He only knew how to steal.

All of this came together in a succession of searing seconds as she looked over his bookshelves. She lowered the pipe in her hands and stared.

Leonard walked toward the basement door with a tray in his hands. When he saw it was open, he dropped the whole thing to the floor with a crash.

"No no no no no no no no," he wailed, pelting down the stairs.

Should I follow him? No, no reason to go out into the open. Stay here. Hide. Leap out at him. Surprise him. Or escape. Or lock him in the basement! Would the door hold? Is there a lock? Why the fuck didn't I check for a lock?

She decided not to follow him, but to try and run while he was still in the basement. She ran clumsily toward the front door, knocking down a lamp as she went. Locked from inside with a flat dead bolt. Frantically, she looked around for a key hook or a bowl beside the door.

Nothing. The keys could be anywhere.

She whirled around, looking for another option. The room was unbearably dim. She kept trying to open her left eye wider, to see what the right eye couldn't. She didn't think it was possible that the ground floor of this house had no windows, but she could see none. There were two lamps in the room with buttery yellow shades that barely made a dent in the gloom.

The house was absolutely spotless, with not a single fiber of lint discernible in the dark rug. The bookshelves held no dust. The framed posters on the wall, including one for *The City under the City* shone without fingerprints.

No windows. What the fuck?

The walls were paneled with dark wood all around. Eli supposed it was possible to panel over windows, but who would do that?

A massive paranoid shut-in! Think of something useful, godsdamn it!

He was coming back up the stairs, taking them two a time.

My phone. The door. Windows. The pipe. The door.

Her thoughts were a tangle. She could see her pulse at the edges of her vision, a beat in her shimmering periphery.

"Millicent," he yelled. "Millicent, where are you?"

Eli backed up until she hit the wall and said nothing.

He came running into the room and she raised the pipe, trembling but resolute.

He saw her and his eyes bulged in his face. She ran at him, bringing the pipe down three times in quick succession, trying for his face or head.

She kept hacking wildly, hoping for the satisfying sensation of landing a good one where it would count. It never came. She couldn't get inside his daddy longlegs reach. His arachnoid arms blocked her out, taking blows on his forearms and shoulders. She could hear herself, the hoarse sobbing sound she was making. Turning her around violently, he wrapped her up in his long spidery arms, her right hand in his left, her own wrist pressed against her neck. He locked his arms together in a triangle choke and her vision immediately began to darken.

She kicked out behind her, strength failing, trying to pull away from him or sink beneath his iron grip.

He choked her out soundlessly, holding her long after her body had ceased its struggle. Eventually, he let her slide heavily to the floor.

December 16

@leonardlobovich: I am truly sorry if I have caused any chaos to interfere with the Hand of Fate series. It was not my intention. However, the current narrative that is being propagated about me is not entirely true. 1/2

@leonardlobovich: In time, the truth of these events will be revealed. For now, I can only offer my apologies to my fans and Bernard Armour's fans. As Prince Vantan would say, "Beyond that storm, the dawn is already touching some far horizon." 2/2

19

Eli was fourteen years old when she found the linen closet.

The Grey family had lived in every kind of cheap housing: apartments that shook like they were made of saltines boxes when someone slammed a door, crumbling modular houses and moldy trailers. They never stayed anywhere for long, and Eli did not attach herself to anyone or anything.

She had tried to explain the facts of life to Benny, so that he would not get attached to this place, either. He was still small, and she knew this kooky old place would delight him, no matter how drippy and drafty life under its roof would undoubtedly be. First, she told him it wouldn't last.

"Look, I know this place looks cool to you. Like something one of those orphans in the movies might live in. It's just another place Mom and Dad threw a month's rent at, so don't get used to it."

"I know, Lizzie."

"The basement is mine. I'm calling dibs right now, and you are not allowed to come down there at all."

"Okay, Lizzie. I don't care. It's fine."

"You might be scared to go up into the attic, but if you're not it's pretty cool. Kinda spooky. Plus it's the highest point in the house, so it'll probably be warmer."

Benny had smiled at his sister then. "Why would I be scared? I'm not scared at all."

"Fine," Eli said, trying to be the smart one of the two of them, but unable to resist the kid's bulletproof optimism. "Better take your stuff up there, then."

Eli's stuff consisted of her Star Wars backpack, scuffed from years of use and stuffed to bursting with her clothes and favorite books, and two pillows tied together with the belt from her old pajamas. There was a sagging, dusty sofa in the basement, which Eli claimed for her bed, pushing it to the far end of the basement, beneath the one window where the space was not quite so dank.

The basement was colder and damper than the rest of the drafty old house, but it did give Eli her first real experience of privacy. The house was big enough and the basement nonessential enough that there was hardly ever a reason for anyone but her to come down the stairs. Eli would take her meals in her room after school, spend her hours reading books and blessedly unbothered by her parents' endless fighting and arguing.

When Eli graduated the eighth grade, no one came to her promotion ceremony. She hadn't expected them to. She brought home her small completion certificate and her registration paperwork for the nearest high school, hoping that by the time she started ninth grade, they would still live in the same district. These she set on the kitchen counter—there was only a yellowing expanse of linoleum, no table—and headed downstairs.

She spiked her certificate on an old nail that jutted out of the wall, and then she saw the seam just beside it.

It was only because she was home in the middle of the day and the light was hitting it just right that she could even tell it was there. Buried beneath coats of paint and at least one layer of wallpaper, she could see the outline of a door.

It took the better part of the afternoon to work a butter knife all the way around it and then to discover the old lock plate without a knob in it. She wrenched the warped piece of wood free with a terrible groaning and blinked into the shallow darkness.

It was an old linen closet. Eli had never used a linen closet before, but she saw that the space had deep shelves that went back nearly four feet. It was dry inside, and empty.

Like most children who grow up frightened and insecure, Eli was attracted to small, hidden places just like this one. In no time at all, she had outfitted it with an old sleeping bag, a few candles, some canned food and water and books and notebooks. Just in case.

As her parents came to the end of their bitterly short cycle of stability, Eli got ready. The day the eviction notice was stapled to the door, she went into the closet and pulled the door resolutely shut. She left her bed exactly as it was and most of her belongings where they could be found. When her mother came reeling down the stairs to tell Eli to pack, Eli wasn't there.

She emerged two days later with her bag packed. No one asked her where she had been.

Mrs. Grey and the two children moved to a friend's apartment less than a mile away. Edward Grey disappeared from their lives and the children did not ask when he would return. He always did, eventually.

But no one else would rent the ramshackle old house for a long time. Eli knew that, because she slipped back in, over and over, to live in the secrecy of her forgotten linen closet.

There, she dreamed long dreams of rescue by Starfleet officers and Jedi and the headmaster of Hogwarts—anyone who would come and take her hand and tell her she did not belong here. There had been a mistake, and they were finally here to correct it and take her home.

The closet was her hideaway for years, until they moved too far away for her to reach it on her own. By then she was almost too tall to scoot into the space, and too big for the sleeping bag by half. She bitterly resented the loss of the thing that was only hers, where no one could intrude on her private thoughts.

Eli went back to the closet now, somewhere deep in black memory that was not a dream, in an unmoving rest that was not sleep. Her notebooks were there, as was her copy of *The Hand of Fate.*

She read it again, starting from the very first page.

What would Armour do? Armour's dead. Lobovich killed him.

No, Lobovich didn't kill him. Cancer did. Right?

Patiently, slowly, she made a cup of tea in a tin can over a candle, just like she used to do.

Somewhere else, her lips and mouth were dry. Somewhere, her eye ached and her vulva itched. Someone was trying to talk to her. She couldn't hear them in here.

Vantan was riding out of the city in the middle of the night with the intercepted message that changed his life. Her tea was warm, but not hot. She added a packet of sugar from her diner-looted stash and drank.

Somewhere else her stomach was empty and her head ached. In here, the candle gave a circle of light and her tea was good.

She wished Nella could visit her here. Or that Joe could bring her more tea; there were only four more bags. But no one could come here. No one even knew where it was, not even Benny.

Vantan was narrowly evading the royal guard in the forest,

taking the secret trails of his boyhood. The pages of the book were blank, but Eli knew the story was inside her. She could see it all taking shape.

Lobovich got them to give him The Hand of Fate. *He's planning to do the same with Millicent, but how? If I'm dead and he's got book eight, that's no good. People have already seen book eight, and I have to tell him that. He doesn't stand the chance he stood with Armour, even if I am dead.*

They'd never let him do it, anyway. Not after the mess he made, the disgrace attached to his name. So what the hell does he have to gain here?

The book changed from *The Hand of Fate* to *The Coming of the Tide*, the seventh in the series and first written by Lobovich. Everything was just one shade off; Vantan's voice was a little more Batman, a little less prudent prince. The metaplot was lost in romantic dithering; the love triangle had taken over.

He changed my hair to make me more like Millicent. He wants to call me Millicent, wants to take credit for creating her. That's not something he can act out when it's just the two of us, is it? What good is it getting me to play Pygmalion around the house? What does he get out of that?

Prince Vantan was whining that nobody loved him like he deserved to be loved. Abruptly, Eli made the blank pages of the book show her *The City under the City* instead. She had worked hard to avoid all the clichéd garbage romance that she disliked throughout the genre. She remembered thinking about *The Hand of Fate* as she learned to edit her own work.

On the blank page, the two stories came together. Vantan rode with Millicent to the Maginaria. Millicent helped Vantan solve the mystery of who had killed his father, the last king.

Eli couldn't straighten it out. She didn't want to leave the linen closet. She sipped her tea.

Somewhere else, her throat throbbed and someone was

muttering. Somewhere else, she could hear the sound of a power tool.

In the closet, she opened up her notebook and began to write. It didn't look like words; it looked to her like drawings of herself, walking on a sketch of a skeletal bridge. She kept going back to underline it, to make it feel safer. The plan took shape in words anyway, despite the self-portrait on the page.

When I wake up, I'm going to call him by his name. I'm going to tell him I know who he is. Remind him that I know him. That's a risk, but now I know what he wants. That means I can keep him from getting it, or at least convince him that he's not going to get it. He's going to have to let me go or kill me.

He must have wanted me to know, at least on some level. Why else would he have created such a display? Who else is that for?

On the paper, the ink bridge ran out. Someone was in the basement with her.

No, that was somewhere else. Nobody could come here.

She made the old wooden stairs to her basement collapse. Somewhere else, Lobovich was coming and going, humming a tune.

It was the theme song from the first Millicent Michaelson movie.

20

Joe's phone vibrated on the surface of his desk just as he was finishing up an email to his client list. More than one of them had noticed that he had been less attentive recently, or hadn't followed up with his usual flawless aplomb.

It was a testament to what a gifted assistant Joe was that none of them were angry with him. The two that had spoken up—an author and a music video dancer—had both done so in a manner that indicated they were more worried about him than anything else.

His email covered the important things: one of his clients was missing. He believed there was foul play involved, and he was doing for her what he would do for any of them. He told them he couldn't get into too many details—privacy was a vital value, as any of them would agree—but that he would let them know if he had to take time off or if he knew he would be remiss in his duties in the days to come.

What he didn't tell them was that Agent Silvestri, who was calling him at this very moment, was beginning to scare him to death.

She had followed every lead. She had logged the case as a kidnapping. But he still wasn't sure that Silvestri understood Eli hadn't just done a runner. Joe believed with every fiber of his being that Eli's life was in danger.

"Agent Silvestri," he said as he slid the answer button briskly to the right. "What news do you have for me?"

"Your girl is tweeting again," Silvestri said shortly. "I'm going to level with you, Mr. Papasian. I don't believe that Eli Grey is in possession of her phone. I think you may be right."

Joe tapped the tab on his computer where Twitter was always open. He found Eli's account with ease.

@eligrey: I'm sorry I have been so quiet lately, dear readers. I have decided to take some time off.

@eligrey: I've elected to stay away from home for a while, to work on the next Millicent book.

@eligrey: I'm with someone I care for deeply and you will all be hearing from me soon.

Joe's veins were like ice beneath his skin. His stomach fell into his shoes. "That's not her," he said.

"Just like that Instagram picture."

"Yes, exactly like that. Agent, I would know her writing style anywhere. Whoever has her account isn't doing a great Eli impression. It might not be obvious to most people, but it's obvious to me."

Silence on the other end of the line.

"Wait, okay. Wait. Scroll back to December...twentieth. Look at Eli's tweets about her publisher's holiday party."

A few more seconds of silence. Then, Silvestri's careful voice. "Okay."

"See how the tweets are threaded so that if you open the

top one, you can read them all in order?" Joe could feel sweat on his upper lip and licked it. It tasted like fear.

"Yeah, I see that," Silvestri said.

"If you look at those tweets just now, you'll see that they're not threaded. This is something Eli has bitched about a billion times. You can find that on her Twitter, too. Agent, somebody has Eli's computer and is making bad excuses for her. This is scarier than a ransom demand to me."

Silvestri was typing, Joe could hear it. He fidgeted with his beautiful watch, then switched his phone from one hand to the other.

"I've gotten cybercrimes division involved in the case to see if they can help trace these events."

Relief flooded into Joe as he realized she'd believed him for a while now; she'd been working in ways he hadn't known. "I think that's a really good idea, Agent. I don't know what I can say to you to help you understand that I'm not jerking you around. If this turns out to be nothing and Eli really did just ditch her life, I'd face up to whatever. Charges, jail time for wasting your resources. I'm that sure."

Silvestri sighed. "It's just not often we have a real mystery disappearance like this."

"I believe that. Do you have any leads?"

Silvestri had the surveillance footage and the switched plates. She was waiting on the local field office to send her the transcripts of eyewitness interviews. She had an unidentified tall white man as a person of interest and a lot of calls from reporters. She couldn't share most of this information with Joe.

"Some, yes. I'll share with you what I can when I can, Mr. Papasian. It's also pretty unusual to be dealing with someone who has no family connection to the missing. I won't be able to tell you everything."

Joe gave an answering sigh just as a message from his boyfriend popped up on the screen. "I appreciate your candor, Agent. I am at your convenience if I can help in any way."

"Thank you." The agent hung up and Joe set his phone back down.

You gonna be home for dinner tonight?

Yeah, just kissing ass to make up for the last week.

Clients pissed?

No, everybody is cool. Just explaining to them.

Still nothing on Eli?

Nothing.

Do you think she's dead?

Joe reviewed his television-based education in missing persons. He thought about the up-close torture porn of anything female in those shows that usually took place for a long time before death.

I dunno. I hope not. You know she's my favorite.

I know. Come home.

Ok.

Joe got a car home to Paul's house in Bernal Heights. The house had a spectacular view of San Francisco and Paul stood by the window with two glasses of wine. He looked like a professor in his shawl-collar sweater and corduroy pants. He kissed Joe and handed him the drink.

They looked out over the hills of the city before Joe's phone went off again.

Eli had posted on Instagram again. It was a picture of all of her books stacked neatly on a table. The caption read: "Sometimes I'm so proud of all I've done, I just marvel at it."

Joe imagined someone standing over her, forcing her to type out the caption. He saw some stranger put two hands on her face and work her like a puppet, making her say the words. He leaned into Paul, comforted by the warm contact and scent of his beloved.

"You okay?" Paul murmured into Joe's shiny hair.

"Eli bites," he said quietly.

"What?"

Joe turned and looked at his boyfriend, who was sipping his wine again. "I think somebody has Eli," he said. "And I think she's the kind of woman who bites. I hope she is, anyway."

Paul's brows came together. "Why don't we sit down and you tell me everything?"

Joe walked to a tweedy chaise and dropped to it as if he were born without knees.

"Easy, kid. That's vintage."

Joe made a face. Paul made one back.

"I'm worried that the FBI agent on the case isn't taking me seriously," Joe began. "And I admit that this is all fucking weird, but Eli definitely did not just skip town and get a personality transplant."

"Slow down," Paul said, crossing his legs like a tailor. "You know I'm on your side here."

Joe gulped wine. "So she's been tweeting again. And when I say she, I mean someone else who is not her at all. I mean someone pretending to be her. And posting to Instagram."

"What?" Paul reached out and took Joe's phone. He scrolled and looked. Joe waited.

"I think she's being held somewhere down south. I told the FBI that."

"You think she got kidnapped in the desert? Or like in LA?" Paul pursed his lips.

"Yeah, I do think that. I know it sounds crazy." Joe stared at Paul as the sun set behind him, rendering him in silhouette. "I'm serious, Paul. I think someone fucking has her. I know it's a weird friendship that involves money, but she is my friend. And I don't think she has anybody else. If I didn't notice she was gone, this might have just not gotten noticed. She has fans, but not really anyone else."

"There's a reflection in this one." Paul was frowning down at the phone again.

"What?"

Paul clucked his tongue. "I know you're all literary now, but don't act like you never engaged in Kardashian Kremlinology with me. Look close right here."

Paul pulled the photo apart with two fingers, zooming in and ruining the clarity of the image. Floating in the glossy book jacket on top of the stack was a distorted man-shadow with the outline of the phone he was holding to take the picture.

"That's not Eli!" Joe almost yelled it. At the curve of the shadow-man's temple, he could make out the hard corner of a pair of glasses. He snatched the phone and shrank the photo back down. He stared at the stranger's reflection as if it had more information to offer.

"You need to call that FBI agent back and tell her that you showed this to your own little in-house CSI."

Joe was already dialing. Silvestri didn't pick up. She knew.

21

Leonard had not saved the FBI agent's number on the phone, but he recognized it when it came up again. He wanted to answer it on the first ring, but thought better of it. Waited a natural interval. He picked it up using his Eli voice, trying his best to sound bored.

"Eli."

"Ms. Grey, this is Agent Silvestri with the FBI again. How are you doing today?"

"Fine," Leonard said, thinking fast. He should be annoyed, he realized. Affronted. Was this harassment? It might be.

"I was hoping to follow up with you about your whereabouts. You see, I've been in touch with your family."

"Oh?"

A beat of silence. "Yes. Your father and your brother. They're both concerned that you haven't been in touch with them for some time."

"I am sorry, did you say you were a therapist? Or are you an FBI agent who is seriously out of her depth right now?"

Silvestri didn't take the bait. She swallowed. She waited.

If they're just pissed off, they're hanging up now, she thought. *If they want to match wits with a cop, they'll stay on the line.*

"Well?"

"Ms. Grey, can you verify your Social Security number for me?"

The person on the phone recited it without missing a beat. *Proving something. Feeling cocky.*

Just wanting to keep the voice on the other side of the line talking, she asked, "And where were you born?"

He answered that and other questions for a few minutes before beginning to huff. Silvestri was recording and listening carefully. She was deciding whether or not to call him out. He might panic and kill the woman. She decided against it. She watched the computer try to locate him while she spun it out.

"What is the point of this, Agent? I do not have all day. I am a very busy novelist."

"I'm just doing my due diligence, ma'am. You understand."

"I can assure you that I am Eli Grey," he said evenly. "I am alive and well and acting with a sound mind. I do not know why you are bothering me like this, but perhaps the next time I hear from you, I could refer you to my lawyer instead."

"I apologize, Ms. Grey. You have a nice day."

"Thank you."

The line went dead. Once again, the locator software could only indicate a vast region of California as the origin of the call, covering parts of two counties. But Silvestri knew that this time there was enough on the recording for the lab to make a positive voiceprint ID. She walked over there in the flesh to press them.

Eli was awake but she stayed quiet. She kept her eye closed, peeking through her lashes when she knew Leonard had moved away. Most of the basement had not changed. The rules still hung where they always had, but Eli could dimly see there had been an amendment toward the bottom.

Eli was dressed in another satin nightgown, this time in a blushing shade of peach. She was cuffed by both feet to the bed, and her hands had been zip-tied to the headboard. She stirred a tiny bit and found that she had almost no range of motion. The plastic ties dug into her wrists and she fought the urge to grimace.

Relax. Breathe in slow, breathe out slow. He still thinks I'm out.

Does he know I'm gonna develop a tolerance to whatever he's giving me? Is he upping the dosage a few milligrams every time? Has he thought about it? How long can he do that without causing an OD? If I keep pretending to be out, can I fuck up his calculations?

Leonard went back to the stairs, and Eli opened her eyes. The top rung of her pipe footboard was gone, and she was cuffed to something much lower and impossible to see from her position lying on her back. Her feet were stuck outside the bedclothes there. She felt the cold air of the basement on them.

Eli squinted across the room to read the new rule that had been added to the list. It hadn't been added hastily, she could see. Leonard wasn't the kind of guy who would scrawl the new rule on there with a ballpoint pen. He had edited the document and printed out a new one, hung it up with fresh blue painter's tape. She thought maybe the font was slightly larger than before.

The amendment read: YOU WILL OBEY ME. YOU BELONG TO ME.

Eli felt her stomach turn over, grinding on its own acid emptiness. Her brains roiled. She took deep breaths to dispel the dizzy feeling of sickness.

I found a way out of this bed and I will do it again.

Millicent would escape this.

That thought was not the comfort that it should be.

She's mine, damn it. I created her. I'm not her, but I made her. I can't let him fuck that up for me. She's all I've got.

Just my imaginary friends. Just my made-up bullshit. Just me and my pity party of one. Just—

Her thoughts were cut clean off by a noise upstairs.

Near the top of the stairs she heard a solid bang, followed by shouts and the sound of a scuffling. Leonard was yelling but she couldn't hear the words.

Grogginess fled as the adrenaline dump valves opened up in her bloodstream. She strained, pulling against her bonds and trying to lift up her head. She stared at the top of the stairs, eyes bulging.

"FBI!" The voice was booming, bass heavy. Eli could picture the agent exactly: a barrel-chested hero made even bigger by a tactical vest and several holsters holding guns and knives all over him. Chinos and Timberlands. Big, square hands double-gripping his gun as he shouted at Leonard, then spoke into the walkie-talkie on his shoulder. A column inching in behind him, a half dozen in FBI windbreakers, all with guns drawn. Leonard sniveling, shrinking to the floor.

The door at the top of the staircase rattled.

"FBI! Open the door!"

"I'm down here," Eli yelled, her voice creaky with disuse and alarmingly weak to her ears. She cleared her throat and tried again. "I'm stuck—I can't get up! I'm down here! Break the door down!"

She felt warm all over. She was breathing fast; she was actually *smiling*. Relief washed through her and the sensation was so enormous that she felt like she might pass out. Her heart swelled and she knew tears were not far behind.

"Thank you thank you thank you thank you," she breathed, not knowing where she was directing her gratitude.

"Here!" she yelled again. "I'm down here."

The moment stretched on forever. She pictured a smaller agent kneeling down beside Leonard's blubbering body, pulling the keys from his pocket while the big guy kept his gun trained on the kidnapper.

Why not just break it down?

The silence unnerved her. What if Leonard had booby-trapped the house somehow? What if he was telling them he had a bomb or something right now? Her heart hammered as relief began to wash away.

Even if he does somehow manage to hold them off, more will come, right? It not like they won't know their agents didn't come back. They can call for backup, even out here in bum-fuck nowhere.

The door at the top of the stairs opened fast, banging against the wall behind it.

For a moment, the FBI agent was so real that Eli could see him coming down the stairs with his gun slightly lowered. He made it three or four steps before he became Leonard. Leonard, smiling like a kid who managed to pull off a prank.

Something like revulsion came up in Eli, tasting like bile and disappointment so intense she quivered with it.

"I realize that I am a gifted mimic," Leonard said, a small smile at the corners of his mouth. "But you must be quite naive to believe that could have been real. I only did that to teach you a lesson, my love."

He came to stand beside the bed and stare down at her. Her shaking did not subside.

"Millicent, nobody is looking for you. Nobody is going to come here. I wrote a really nice explanation on our social media accounts that we're taking some time off to reevaluate what we really want. Our fans have been really receptive! They know you're in no danger. I can't wait until we tell them the good news!"

Eli stared up at him and said nothing.

"And I have been speaking directly with the FBI. They understand the situation. They have no reason to believe you're in any kind of trouble."

There's no way, Eli thought. *No way he's been talking to them. What the fuck is any of this?*

He followed her facial expressions and nodded gravely. "Yes, I have handled that. I explained to them that we are just taking some time away for artistic reasons, and we are doing quite well. They are not going to search for you. No one is. Your place is at my side, after all. Rule number two, remember? I want you to get used to that, and come to love it. However, I can't have you leaving this room again. I trust you saw the new rule on the list?"

Eli said nothing. She closed her eye for a minute and tried to think. In the darkness, she saw the FBI agent who had only ever existed in her mind. She tried to decide whether he was lying about talking to any cops on the phone.

What would he say to them? Did he call them to taunt them about having me? Did they call my phone and he just picked it up saying, "Yes, hello, kidnapping asshole here"? Does any of that matter? No, nothing outside of this basement matters. It's just me and him, day after day.

Leonard smiled. "So quiet today! Well, no matter. The important thing is that you understand the new rule."

When she opened her good eye, he was still standing in the same place, staring down at her.

"I understand that I'm tied down way worse than I was before," she said. "What am I supposed to do? I can't even move. I can barely see."

"You're supposed to be a good girl. You can do that from there."

The tears that had threatened to spill in relief were still hovering, waiting. Eli bit the insides of her mouth to keep them below the surface.

"Good girls do not go upstairs. Do you understand, Millicent?"

She did not answer him. She went back to the moment when she first heard the FBI upstairs. The relief. The triumph.

"So you'll have to be punished."

Eli's eye flew open as she remembered the cattle prod. "Wait."

"I knew you were crafty," Leonard said. "How else would you have caught the Spider Conjurer all on your own after your partner was kidnapped? How would you have freed the captive prince when all your magic had been taken from you? So I should have been more careful with your keeping."

He picked up a long, flexible rod of clear acrylic or plastic. Eli recognized it as the wand used to control a set of venetian blinds. She couldn't ascribe any harm to it after the fights they had had, using jagged metal and high voltage. She stared at it, uncomprehending.

"But just in case you manage to escape again, I need to make sure that you are slightly less mobile until you are better behaved."

"Less mobile?"

Leonard didn't answer, but lined himself up at her feet, which were still exposed and cold.

"What are you doing?"

"This will only take a second," Leonard said, staring at her feet.

Eli took a deep breath and said the only thing she thought might derail him and his hellish plans.

"Leonard Lobovich!" Eli relished the full-body reaction that she got by saying his name. His long spine curved, diminishing his terrible height. His face fell into the sinkholes of open eyes and open mouth. He looked like a kid found out by his parents just before getting into the cookies.

He turned to stare at her, his glasses slipping down his nose.

"That's right. You like that, you fucking pig? I know who you are, motherfucker. You know what I saw? I saw your books upstairs. Well, they're not really *yours*, are they, Lenny? Your name is on the cover, but you didn't write them. I remember the whole story. I saw your bullshit apology and then you disappeared. You slunk away like the lying fraud that you are. You changed your look and grew a beard and moved to the boonies to get away. But you can't get away from what you are."

Lobovich's mouth fell open.

"I know what you're after, Lenny. And you're never going to get it. I knew you were nobody, way back when we first met. That's why I'd never responded when you contacted me. I barely remembered your name. You were never on your way somewhere, and everybody knew it. You'll always be nobody. You'll have to kill me to change that, and then you'll only be famous for fucking up again. Lenny, you fucking loser, I'd rather die than let a hack *thief* like you touch my work."

His face colored fast, red racing up from the collar of his flannel shirt to his hairline. His face then purpled, swelling, his mouth open as though he were choking on a bite of poorly chewed steak.

Savage pleasure rose in Eli. Fear fled. Tears were miles away. She smiled at him like a predator showing its teeth. God, it felt so good to get to him like this after what he had done to her. The pleasure of it was like nothing else.

Shaking with rage, he turned away from her face and back to her feet.

"How. Dare. You." He raised the acrylic rod again and Eli

had a final half second of doubt before he snapped it down against the soles of her feet.

The impact came first, heavy enough but queerly non-threatening. A lancing, searing pain followed that made her suck air in so fast she nearly choked on her own tongue. Lobovich swung again and again like a man trying to chip a golf ball out of a sand trap.

The pain was incredible, huge and unthinkable. Eli was sure the skin on the bottoms of her feet was split open but she couldn't open her eye to look for blood. She couldn't do anything but shriek again and again. Tears flowed out of her eyes and into her ears. Her nose ran and she couldn't wipe it away, nor rub her face against anything at all.

"How. Dare. You. How. Dare You. You. Fat. Pretender. You. Fake. You. Dilettante." He spoke through clenched teeth, his voice rising in terrible frenzy.

Eli's resolve was gone almost at once. Her strength was wiped out. She cried, she begged, she screamed at him to stop. She said please. She said she'd do anything at all.

Leonard did not let up.

Her knees creaked and popped. Her calves and quads and glutes seized in cramps as she fought to pull her feet away. She was a moment from begging for death when the rod snapped on the side of her right foot, farthest away from him.

For a moment they were silent together, their ragged breathing filling the room like the beating of wings.

Eli whimpered, trying to pull herself into a smaller shape, to become a ball, to become nothing and get away from this endless horror.

Leonard said nothing. He turned away with the broken piece of plastic still in his hand and walked slowly up the stairs, head lowered, breathing in hot snorts like a bull. When he was gone, the lights in the basement went out and Eli was left with nothing but her wet face, wet diaper and the smoldering sting and stickiness that was her bloody feet and ankles.

He shut off the lights and Eli sobbed in the darkness. Leonard watched her in the green of the night-vision camera. He set the Klaxon and light alarm to go off in five hours. He did not return for two days.

Eli was back in her own basement. She was out of the closet and sitting on the old sprung couch. She looked up at the dingy window to enjoy the indirect sunlight.

She had her spiral notebook and a handful of pencils that she'd sharpened with her knife.

She could not go where her body was. It was on fire; it was dying of shame and thirst and futile rage. It was sitting in a dirty diaper. The alarm had returned to keep her from sleeping, so she fled from all conscious thought and sensory input. She floated in a twilight stage of deep fugue, something without envelope or edges. Her body was somewhere else.

Here, she was in charge of her head. In here, she could get some quiet and some privacy. Here she got all of her good ideas, wrote her endings and got herself together when things got bad.

She put the carved point of her pencil to the page.

There is something about constant pain that removes most of one's higher function. Eli could not distract herself with any thought, not even that of escape. She groaned and tried to toss and turn, but she could not move. The iron manacles that bolted her to the wall did not give in the least.

Eli slept fitfully in the cool darkness of the dungeon, her heels sticking to the sheets with congealing blood. In the corner, a torch burned in a sconce high up on the wall, casting faint shadows in the corners. Though her injuries were life-threatening, Eli's powers still answered her call when she managed to whisper them through her parched lips.

When the final word of the chant left her lips, Eli felt herself hovering above the oaken bed. She ascended slowly, gathering momentum. The stones of the stronghold parted for her, clanking and scraping against one another as they moved. Her miserable hooded gaoler saw the tumult and stared up at her as she rose. She killed him with a thought.

The roof timbers split and the thatch cracked apart to reveal the brilliance of the night sky. Eli spotted her black dragon, Nightcrest, as he rose to greet her, elated at her sudden freedom. He swooped beneath her, positioning himself so that she slid into her saddle.

"I am very tired, old friend. Thank you for coming. Can we go home?"

The sparkling night-colored mount nodded his assent before ascending toward the moon.

They would be home by daybreak.

Somewhere else, Eli felt a tiny bit better. Control was the ultimate palliative.

Leonard could not get ahold of himself. Millicent had been so ugly, so disagreeable that he had no choice but to discipline her. He hated doing that, but there was no other path to order.

He went about his calming routine, starting with the first and most basic steps. He took off his soiled clothes and pushed them into the washer. It was permanently set on the sanitize setting. Next, he climbed into the shower and vigorously scrubbed himself with Irish Spring, the only soap he ever bought. He washed his hair with clarifying shampoo until it squeaked beneath his hands.

He stepped out and toweled off, buffing his skin roughly. He stood before the mirror, saying his own name to his reflection again and again.

"Eli Grey. Eli Grey. Eli Grey. Bestselling author, Eli Grey."

He wanted to talk to the FBI agent again. He wanted to feel like he had his hands wrapped around the situation.

He slipped into a new pair of briefs, straight out of the bag, and a new pair of socks, as well. In his closet, he found a perfectly pressed pair of jeans, undershirt and starched button-up.

He stalked the house, looking for where he had gone wrong. The sink was empty and sparkling, smelling of artificial lemons. His linens were crisp and folded and squared in the closet. The refrigerator held perfect faced and fronted boxes and jars, their dates all within acceptable parameters.

Leonard seethed. He smoothed down the front of his shirt over and over again. Nothing helped. Millicent would not come to him, or comfort him.

He sat down at his new laptop again and tried to find the file holding his new novel. He tried every file-hosting website he knew to see if there was a saved login and password that populated automatically. Nothing worked.

She hadn't known him at first, but she did now. Did she remember all the conversations that they had had via email? He had reread them so many times that he could recite them as well as he could any of the Millicent movies' dialogue. How could she use their connection to try and hurt him? How did she dare?

Thinking about this and sitting at his computer brought it all back. That awful, endless day when the accusations had risen up from the unreasonable mob to destroy him on the eve of his triumph. He had been about to reveal the final sequence of book covers. He knew how *Hand of Fate* was going to end. He had signed the contract for the film series option. It was supposed to be the best day of his life.

He had sat in front of his computer, barely moving, for the next thirteen hours. It had come in restless, terrible waves. The vitriol and poorly disguised envy masquerading as righteousness had poured out of the machine. His email seized up as notifications came in like malevolent snowflakes in a blizzard. His Twitter was an unnavigable, rapid churning river, and all of it was abuse. His phone had begun to ring without end and voice mails showed themselves, transcribed on the screen.

His agent: We have to talk.

His editor: You son of a bitch.

His IP lawyer: It's not looking good.

The reporters: We want to get your side of the story.

Bernard Armour Jr.: How could you? We trusted you.

Leonard found that he could not breathe normally. He was pulled back into the maelstrom of memory, unable to transcend it. He clicked his way to Eli's Twitter page and soothed himself. Another outpouring of love in the notifications. The constant reassurance that the work was good and people cared. All that could be his. Would be his. He would never have to relive that terrible day.

He was beginning to calm down. He could think about the future rather than the past. Leonard pulled up a YouTube video of the author talking about the eighth book again. He turned the sound off while she was introduced so he didn't have to hear her false name.

"It's all ready to go," Millicent was saying. She was dressed terribly wrong, in a man's green vest and no makeup at all. She was so unappealingly fat, her belly pooching out over the waistband of her slacks. She wouldn't even sit up straight! He thought of her safely downstairs, thinner, lovingly chastised into obedience. On the screen, Millicent laughed. He made a face but kept watching.

"I put all my books in a special place, and then I wait to submit until April first. That's my private joke."

The questioner, a short woman with an academic-looking brooch on her lapel, tittered prettily at this. "Yes, that is a great story. So can you tell us anything? You left us hanging after the big wedding. Can you give us any hint about what's going to happen?"

Millicent smiled and dimpled prettily. Leonard loved when she smiled; he could see the real her when she did that.

"I can't tell you much, but I will say that the wedding doesn't end in the way that you'd expect. There's a big surprise coming."

She was still smiling when the video came to an end.

He watched it again, his mouth moving when hers did.

There's a big surprise coming. He smiled, wishing he had dimples, too.

22

Leonard shut down the alarm system on the third day. He set a timer for five hours and worked on his surprise for a while. He had a task list taped to the wall and had marked off the days on his calendar with a careful, even X on each day. He had cleared out the guest bedroom completely and was starting from scratch. This had to be perfect.

When the timer went off, he set down what he was working on. He was midtask and it would have been better to finish it up, but that just wasn't the sort of person Leonard was.

He showered in very hot water, his skin lobster red in the heat. He shaved with a brand-new blade and deodorized himself. He carefully inspected the picture of the author he had printed out from online. The hair was a few inches longer than he could stand his to be, but his clippers could shave the sides just so and the resemblance would be clear.

He chose a plain white button-up shirt and black pants. The effect was very different than his usual flannels and he could see that he already appeared more professional.

He looked in the full-length mirror at himself. This was a man people would listen to. Nobody would talk over him, or tell him that he was way off base.

"I wrote Millicent Michaelson, so I think I know a thing or two about female characters," he said to the mirror, a wry smile at the corner of his mouth.

He turned the other way. "The thing that people really do not understand is that the work is so freeing. It allows me to be god and the devil and fate and the weather all at once." This was a line cribbed straight from an interview with the author. There was such power in it. He changed the angle he was standing at and said it again.

He saw his socks while adjusting and frowned. That was unfinished business. He went to the drawer under his bed where each pair of shoes was lined up, toes together, with a few inches between. He pulled out the author's black leather oxfords. He had of course shone them and replaced the insoles before putting them away. The matching ones he had ordered in his own size had arrived at his post office box just days before. He compared them and found them almost identical. She would think he was standing in her shoes. It was a good sign. A proof. They could pass one another in the middle and assume their correct roles. He stood before the mirror again.

"It is so gratifying to hear from fans all over the world and know that my work really reaches them. It is the best part of the best job in the world."

He smiled and felt giddy, felt like his fortunes were looking up for once.

He went into the kitchen to prepare Millicent's shot.

Leonard was able to creep all the way down to her and administer the shot without any fuss. Once he was sure she was out, he went to work on her.

★ ★ ★

Silvestri got proof positive from the lab that morning: the person on the phone identifying themselves as Eli Grey was not the author. Data said he was almost certainly a man, white, in his thirties and had grown up speaking English. There was no background noise that could help them place him: no birds, no train whistle, absolutely nothing to go on.

She read over the transcript of the call, trying to find anything that she might be able to use. Paranoia, but that was to be expected. Indignation and superiority. Silvestri thought back to her training in profiling. It had not been her strongest suit; she favored the provable, fact-based techniques of good detective work to the dreamy, unprovable stuff that profiles were made of. Still, she made a note to look for someone who had offended against other women authors or celebrities. Had this guy maybe stalked the actress who had been in all Grey's movies? That seemed in line with this kind of thinking. But when she searched, she found that Alice Stample had one documented stalker: a woman who had killed herself two years before. No other authors in Grey's genre had marked anyone in particular. The agent was sure this guy had offended before. Nobody jumped straight to this kind of elaborate kidnapping. But the pattern did not reveal itself to her.

Silvestri went to cybercrimes and began to work toward finding an address for which she could get a warrant. This case was unlike anything she had ever seen, and she didn't want to wreck it through procedure. She updated every connected department, filed every report exactly as she was supposed to do.

A man who holds a woman and takes her name and her voice from her is not someone I want getting out from under on a technicality.

Still, Silvestri could not help counting how long this guy had been holding Eli Grey. How long could this go on? How long could the writer take it?

Silvestri took the stairs two at a time. In the conference room at the top of the stairs, she met with the two lab techs who had analyzed the recorded calls she had handed over, and a specialist in celebrity stalkers. Nobody had good news for her. A young woman from cybercrimes walked into the meeting late, and Silvestri looked up with such hope in her eyes that the kid swore when she saw it.

"Nothing yet," she told the agent. "This guy is a ghost. We're working."

23

Eli hadn't consciously known when the alarm and lights stopped, but she had slipped into a deeper, more recuperative sleep. Her feet were crusted with dried blood. Her diaper was unspeakable. She was sore from both not moving and attempting to move. Sleep was dreamless and she threw herself into it.

She did not feel the sting of the needle.

She awoke disoriented, not sure how much time had gone by, with her mouth dry. For the first time in all these unnumbered days, she was sitting up.

The sensation was not quite right. She was pitched forward with her chin on her chest, but still upright. As she breathed in deeply, she found that she had been bound at the shoulders and chest to something behind her. The bed frame. She was sitting up in bed.

She opened her eye to find she was lost behind a curtain of blond hair. This was not just the wispy blond remains of what Lobovich had done to her; this was long blond hair, luxuriant and strange. On impulse, she moved her hands to get it out of her eyes. Her right was cuffed to the frame, but her left was free.

She flopped the hair awkwardly back, not sure how to manage it. Experimentally, she brought her head close to her hand and tried pulling it. A wig would have slid off, but this was no wig. She felt her scalp with her fingertips and discovered the hair was extensions of some kind, affixed to her own hair in long, bumpy ribbons running horizontally across her head.

She scanned the room. She was alone, but saw in her peripheral vision that she was also wearing false eyelashes. She looked down and saw that she was freshly dressed in a white blouse with balloon sleeves and a loose-fitting houndstooth check skirt. It was an old-fashioned outfit, and the fabric felt weirdly synthetic.

Costume stuff. Looks like the cheap version of Millicent's school uniform.

"Hello?" she called out, looking up at the wan red eye of the camera. "Leonard?"

Looking to the shadowy top of the staircase, Eli remembered the terror and exhilaration of escaping the basement.

How did it end? How did I get back down here?

Does that matter?

She flexed her feet and felt scabs crackle beneath bandages and socks. She stopped that right away.

Don't do it again. For fuck's sake, I can't go through that again.

Eli shivered. Each need was coming awake in its own time. Hunger followed thirst; fear followed pain. Cautiously, she slit her right eye open. Her vision was still cloudy, but the swelling had gone down considerably. She let it stay open, trying to accept the information it was bringing her. It was imperfect, but it was better than nothing.

She heard the sounds that always prefaced his entry to the

basement. The door opened and Leonard came down, bearing a tray.

He had dressed differently than he normally did, she saw. *We're both dressed up. Are we going somewhere?*

He was carrying a tray and she could smell warm food coming.

"Good morning, Millicent." He settled the tray over her lap. It was an old-fashioned TV tray, aluminum with spindly fold-out legs. It sat over her lap with glasses of water and juice, a covered plate that he revealed bore egg whites and toast, and a small bowl with apple slices. "I picked this up the last time I was in town, since I thought we might be needing it. For breakfasts like these."

"Is it morning?" She shoved an apple slice into her mouth and washed it down with juice. The juice had been watered to barely sweet, but the remaining sugar tasted like life itself.

"It is!" He sat in the chair beside the bed. "I like to see you eat something healthy," he said, smiling.

She did not look up at him. She forked egg whites onto the slice of unbuttered wheat toast and made a crude sandwich. She took large bites and swallowed hard. The food tasted like nothing without salt or seasonings or fat, but she could feel precious calories coming up the on-ramp into her bloodstream. She did not speak with her mouth full.

Leonard did not seem to mind. He watched her with amusement and pleasure. She wiped her plate clean, drank the cool water, washing it all down.

"Well?" He smiled as mildly as the mother of a young child.

"Thank you for breakfast." She said it looking at the plate.

"This was my father's favorite breakfast. He would make it for us after we had done our morning exercises. He had real discipline. Not like most people."

Leonard looked away a moment, preoccupied.

He cleared his throat and looked back at her. "I am so pleased you are in a better mood this morning, Millicent. I was really hoping you and I could have a chat."

I'm sitting upright and eating solid food. I'm dressed up like a life-size sex doll, but I'm alive. I can play along. Yes, I can. Yes, I can.

"What would you like to chat about, Leonard?"

He blanched for a second, but his smile stayed on. "So you know that we have met a few times."

"Well, before your shaming and the end of your career, we were something like colleagues. I remember seeing you at conferences, and I think we've emailed a few times. I didn't recognize you at first, but I know who you are."

He looked away for a second, as if he could edit her words as they came to him, and take only what he liked.

"So much is different now," he said, turning his eyes back to her. "I wish I could do it over again. I never took advantage of our connection the way that I should have. I see that. I always hoped to get a moment or two alone with you. To talk about your story and your process. To get to know the real you."

"Me?"

"Yes, you. Millicent Michaelson."

Eli sighed. She dug deep. *The everyday. Not the underneath. Play along.* "Okay. What do you want to know?"

Leonard was rapt. He looked up for a moment and the reflected light made the lenses of his glasses go white.

"How did you get started?"

I have to answer as Millicent, or he's going to get angry. I have to figure out how to talk around myself.

"The author of my story had a much harder life than most of their friends."

Leonard was nodding. "I did—it's true."

Eli gritted her teeth. "So my life started off as a kind of wish fulfillment. What if a small child was orphaned, not because they were unwanted, but because they were special? What if a kid fought their way through public school and the police academy, only to find out they had powers they knew nothing about? My story is really about life getting easier and more interesting as the result of luck and hard work."

Leonard was leaning forward, putting his elbows on his knees. "And then, each story after that—"

"Was another what-if like that, yeah. Wish fulfillment gets old, and that first book wouldn't have worked a second time. So...the author decided to see how far they could push the magical world into mundane law enforcement and vice versa, while still keeping the secret."

"And the author sits down to write, and the ideas just come to me. With you as my muse, I never run out of things to say."

"So as your...muse, what do I do, exactly?"

"Inspire me," Leonard said. His mouth was suddenly loose and sensuous. He was deeply pleasured by this concept. "Whisper the right words in my ear. Read my pages and tell me where I have been brilliant and where I can do better. Excite me with courses of action I have never considered before. Help me outline and plan things."

"I see. And where will we do this work?"

"Right here." He gestured broadly around them.

"In this basement?"

"Well, once you are feeling better, you can move upstairs."

"Into your room?"

He pursed his lips sharply, as if she were spoiling something. He didn't answer. Editing again.

"And why am I wearing blond extensions? And false eyelashes? And this ridiculous outfit?"

Leonard stood and began to amble around the room, not looking at her. "You were not looking your best. You were not comfortable with yourself, so you pretended to be something else. I am helping you be your true self, Millicent. Just like I dreamed you."

"What about you, Lenny? Are you being your true self?"

"That is not my name. Father said nicknames were for sailors and streetwalkers." He looked back at her sharply.

She was starting to lose control. "Do you really wanna have that fight with me? Right now? You won't use my name at all."

He looked away.

I can get him to meet me in another world. I can do this on our shared turf. "Answer me. Is this your true self? If you went with me right now and looked in the Mirror of Kalta that strips all masks away—"

"Do not bring up *The Hand of Fate!*" His voice got high when he yelled, a world away from his impression of the booming FBI agent's call.

"Why not? They're your books, aren't they? Lenny? You are a writer, aren't you?"

"You could never understand. No one understands."

"Explain it to me, then. Try me. As your inspiring little muse."

He walked back over slowly, sinking down into the chair again.

"*The Hand of Fate* was always mine, in a way. The fans are the ones who really own a work of art. It becomes ours the minute it is released. But to write the books themselves... I wanted to cross over from fan to creator, to be the giver and the gifted all at once."

Leonard was lost in his vision, his head tipped back. He looked at her over the twin plateaus of his own cheekbones.

"Do you understand?"

"Sure, every writer has a book they wish they had written.

Like, if I could wake up tomorrow in a world where Agatha Christie had never existed, I would re-create her works from memory." Eli worked hard not to roll her eyes at all this.

He smiled at her. "See, that is exactly it. Bernard Theodore Armour died, and suddenly there was a way. I was his true heir. I knew it in my soul. That was the work I was put on this earth to do."

Eli blanched at the way Lobovich invoked Armour. She hadn't even known Armour had a middle name.

He doesn't have anyone to talk to. It's usually just him out here. Can't get him in fiction, but I can get him in loneliness. He must be lonely, despite how crazy he is. Has to be. Can I use that? Find a way to use that. Wanting is weakness.

"I knew I was chosen by destiny. When Armour died, I knew that was my moment. I could become the author. I could step right into his place. So I worked and worked at my submission until it was perfect. I created a database of every word in the series. I analyzed his sentence structure and copied it exactly. I never deviated once from how he framed each act, and how each chapter ended. But I made certain improvements, as well. I brought my own precision to it. That is the true nature of my art. Purity. Mathematical perfection."

Eli tried to bring him back to his feelings. This had gotten so cerebrally masturbatory. "Did your folks know? When the seventh book debuted on the bestseller list, did they find out? Were they proud?"

Leonard looked at her sharply, as if he had forgotten she was there. "What? No, of course not. They never noticed."

"Why not tell them yourself?" Eli fidgeted, tossing the fake hair out of her eyes. "Didn't you want to make them proud?"

"We were not in touch."

Restraining order? Or just orders from dear old Dad? Fuck, I'm not Freud. What would I do if he told me his tragic childhood? Accept my fate because he had it so hard? Stay in the writing.

"But your success! The money was good, right? You were on top of the world."

"I was one of the best. You know, it is hard for a highly sensitive, creative person to expose their art to that broad an audience. People say cruel, terrible things."

Eli thought of the file she kept for the FBI, just in case. "They say nice things, too. Maybe your family didn't get you, okay. You must have gotten fan mail."

Leonard actually blushed. He leaned forward, putting his hands on the seat of the chair in the V between his thin thighs. "I did. It was wonderful. To be so loved."

Go carefully now. Careful. Find out. But be careful.

"If you had that much going for you, why did you end up plagiarizing? You could have just kept doing your Armour impression until the series was done."

He shook his head slowly, sadly. "I did not plagiarize."

"What?"

He raised both hands out in front of him as if to show her his innocence. "Those were *my* stories. I wrote them. Some of the best ideas I have ever had were in the stories I uploaded to Fic & Fan. Other people with more followers used and rewrote my stories, but when *I* used them, people said they were stolen. They were—from me."

Eli goggled at him, her mouth open. She leaned back against the bed frame and took the strain off her chest. It was a lie— she knew it was a lie. But he believed what he was saying with every fiber of his being.

"But if you wrote and published them first, you'd have the time stamps to prove it. You'd have the evidence on your side. That can be proven."

"I published the evidence. And I sent screenshots to journalists, but they ignored me. Once the internet mob decides you are guilty, you are dead."

Unbidden, Eli felt understanding and pity clamor inside her. Was that true? What would she have done if someone else claimed credit for her work—and her fans believed them? She had seen internet pile-ons in action, of course. She had even participated, adding her voice and her follower count in moments of righteous anger only for a situation to prove more nuanced later. Eli had been on the losing end a few times—over her silence when she won the Supernova, and when someone with enough clout decided to take her to task for not writing more queer characters. She knew it was unfair and inescapable. She knew how Leonard must have felt.

Don't start fucking identifying with him now. Don't you dare. But use it.

"There was so much pressure. Thousands of voices, all screaming at me as if I had committed a murder. You could not possibly imagine. The series had to be good. It had to be perfect. They wrote me letters. You must do this. You must not do that. I used my best, my absolute best material. And it was never enough."

Despite herself, Eli's thoughts flashed to when the director of the *City* movie told her to end the next one on a cliffhanger or the series would die. And when fans had written to her to say the books were too feminist. An equal number wrote to complain that they were not feminist enough. People demanded she include aliens, polyamory, claimed that she was a self-hating queer because she didn't write Millicent queer, too.

Eli wasn't the healthiest, most well-balanced writer in the world. She drank and she pushed people away from her heart, but she could take the garbage in her in-box and contextualize it properly. She knew that to the people who read her work, she was like the blank screen at the front of a movie theater.

She had a starting point and an end point and her physical properties that hardly mattered at all. People who read her books could only see what was projected on her. They were talking to light and shadow, and she was the unknown surface they forgot was there.

But Leonard. Eli didn't know everything, but she was sure that there wasn't enough solidity in his sense of self to take what a frenzied fan base would dish out. When they waved their hands through the air to catch his work in their palms, he would see the black eclipse they cast upon him and think they were holes in himself. He'd never be able to take it. He was already too damaged. When his audience turned on him, he had had no inner reserves upon which to live.

Christ, am I feeling sorry for him?

She knew that it wasn't pity, not exactly. Pity wouldn't make her fear for her own stability; it would keep him beneath her, less than her. She understood him, and that was far more dangerous.

Leonard stood up and ran his hands through his hair. He was talking faster now, licking his lips. He walked, taking his long, stilt-legged strides around the small underground room.

"The publishers wanted it fast, and they wanted to talk about movies and merchandising and all the potential the series had to make money. They had all these questions and contracts and every day they were asking me for something. Deadlines. The deadlines hung over me. The sword of Damocles! I could no longer sleep."

He looked at her suddenly, wounded. He needed reassurance. Instantly and unerringly, she gave it. This was what he had always wanted from her. This was the kinship, the friendship, the collegial intimacy he had made his goal. He wanted to be a writer among writers. It was the only thing Eli had ever wanted, and she knew the shape of that driving desire at the core of her being. This was the only feeling they had in common. She nodded, sympathy on her face.

For one brief moment, they connected. They saw each other whole.

He broke that contact. He went back into himself.

He went on.

"I could not write the book with all that pressing down on me. I sat down to work and nothing would come. I went back to the forums where I had gotten started. I read my best work for inspiration. Those people were my real fans. When they turned on me, I lost everything. I had no credibility. No community. I am a white heterosexual man, the lowest of the low. I had no allies, no identity group to take my side. I had nothing. I had this screaming mob chasing me away from my dream job. I did not deserve this. I had done everything right."

Leonard struck himself in the chest with both fists. They landed so hard that Eli knew there would have to be a bruise there tomorrow. The sound of it was terrible, a drum made of bone hit by bone. She stared up at him, stunned.

Leonard turned again and resumed pacing. "When I posted my proof, the time and date stamps, those tweets and blog posts got less than a tenth of the engagement that the accusation enjoyed. When they did get noticed, people pointed out that time stamps on the archive are easily manipulated. They said I had fabricated that, too. They all wanted a scandal. They wanted a fall from grace. Nobody wanted the truth. They had an agenda—I was convenient."

Eli swallowed and tried to get herself under control. Not to laugh at the absurdity of it.

"You could not possibly imagine that terrible day it all came crashing down. It was like being burned alive. The whole world turned against me and I had no chance to redeem myself. It was all over. *I* was over."

Keep him talking. He's hurting and vulnerable. He needs some-thing. Someone who gets it. Connect. Build a bridge. Find that feel-ing again. Let him know you're listening.

"I... I understand that pressure, Leonard. After I won the Supernova, I had to deal with that. I got death threats and had to lock down my Twitter account. People were mad at me for winning, and other people were mad at me for not making my win more political. I felt like I couldn't do anything right. I couldn't make anybody happy. I had to just... I had to just make myself happy, and ignore most of it."

"I could not ignore it," Leonard said quietly. "It took my career from me. It took everything. It took my sense of self."

Eli looked up at him again. "You can't let anybody in. Not all the way. Not to the center of yourself where you decide whether you're enough or not. You do that and you lose, every time. I had to make that decision a long time ago."

She swallowed, and her mouth tasted like bile. She hated what she was about to say, but she forged ahead.

Fucking get on with it.

"I'm sorry for what happened to you. You didn't deserve that. Your publisher should have helped you out, backed you up. Released a statement of some kind. Or your agent. Or somebody."

"I had nobody," he said sullenly. "I should have had you here with me. You belong with me."

Eli's heart hardened again. "I belong to myself, Leonard. I belong to my work. That's what I'm saying. Yours should belong to you, and it's not too late to fix that. You can have your life back."

"It is too late for that," he said curtly. "Reputation is the easiest thing to ruin and the hardest thing to regain. A man like me does not stand a chance. It is time to become some-one new."

"You don't have to do this," she said, starting to break down. "You can still fix this. I could help you fix this. I've come back from the brink myself. I figured out who I was by diving into my books and holding myself to my own standard. Millicent is good because the pressure comes from within, not from without."

"Pressure comes from within, not from without."

He was staring at her hard, like she was a book he was reading closely to see how the work was done. His inflection was exactly hers, mimicking her voice like he was doing an impression of her. He even adjusted the shape of his mouth to something slightly more feminine.

Eli saw him doing it. She felt the change in the room like a turning of a tide. She had been real to him, for just a moment. Now she was like some gaudy talking doll again. She shivered.

Keep trying. Yes, he's crazy. Yes, he was probably crazy before all this happened. You can't fix that, even if you could help him with all this. Don't give up. Connect.

"I realize your public shaming must have been very hard for you, but you can make something of it. You should start writing again. You could go on the convention circuit and talk about your experience. Set the record straight. Speak up about how terrible this was. Public shaming has become a real topic in the community these last few years. You could even write a book about what you di—what you went through. I could blurb it for you. Nonfiction can be very prestigious."

Her hope was like a sheet of ice over a frozen lake. This was close to what he wanted. Maybe it was close enough.

He stood with his back to her, giving her nothing.

When he spoke again, his voice was perfectly calm. He skated across the ice on heavy feet. He lifted his chin. "That story does not matter. It did not happen to the real me. The real me is a great author and doesn't need blurbs or favors from anyone. Eli Grey is at the height of his career, and he is about to finish his triumphant series."

Eli swallowed hard. The ice was cracking. Cracking.

He turned on his heel and stared back at her, his face haggard. "This is why I need you, Millicent. I need to show them I can do this. This is my destiny. I can be trusted with a series. I can improve and perfect your series. I can keep the work going once the author is gone."

"I'm not gone." Eli said it without thinking. She crashed through the ice and into the black water. "And I'm not Millicent."

Leonard sighed deeply. "I have done so much to help you already. I have tried to free you from a life that makes you unhappy, to show you your true purpose. Is it not time to let someone take care of you?"

That's another line from Captive Prince, *except he tortured it to keep from using the contraction. Disgusting. He never uses them, does he? Why in the fuck does he do that? Purity?*

She struggled fruitlessly against her bindings, trying to get as upright as she could. She felt sapped, despite being fed and mostly sober. Captivity was draining her in ways she couldn't anticipate.

Fuck it. I am so tired and so weirded out and so done.

"Listen, Leonard. Listen to me. This is the awful truth. Nobody gets to be the person they really want to be. Your identity is based on your actions, but also on the way people perceive those actions. Intent is rarely understood. If anybody knows that, it's writers like us."

For one brief second, she thought she saw him wavering. She had almost made a connection, almost made him see her. Then it was gone.

"This is the awful truth." He was mimicking her again. He adjusted his posture, then said it again. "The awful truth."

"Stop doing that! You're not Eli Grey! I am Eli fucking Grey. The one and only." She fumed in defeat and frustration.

"Millicent, honey, you are not making sense." He walked over and picked up her tray. "Do you want to lie down?"

Eli shook her head. Tears were gathering at the corners of her eyes, making them hot. She was still so hungry. And this interaction had gained her almost nothing. Nothing.

Disappointment. The disappointment is worse than anything. Worse than the fear, the boredom. These moments of hope are going to kill me.

"Leonard, I'm dying here. I'm dying slowly. I can't be your muse. I won't live like a caged bird on measured seed. I want my phone. I need to read and I need to write. I have people who care about me, who will be looking for me."

"I have been in touch with them," he said, straightening up. "I let our followers know that we are taking a break."

"What? What are you telling them?" She was surprised how bad that shocked her.

"Our fans want to know why we are not as talkative as usual." He gave her a small smile. "They are desperate to know what happens next. About the wedding."

Eli tried to shake it off. Tried to stop begging. "I have friends, too. And an assistant. People who aren't fans, who know me in real life."

He cooled down in an instant, back to the icy lake. "I know you have friends. I have watched them. I can bring them here, too. If you need me to do that."

"What do you mean?"

He did not warm up, but he looked away from her, looked up as if he were doing hard math in his head.

"A lot of people might not understand what we have. It is an unusual story, how we met and you became my muse. How we corresponded over the years, until you were ready to come to me. How we wrote these books together and decided to pretend they were only by you, because there is such a bias against white men in this business."

"What?" Eli was shaking.

"But it is time we told the truth. I am going to bring someone here, as a test. Someone young and impressionable, a fan. A book blogger. I have her all picked out. She writes wonderful reviews. She loved my *Hand of Fate* books before all the unpleasantness began. And you are going to tell her our whole story. You are going to explain how you have always been a muse to my creative process, that you were Millicent all along. That we have a long love story, beginning with small interactions online and at conventions. That my genius brought you to life and you owe me everything. And that you are finally ready to go public. That you adore me and you could not lie about it anymore."

He was close to her now, close enough that she could see her own scared face in the reflection in his glasses. She was not quite herself there. He looked lovesick. Her stomach had floated away like a helium balloon, only tied to her by a thin ribbon. She couldn't keep the various parts of herself inside her body.

"And if I refuse?"

"Well, we will just keep trying new bloggers until you get it right," he said cheerfully. His voice was quiet, even, maddeningly placid. He turned away from her and walked toward the stairs.

She wanted to scream at him that he would never get away with this. That she would be found, that he had failed at this and would fail again. But how long had it been? How cold was her trail? Was there any chance now that she'd make it out of here alive?

Let him bring someone here. Let him try and tell this story to the world. That might actually get someone to help me. Kidnap some other woman—

The cold, selfish cruelty of the thought broke her cleanly off and she couldn't believe she had thought that. *Who the fuck am I?* She watched his back as he retreated up the stairs.

"Rest well, my darling!"

Before his feet were gone from view, she saw something that took her breath away. Peeking from the back of his right foot, she saw the sewed black-and-yellow tag from her oxfords, the shoes she had been wearing when he kidnapped her.

The son of a bitch is wearing my shoes. Tweeting as me. Emailing god knows who, pretending to be me. Repeating what I say. Becoming Eli Grey.

That's why I'm not dead yet. He doesn't want to kill me. He wants my life. He wants to rewrite reality so that I just hand my life over to him. I'm not going to let him do this to anyone else. I'm not going to let him do this to me. If nobody is coming for me, then this is it. Me and Leonard. I'm going to end this.

Nobody is going to be me but me.

Eli sat up for a long time, thinking. She went back to her closet to write.

24

Joe had been up all night. He was way behind on work for his other clients. He had booked hotels and contacted guest liaisons. He had put together itineraries and fired off twenty-odd cheerful emails. His espresso machine was gummed up when he went back for the fifth cup.

As he passed by his bedroom door, he paused a moment to watch Paul sleeping. Paul had the cutest imaginable sleeping face. His lips pursed and pooched forward like a nursing piglet. His brow was serene and he did not snore, despite his chubby-bear build.

Joe watched him a moment, his head tilted tenderly to the side.

If anything happened to Paul, he did not know how he could stand it.

Paul's jeans lay in a heap on the floor, because adorable though he was, the man was an abject slob. Joe padded into the room in his storm-gray shearling slippers and picked them up. Paul's pack of cigarettes slipped out and hit the floor. Joe shook his head, pocketed the pack and dropped the jeans into the hamper where they belonged.

Back in his office, Joe lit one of those fancy hipster cigarettes and opened one of the broad, crank-operated windows on the back side of the house. He blew a huge cloud of smoke out into the night, both irritated and comforted by the taste and sensation of a lungful of smoke.

He knew a cigarette wouldn't calm him down, but ten years of an old habit sweetly promised otherwise. He had not been able to sleep through the night for the past week. He kept dreaming that Silvestri called him to identify a body.

There's no one else, his dream kept saying. *It's got to be you.*

Joe had gotten ahold of the only real friend he knew Eli had, Nella Atwiler. Nella had been less than helpful.

Over oysters and French vodka—her favorites, he knew— he had brought her up to speed.

Nella's voice was careful, but she was clearly worried. Verging on upset. "Joe. I'm saying this as someone who's known Eli a long time. Have you considered the possibility that she might have killed herself? She's a planner, you know. She might have made arrangements to go somewhere she couldn't be found and just done it. Like an old cat. She would want privacy."

Joe shook his head, raising his glass to the waitress for another drink. "I know the last time you saw her she wasn't in good shape, but she was really doing okay. She was happy about the tour, she wasn't drinking so much and she was really excited about the next book. She said it was going to really surprise people."

Nella sighed. "So, the FBI, huh?"

"Yeah, I'm surprised they haven't come to you. They called her agent, dropped in on her family, you name it."

"Well, she and I haven't spoken in a while." Nella looked down at the empty shells resting on crushed ice on her plate. She toyed with a lemon wedge. "I'm not even sure I was in her phone."

"Oh? What happened?"

Nella took a drink and patted her head wrap. "It was work shit. We both got dragged into one of those Twitter fights and I think we were actually on the same side, but it was ugly. It didn't end well. I was planning to call her up soon and take her to tea. You know how she loved that fancy tearoom in the city."

Joe, who knew everything about Eli's taste, just nodded. "Please don't use the past tense," he said gently. "We're not there yet."

Nella shook it off. "Anyway, I'm not saying I was wrong, but I missed her. I was willing to just bury it. Now I feel like a perfect ass that the last thing we did was fight."

"Don't say *last*," Joe said quickly. "Please don't."

They sat in silence a moment. Fresh drinks appeared on the table. Nella sipped.

"Anyhow, I wanted to ask you if you know anybody who had it in for Eli. You did a lot of events and cons with her. Did you ever see her around a creepy guy?"

Nella slurped another oyster and shrugged her shoulders. "She had a couple dudes who tweeted at her now and again. Reply guys. Sometimes they'd say creepy stuff, but that's just an occupational hazard."

Joe thought of the file he had passed on to the FBI. "Nobody in particular, though, right? Like, no ringleader, no standout?"

"I mean, all those guys have a dozen sock puppet accounts." Nella sounded morose as she turned her big brown eyes to her next drink.

"I want to show you something."

Joe pulled out his phone and showed Nella the two Instagram posts. He outlined the reflection of the faceless man with the tip of his finger.

"Weird, right?"

"Very." Nella's full lips had settled into a hard line. "Does the FBI have all this?"

"Yeah, they do. And there's these tweets now that are coming from her account..."

Nella looked at him funny. "The ones that don't sound like her at all?"

"Thank you!" Joe exclaimed with relief. "Why is that such a hard concept?"

"I was thinking that she'd handed the account over to you," Nella said frankly.

"God, I could do a better job than that."

Nella nodded and sipped cold liquor.

"So yesterday, Mickey forwards me this email." Joe pulled up the app and showed Nella the email that had come from Eli's agent.

TO: mgriffin@pgr.com
FROM: eligrey@maginaria.com

Good morning,
I am just touching base with you about Book 8. I was not sure if you had had the chance to review it, or if you had any notes. If you do not mind, could you reply in-line on any changes you would like to make and send it back to me? I am in the middle of rewrites and I want to keep different versions straight.
Sincerely,
Eli Grey

Nella frowned at the screen. "That's not Eli. That's somebody who's never even *seen* an email from Eli."

"Right? And she hates in-line comments. It's almost like someone is trying to trick Mickey into giving them the next book."

"So Mickey sent this to the police, right?"

"Of course! Mickey's no fool. And she's very protective of her fifteen percent, even if she and Eli aren't best buddies."

Nella scanned the email again. "I mean, this is just sloppy. They could have looked at her sent folder, if they have this much access. They'd see that she always just signs as 'E.'"

"She wouldn't call it 'Book 8,' either. Something is seriously weird here. If you get anything from Eli before she's back—"

"I'll go straight to the cops with it," Nella finished. "Oh shit, I hope she's still alive."

Joe had given her Silvestri's direct number. He gave it out to anyone he thought might be able to help. He didn't care if the agent's phone blew up nonstop. He needed to feel like he was helping.

Keeping his exhalations close to his office window, Joe smoked the cigarette down to the filter and looked at the last one in the pack. He knew that two might make him throw up, since he'd been cold turkey for four years now. He was on the verge of doing it anyway when an email came in.

He sat down at his computer and was shocked to see that it was just after six in the morning. He really had gone all night.

Joe tapped on the tab where his email always sat, on the far left side of his browser. He stared.

TO: *j.papasian@gmail.com*
FROM: *eligrey@maginaria.com*
RE: *Help: Joe, I messed up.*

Dear Joe,
I hate to bother you with this, but I cannot seem to find my clean copy of Book 8. It is not in my Dropbox or in Drive. I am worried that I may have deleted it while I was drunk or something. Can you help me figure out where it is, or share the file with me if you have it? I know it is out there somewhere. Thank you,
Eli Grey

Joe almost laughed out loud. It wasn't a terrible impression of Eli, but it was as if someone had written it based on Eli's books rather than any kind of personal relationship. Eli never apologized like this for asking Joe to do his job. She never admitted to fucking up while drunk, and she never signed her full name with him. She rarely included a subject line at all. The whole thing was formal, stilted, bizarre. It was absolutely not her.

Most of all the idea that Eli could ever lose hold of something she had written. Eli had a bracelet made after the second Millicent book had sold. It concealed a tiny USB key of rather enormous capacity. On it, Eli had a copy of everything she had ever written. She would never lose her work, she told him and only him. Nobody else could ever know, and it was Joe's job to retrieve it if she were to die or become incapacitated.

"There's no such thing as the cloud, Joe. It's just someone else's computer."

The bracelet was an ingenious and elegant piece of engineering. It didn't reveal itself when it opened; it took springing a secondary catch to show the drive itself. He had laughed and called it spy shit.

She had looked very seriously at him. "The only thing that matters is being able to put your hands on what's yours," she had told him. "My work is the only thing I have that can't be taken from me."

"Hey, that's not true."

Eli had smiled at him in that way that she had when she knew he was wrong, but wasn't going to say it.

"That's not you," Joe said to his computer. He was full into the jitters now, murmuring out loud. "Let me count the ways that's not you. You don't get up at six in the morning. You don't ever apologize for bothering me, because I fucking work for you. You don't number your books. You don't lose track of your shit. You don't sign your name. That's not fucking you. Fuck."

He sat back in his chair and lit that second cigarette.

After a minute, the muttering and the smoke brought Paul.

"What is it now?" Paul asked, yawning through the words.

"Look at this shit."

Paul bent over and read the short email. "That's not your boss, right?"

"Right!" Joe bit the filter of his cigarette and then hit Forward. "I gotta send this to Silvestri."

"Nah, fuck that. Answer it."

Joe turned in his chair and looked up at Paul. He had pillow creases on the side of his face and his hair was tousled, but his eyes were absolutely clear.

"What do you mean?"

Paul thought a moment. "Tell him you only have the printed copy that she gave you to copyedit. Say you can overnight it, you just need an address."

"There's no way that will work," Joe breathed.

Paul shrugged with one shoulder. "Worst thing that will happen is he won't answer. You can still forward it."

Joe bit his lower lip a moment. Then he began to type.

TO: *eligrey@maginaria.com*
FROM: *j.papasian@gmail.com*

Dear Eli,
It's such a relief to hear from you! I was getting pretty worried.
So, I still have the paper copy that I copyedited for you. I can overnight that to you if you send me an address.
Thanks!
Joe

He hit Send and sat there a moment, deciding whether he should call Silvestri or just forward this chain along.

The response came immediately.

TO: *j.papasian@gmail.com*
FROM: *eligrey@maginaria.com*

Joe,
That is perfect. Will you scan it and email as PDF?
Eli

"Shit," Joe said, sitting back.

"I didn't think of that," said Paul from just over his shoulder.

"I should have," Joe grumbled.

He spread his hands over the keyboard again.

TO: *eligrey@maginaria.com*
FROM: *j.papasian@gmail.com*

Sure thing. My scanner is dead, though. I'm going to have to
wait for a printshop to open.
Joe

Joe pulled out his phone and searched his recent call history. He didn't need to go far; nine out of ten of his recent calls had been to or from Silvestri.

Silvestri was not thrilled that her phone was ringing so early, but she perked up at what Joe was telling her. Cyber-crimes had told her that these emails were coming from behind a proxy server, but that the guy doing it was no wizard. A few more and they'd have him.

"You answered the email?"

"Yeah," Joe said, sounding sheepish. "I thought I might be able to get more info if I was prompt."

Silvestri read the whole exchange. "So he's expecting something from you...what, after nine?"

"Yeah, that's kinda what I was hinting at."

"Do you have this book he's after?"

"I don't, but Eli's agent does. Mickey Griffin. She's been in touch."

"Yes, she has," Silvestri said, sliding out of bed. "Alright. Don't send any additional emails. Don't do anything at all until you hear from me. Alright?"

"Alright." Joe nodded at the phone as if she could see him.

Silvestri called Mickey Griffin. The agent picked right up.

"Ms. Griffin, I need to come to your office with a few other agents and we're going to have to manage something awfully delicate."

"Of course," Mickey said. "Whatever I can do."

Silvestri arrived at the downtown agency in its art deco building that had long since gone to seed. She gritted her teeth when she saw the news van outside. She had her badge on her belt and knew that her gun was obvious inside her unbuttoned blazer. The other two field agents wore FBI windbreakers against the San Francisco fog, but still wore their habitual sunglasses. They looked like a walking pair of stereotypes.

"Agent Silvestri! Do you have any leads in the case of this missing writer?"

Silvestri put her right hand up before her face and shouldered her way toward the building. Her flanking agents did the same.

They rose in the brass elevator in silence. The receptionist pointed them toward a deep corner office. When they came through the door, Mickey was talking to a redheaded journalist who had her recorder out on the desk.

"Ms. Griffin, I'm afraid you're going to have to cut this short. We don't have any time to lose."

The journalist was keen. "Let me get out of your way." She picked up her recorder and retreated to a corner without turning it off.

"Out," Silvestri ordered. "We're in the middle of an investigation."

The redhead sulked to herself, but she cleared out.

Mickey was apologetic, but still smiling. "You have to understand, I'm very concerned about Eli. But I also have to manage her brand, no matter what happens."

Silvestri ignored her. "Katsopolis, set up here on the desk. Wright, you're on the door."

The two agents moved as if they were one body. Katsopolis, the tall, dark-haired cybercrimes agent, began to connect his equipment to Griffin's Mac. Griffin stepped back.

"What are you going to do?" Her smile was faltering, as though she were just realizing that this was serious.

Silvestri squared off, facing Griffin. "I want you to transmit the file that Eli is asking for, to her email. But first we're going to break it into a couple of pieces and attach some of our own code so that when it gets opened, we can find the person who's receiving that email."

Griffin nodded vigorously.

Silvestri reached out and put a hand on the older woman's shoulder. "I won't tell you not to talk to the press, Ms. Griffin, but I can tell you that you cannot discuss our particular methods of finding this guy. We don't want him finding out on the news. He'd probably panic and kill her. Do you understand what I'm telling you?"

Griffin looked progressively more and more rattled. She pushed her perfect platinum-gray hair behind her ears. "She really was kidnapped, then? I thought she had just gone off the grid. She's kind of…eccentric like that."

"We believe someone is holding her against her will. That person is also pretending to be her, in a couple of different ways. And so far, the only thing that someone has told us they want is this book. So we're going to bait the hook with that."

"Okay. Okay, sure, okay." Silvestri saw that Griffin's hands were shaking.

Katsopolis spoke up a minute later. "Where's the file on your computer?"

Griffin led him through it verbally. Though it was her computer and her office, she didn't seem comfortable trying to take control of it from him.

There were a few minutes of silence punctuated by furious typing. Katsopolis pulled out his FBI laptop: a brick with hard corners that looked armor-plated. He woke it up with his fingerprint and pulled up a satellite map of the US.

"It's away," he said curtly.

"How long will it take?" Silvestri asked.

"Depends on how eager this guy is to open the file." Katsopolis raised both of his bushy eyebrows as he looked at his screen. "Like, say for example he opens all three packets immediately and I get a lock on him."

On the brick's screen, a red dot appeared on the map. Katsopolis switched to satellite view and saw a small house in Los Angeles.

"That's where the assistant said her last gig was," Silvestri said, gathering up to leave. "He was right. Ms. Griffin, we'll be in touch."

The three agents hustled out and impatiently rode the elevator back down to the street. They ignored the press. They jumped into their illegally parked SUV and fought their way to the freeway. By the time they reached the airport, Silvestri's flight was boarding and the LA field office was on their way. She planned to meet them around nightfall. For a moment, she allowed herself some happy anticipation of showing the writer on some local LA news channel, wrapped in a blanket but glad to be alive. Then, she slept with her head against the cool glass of the window.

★ ★ ★

The LA field office sent ten men by two SUVs to the location that Katsopolis had pinpointed as the address where the files were downloaded. Easy peasy, neat as a pin. The agents were mostly silent. The rate of gun ownership in the city led them to expect a firefight. They shifted beneath their Kevlar as the vehicles rolled across the broken, sunbaked streets of the city. The sky above them was flat, heavy and more white than blue.

The address they'd been given belonged to a small white house. There was no car in the driveway, no mailbox on the curb. Agents swarmed silently around the sides and back of the house. They posted at windows and the back door. They listened. They waited.

The doorbell rang and rang. Two men with a battering ram broke the door down and the FBI swarmed in.

The house was carefully, even precisely arranged. Every piece of furniture, every frame on the walls was at a crisp ninety-degree angle to everything else. Agents stalked around the islands of coffee table and footstool, touching nothing. As they passed, a thick layer of dust puffed into the air and trailed in their wake. One by one, agents cleared the living room, the attic, the bedrooms, the kitchen. No one was home. No one had been home for some time.

By its sound, one of them found a bank of servers running in what should have been the water heater closet.

Leonard Lobovich was able to access his servers remotely. The program was slow, but reliable. He had managed to retrieve two of the files and was working on the third. He smiled gleefully at his monitor as he watched the progress bar. He was so close. He almost had the entire Millicent book in his hands.

An FBI agent gloved up, miles away, and unplugged the server bank from the wall. Lobovich's final download failed and the file was corrupted.

Eli could hear him wailing above her head.

By the time Silvestri made it to LA, the field agents were back in their office. They had lifted a few partial prints from one of the power cords in the server stack. Everything else had been wiped clean.

Silvestri stood in the small office, staring at the tacky faux wood paneling on the walls. She couldn't believe they had been faked out by this guy. Katsopolis had been sure he was correct, probably because it had rung back a residential address.

She sat heavily in a chair, rewriting her part in all this. No rescue. No touching moment on the local news. No catching a kidnapper. At this point, she may have to catch a murderer instead.

"There are two possible matches in the system on this print," the local agent was tapping his screen, leaving his own prints in grease. "One matches a guy currently in lockup in Chino for arson. The other is from an unsolved sexual assault case in Seattle."

"Link me the SA case file," Silvestri said.

She read over it quickly. A twenty-six-year-old Caucasian female had been drugged and raped at a hotel over a convention weekend back in 2017. The victim had showered thoroughly upon waking, and had contacted law enforcement too late. Hotel staff had changed the room and no DNA evidence was collected. Victim stated that the perpetrator had handled her cell phone. Prints revealed hers and one other, assumed to be the perpetrator. No match in the system.

Victim drank in hotel bar from 1700–2200 with a large crowd from the event. Suspected she had been drugged around 2145 and began to tell people good-night. Victim admits she may have just been very inebriated. Credit card slip showed nine alcoholic beverages on her tab. Victim reached hotel room door around 2150. States adult white male, approximately six foot seven inches, slight build with glasses, met her there and pushed his way inside. Victim has partial memory of sexual assault. Physical exam shows vaginal and anal abrasion and tearing.

Victim awoke around 0930 unclothed. Immediately showered and allowed hotel staff to change bedding. Called local law enforcement at 1310. Victim gave full statement. Hotel and convention liaison cooperated fully. Attacker's description matched several participants, including a number in costume with lifts.

Just like the guy on the hotel security tape from that desert hotel. Tall, thin, glasses. Same guy?

Silvestri clicked away from the report to examine the attached documents. Photos of tearing and bruises came up first, making her face twist up and away, though her eyes kept doing their job. Photos of the victim's face reminded her of something, though she couldn't say what.

The attached list of individuals matching the victim's description who had been questioned was short, she was glad to see. None of them had a record or a warrant. Each of them had an alibi for the time of the assault.

Silvestri scanned down the list until her eye caught on one. Leonard Lobovich, age thirty-one. Occupation: writer. Residence: California City, CA.

She clicked back to the victim's tired face, soft with exhaustion and washed-out with shock.

What was it about her? She doesn't look like Eli Grey.

In another tab, Silvestri image-searched Eli Grey. Photos of the author came up immediately, from dust-jacket photos to convention shots.

One drew her. It was Grey helping a woman out of a limousine onto some red carpet somewhere. The woman stepping out onto the carpet was a stunner, blond hair and green eyes that were hard to forget. The photo identified her as Alice Stample, star of the Millicent Michaelson film series, age twenty-four. Silvestri recognized her, but something else was coming together. The pieces were connecting.

Silvestri clicked back over. It wasn't the same woman, but it was damned close. The assault victim could have signed up for a look-alike contest. She paged back to the vital stats on the victim and saw that her eyes were listed as blue in one place and green in another.

Agent Silvestri bit her lips savagely while hunches began to coalesce into a certainty. *No ransom demand. No body. Someone so obsessed that they'd know where to find Eli Grey, where she'd be most vulnerable to capture. Somebody who's done this before.*

I looked for someone stalking the actress, but I didn't think to look at cosplayers. I wonder if we document a pattern in that—what if a perp always stalks or assaults women playing the same character? It's not even in the report that she was dressed up as Millicent.

Silvestri did not live or work in fandom. This case had brought her to the edge of subcultures she hadn't dreamed existed. She wondered dully whether there might be a serial killer on the loose who only killed women dressed as Princess Leia. If they were all from different cities, different races and different jobs, would he ever get caught?

She looked over the page of images from her Google search again. There were people in costume from Grey's books, girls and women of all ages. There was fan art and fan fiction and suddenly it all looked like obsession.

"Hey, do you guys know a town called California City?" she asked the locals.

An agent in a Patagonia vest looked up. "Yeah, I know it. It's real weird. Half-built. Middle of nowhere, out in the desert."

"How long to get there?"

The agent looked up at the ceiling. "Couple of hours, by the freeway."

"Shit. Okay," Silvestri said, sitting back down. She hadn't even known she had stood up until this moment. She put Leonard Lobovich's name into the computer. She had his address, his license plate number and his Social Security number. He had no priors. He didn't own the house in LA where his servers were running, but he might have been renting it.

She returned to the tab with Alice Stample grinning in it, and took a quick look at Eli Grey again. She clicked a few links until the page showed cosplayers from different series grouped together, their arms around each other. Prince Vantan locked arm in arm with Millicent Michaelson. Leonard Lobovich and Eli Grey. There were no pictures of the authors together, but they certainly had fans in common.

Silvestri told the agent she needed a new warrant. "And get the squad to head back out."

I'm coming. I'll be there soon. Hold on.

In the search bar on her phone's browser, Silvestri typed "Leonard Lobovich author." She began to catch up.

25

When Eli heard Leonard wailing, she had a momentary spike of hope. The police were out on the dirt lawn. He had dropped a steak knife in his foot. He had realized what a terrible mistake he had made and that he should drop her off at an emergency room and run like hell.

Hope is the thing with feathers, so it also has hollow bones that are easy to crush. It's nobody. It's nothing. It's his crazy brain. Anything could make him crazier. Don't give it meaning. Don't hope.

She was out of her closet. She was still sitting up. The ties felt slack so she worked against them. Her hands and feet were still cuffed, but she could at least make some room for her body. She shimmied hard to the right, then twisted back to the left. The resulting roominess felt almost luxurious by comparison.

Joe never even called the cops. My agent didn't do shit. I ignore them both for days at a time—why wouldn't they just accept this? Nobody reported me missing. No girlfriend. No close friends. My empty apartment. My rent gets drawn automatically. I'm all I've got.

This is it. I'm out of time. I'm going to die here if I don't find a way to kill this guy myself.

On the other side of Leonard was the problem of escape. If there wasn't a way out, she'd burn the house down. That would bring someone. Probably.

One thing at a time. I have to get out of this bed.

Her stomach growled and she growled back at it. Eli flopped her blond extensions away from her face by tossing her head back.

If I get a hand free, I am ripping these fucking things out. I don't care how much it hurts.

But just thinking of pain made her quail and remember the prod in her eye, the rod on her feet.

It's different if I do it to myself, she thought stubbornly. *It's different if I'm in control.*

Leonard couldn't stop himself from reading the whole thing up to the point of the lost file. He sat hunched over Eli's laptop for hours, scrolling through the finished manuscript. Millicent's wedding to her on-again, off-again magical love interest, Marcel, had been just as beautiful as he had dreamed it. Their lovemaking was all the more special because the sorceress's curse had made them wait until their vows had been said. But Eldivar's forces had struck the Maginaria just as the honeymoon was getting started. All magical law enforcement was called to defend their ancient stronghold against the cartel and keep them from stealing the last Tear of Ymir: the source of all the magic left in the twin worlds.

Leonard sat weeping over the deaths of Madame Olitti, Millicent's own teacher, as well as Ganji and Hak, the archers of truth. Beloved minor characters were slaughtered left and right and Leonard thought his heart could take no more. He knew he was close to the end of what he had, but he couldn't stop himself. He couldn't even slow down.

Millicent had Eldivar right where she wanted him, and he knew it. His red mustache quivered with fury as she pinned him to the great black stone columns of the Maginaria with a powerful magic she had never used before. It simply coursed through her, making his efforts to escape seem utterly pitiful.

"You killed my mistress. You killed my parents." Millicent spoke with a voice that threatened tears, here at last with the power to end the greatest villain of her time, as well as her own life. "You're going to the Barge of the Infinite for what you've done. You'll suffer eternally, just as you deserve."

"I...didn't..." Eldivar's breath was shallow. A trickle of blood came from the corner of his mouth.

"What?" Millicent stepped closer, subconsciously easing the pressure on his rib cage.

"I didn't kill your parents," he hissed, his black eyes opening a tiny bit to reveal a sadistic gleam. "I took the credit, oh yes. But they were just killed by random chance. Their deaths meant nothing. No death means anything. There are only two things to be in this life, young witch. The eater. Or the eaten."

Eldivar raised one hand and drew it down slowly, majestically.

Millicent looked over her shoulder and saw gray jaws made of cloud and nothingness envelop Marcel just behind her. She had no chance to say goodbye. She saw his feet last, still in his shiny wedding shoes.

She turned with sudden savagery to Eldivar. She put the flat of her powerful left hand against his chest.

This is what he wants, you know. Don't kill him. Prolong his suffering. Don't give in and end it for him.

But her rational mind was gone. Blind fury took her for its instrument. With one hard exhaled breath and all her chi, she obliterated his heart. Eldivar sagged to the floor, no longer a villain. Just another dead man among the ruins.

Millicent walked calmly to the breached sacred chamber. She laid her hands upon the Tear of Ymir and gently took it to her breast.

"Now," she said. "Now, we begin again."

Leonard gasped out loud when he realized he had reached the end of what he had. He stood up and paced the room, talking to himself.

"The only person who can touch the Tear of Ymir is the mother of the Whisper King. But Millicent doesn't even believe! And even if she did, she couldn't be… I mean, she could be perhaps a few hours pregnant? I guess?"

He ran his hands through his hair, then reached for the comfort of a pen. Not his grail pen, but the one he thought of as the most sensitive. It was carved from rosewood, red as a heart in a butcher's window. He uncapped it and capped it again, his long fingers pulling the trick with one hand. He thought about the best ink to sign a legal document with, then pulled open his inks drawer. The neat, orderly bottles stood like soldiers for inspection, presenting their magical names. Diamine, diopside, dragon's blood. Marine, magenta, midnight. He thought about writing his new name in one of those sumptuous inks with the sheen that glowed gold when it dried. Leonard was pleased and soothed, picturing the way that good ink sank into proper paper, not feathering, not spreading. Indelible, how he loved the word *indelible*.

His mouth formed the word again, lingual and liquid, bilabial and buxom, as he glanced over at the closed door of the guest bedroom. The surprise was almost ready, but now that he had read most of the book, he could finish it. It was almost time.

★ ★ ★

Silvestri had her warrant and the same group of agents was in a van, barreling into the California desert. She watched the fields of wind turbines slide by outside the window. The same battering ram lay on the floor at her feet. The air in the vehicle was electric.

She hoped it could be done in time to save Eli Grey, if she was still alive.

Silvestri, unable to sit still at all, kept reading the details of Lobovich's fall from grace and Eli Grey's simultaneous ascension to fame. This case unsettled her. She was unprepared for the enormity of the drama behind it; the years of industry gossip and connections to larger social movements. She had heard about details like these becoming relevant in celebrity stalking cases and industrial espionage before. She typically worked cases of kidnapping, human trafficking and other forms of sexual violence. She was accustomed to the ways in which money became power became sex, and the human depravity that followed that evolution. It came to her all at once that the same was true of this case, of Eli Grey and Leonard Lobovich. This was the same old story of money, sex and power. But the power aspect was complicated. There was an entire underworld to these fandoms, each bearing its own current of political intrigue, professional jealousy and public shaming.

Gradually, Silvestri came to understand how insular and particular this case really was. She had worked on cases that involved professional athletes and drug kingpins; the FBI often brought in consultants on these specialized, byzantine worlds in order to decode the cultural nuance required to understand them. She had realized too late that she should have had the same kind of help here. Joe Papasian had held the key to all this, and if she had listened to him she might have gotten to Grey sooner. His haste and understanding might have made the difference between her being found alive and her skin being tanned on the side of some barn out in the desert.

Silvestri needed Grey to be alive. She was invested, sure. But she was also worried that she was catastrophically late and only dimly aware of what kind of case this really was. She was agitated, not only because Grey was in mortal danger, but also because she knew all at once that this case could ruin her career.

I should have called in more help. I should have known that wasn't her on the phone. I should have tracked all this down days ago. How much faster could I have caught on if I had taken Papasian at his word? How much sooner could I have gotten her out?

She put her phone down and prodded the driver again. "How much longer?"

"About another hour."

Outside the van, the wind blew sandy dirt in whirling dervishes. The expanse of nothingness out there made Silvestri's mouth run dry.

Eli awoke as Leonard came ambling long-legged down the stairs. His face was puffy, his eyes red.

"Leonard, what's wrong? I heard crying or yelling earlier. What happened?"

"Our book…" He sniffled, collecting himself. "Our book is beautiful. I am so, so glad we are doing this together."

"What book?"

"The Siege of Maginaria," he said, his voice full of wonder.

Icy terror took her. "How do you know that's the title?"

He smiled beatifically at her. "Our agent sent it to me. There was a minor mix-up and I have not read the ending yet. But I know what is going to happen, my dear. I always knew Millicent had a greater role to play in the history of the magical world than just a constable's legacy. I am so excited you're on your way to your greatest adventure. Motherhood." His voice broke on the final word.

"Leonard, wait." The whole room wavered in her view. "You haven't read the ending. You don't—"

He closed the gap between them with one long step and plunged the needle into her biceps, barely looking down.

"Millicent, my love."

His voice carried her down into the deep. There was no fight. There was nowhere for her to go. It was over too fast.

Leonard had made everything absolutely perfect upstairs. It was time to prepare her for the special room.

Eli came to only halfway, her vital defenses at war with another massive dose of drugs. Her heart was pounding so hard that it knocked her teeth together.

The sensation was familiar and yet alarming. She was in her body and not quite of it. She could not move at all, not confident that she could scream if she wanted to. This was much worse than sleep paralysis as she had known it. She swam in a thick river of consciousness, unable to draw a deep breath despite insistent, circulatory panic.

The duckbill of a speculum slid slowly into her vagina. It had been carefully lubricated with something thick and oily, but its shape and cold intrusion was unmistakable. She could not gasp or cry out. She could not lift a finger.

The jaws of it spread apart methodically, the metal warming incrementally against her insides. It cranked to its widest and cold air snaked its way into her; a robber in a vault. She could not open her eyes.

Eli had had an IUD for eight years. She got it while she was still occasionally having sex with men, and had kept it just in case. She remembered having the last one removed. The nau-

seating twang as it passed the nerves in her cervix. The tor-
turous look of the ring forceps used to pull it out.

She pictured that tool now, long steel beak in the long,
gloved fingers of Leonard Lobovich. She couldn't even shiver.
She tried to scream and only puffed air out of her nose.

The pain was just as intense as it had been last time. It sent
signals that cramped her gut and panicked her brain. Her
whole body flinched.

Leonard laid a latex-clad hand against her right thigh and
whispered, "Shh, darling."

Once he had it out, he closed the speculum. Eli could feel
the dry tackiness of her vaginal walls, unused to the long exposure to the air. Leonard was gone a minute, disposing of
his tools. When he returned, she realized she was no longer
cuffed down because he lifted her out of bed with one arm
behind her shoulders and the other behind her knees.

Now! If I can just get my hands around his neck now!

But her hands dangled limply at the ends of her cooked-
spaghetti arms. Her abs were a slack sea where nothing lived.
No muscle group in her body would obey her command, not
even her eyelids.

Desperate, the spark of her consciousness left her body behind and fled to the closet in the basement.

It was raining there, raining as it had never done before.
The floor squelched beneath her feet. Her oil lamp would
not light. She perched on the edge of a shelf in the darkness,
smelling the plaster. She reached for her notebook and found
it by feel. She found her pen and scratched out unseen words.

Leonard laid her body in the bathtub, full again of warm
water.

*Eli Grey was secretly a mermaid. She shrank herself using her
mermaid magic and swam down through the tiny holes in the drain.*

The pipes took her to the river. The river took her to the ocean. On the back of a tuna, she rode south.

He shaved her legs and pubis again. He lifted each arm on to his shoulder and shaved her armpits, as well.

Eli's communicator lit up in her leather satchel. The ship was in a low synchronous orbit, searching for her signal. Once they had a lock on her, they beamed her out immediately. She was wet and disoriented, but Sick Bay was able to sort her out immediately.

He rubbed her down with a distinct-smelling soap, gently lathering her neck, her breasts, her belly. The old-lady reek of it filled her nostrils. She knew if she vomited she'd die. She had no way to stop it.

Eli shot suddenly out of the bathtub, through the roof and straight into space. She shed her mortal body and became a star-wraith. She never thought about life on earth again.

Leonard's hand, now ungloved, cupped her freshly shaved sex with a filmy slip of soap between his skin and hers. He rubbed sensuously, sliding over and over the mound, but avoiding the cleft.

"You are so beautiful, Millicent. You are going to be perfect. We are going to be very happy."

Her head slipped backward and banged the heavy enamel at the back of the tub. Stars exploded behind her eyes and she hoped death would follow. But it was just a bump.

"Oh, oh, oh, oh, oh," he said solicitously as a father whose toddler has taken a tumble. "Careful, baby, careful."

He scrubbed her hands and feet. The soles of her feet were not fully healed and they tingled and stung throughout this operation. She could make no sound. He carefully combed out her hair and extensions. He lifted her out of the tub and laid her down on towels he had spread across the floor.

This isn't happening, she wrote in some other world. *Eli Grey is free. Nothing is happening to her right now. This is not happening. I am in my closet and all is right with the world.*

Leonard leaned down and lightly kissed a spot just below her navel once she was dry.

"That was naughty of me. Well, soon enough it will all be okay."

Nausea threatened, then rolled away. She was adrift, unable to hold on to anything. Even her horror.

He lifted her again, this time in a fireman's carry. Eli felt blood rush into her face as she hung limp as a ragdoll down Leonard's back.

Drag you down the stairs and break your neck.

But she could do nothing.

Upstairs, another room unseen until now. Leonard slowly dressed her lifeless body, starting with lacy-feeling underwear. He wrapped his arms around her to get her into a strapless bra. His neck was just beside hers.

Turn your head and bite him. Bite and never let go. Drain him like a bloodsucker.

But she could do nothing.

A long, synthetic-feeling dress came next, tugged up over her hips and below her armpits. Arms around her back again as he zipped her up.

She fogged out, blessedly unaware for twenty minutes or so. There was nothingness within while ruin carried on. Without, Leonard was tenderly applying her makeup and pinning her extensions into a rough but lovely updo.

He clasped her Maginaria pendant around her neck and slipped tiny diamond studs into her ears.

"A surprise for you, my love," he whispered as he bestowed these gifts. "To celebrate new beginnings. Now, we begin again."

Silvestri and the van full of men had reached the edge of California City. The GPS had failed and someone whose phone still had reception was attempting to navigate them. One field agent had a *Thomas Guide*, but the streets on the map didn't match up. They cruised up and down streets that had two or four houses spread out sparsely against the backdrop of nothing. They rolled on to the unpaved streets. The satellite lost them and searched, lost them and searched.

Eli's nose twitched. That brought her more into herself than any other input. It was involuntary movement, but movement still. She was dizzy and could open her eyes only to slits. The light she could see was warm and yellow, and radiated long spikes across her vision. Her false eyelashes made this effect far worse.

The floor seemed very far away. She realized she must be upright, but she didn't know how that was possible. As she came further into herself, she sensed she was tied to something rigid that was holding her up. Even her head was strapped to it.

Leonard was standing before her, dipping his head to meet her eyeline nearly a foot below his.

"Millicent? Are you with me, darling?"

"What?" Her mouth felt gummy. She could barely get the word out.

Leonard put a straw in her mouth and used it like a dropper, putting his finger to the end and depositing cold water. The reflex to swallow was sluggish, barely enough to keep her from drowning.

As she forced her eyes open farther, she saw that the room was full of people. Startled, she tried to look around but found that she could not move her head.

"Do not tax yourself now," he said softly. "Be careful."

"Help me," she whispered to a face to her right. It looked familiar. She strained to see it more fully and realized that it was Reina Orbach, the actress who played Madame Olitti in the first Millicent film.

From her limited vantage point, Eli could finally make out that the room was crammed with cardboard cutouts of the actors from her movie. Some were in costumes from completely different films. One or two were old and faded, as if they had sat in some video rental's window years ago, watching the sun come and go.

They were smiling on three sides, lining the walls of the room.

Shelob. You're in the web of Shelob.

The carpet was strewed with white bits of what might be paper. Looking down, Eli saw her own bare feet on the metal bottom of a tall, sturdy appliance dolly. She saw the hem of her white dress. She saw Leonard's crab knees, slicing through the air as he pushed the dolly and tried to crowd close to her while he did it.

"Darling, the time has come." She could sense him coming around to face her.

Eli had to work hard to look up at Leonard. Everything swam in her vision as she moved her eyes, leaving smeared trails of color like she had dragged it all through wet paint. Her eyes wanted to close again. Even the smallest effort felt exhausting and her stomach roiled angrily, emptily. It took her a moment to settle and focus on him. When she did her shock was near total.

He was wearing her clothes. That was her tailored white shirt, straining to contain his much broader chest, failing to cover his knobby wrists. That was her blazer, open and clearly tight across his shoulders. Her black pants couldn't have begun to fit him; he had opted for a pair of his own. But those were her oxfords again, shone like black mirrors.

He had styled his hair to look as hers had on the day that he kidnapped her: shaved on one side and combed over long to the other. She saw that he had used pomade of some kind, probably hers, and that he had darkened his hair, as well. He was clean-shaven.

"What in the hell?" Her words were badly slurred. The room swam, faces swinging past like streetlamps when she drove in the rain. She struggled to get a deep breath. Leonard was behind her, pushing the dolly to the far wall of the room. The dizziness in movement was unbearable.

There was an arch there, an absurd white-wicker affair woven with artificial white flowers and greenery. A tablet stood at Eli's eye level, zip-tied to the head of a cutout dressed like a Catholic priest.

Leonard circled around to face Eli before the cardboard priest. He tapped the screen a couple times, then turned to face her. Incredibly, he reached out to take her hand, though it was strapped to her body. Awkwardly, he held the outside of it with the tips of his fingers.

"Dearly beloved," the tablet said in the voice of some movie actor Eli could not place. "We are gathered here together to witness the marriage of—"

Here the voice cut out and Leonard's bad dubbing cut in. He had recorded it with his mouth too close to the microphone so that it distorted, booming and breathy in the midst of a well-mixed soundtrack.

"Eli Grey," his voice said.

"And," the priest said.

"Millicent Michaelson," Leonard's voice bellowed once more.

Leonard was busily working to free Eli's left hand while the priest got into a sappy version of the traditional Catholic vows.

When he got to the sticky part, Leonard produced a ring from his pocket. Eli didn't look at it.

He repeated after the priest's mangled prompting, "'I, Eli, take thee, Millicent, to be my lawfully wedded wife. With this ring I thee wed. With my body, I thee worship. With all my worldly goods I thee endow.'"

Eli shuddered and closed her hand into a fist. Her strength was nonexistent and Leonard forced it open again. He pushed the ring down on the fourth finger of her left hand.

"Now, repeat after me. 'I, Millicent…'"

Eli said nothing, but Leonard had been ready for that. He had painstakingly cut clips of Eli speaking from interviews for the last few years and pieced them together. Like the audio equivalent of a scrap quilt, Eli heard her own voice come out of the tinny, flat speakers.

"I, Millicent, take you, Eli Grey, to be my lawfully wedded husband. With this ring I thee wed. With my body I thee worship. With all my worldly goods—my copyright, my image, my story and my intellectual property—I thee endow."

The inflection was all over the place, some words rising like questions, others obviously chopped into pieces to knit phonemes together like Frankenstein's monster made of word parts.

Leonard placed her hand on top of his own as he put a matching ring on his own finger. Then, he wheeled her slightly to one side and pushed his rosewood pen into her hand. He clutched hers in his own and together they made a jagged scrawl that was meant to be *Millicent Michaelson*.

He hated how it lacked neatness and romance, but there it was. On the page. Indelible. He took the pen smoothly from between her fingers and Eli felt a swipe of wet ink land in the webbing between her first and second fingers. She twitched them, spreading the rosy color of it, too cheerful to be blood. Looking down through hazy eyes, she saw Leonard write out "Eli Grey," looking like a computer's approximation of her professional autograph.

Leonard carefully capped his pen and set it beside the document he had typed up to look like a marriage license, making minute moves so that the pen lay exactly parallel to the thick paper's edge. He turned back to her, lips parted, eyes shining.

He looks like a bride, she thought. *He's dreamed of this moment for fuck knows how long.*

"What God has joined together, let no man put asunder," the priest intoned. "You may now kiss the bride."

Leonard came in close to her trapped head, breathing in her scent and looking into her eyes. She wanted to deny him anything resembling intimacy, but she found that she could not look away.

"At last," he said, his voice trembling. "At last, you are mine."

It was nearly impossible to tongue-kiss an unwilling person. The best one could do was to explore the mouth of another with one's own tongue, making the best of a sour and slack place. Leonard did not seem to miss anything in his experience. His breath quickened as he kissed her unmoving mouth, mashing his teeth against hers and breathing against her gums.

Eli kept her eyes open.

He wrapped his arms around the appliance dolly and crushed himself against her at full length. He put his mouth to her ear. "I have waited so long for this. To feel you here, completely under my command. To be Mr. Eli Grey."

Eli said nothing. She went away. She tried to coax herself back to the gray foggy nothingness of the drug, but it was wearing off.

She closed her eyes and went as limp as she dared. Leonard sighed and got behind her again. He pushed the dolly out of the room as the wedding recessional music played.

Breathing. Breathing as deep as possible. Got to get ready. Got to at least be able to see clearly. No time left now. No time at all. Get yourself together or there will be no self.

Everything was perfect in his own bedroom, as well. Candles shone all around the room. The bed was made with fresh linens with a rubber sheet beneath, to protect the mattress. A bottle of sparkling cider sat at a perfect angle in a bucket of ice on the gleaming table beside the bed, with two perfect shining glasses.

He unstrapped her slowly, opening ties from bottom to top. When she slumped, he pressed her and the dolly against the wall with his body.

She tried to remain as limp as possible, but she had been experimenting with different muscle groups, trying to see if she could clench her quads, if her abs would obey her at all.

Her body responded sluggishly, but it did respond.

I can get one shot at this guy. I have to get it right the first time. There's no other option. If he overpowers me, I'm done.

He picked her up and laid her tenderly on the bed. He slipped his shoes off and joined her almost shyly, lying beside her so close that his hip touched hers.

Stall. Stretch it out. Make him wait. Oh, for fuck's sake, wait.

"Leonard?"

"Eli," he corrected her, moving a stray wisp of hair away from her eyes.

"Eli," she said, her own name a powerful thing in her mouth, no matter what he might think. "What happens next?"

"We tell the world," he said.

"But it's just the two of us, right? Why bring anyone else into it?"

"True," he said, laying a hand on her lower belly. "This is our honeymoon, after all."

Honeymoon cystitis, they used to call it. That UTI from having sex for the first time. Got it already. Honeymoon's over.

"We could make a YouTube video," Eli murmured, trying to sound enraptured instead of stoned and desperate. "Explain it in our own words. Together. Wouldn't that be best?"

"Yes, my darling." He scooted closer to her, inching like a worm.

Slowly, like a crab, her left hand crawled toward him on the bed.

Stall. Distract him. Anything. Think of anything.

"We can tell them everything, okay? We can make it part of the release PR for *The Siege of Maginaria.* It'll be a huge story."

He pulled his glasses off and hooked them over the top of his headboard.

"I love it when you talk publishing business."

She smiled for him, knowing that the expression must look sickly and insincere. He didn't notice at all.

Her left hand crawled again and it lay lightly but deliberately against his thigh.

"Why, Millicent!" His eyes were alight as he looked at her hungrily. He took her hand and enthusiastically pressed it against his erection. "Was this what you were looking for?"

Quivering with adrenaline and disgust, she flexed her hand to squeeze him. His eyes closed and he leaned in to kiss her.

She kissed him back, eyes open and working like an automaton. It had been a while, but she hadn't lost the habits of driving a stick shift.

Her left hand crawled away, toward the nightstand. Waited. Crawled. Waited.

"My darling wife, let me dip my pen in your ink now. You need me—I can feel it."

She groaned into his mouth with hatred and dread, but Leonard heard only desire. She unzipped his fly and reached inside. His hands flew to her breasts and he came closer to her still, pulling up her dress in jerks while manhandling her body.

Bile rose in Eli's throat. This was the moment. The only moment there would ever be.

Her left hand found the candle behind her. She gripped it

in one hand and the root of his penis in the other, taking a breath and gathering her strength.

"Millicent," he moaned.

"Eli," she said, bringing the candle around her body with all the force she could muster, and plunging the burning end of it into his left eye.

His scream split the air like an ice pick to the ear. He clawed at her, pushing her away and then off the bed. She hit the floor with a thump and everything slid sideways. She took a deep whoop of air and tried to pull herself up using the bed. She made it as far as her knees.

The candle had only sunk into the eyeball, not past it and deep into his brain as she had hoped. There was a mess there of blood and boiling char, dripping black and red and viscous on to his cheek. He was standing, throwing the candle to the floor. He put his palm over the gore and stumbled toward her.

"I wrote you into this world," he screamed. "And I will erase you out of it."

The corner of the bed tripped him and she crawled away, toward the open door. She pushed the dolly away from the wall with her bare foot and turned away before she knew whether she had been successful or not. She heard it crash to the floor, but kept moving. The house was an unfamiliar landscape, dark and full of obstacles. She shambled on her hands and knees, unable to get to her feet at all. She reached a desk and tried to pull herself up again.

He was behind her an instant later, hands wrapped around her throat.

"You...you..." His voice was strangled with agony.

Eli's hands grappled desperately with the surface of the desk, searching for anything that she could use as a weapon.

Her right hand found Leonard's perfectly lined up fountain pen collection. She ripped the cap off one as she began to lose consciousness, and stabbed wildly behind her, catching him once in the thigh and then missing entirely.

He howled and let go of her. She collapsed, banging her face against the edge of the desk. She scrabbled after the pen on the floor, found it, then slashed Leonard through the snowy blameless white of his clean cotton socks.

The pen stuck deep into the meat of his foot, the sock reddening at once. Savage joy struck Eli and gave her a minuscule rush of strength.

She twisted and ripped a drawer out of the desk.

"You bitch!" He was screaming now, bedraggled and bloody. He had flexed his upper body enough that he had ripped himself out of her shirt. He looked half-mad, the spider monster in man-tatters, his one remaining eye wide.

Eli laughed with a satisfaction so deep that she could not connect it to any previous experience of her life.

He stumbled backward, away from her. On the floor, she found another pen and seized it. This one the cap wouldn't pull off—it was a screw top and she gave it up after a second. The second one was dark blue and the cap ripped free, showing a wide calligraphic nib like a monk might have used to draw the illuminated drop capital at the top of a gospel page.

She lunged for him with it in her right hand and swiped a hard backhand, left to right, and cut him high, across the collarbone. Midnight blue ink spread out over the white of his tattered shirt, dyeing the edges of the sliced material. For one lunatic second, she saw the color of it spread beside his blood, blue to red and then together into a misbegotten purple.

Bloodtalking, she thought.

Leonard flailed and knocked the pen out of her hand, but then moved both hands to his chest to inspect his new injury. She saw blood still oozing out of his ruined eye, sliming down to his chin and smearing against his collar. She bent to the floor, barely looking, and snatched up another pen.

He reacted a second too slow, closing in just as she stood up fast, her vision darkening as her blood pressure bottomed out. She drove this one into his belly, just above the waistband of his slacks. It sank inches into him, with a stomach-turning sensation of busting through gristle with a cheap knife. She hadn't had time to see the nib, but she saw the haft of the pen itself jutting from his gut, jerking as he screamed. The shaft of the pen was emerald green and hung downward from Leonard's lower abdominals like a misplaced, half-tumescent penis. Eli could see matching green ink in a ring around the wound before the bleeding began.

Got him now. Got him. He's all focused on the pain—he won't even see me. Do it now. Do it. Finish. Finish this.

"You are not real!" he screamed as he yanked the green fountain pen out of his flesh. He raised it over her, his own blood dripping down it.

She went down as he grabbed at her and she scrabbled for one last pen. *If it's a screw top, I'm screwed, too*, she thought as her hand closed around his grail pen, his black beauty. Eli didn't know, would never know, that the pen was a Visconti Homo Sapiens, made of black basaltic lava from Mt. Etna, bearing the name of a medieval family of robber barons from Milan. The cap came off with a vacuum-sealed snapping sensation, satisfying and sleek, and she gripped it as she would a knife.

Leonard had bought it for himself to celebrate the *Hand of Fate* deal; he had signed the contract with it. To him, it had symbolized finally becoming a real writer. It was the sort of pen a real writer might casually uncap to give an autograph.

A real writer stabbed it, low and vicious as a snake, into the meat of Leonard's left calf muscle. Eli didn't let go this time once it cut through the leg of his pants and found flesh, but kept driving it in, digging and jerking it savagely, fighting her way into the belly of the muscle there.

Leonard's leg folded beneath him, agony and weakness coming as one. His screams became a long, bovine wail as his bony weight crashed to the floor. He reached for Eli with both hands and Eli thrust again, digging with the eighteen-karat gold nib to find nerve endings, not stopping until he jerked hard and his voice soared back into its upper register. He keened and his hands clenched into fists in midair.

"You like that, you fucker? You like it when I dip my pen in your ink?" She pulled the Visconti out and stabbed again, this time in the back of his knee. Black ink seeped into the wound, and Eli thought wildly for a second that she was impregnating him with it.

Pen and ink. Inside you forever. An IUD wouldn't have saved you, you fucking rapist.

She dug the knife in again.

Eli was looking at Leonard dead-on and saw his eyes roll up, his face turning blue green as she drove the point into the network of veins and nerves and ligaments there, cutting through skin and fabric again to tear into his most vulnerable places.

"The pen is…" He was mumbling, just on the edge of losing consciousness.

He's not seriously going to do this now. Eli was crazed, covered in blood and multicolored inks. She quivered like a greyhound, her hand still clutching the black-lava pen as it protruded from his knee pit. *I'm going to kill him if he says it. I'm going to kill him either way. I'm going to pull this pen out and write "THE END" on his fucking forehead.*

"The pen is mightier," Leonard said in a faraway voice. His lids fluttered and he was out.

Eli jerked the pen out of its well and looked at it. The tip was bent, the soft metal destroyed in this, its final purpose.

Black ink beaded sluggishly out through the oily, dark red gore that streaked the gold. Everything was intensely clear to Eli, an image she would never be able to shake from her mind. Indelible.

She looked at his still form and thought for a second about the quickest way to kill him.

"FBI!" The shout came just as the door burst inward. "Down on the ground! Get down on the—"

Eli looked back over her shoulder just in time for the shouting cop to stop. She was crouched on the floor over Leonard's body, her wedding dress ruined in sprays of red and black and green and blue. She did not drop the pen. She did not raise her hands.

It took her a minute to believe it was real: the barrel-chested agent with the short beard, just as she had imagined him. He lowered the battering ram to the ground. Behind it, tall and curly-haired, came Agent Carla Silvestri.

"Ms. Grey? Eli Grey?"

Silvestri was standing over her, looking into her face.

Eli looked up, unable to speak.

"That's not Grey," another agent said. "She doesn't fit the description at all."

"She looks like Millicent Michaelson," another one said, stepping closer.

Eli began to laugh. The laugh was short and mirthless, ending in a long cough that left her gasping.

"I'm Eli Grey. I'm Eli fucking Grey."

Slowly, deliberately, Eli put down her pen.

26

EMTs arrived and strapped Lobovich to a gurney. He left in an ambulance with two officers escorting.

Eli regained consciousness but did not make much sense. She was able to identify herself. She scowled continuously at the agent who had called her Millicent. She said she wasn't injured, but she could barely stand and had livid bruises all over.

Silvestri wrapped the writer in a blanket she pulled from a squad car. There was nothing they could do about her bare feet; her oxfords were bagged as evidence. Silvestri spoke to her gently about the hospital and began to shepherd her toward the door.

Eli balked. "My phone. And my laptop and my bag. My bracelet," she said. "I have to find them."

"They're all being entered into evidence, ma'am," the barrel-chested agent said, leaning over an end table spattered with Eli's blood. "You'll get them back after that."

"Where are we going?" Eli looked at the doorway, unsure of where it led.

"To the hospital," Silvestri repeated. "We can get you home, after you've been checked out."

"Home," Eli said, her mouth numb.

"Is there anybody you want me to call? Your assistant will be so happy to hear that you're alive."

"Joe," Eli said, soothed to think of him. *There should be someone besides my assistant to tell I'm alive. But there isn't. That's it. That's something.*

"Yes, please let him know." Eli found she could not look at anyone while she spoke to them. She could not accept that it was over. She expected the charade to break at any moment, for each of the cops to unmask themselves and be Leonard underneath. She found herself smelling Silvestri in the car as they drove.

Sitting in the passenger seat of Silvestri's van, Eli watched the mile markers tick by as they headed for the freeway. The desert highway sloped gently up and down past ghostly Joshua trees and grand expanses of naked yellow-brown earth. Birds of prey wheeled lazily overhead. Silvestri swore each time the GPS signal dropped out, but she kept following the route she remembered from the way in. It was a long time before they saw other houses, and even longer still before they began to pass other cars.

Never would have made it. Must be sixty, maybe seventy miles out now.

Eli looked at the speedometer. They had been on the road nearly an hour, and Silvestri drove with the red lights flashing, heedless of the limit.

No chance I could have made it. But the feeling that she had not tried hard enough would not leave her. She hooked her fingers into her hair where the extensions had been sewed in and began to yank. Handfuls came out as her short bleached strands gave way, breaking and ripping out of her scalp under the strain.

"Don't do that," Silvestri said. "Please? Just wait, okay? We'll get you some help with that.'

When Silvestri saw that Grey was not going to stop, she flailed behind her to her backpack and handed the writer an evidence bag. "Can you put those in here, please?"

Eli did.

Eli stripped off the necklace, earrings and ring that Leonard had put on her. Silvestri fished out another plastic baggie and Eli filled it. Eli wanted to take off the wedding dress, but she had nothing else to put on.

Silvestri wanted to say something, anything. She had driven survivors to the hospital before. Most of the time they cried, or they made phone calls to people who were worried about them. Grey's silence was impenetrable. Silvestri looked at the bag with the jewelry in it and saw the wedding ring.

The hospital was ready for them and had a trauma nurse meet them under the awning to take Grey in. Her ruined, bleached hair stood up in peaks from her head like the shorn ruins on an abused Barbie doll.

There were so many things that could go wrong in circumstances like these. Eli had heard some about them, but experiencing them was another.

The hospital assigned a nurse to strip her and bag her clothing and underwear. They photographed her naked body to get high-definition proof of bruises and wounds. They looked carefully at her damaged right eye. Mentioned needing a specialist. Eli's vision would still not come clear. She was now convinced it never would again. Wordlessly, Eli grabbed on to the scrub-clad shoulder of the nurse with the camera. She wanted them to stop talking about her ruined eye. She pulled up a foot to show them her soles.

The nurse tutted.

Eli spoke softly, asking her, "Do you think that's going

to be permanent?" She could not ask the question about her sight. Her feet seemed farther away, less a part of who she was.

The nurse said she had never seen anything like it and had no idea. The shrug went all the way around the room until Eli wore it again.

Eli eased herself into the stirrup chair and scooted down until cold air washed over her exposure and she was in the familiar position known to anyone who had ever undergone a gynecological exam. The sight of the speculum made Eli vomit water and bile out of the corner of her mouth.

The doctor informed her in a low, reassuring tone before collecting each small piece of evidence for the rape kit. Eli stammered, trying to explain what had happened to her, to tell them that it was not rape in the traditional sense and they weren't going to find anything but a missing IUD. The doctor told her he was just following procedure. He noted the profound inflammation and rash caused by Eli's ongoing UTI and yeast infections. He wrote the notes for the over-the-counter medicines that would put them both down, along with emergency contraception and postexposure prophylaxis for HIV.

When the nurse brought her the meds, Eli took them all without looking or counting. She pushed the tiny syringe of antifungal ointment into her vagina while she was alone, hating the crawly feeling of it, knowing it was necessary to stop the awful burn that consumed her.

Silvestri came back about an hour later to take Eli's statement. She found that the author was surprisingly bad at describing what had happened to her. Maybe it was shock, or maybe she was still adjusting to being out. Silvestri asked the questions she had to ask kindly, in a low, soothing tone of voice like her training had taught her. Eli answered, delivering every detail as flat, matter-of-fact discourse. Silvestri stopped her to clarify a few points.

"You got into his car willingly?"

"Yes, I had chartered a flight and he told me he was there to transport me from the airport." Eli felt very far away from herself.

"Did you know him?"

"I did, but I didn't realize I did at first. We were former colleagues. I had seen him around, but didn't recognize him."

"He freed you from the house, yet you were unable to take advantage of the situation?"

Eli flinched. She had never been questioned by police before. *Is she really asking me this? Does she think I'm lying?*

"You saw how far away we were from everything. The heat. I had no water, I was naked. I got stung by something and he dragged me back."

"And you signed this document," Silvestri said, raising the contract Leonard had drawn up and signed. It flapped there in a plastic evidence bag. "Granting him permission to assume your pen name and wield your copyright. You signed it under duress."

"I didn't sign it at all. He signed my name, then his."

"Does it match your signature?"

Eli looked at Silvestri with pure, unadorned hate. "Anybody can Google my autograph. And Leonard is good at copying. Maybe it's the only thing he's good at. The name that I wrote, right there beside it, is the result of the medication he injected me with. You'll notice Leonard did not write his own name, because he had decided to become me. Which is a fun and normal thing that people with willing partners do."

Silvestri had never seen this kind of cold hostility from a victim before. She took a deep breath. "I'm on your side here. I got you out of there. I just need to know what happened, so we can put him away. I know you don't want to go through this again, but please try and help me."

Eli looked at her with eyes that blazed. "Why do your questions sound like you're trying to catch me in a lie?"

"Because... Shit, you know why." Silvestri sagged into a chair. "You know he's going to say you were asking for it. They always do."

"This wasn't date rape," Eli spit. "There's no gray area here. I'm covered in evidence."

Silvestri flattened her lips. "No fluids in your rape kit."

Eli nearly screamed in frustration. "He didn't rape me. Not in the technical sense. But he did this," she said, pointing to the bottoms of her feet. She brandished her ankle with its cuff mark. "Does it look like any of this was my idea?"

"I believe you," Silvestri says. "I just have to get it into my report for the judge. The DA. Okay? They won't see you for a while, and you'll be better by then. They need to know what happened, see pictures of you now. Okay? So just talk me through it."

"Fine," Eli said. "Where were we?"

"So, after the wedding. He put you into the bed against your will, but you voluntarily began to stimulate his penis with your hand?" Silvestri's voice changed appreciably here. Eli could not tell what the change meant.

Silvestri was slipping back into her professional mode, her distance from the emotional weight of the case. She was trying to be a good cop.

Eli, who had only ever talked to cops so that she could convincingly write about magic, did not understand. This felt like abandonment and betrayal. She did not help Silvestri any more than she had to. She had no reason to trust anyone.

"Yes, as a distraction. I needed his attention to dip so I could get a clear shot at him. You understand that, don't you?"

Should I have lied? Nobody else was there. What good is telling the truth? You say you believe me, but then you pull back like you don't. I'm on my own here. Just like I was there. You should have left me there to finish the job. He'd be dead, and the story would be only mine. This would really be over.

This will never be over.

Leonard had gone into surgery in the same hospital where they were holding Eli. She had known he was in the building and could not be calm. They sewed him up and stabilized him. His eye was gone for good, so they cleaned out what was left of it and put a patch over the place where it had been. He had slept under heavy anesthesia. Silvestri told Eli that he would recover and stand trial. Silvestri left. Eli did not sleep.

27

When the case went to trial, Leonard's defense attorney did everything he could to cause the jury to question whether Eli had put herself under those circumstances out of creative curiosity, or because of love.

He entered into evidence letters that she did not write to Leonard about his *Captain Ampari* stories. Leonard had copied her handwriting from her Instagram, and mailed them to himself from San Francisco. In them, Eli confided that she loved these stories of sexual submission and that she'd like to explore that in herself.

Also entered into evidence were emails from years ago, when he had tried to engage her or ask her for a blurb. Despite the curtness of her replies, the defense argued they proved that Eli had known her captor, and must have recognized him when he picked her up.

When he cross-examined her, Leonard's defender worked hard to poke holes in the concept of her will. Eli tried to stop reliving the things that brought her here and focus on his efforts to destroy her.

Like Leonard needs your help. He did fine enough on his own.

"Going back to the alleged kidnapping. You got into his car, even though you had no idea who he was?"

"I had summoned a car through a rideshare app. He posed as my driver."

"And you got into the car without verifying that. Even though you had no idea who he was?"

"I use rideshare all the time," Eli said tiredly. "I had a habit."

"And my client knew where to find you just then."

"Yes. He was stalking me."

The lawyer's mouth flattered. "Move to strike. It was a yes-or-no question."

The judge nodded and lifted a finger.

Eli shrugged on the stand. She looked up wearily. Her face was puffy and her eyes were glittery, dry. She did not look toward Leonard. She tried to breathe deep, to focus. She flexed her ankles and pulled them apart to remind herself that she was free.

"You and Leonard corresponded over the years."

"I've seen the evidence. I can't deny that we did. I think my responses are pretty clearly short and cold in each of them. I didn't know him. I didn't even remember us having conversations."

"You don't remember writing three-page-long letters?" His voice heated up.

Eli's eyes narrowed. "No, I don't."

"You don't remember expounding on Leonard's, and I quote, 'brilliant use of chiaroscuro'?"

"I often have to placate men's egos when they write to me. I am a professional writer. I embellish without much thought." Eli crossed her legs, then recrossed them. She saw her lawyer sag a little across the room.

"You don't remember that you had several specific interactions with Leonard at five separate conventions over the span of three years?"

"I saw thousands of people at each one of those cons. He was nobody."

He rounded again, looking away from the witness stand. "Yes or no."

Eli sighed. "No, I don't remember."

"But you can't tell us what you were doing during those times."

"As I've said, I was generally drinking in the bar during conventions. Alone."

"You drank excessively?"

"No."

"But you don't specifically remember what you did."

Eli's lawyer raised a tired hand. "Objection. Your Honor, she has personal knowledge about her own behavior in the past. This does not need to be dissected."

The judge did not look up. "Overruled."

The lawyer pulled his slightly too tight jacket and began again. Eli's eyes zeroed in on the strain in the fabric. She was thinking about the wedding dress again.

"In the car, when my client first picked you up. When you claim you were kidnapped. You were not tied up."

"No, I was drugged."

"Forcibly?"

"No, I was given a Gatorade that was drugged without my knowledge."

"Where did the Gatorade come from?"

The attorney's eyes were everywhere. He did not look at Eli. It began to grate on her. She sought to make him look.

"It was in the door of the cab."

"So Leonard did not give it to you."

"He told me it was there, and suggested that I drink it."

"So you found it and drank it. You never saw it in his hand. He did not make you drink it."

"No, but—"

"Did you ask my client to supply you with recreational substances?"

"Never."

"You never sent Leonard any messages promising wild weekends where you would fulfill his every desire, if he could just help you get past your inhibitions?"

"No, godsdamn it, never." Eli saw her lawyer's shoulders pull up around her ears. She tried to relax. "This guy got into my email. Impersonated me. You have proof of that. He had a shrine to me in his house. This was all one-sided. I had nothing to do with it."

The attorney paced a short track in front of her. She saw the fluorescent light reflected in the sheen of his suit. He pursed his lips and she wished for death.

"One-sided?"

"Completely. I don't even date men."

"But you do. Your personal history—"

"I used to. I don't anymore. And even if I did, it wouldn't be Leonard."

"Because of his personal problems. His trouble in your industry. His fall from the heights of popularity. You'd have to keep it a secret, because of your career, your status."

"Objection," the prosecutor called from her desk, her mouth compressed into a line.

"Goes to credibility," Too-Tight Jacket said, almost lazily.

"Overruled. The witness will answer," the judge said again. Eli thought he sounded awfully bored. She focused on the sound of the court reporter typing.

"You're asking me to explain why I wouldn't consider dating a huge fuck-up who destroyed his own career and then kept me captive in his basement for weeks? Is that seriously the question?"

"Is that why you deny that you two used to correspond?"

"No! I just don't remember his emails. Because he was nothing to me. Nothing at all. I did not know him, only of him."

He took a few long strides. "Back to the night of your sexual encounter. You said in your statement to the FBI that you willingly engaged in sexual activity with Leonard before attacking him with a lit candle?"

Eli sat up very straight. "That's an inaccurate way to describe what happened."

"But you did say you willingly engaged in sexual activity with Leonard? To the agent who took your statement. You told her that."

Eli made an exasperated gesture, dropping her hands into her lap. She could feel herself beginning to sweat.

Silvestri had testified already, outlining how hard Leonard had worked to sound like her on the phone and delay their action. His lawyer had argued that Leonard was identifying himself by his pen name, no more. Silvestri's testimony about Leonard giving her Social Security number might have helped, Eli thought. But it might not be enough when paired with this muddied mess.

I should have lied.

"I wasn't in the best frame of mind. That wasn't an accurate description."

"What would be more accurate?"

"I tried to distract Leonard, who was trying to rape me, by touching his penis until I could get a weapon."

"How was he trying to rape you? Did he get his penis out?"

"No, he drugged me and laid me in his bed. He put my hand on his penis. He pulled my clothes off. And by my clothes, I mean the creepy wedding dress he forced me into, so that he could pretend to marry me."

"My client has testified that that wedding was a role-playing game, in which you were an active participant."

"Yeah, that's why I was strapped to a furniture dolly." Eli saw her lawyer's hands go up and tried to remember what she had been told about sarcasm on the stand.

"You never role-play?" The question was designed to embarrass her, and it did.

Eli felt her face grow hot. She hesitated too long before answering. Anything she said now was going to look like a lie, and he knew it. "Not with Leonard."

The defense attorney picked up a bagged piece of evidence. "But you wrote this email, asking him to reenact a wedding scene from a movie."

Eli grimaced. "No, I did not. Anyone who has ever read me knows I didn't write that. And that," she said, pointing to the iPad that had been the priest's head during the wedding, "wouldn't have had to be edited to speak for me, if I had wanted to be there. Don't you think?"

"You said you wanted to be 'in a wordless and dreamlike state, induced by hypnotic nepenthe, subject to your will' in this very email."

Eli could not help but roll her eyes. "Does that prose sound like a professional author to you? Or does it sound like a plagiarizing, smut-peddling hack who's addicted to purple prose and incapable of saying what he actually means?"

Out of the corner of her eye, Eli thought she saw Leonard sit up rigid at this offense. His eye patch was very stark against his pale face. She had read in a magazine article about him that the pens she had stabbed him with had left permanent deposits of ink under his skin, like jailhouse tattoos.

Good. Fuck you. Call you a rapist or an attempted murderer and you don't move. But make fun of your writing and your egomaniacal ass sits right up.

Eli almost laughed at how ridiculous it was.

But then her eyes fell on the jury.

They're not writers. They're not fans of mine or his. No way they didn't screen for that. They can't tell the difference. Oh fuck, they might believe him. They probably do. I probably sound like a kook and a drunk and fuck. Oh fuck, oh fuck. Get it together.

"So back to this alleged sexual assault. The one for which there is no physical evidence. My client did not attempt to penetrate you."

She focused again, clenching her jaw and trying to remember the preparation to testify rather than the events themselves.

Safely solipsized. Guess I became a character in the story after all. Leonard, you son of a bitch.

"No, he didn't attempt to. He did. Earlier in the day. With a speculum, while I was half-conscious. He removed my IUD. That's in evidence, too."

"He did not attempt to penetrate you with his penis."

"No."

"You told Leonard you wanted him to get you pregnant."

"No, he told himself that, using my email address as a sock puppet. You can tell, because he's too fucking weird to use contractions." Eli had gone back into his *Hand of Fate* work to discover if he always kept his books free of them. An editor had clearly cleaned it up, but the tendency was obvious in all his writing.

"So you know Leonard's style rather well."

Eli bit her lips. "I do now. I didn't before I had to prepare to defend myself against this."

"You are familiar enough with Leonard's writing to recognize a similar style."

"Yes, as I said. I am now."

"After beginning your relationship with Leonard, you began incorporating some of his stylistic preferences into your own writing."

The son of a bitch was almost smiling. Eli went back to looking at his jacket. The way it strained to fit him. Leonard wearing her clothes, at the end. His copy pair of her custom shoes. His spidery body bursting out of her shed skin.

"No, I did not. His style is laughable."

"Did Leonard ever attempt to penetrate you with his penis? At any of these points when you claim he had you completely knocked out and at his mercy?"

"That was obviously his intent."

"How can you know what he intended? He had multiple opportunities to assault you when you testify that you were unconscious. And you're sure rape was his intent." The lawyer's voice was climbing, getting louder as he built to his point. He rounded on her. "So why didn't it happen when he had all the opportunity in the world?"

Eli was silent for a long minute. She took a deep breath. "I think there was something Leonard wanted that he couldn't have. I think he was waiting until he thought he could actually take me over. To get me to the breaking point. He wanted another shot at being a legend, like the one he blew when he wrecked his life and the *Hand of Fate* books. So he wanted my life. My books." She took her gaze away from the lawyer and stared Leonard down across the room. He did not meet her eye.

"Rape is a small thing, compared to what Leonard really wanted."

The prosecutor had counseled Eli to cry on the stand, but only if it was genuine. She found that she could not. Her eyes crawled over her ruined satchel, her Montblanc fountain pen. She wasn't sure she could ever use a fountain pen again. She saw her black bracelet in the array of evidence and rubbed the spot on her wrist where her whole identity should be. The FBI had checked it, writing out a description of the contents on the evidence list. In discovery, she imagined Leonard's lawyer had told him what was on it. That he had had her next book in his grasp the whole time, plus more that would be published soon and some that never would. Eli hoped that he hated knowing that as much as she loved it. It was coming back to her untouched by him. Her work was purely her own, and he had failed to steal the one thing he had wanted most. After the trial, Eli waited months for the bracelet to be returned.

The jury found Leonard Lobovich guilty of kidnapping and assault, aggravated assault and assault with a deadly weapon, but not of attempted rape, unlawful imprisonment or attempted murder. During sentencing, his defender dug up his juvenile psychiatric records, building his case on an abusive childhood and begging for leniency. When those things proved less persuasive in the trial, he had hammered reasonable doubt on how much of this Eli had asked for. He found that the jury responded much better to that idea.

Lobovich was sentenced to nine years at the California institute for men in Chino.

Six months into his sentence, Eli began to receive letters from herself.

28

A year after the end of her ordeal, Eli Grey was living in a condo rented under Joe's name in San Francisco. She could not live in her own house, so she rented it out. Joe collected all her mail and promised never to tell her when anything came from Chino.

The Siege of Maginaria had gone to print and outsold every Millicent book before it. The next two movies had come out and the studio was hard at work on number four. Eli did not attend the premieres. Alice wrote and she did not answer.

Joe fielded inquiries from her agent, her publisher and all attempts to book the author for interviews and events. He said no to absolutely everything.

The Siege of Maginaria won Eli another Supernova award. She asked Nella to attend and accept it on her behalf.

Eli slept poorly. She studied Krav Maga in a women-only class and bought several guns. She had taken to shaving her head and wore dark glasses, rain or shine. Her vision was better but would never be what it once was. She accepted that, but she hid it as well as she could. She drank every day.

She could barely walk past a window display of wedding clothes without feeling like breaking the glass and eating the shards of it on the street. Her agent asked her once whether she'd work with a ghostwriter to tell the story of her kidnapping. Eli had not answered the email.

She lay in bed sometimes, feeling the basement take shape around her as soon as sleep set in. She'd jolt awake and stare at the door for hours, waiting.

Awards season became convention season and Joe came to her with an offer.

"SphinxCon wants you as a guest of honor," he said. "They've made a really sweet deal, with two handlers and a lot of control. It pays a butt ton."

"No," Eli said, pouring whiskey into her coffee at the dinner table, unable to care who saw.

"Eli," Joe said, trying to lay his hand on hers.

She jerked it backward like a feral cat. "Don't," she said. "You know better."

Joe shifted uncomfortably. "You need to get back out there. Don't let him win. Don't let him take all of this from you."

"Fuck you," she said quietly. She drank her coffee. It tasted like gasoline.

His voice lost its sweetness and he spoke sharply now. "You know, you don't really need an assistant anymore. You need an automatic reply on your email that just says no every time someone contacts you. You can do the same with your voice mail and stop paying my salary."

Eli looked at Joe, some feeling trying to crack through her. "Look, you know I'm grateful for all that you do," she began. "But I'm not ready. Not yet."

"It's been a year. I know I can't possibly understand what you've been through. But I know you. Or I knew you before all this. And the old Eli would tell you to get the fuck over it. You have work to do."

She goggled at him, perfectly shocked. He was right, but she hated him for saying it anyhow.

She took another swallow, putting her hand against the plate glass window beside their booth. It was warm with reflected sunlight. "What con?"

"SphinxCon," he repeated. "And drink some water with that."

She took a sip of water. "And you think I should do it?"

"I'll go with you," Joe said quickly. "You'll have two handlers and me. Nobody will get to you. And if you hate it, we can bail. I'll handle the fallout."

Eli took another sip of water. *Joe is the only reason you're sitting here right now. Do this for him.*

"Okay. Tell them I'll do it. And you are coming with me." Joe smiled slowly.

"You're the only reason I'm here to tell the tale."

Joe's smile faded. "Not really. In the end, you did it without anybody. Without me. I was too slow."

"Knowing you were out here mattered to me," Eli said. "I might have given up otherwise. I knew you'd figure it out. You'd never let it go."

He reached out and put his hand on hers. This time, she did not pull back. She took a deep breath as they looked at one another.

"So you're coming, right?

Joe nodded. "No other option will be entertained."

SphinxCon trumpeted the news as soon as the deal was signed: the triumphant return of Eli Grey! Her old head shot went to the top of their website and all their promotional materials.

Eli started to grow her hair out. It wouldn't be long, but

it'd be enough to part with a comb by the time the con rolled around. She was still too thin, but she let Joe order her lunches and she actually ate. She had thought that when she got out of that basement that she would eat herself into a coma, but she couldn't face food at all. She couldn't choose it for herself and she hated having anyone bring plates to her table. At night, she ate standing in front of the freezer, listening to the sound of the condenser pumping cold air, hearing the air conditioner in the basement.

She left the condo a few times a week to take walks. She always read the street signs and stayed in the most crowded parts of town. Her shoe size had changed permanently, with her soles seeming always to be round as pancakes along the bottom. But she walked without pain, no matter how bad her feet looked.

Eli would not board a plane, so they took a train to Sphinx-Con in Phoenix. The crowd set her on edge immediately, pointing and whispering. Taking pictures less discreetly than they imagined. The con handlers and Joe got her to her suite. She began to drink before the handlers left the room.

Joe stood before her, looking her in the eye. "Look at me. You cannot be drunk the whole time. People will notice, and they will take video. You can drink when your shifts are over, but not before. Got it?"

She gulped the one she had already poured. "Okay."

Gently, Joe took her sunglasses from her.

She had three panels and one keynote. She made it through the first two panels, no problem. Joe helped her write a speech about the importance of the arts in elementary schools for the next generation of writers. It wasn't brilliant, but it was passable. She delivered it calmly, in a steely manner. The applause was more than kind.

Everyone was terribly warm and careful around her. More

than a few people told her it was great to have her back, but seemed miffed that she was not in the market for hugs.

Her final panel was on Sunday, and she was already packed and ready to head to the train station before it began. Joe had her bags stashed in the greenroom and was standing anxiously by to usher her out, cutting off last-minute talkers. They had made it all the way through. She might go back to doing the work of being a public author. This could be the way back. Joe smiled thinking about it.

When the session opened up for Q and A, one man stood up first and asked for the microphone. When he got it, he crammed it too close to his face and spoke too fast. Eli could see that he was shaking. She could also see that he was holding his cell phone down at his side, angled to record her as he spoke.

"Yeah, my question is for Eli. Were you really kidnapped by that *Hand of Fate* dude? Lobovich? A lot of people say that's not really what happened. There's a lot of talk about how you were into it, how you two were in a secret relationship for years and whatnot. Don't you think you ought to set the record straight, since you sent a man to prison? Weren't you kind of, like, asking for it?"

Eli sat for a moment, feeling pressure welling up from her chest into her throat, as if she were strangling herself from within. She turned to the moderator, pulling her face away from the microphone.

"Can we get another question?"

The moderator smoothly refused the man and a woman stepped forward to the mic.

"Are you worried that your testimony was too weak to put that guy away? What if he does it again?"

Leonard was awaiting trial for the sexual assault he had committed in Seattle, the one that had given Silvestri a hit on his fingerprint. Eli knew that and couldn't bring herself to point it out. It sounded like she was trying to get credit for someone else's work.

She swallowed and her throat was too dry. She reached out to the tall, sweating water pitcher on the table and tried to pour herself a glass. She succeeded in knocking both pitcher and glass over. The tablecloth darkened as the wetness spread out.

So disgusting and disrespectful, Leonard's voice sang out in memory. *You will be a good and tidy girl.*

Almost unseen, Joe appeared at her elbow with a plastic bottle of water. She missed it with her hand, then took it. But couldn't thank him. Couldn't open it. Couldn't drink.

The moderator tried again. A person dressed as Millicent came forward. "I know it's hard to expose your trauma, but do you ever think you'll be able to tell the story of what happened there? I'm a big fan of your work, but I'd like to know more about the person behind it."

Eli looked at the blond wig, the uniform. She shivered visibly.

The moderator's eyes were wide with distress; she knew this was not going well. She tried a smile and leaned into her microphone.

"Can we have a question about *The Siege of Maginaria*? Anyone with a question about the book, please step forward."

One by one, people fell away from the line, making space for the right kind of questioner to come forward. When none did, they looked back to the dais, expectant.

Eli stood up and walked out of the room. Water dripped off the tablecloth onto the floor behind her.

Joe put their bags into the trunk of a cab. They rode the train home in silence.

SphinxCon sent their apologies that her final event had not gone well, and their hopes that she would join them again in the future.

Joe answered them, signing "EG."

29

It took Eli forever to find the house. It had been remodeled significantly since the last time she saw it. She circled the block it was on, refamiliarizing herself with the landmarks until she was sure.

The family in the house did not want to move. She ended up offering them twice as much as the place was worth in cash if they moved in thirty days or less. Stubborn but not foolish, they complied. She waited three weeks, then began to watch the house every day. In the last week, she found that she could not stand being anywhere else.

Eli slept in her car for the last few days. She texted Nella and told her friend where she was.

The house you told me about? You found it?

I bought it.

Eli dropped a pin and transmitted her location. She sent it to Joe, as well. She did this often.

You can come see it, if you'd like. Maybe we could get dinner and talk?

Nella's answer was immediate:

I'd like that. It's been a long time.

I know. I'm sorry. I'm ready now, if you are.

About damned time.

Joe texted back after a minute or two:

Thank you for checking in. Can I set up anything for delivery to that address? How about a water cooler and bottles?

Eli thought for a second. Joe knew she couldn't stand to be thirsty.

Yes, please. Thank you, Joe.

Here for you. ♥

On the third morning, the father of the family tapped on her car window to give Eli the keys. She was only dozing, after having decided not to go for coffee. She awoke with a thin scream. The family's truck pulled out of the driveway with a final roar.

The basement had been finished and made into a games room. The stairs were carpeted now, and the walls had been paneled. New light fixtures warmed the place when she flipped on the switch.

Eli pulled a short sharp knife from her bra. She hacked and chipped at the wall for a long time before she found the seam. It took hours to pry the layers of paint and spackle and paneling away from the tiny crack. She excavated patiently, digging into the wall without stopping. When she could work all her fingers in at once, she wrenched the whole section backward with a staggering yank.

Paneling snapped off the door and old plaster rained to the floor in sheets and large chunks. But it was open.

The closet was exactly as she had left it. The oil in her lamp had evaporated, but the tall glass with the dusty brass hardware was still there. Her last composition notebook had been bitten and shredded on every side by mice, but the bulk of it was still in one piece. The smell was the same. The fortress was secure. No one could come in here but her. No one ever had.

From her black leather bag with the monogram scraped off to a rawhide spot, Eli pulled her wide tablet with its keyboard. She propped it up, opened a blank document and hovered her hands over the keys. She adjusted her USB bracelet so that it would not slide as she wrote.

She typed out the title page first: *Maginaria Fallen*. Then, slowly and with relish, she returned down and centered her own name: *"By Eli Grey."*

And no one else, she thought.

"Now it ends," she wrote. "Because I am the only one who can bring about the end. It is my destiny."

She thought a moment, went back and changed "it is" to "it's." And the words began to flow in like ink poured from a bottle without need for a pen.

It's my destiny.

Eli did not emerge from her stronghold for a long, long time.

30

**AN EXCITING ANNOUNCEMENT
FROM FATECON 2020!**

We've been BURSTING to tell you patient folks, but today's the day.

Maginaria creator, Supernova winner, Herbert winner, P. G. Whitecroft winner and *NYT* bestselling author

ELI GREY

is FateCon's 2020 guest of honor! Get your tickets now, because this is going to be the event of the century. Grey is dishing the details about the conclusion to her epic series: *Maginaria Fallen*. She will also discuss her next fiction release. No title yet, but a little bird in publishing told us that Grey has created a whole new world for the fans who just can't get enough of that magical stuff.

BONUS ROUND!

Newly minted *Hand of Fate* finishing author and screen-play adapter Nella Atwiler will also join us via Zoom from LA!

Following the blockbuster news that a mysterious emerging author had signed on to finish the long-awaited and much-debated *Hand of Fate* series at last, our entire community has waited on tenterhooks to find out more. Ent publishing has kept the entire story under wraps until today, and we're so pleased to be able to share this news with you.

We're sure we're not the first to tell you *The Hand of Fate* books have been optioned as a major motion pic-ture series, starring none other than fan-favorite Derek Patel as Prince Vantan. The first trailer for this film will premiere EXCLUSIVELY at FateCon. It won't hit the internet for five days. BUY TICKETS NOW.

This movie deal was finally made when Ent signed a new author to finish books nine and ten in the series, ti-tled *Vantan's Destiny* and *Binding the Hand of Fate*, respec-tively. This author's identity has been shrouded in mystery until recently, with critics and fans alike guessing every giant of genre from Jerry T. T. Larkin to Vincent Lavelle.

In an exclusive interview, live and streaming from FateCon's main stage, Eli Grey has agreed for the first time to talk publicly about her experience with disgraced *Hand of Fate* author Leonard Lobovich, in support of her forthcoming memoir, *The Agonist and the Protagonist: The Untold Story of Leonard Lobovich's Basement*. All proceeds from Grey's nonfiction work have been assigned to the Rape, Abuse & Incest National Network (RAINN).

★ ★ ★ ★ ★

Acknowledgments

Every writer has a colleague or a friend to whom they complain when the work is bad, the work is recalcitrant, the work is stuck. I owe more than I can say to Eric Scott, who lovingly indulged my gloom, and Maggie Tokuda-Hall who utterly refused to do the same.

Every writer is part of a team of folks who bring a book into being, but still takes all the credit, so I want to share some here. I am grateful to my agent, Dara Kaye, for finding the right home for this fiendish novel in the year of the plague. I am also humbled by the work of my editor, Margot Mallinson, who pushed a good idea into the territory of great more than once. It is good to be a pearl among pearls.

Every writer is indebted to specialists who consult thoughtfully over dinner about poisons, anatomy, psychology and other disciplines in which the author herself is not an expert. I owe my thanks to Brandon V. Stracener for his help on criminal proceedings. I owe my thanks to Trevor Z'Dorne for his help on pharmacology and nursing procedure.

Finally, almost every writer derives the privilege of time

to write from the support of a partner who helps pay the rent, makes coffee, and keeps the writer's health insured. For these reasons and many others, I am grateful to my husband, John Elison, a union man.